A Bloody Deal

A Vampire Thriller
by Z.L. Johnson

Published in the United States

First printing, 2025

Cover design by GetCovers.com

Paperback ISBN: 979-8-9992711-0-5

EBOOK ISBN: 979-8-9992711-1-2

To my mother, who will probably be terrified of this story but nonetheless, to whom I owe everything.

Content Warnings (if you consider these spoilers, please skip): PTSD, confinement, kidnapping, alcohol use, emotional abuse, human trafficking, xenophobia, gore, violence, and scars from torture

Grace's body locked her inside.

THIS MUST BE A dream, a night terror. She'd read about them, how your body turned against you and refused to obey. Although, she had never had one before. Was that normal in your thirties? Made sense though. Life was always looking for a way to kick her in the amygdala.

A door slammed. Her body shook with its impact. It felt close, next room close. Her mouth went dry. How had they gotten past her locks?

Keys jangled and approached. Grace's breathing grew ragged as she tried not to hyperventilate. Someone was in her apartment. Someone with a needle.

No, that wasn't right. The needle was inside her.

The gloved hand. The empty syringe. The black swallowing her whole.

Where was she? Who did this?

Worse, what would they do next?

A sharp click flooded her world with light. A slit before her opened wide, a metal toothy maw she was on the wrong side of. In the belly of a beast.

One last thought slipped in before the terror closed her mind for good: This was not her apartment.

Then came the hands at her back. Scrambling, pawing. Finally, a flick and the opening to the duffel bag she was paralyzed inside of zipped closed.

Part One

1

Three days earlier

To most people, the prison camp was just another part of the scenery, like airplanes or closed storefronts. Asbestos was more of a threat than the eighty-odd vampires caged within.

But Grace's job was to make the public care about the bloodsuckers. Too bad she worked for print. Soon even that might change.

As she exited the Cleveland *Plain Dealer* building, heat accosted her from all sides like a crowded bar, worsening her mood.

She should prepare, use these last few moments to get in the right mental state for the night of cases ahead. Instead, she reread the memo on her phone, the overtaxed battery trying to burn a hole through her hand.

```
To: allemployees@plaindealer.com
From: p.kent@plaindealer.com
Subject: GREAT NEWS!
This is it! The paper has been acquired by
Klosky Services, Inc. Paperwork is still being
finalized but soon we will be a subsidiary of
the largest information company in the world!
It's unclear what this will mean for day to day-
```

That was as far as Grace made it before a massive rage migraine ballooned in her temples and turned the world crimson. A billionaire bought the paper. Soon she'd be fired or worse: forced to come up with endless lists for bored morons to scroll through.

Awesome, now she was in a stabby mood. Maybe she shouldn't have stress-binged that bag of Sun Chips, even if they were the only things to spark joy for her all day.

Giving the email one more try, Grace thumbed back to the top and started skimming. And that was when she walked straight into a person with an oomph.

Great, Grace thought, massaging the spot on her chest where she'd bumped into the person's elbow. The stupid billionaire nepo baby was already infringing on her job.

She looked up to apologize but darkness met her, her eyes not used to the night after staring at her phone. The streetlights along the main drag were too far away to illuminate this part of the fence.

"Sorry," she said anyway.

"It's okay," a deep female voice responded. Unfamiliar, though a bit sultry.

"Phone off, miss."

Easy to tell who that second one was. Cop.

Muttering another curse, Grace quickly pocketed the offending device and dug through her purse to excavate her night-vision goggles. When she put them on, the world shifted to shades of emerald. The battery blinked low in the corner of her vision. Oh joy, she must have forgotten to turn them off last time. Now she'd have to charge them every thirty minutes or they'd die. This night could screw all the way off.

The woman materialized, her dress way too formal for a crime scene. She was Black, though the green night vision cast her in unflattering light. Which was typical. Grace's own pasty white skin and frame made her look like the Wicked Witch of the West. Still, Grace would kill for the woman's wispy bangs and high cheekbones. Who was she? Someone from the city? Couldn't be a rival paper—there weren't any left.

"ID," the cop demanded.

Grace handed it over and turned her focus to the officers behind him. Luckily, none of the other policemen behind the makeshift barricade of plastic and riot shields paid her any mind. Their attention remained centered around a hole in the fence three men wide.

But the ambulance parked flush along the curb sat empty. The paramedics must have already been dispatched inside with their mixed SWAT and special forces escort. Perfect. She was right on time and somehow already late.

She tried to spot the mixed battalion inside, but no luck. Darkness blanketed the houses leaving the sole point of light the looming, spear-shaped main gate, A.K.A. the Hellmouth, opposite her current position. She squinted, the Hellmouth's spotlights of faux daylight bright enough to burn her eyes. The gate was nicknamed after a show about a vampire slaying cheerleader. Technically, it was the only gate in but strategy dictated rescues take place from the nearest fence sector.

A dark shape sidled in, eclipsing the monstrosity. The fancily dressed woman's head leaned in, blocking Grace's line of sight. "Can I...help you?" Grace asked.

"Hi, I'm Tracy." A few officers, huddled behind their patrol cars, winced and glanced back in the woman's direction.

Just as Grace feared—a newbie. She sighed. Of all nights. "And you're with…?" she whispered back, hoping the woman would catch the hint.

She did. "The…*Plain Dealer.*"

"Oh." *Thanks for the heads up, Perry,* Grace thought. A new intern meant training, which meant questions, which meant a lot of talking on Grace's part on top of her regular beat. Far more energy than a bag of Sun Chips could give.

Grace bit her lip. She needed to play nice, like Perry said on her annual evaluations. Still, it was odd. If she had to guess, this Tracy was in her thirties, making them practically the same age. What had happened in her life that led her to this zero-dollar career choice?

"Ma'am," the cop said, handing back the ID, "all clear." He lifted the police tape for her to cross. Truly, a gentleman among swine.

"Thank you," Grace replied. "She's with me."

"…you're Grace Clemons?" Tracy asked.

"What gave it away?"

"I'm, um, I'm supposed to report to you. I'm the new intern."

"Great. Can you report this way?"

Tracy looked from Grace to the cop still holding the tape. "Oh, sorry. Yes." She scampered—there was no other way to describe it—over to Grace like she was a mouse and Grace was a hidey hole in the wall. Jesus, this woman was shaking. Terrified. She hunkered in close, no consideration for Grace's personal space. Which wasn't too bad, but she reeked of Memorial Day barbecue.

No one had seen a vampire in fifty years but Grace wished one would come out right now and eat her. She sighed and pinched her nose. There was a bright side. Sometimes during training, the cops and the Quarter guards overheard and corrected her, providing a new insight. *It's not about you,* Grace reminded herself. *Nothing is ever about you.*

"I'm sorry. I thought you'd be..." Tracy began.

"Yes?"

"...taller."

"Wow."

"I'm sorry. I'm sorry. I didn't mean—"

"Shut the hell up!" a uniformed officer nearby rasped.

Clutching her bag's strap, Grace faced the gap in the fence. The dark shifted several dozen yards inside. Her breath caught. If the vampires did attack, they'd go for the one who smelled like cooked meat first. But she was Grace's responsibility.

"This way." Grace led Tracy behind the nearest cruiser, the officer there already positioning himself to shield them.

The reek of the new intern was overpowering. By the looks of it, the officer with the shield wanted to say something biting, but refrained.

After a few tense moments, the Quarter settled back into its usual impenetrable self. Someone gave the all clear. Grace stood up.

The intern whispered so softly, Grace barely heard her: "Can we talk...somewhere far away?"

"Good idea." As they walked, Grace took deep breaths.

What would her sister, Joy, do? Let every opportunity be a chance for a big story. Help one more person the best she could. Grace rolled her shoulders and stretched her neck until it gave a satisfying pop. That paper-buying billionaire didn't know who he was dealing with. Take her off of the vamp beat? Likely story.

She readied her notepad and recorder app.

"My name is Tracy Wright, Grace Clem—*Miss* Clemons," she sputtered as they stopped by an off-kilter police cruiser. She adjusted her grip on her coffee cup and scratched the back of her neck. "It's an honor. I like your outfit. Designer?"

Grace resisted rolling her eyes. Was this lady serious? Attempts at flattery did not work when the subjects involved—a dark tan blouse and wide legged pants that swished—cost a mere twenty dollars at an outlet.

Crossing her arms, Grace leaned against the car's hood and studied the woman. Tracy gulped. Under her press badge photo, the American flag had fifty-six stars instead of fifty-eight. Most likely a misprint. But if the boys in blue caught it, there'd be hell to pay: bogarting any knowledge about cases tonight and leaving Tracy without a single story by morning.

But was this intern worthy of Grace's protection? She hadn't decided.

"Uh, I have a couple questions." Tracy pulled out her own notepad – she was prepared, a rarity. But the pad soon slipped through shaky fingers. "Sorry." She bent to pick it up. "It's just so...quiet."

"Yeah, I used to think something nefarious was going on." Grace grinned at the memory. "But you already figured out why it's like this."

"Right." Tracy cleared her throat but that didn't stop her voice from squeaking. "So, uh, why the gothic houses? Some kind of joke?"

Grace knew the answer. A fun one, too, but first, she needed some info. Once the battalion returned through that hole, everything here got wrapped up with military efficiency and she'd be working twice as hard for any information. "Hold that thought. I have to find the officer in charge and get the info on our victim."

"Oh, I have that."

"What?"

"Um. If that's okay? I got here before you and heard them on the radio. I've got everything right here." Tracy lifted her notepad.

Grace pursed her lips, impressed. Maybe this intern had some promise after all. *Okay, new plan.* Tracy looked about to fall over, pupils dilated, her breaths coming out shaky—when she was breathing at all. She needed a distraction. Or better yet, a game. "Tell you what. I'll answer all your questions about the Quarter if you fill me in on the victim."

Tracy bit her lower lip as she considered. It was somewhat cute. She nodded.

"Great." To put her at ease, Grace flashed her best smile, which she had been told was dazzling when her head was tilted just so. Of course, the complimenter had been drunk at the time. "To answer your question, yes, the gothic stuff is a joke. The city planner thought it was hilarious to design the vampire's living quarters off the movie Nosferatu. He didn't seem to realize that no one but him, some cops, and a few soldiers would ever see inside." She made a dismissive gesture toward the gathered cops. "Not many horror fans here."

"Huh. Well, how about the Green Beret—"

"Uh uh. My turn." She flipped through her notepad to a blank page. Her phone would catch every word but something about pen on paper helped to focus the mind. "Let's start easy: cause of death?"

"Exsanguination through the neck."

That couldn't be right. "Killed inside?"

"I guess," she replied with a shrug. "Why? Is that unusual?"

"It happens on occasion. But we'll get to that. What did the prelim show?"

"Um, I didn't hear that part."

Grace grumbled. Had to talk to an officer for that bit. If she missed out, she'd have to wait for the medical examiner for the info. And that meant calling her backup to wait around the morgue for a couple hours. Betsy always loved that. "Your turn."

"Why are the Green Berets here?"

"That's your question?" Grace rubbed her brow. "You really don't know any of this?"

"Only what you write." Tracy coughed. "I'm from a small town in Alaska. Barely any internet."

"Ah." Grace peered at her. Ignorance like this was so rare, it bordered on the absurd. "So you're probably thinking about the Comitatus Act, right? No troops deployed on domestic soil? Originally this place was manned by the National Guard. Then Kent State happened. So the Quarter was declared its own territory, and special forces were sent in. They partner with local police on retrievals."

"Oh, retrievals!" Tracy thrust her finger out, the tip stopping shy of jabbing Grace in the ribs. "Sorry. How the heck are people getting in there?"

"Dude..."

"What?"

"You suck at this game."

Tracy sighed, aggravation clear in her resigned tone. Good, a new emotion. "Fine."

"What's her name and physical description?" That was technically two questions, but who was counting?

But Tracy narrowed his eyes. Uh oh. "How did you know it was a 'her?'"

Grace kept her tone breezy and light. "Over eighty percent of victims found in the Quarter are female."

"Oh." She frowned. "First name Joy."

Grace straightened. "Joy?"

"Yeah. With a Y. Fifteen. Temp license found on her was new. Brown eyes and hair. Indigenous descent. They haven't checked missing persons yet, as far as I know."

Indigenous? It wasn't her. But still, Grace's heart pounded. She found herself lifting her phone out of her purse and up to Tracy's mouth. "Any relatives? Background? Motive? Suspects?"

"Um," Tracy stammered under the onslaught of questions. "Isn't it my turn?"

Grace glared. When Tracy didn't answer, she set her phone back where it had been and spoke through clenched teeth: "What's your question?

"Who's ending up in..."

Tracy trailed off, her eyes settling on the fence gap. A squeak made Grace turn. Inside the Quarter, a stretcher emerged from the last line of houses and eked its way toward the wall, the joint task force surrounding it in a defensive phalanx. They moved as one, everyone keeping a practiced, steady pace despite the terrified faces of the EMTs. Last time they forget to oil their wheels, Grace thought.

"The retrieved," Grace said, stepping close to Tracy and dropping her voice even lower. "The best way to explain them is to break them down by type." She counted on her fingers. "The first are the wannabes. Humans who drink blood, only go out at night, and wear black. You know, your average teen. Of those, the real zealots dig tunnels under the fence from surrounding properties."

"You never mention them in your articles."

"People aren't interested in that kind of crazy. Speaking of which, the second group are the prize seekers. These idiots want to get the cash prize for being the first to capture a vampire on film."

"Seriously? Even with all the warnings? And the Plain Dealer right there?"

"The PSAs about vampires not showing up on camera isn't the deterrent you'd think. We live in the Age of Conspiracy Theories, after all."

Grace paused, taking in a deep breath before continuing. "The last kind are my people: the victims of crimes. Undiscovered tunnels dug by the fanatics are found by opportunists. These entrepreneurs provide a first class ticket to a supernatural dumping ground where vampires act as quasi-human garbage disposals."

Tracy went quiet. Grace thought she had scared the woman mute but she only said, "Garbage disposals?"

"Yeah," Grace said. "We aren't sure why, but every now and then, the vampires drain instead of," she paused, trying to think of a better word, and failed, "feasting."

Tracy lowered her face, scanning her notepad to hide her discomfort. Didn't work that well.

Grace decided against mentioning the fourth kind of people: suicides. Too cruel. With how powerful the electric fence was, they rarely made it inside anyway. And besides, that particular cherry would get popped soon enough.

"The victim's address," Tracy said, unprompted, "was tied to a local youth hostel. So they have no leads."

"What's her last name?"

"Hatathli."

"Tell the detective in charge to try the Navajo Nation in Arizona. It's no guarantee but they might know something. Plus it'll give you a foot in the door with the blue frat here."

Tracy cocked an eyebrow.

"Yes, I'm capable of being nice."

"No, it's—so, you're from Arizona?"

"Yep." Was that some heat in her cheeks? Good thing night vision didn't pick up on blushing. "Give me a moment."

Tracy went with hesitant steps to fulfill Grace's request. Crazy, her inner bitch usually drove everyone away. Still, it was good Tracy left before asking more personal questions. Anyone, especially strangers, knowing anything about her always set off the repellant shields, as her dad would say. Best not to bite the new intern's head off.

The stretcher reached the ambulance. There she was. The victim's name being Joy was a coincidence. That was all. At fifteen, it couldn't be her. Still, Grace could barely resist the urge to charge forward and tear the body bag open.

Ladders rose up on either side of the gap. SWAT members climbed, mounting a temporary defense. The Green Berets started to weld the fence closed.

"Detective in charge isn't here yet," Tracy said, strolling back with more confidence. "Can I ask, if it's not too personal, what's your interest in all this?"

"This...what?"

"The Quarter."

Grace's tongue felt thick in her throat. *Her name is Joy.* "I, uh, would rather not talk about it."

"Okay." Tracy's breathing changed. "It's just so strange to me. People are really obsessed with this stuff, huh?"

You have no idea. "It keeps the lights on."

"Still. Day after day, reading about the most horrible things these prisoners do—"

"They're vampires. They're the damned."

"And what does that make us? If we imprison them and buy up their stories?"

Grace sighed, barely able to keep a growl from escaping. "How about you tell me your story?"

Tracy's mask slipped. "Mine?"

"Sure." Grace shrugged, feigning nonchalance. "Alaska must be interesting." *Since you seem to be so much better than us,* she wanted to add.

"Uh, well," Tracy started. "My cousin's friend ran away about...fifteen years ago? We all suspected the worst."

Grace nodded. It was a common fear among families with runaways teens. So common the paper had assigned a full-time secretary devoted to the tip line.

"Three weeks later, we knew. His body was discovered inside." Tracy faced the ambulance, its doors slamming shut. "I never cared to learn about what happened to him, about what went on...in there. But the way you breathed life into him, humanized him—it was like you knew him better than we did. You pushed the cops to continue the search for his killer." Here it came: "You're why I wanted to be a reporter."

More damn heat rose in Grace's cheeks. Her articles had that effect, and not only on reporters. The number of cops who joined the force because of her, one could think everything had changed, that the system was different. Yet here she was at another victim retrieval before ten on a weeknight. She shivered, the night finally growing a chill.

"Excuse me a moment," Grace said.

"I, uh," Tracy sputtered. She was way too timid for this job.

But she deserved a shot. Grace smiled and pointed at Tracy's press badge. "You might want to change that flag design. It's four months out of date."

Tracy's face paled. Grace would finish with her later; the sun was a long way off. She made her way over to the same officer who had checked her press badge.

"Where's Faison?" she asked.

"Struck gold."

"No way." So the lead detective had retired. That was great. He earned that gold watch a decade ago. "I didn't get a chance to say goodbye."

"Party's this weekend."

She nodded and made a mental note to call him after her shift. Cops weren't exactly welcoming to her in social situations. "Who's the new lead?"

"Yukawa."

Her gut soured. "You're kidding."

"'Fraid not."

"Where is he?"

"On another case."

Grace groaned.

"Is he really that bad?"

"Only if you want a mystery solved this decade."

The task force finished up. She glanced out into the Quarter, wondering how many more times she'd see these homes tonight.

Something moved. There, on the second floor, three houses from the end on the western side. It was only a flicker, a swish of white lace. Had she imagined it? No, the curtain still swung the tiniest fraction. A vampire had walked by, possibly looked out. She peered closer.

"You know, it's weird," Tracy said, sidling over, jolting her.

"What's that." Grace said with all the enthusiasm of a corpse.

"All this rigmarole 'cause the feds built a dumping ground in the middle of a city. Why not in the middle of the desert or at the center of a mountain?"

Grace looked at her. It was clear from Tracy's tone and eager expression that she was trying to get back onto Grace's good side. Didn't work, but she was cute. Odd...did Grace just think someone was cute twice in one day?

Shoving that thought down deep, Grace focused on Tracy's point. It was one Grace had made years ago and forgotten. Why place the camp here? And how, if there are so many involved in these retrievals, had no one seen a vampire? What else were they hiding? She smelled a cover-up.

"Yeah," Grace said. "It's irresponsible is what it is. Damn irresponsible."

Tracy beamed, proud. But Grace hardly noticed, her spirit giddy with a new story.

2

FOUR MORE BODIES, ONE a possible suicide, punctuated the rest of the night in uneven beats.

By body number three, Tracy was heaving in the gutter. It seemed that, without an interview to focus on, her facade cracked. Grace fetched her a coffee, a couple packets of saltine crackers, and sent her home. First shifts should be capped at caseload, not hours. Hopefully being given the bylines for the third and fourth victims would lift the newbie's spirit.

It was the least Grace could do after Tracy set her fingers alight. Grace's hands thrummed even now as she reached the final page of her proposal. Thank Gods for computers. If it weren't for spell check, she'd have been sent to a mental hospital years earlier. Though the software was being strained to the breaking point now.

She was on fire, like she hadn't been in years. Not even the A/C's brisk November morning temperature could dissuade her. Neither did thanking both capital-G "Gods," a religion her father had set her on with all his drunken ramblings years before. No, she was untouchable.

Finished, she speed-read through the proposal. Her palms grew clammy from the mistakes, but she hit Print anyway. Better to be done than perfect. Opening her office door, the blinding light of day struck her.

Crap, crap, crap! This was bad, worse than bad. She had only sat down, hadn't she? Gods, this freaking closet they stuffed her in!

She rushed to the copy room and huddled by the printer, hoping the warmth of the churning pages could still her tremble.

Perry was here. The old man was like a reverse vampire, arriving at the ass crack of dawn and slithering off to his putrid abode at sunset. All her plans–slipping the proposal under his door before he arrived, then sprinting back home to snuggle with Mr. Pawcy as she scarfed down hush puppies before turning in—everything was off the table. Now instead of over email, she had to defend this to his scowling face, its wrinkles etched from a lifetime of unforgiving frowns and never-ending disappointments.

Maybe she should just head home, drop the proposal off tonight before her shift when he wouldn't be around. An investigation like this would take months. What was one day?

Better to continue the way she always did: avoid the man who held her life in his hands.

Keep to the night. Fight in the shadows.

Her name is Joy.

The victims deserved better.

She'd promised.

Grace took a deep, steadying breath. Then another. No, there was no running from this. She smoothed out her shirt and fixed her hair using her phone's camera. A dot of Tracy's vomit blotted her chin. Her shaking fingers barely managed to wipe it away.

The victims needed her. And she would be here to serve, no matter how much she had to sacrifice: her relationships, her career, her life. What was one more measly little meeting?

She marched up to Perry's office and the Door. To her boss, reporters needed to earn their stories. He grew up in a time of struggle, so why should it be any different for them? Of course, he'd earned a living wage during all of his "struggle." Still, he installed the Door: a hundred pounds of solid, unvarnished dead oak that had last been oiled in the Silent Era.

Biting her cheek, she leaned forward, set herself, and pushed. The hinges moaned like a beached whale. Her shoulder made a similar noise. Once there was a gap wide enough, she slipped inside and let the Door bang shut.

Not one but two pairs of eyes glanced over at her.

Perry sat behind his desk, frowning under his crooked halo of hair, framed articles winging him on both sides. He regarded her from behind wide reflective lenses that blared a shrunken image of her back to herself.

In the chair nearest Grace sat Tracy. Her mouth widened in an O, like she'd been caught with her hand inside Grace's purse. Grace didn't see why. Being able to recover enough to return here was God-level work ethic.

Grace clutched her purse strap tight. "I'm sorry. I didn't mean—"

"No, you didn't," Perry interrupted, "but it's already done."

Strike one.

He addressed Tracy. "This has been quite productive. Thank you." She nodded and proceeded to pack up.

Perry turned to the wall, not staring at anything in particular. The minutes stretched. Grace almost excused herself until finally, he sighed. "What can I do you for, Grace?"

"I-I think I have a story." She cleared her suddenly dry throat. "I mean, I know I have a scandal involving the Hellmouth."

"Wow, original." His tone was less than bored. "This better be good. Even thinking about exposing anybody tied to that place will cut your access off in a heartbeat."

Translation: He wasn't gonna protect her from jack. Strike two, already.

"It is."

Tracy stopped packing. Perry finally looked at her. "What you got?"

The sudden attention made her neck hot. She spoke slowly. "So, um, the government took the paper's land back in the '60s and built the Hellmouth on it. The city told them to and..."

What was the next part? Her fingers slipped inside her purse and stopped. If she pulled the proposal out to check her notes, she'd lose him.

"And?" Perry spat.

"Um..."

Her notes burned a hole through her purse and into her thigh.

"Get to the meat of it, Clemons."

Hellmouth, our land, the city—the city! "At the time, we thought the city was getting back at us. It made sense: We exposed scandals and racist housing practices."

Perry twirled a finger through the air.

"B-but," Grace stammered, "what if their revenge was hiding something far worse?"

Perry's shoulders sagged. "Corruption?"

"I know, it's been done before—"

"More than a few times." Perry's face grew slack. He was almost comatose.

"Uh, yes. But..." No hope. Grace had to risk it. She reached into her bag. "Hold on..."

She pulled out her proposal and skimmed through it. Gods, so many typos. Perry's chair creaked; he was turning away. Grace panicked and read the first line she saw: "Why not bury this underground next to UFOs and the Ark of the Covenant?"

But Perry had already started typing on his keyboard. She had struck out. Grace gripped the proposal close to cover her face. She'd failed. Not just herself, but every single person who'd died in the Quarter and every single person to come. She pictured Joy shaking her head, disgusted with her.

"Good PR," Tracy said.

Grace's breath hitched. "W-what?"

"All the territory we stole," Tracy explained. "Other countries thought we were bullies. An empire. But treating vamps nice. It looked good for our image. But behind closed doors, who cares how we treat vamps?"

Perry cocked an eyebrow at Tracy.

"What? I-I read."

"Uh, right. But—" Grace sniffed and flipped to the last page of her proposal "—that doesn't explain the controlled human trafficking."

Perry swiveled her way again. The squeak of his chair cooled the heat in her chest a noticeable degree. "Controlled?" he asked.

She unlocked her phone, made sure the correct website was up, and handed it over. He took the phone but continued to watch her.

"Ohio's missing persons stats claim to be only slightly higher than the national average, but..." Perry started to scroll. "...but that's nowhere near true. I did some digging last night—in between incidents," she added when his eyebrow rose. "Then I reached out to some contacts in neighboring states. I think the real numbers are at least five times higher and almost double in all states surrounding us."

Perry set down her phone and started shuffling through drawers and folders, her words spurring him into motion. "Human trafficking angle.

People eat that stuff up. Plus, it'll be a nice change of pace from all this North Korea stuff. How fast can you get it to me?"

"Depends. I'll need to conduct some interviews."

"Like?" The shuffling whirred down, waiting for her to provide more fuel.

Grace pocketed her phone in an attempt to buy time. This was the part she was unsure about.

"I would need to speak with the mayor," Grace said, "and arrange interviews with the Green Beret and chief of police."

"Doable."

She took a deep breath. "And I'd need to speak with a few of the vampires themselves."

"Well—"

"Without Green Beret interference."

Perry went white. The shuffling ceased.

"They are the only ones with firsthand knowledge of who might be behind these disappearances."

Perry lifted his glasses and rubbed his eyes. "And you suspect the Green Berets are involved?"

"No." Grace said, measured. "But the Green Berets might influence what the vampires say. They're prison guards."

"Are you aware how many toes you'd step on doing this? At best, we have a rocky relationship there. After my predecessor retired, no one in our office is our point of contact."

Not technically true. Grace was. But even though she worked with them almost every night, they hardly spoke.

Perry went on. "If I arrange this, and it goes south, it might mean goodbye to your beat altogether. Are you willing to bet the body farm?"

Grace hadn't thought of that. Could she live with never helping another victim's family find closure? With losing what little influence she had over the police to improve? With failing the vow to her sister?

But if she didn't do this, she'd fail anyway. "Perhaps if you join me on the interviews—"

"What, damn myself, too?"

His response hit so hard, the neutral mask she'd kept cracked. "But you're–"

"I'll help her."

A beat passed before the two of them swiveled toward Tracy. Grace had forgotten she was in the room, and judging by Perry's expression, so had he.

Tracy shrank back from her upraised hand as if it had betrayed her. The barest squeak came out. "If Perry's...okay with it."

Perry cleared his throat, shifting back into genial boss mode. "Of course I am, but Grace, I hate to say it, the higher ups might need more before okaying this. Luckily," he held up a hand when Grace opened her mouth to object, "I have just the way to persuade them."

He pulled out a folder and offered it to her. She opened it, speed-reading its contents.

"A gay mob boss interview for Pride Month?" So many questions passed through her mind in the time it took Perry to nod. She settled on, "Are you serious?"

"We've had a hard time getting anyone to agree to doing the interview."

"Well, yeah." She held the folder out at arm's length. "There's been gay people in the mob for as long as...well, the mob. Hell, the mob controlled gay bars and raided them constantly. Do they really expect people to rejoice that the rainbow glass ceiling has been broken in organized crime?"

"It's what the brass wants," Perry replied with a dismissive flourish. "Do this, and you'll get your story. I'll give you the night off to prepare."

Grace wanted to say more, to shred the board's proposal into ribbons, but she held her tongue. To make change, one had to sacrifice. Joy had told her that once.

"I'll do it."

***

Grace rushed to her office before anyone could follow. Once the door was locked, she shimmied through the stacks of folders to reach her desk. She threw open drawers.

A heavy drawer came off and smashed her shin. She sank to the floor, nursing what most certainly would become a bruise. Screw this new billionaire owner. Screw Perry and his higher ups. She should have stuffed the proposal in the shredder. How in the hell was she supposed to do this? She'd interviewed people that made her skin crawl before but this was so much worse. Was compromising her morals really what getting justice meant?

When the pain ebbed, she scoured through the drawer's contents, past old awards and research notes until she unearthed a flask. The picture splayed across its surface showed two girls smiling wide toothy grins, their eyes full of mischief, a forest at their backs promising adventure.

She uncapped the flask but didn't drink. The age old liquid inside reeked. The odor seeped out into the office. Just a taste, she thought. One taste. What's a sip, really?

A knock at her door made her start. Grace coughed and put the cap back on the flask, then buried it once more. "Just a minute!"

It was probably Perry, ready to chew her out for still being here. But instead, there stood all five-foot seven-inch Tracy, wearing a new red blazer, mouth agape, her fist raised to knock once more. "Hey!" she said after a moment. "Glad I caught you."

Grace shrank back from the doorway. Everyone was taller than her. Why did Tracy freak her out? "You are?"

"Of course!" Tracy's eyes shifted from Grace to the garbage dump of a room beyond. Grace sidestepped to block her view. "I'm on my way out."

Tracy offered a warm smile. "Of course. You must be tired. Can I walk with you to your car?"

"Um. Give me a minute?" Grace closed the door. The flask called, enticing her with its lingering odor. *Deep breaths, just deep breaths.* With each exhale, the urge receded. Finally, she could pack up, which mostly involved emptying old chip bags from her purse into the garbage.

"He's an asshat," Tracy said as Grace joined her.

Grace chuckled. Asshat wasn't even the half of it.

"Don't sweat it. About the office."

Grace frowned and hurried to tap the elevator button.

As they waited, Tracy leaned toward her. Grace froze. Did she smell the booze?

But then Tracy whispered, "How do you even find your chair?"

The ridiculousness of the question, as if it was the most offensive thing in the world, made Grace laugh. "Oh, I don't. I just grab somebody else's."

"You're kidding."

"Nope. Some have taken to securing their chairs to their desks with bike locks."

Tracy cackled and Grace joined in. It was good to make someone laugh for once. The elevator arrived and they stepped in. But as Tracy hit the button for the parking garage, a thin blue paper bracelet slid out from her sleeve.

"I didn't realize your first night was that bad," Grace said as the doors closed.

Tracy pulled the cuff of her shirt over the hospital band. "It wasn't. My mom, she..."

Grace planted her feet and tried to project herself into the floor.

"But everything's fine, doc says." Tracy's thin-lipped smile creased the dark circles under her eyes. "Wonder who worried more: me over her today or her over me back when, you know?"

Grace didn't. Worry? Her mom? That implied at least liking your daughter. But Grace nodded all the same.

The elevator dinged. Here's where they separated, the mood earlier lost. But as Grace shuffled forward, Tracy strode right along beside. "Can I ask you something? How do you stay objective?"

"Objective?"

"I've read your column. You write about so many tragedies. I followed up on some of them. Less than a quarter see any improvement in their circumstances. How are you not discouraged?"

Less than quarter? Was that true? She had never checked, there was never time. All the more reason for things to change.

"I don't know if I'm all that objective," Grace admitted. "But I guess, to me, I have to keep writing. No one else will tell these stories. There are so many families who need help. So many no one cares about. It's a—"*promise I made to a dead girl*"—a need in my bones. To write, even if no one reads it."

"Hm." Tracy shook her head, as if that wasn't the answer she hoped for. "I've worked at other places. Before this. Law offices, retail, real estate. I've never dealt with so much before."

It was then Grace looked at Tracy, really looked. The woman wasn't as short as she appeared. Her shoulders stooped, bowing under an unseen pressure. But her feet never stilled, dragging along the floor as she swayed.

Grace thought she had the market on suffering, isolated as she was on the night shift, but here was proof others felt what she'd grown jaded to years ago.

"I knew I'd have to be objective," Tracy said, "but this is inhuman."

Shakily, then with a bit more confidence, Grace laid her hand on the woman's shoulder. It was strange, but nice. "Things will always slip through the cracks, but the tiny differences you make in people's lives are worth it."

"Yeah?" A hint of a smile tugged Tracy's lips. "And how do you deal with the stress?"

"Did I mention I like to work in bars?"

"That so?" Dimples. Of course, this goddess had dimples. "Do you want to get lunch with me?"

"Uh," Grace said, flying through dates in her mind. "Can we make it breakfast or dinner? My lunch is usually around last call."

"Oh, right." Did her cheeks flush a little?

"Thursdays work best for me," Grace said, pulling out her phone. "We can meet and discuss the investigation."

"...the investigation?"

Grace looked up. "Yeah. You said you'd help with—"

Tracy's face crumpled.

"Oh, you meant..."

The levels in the parking forked, and Tracy stepped toward the opposite way. "It's fine."

"Look-"

"It's fine! I thought I got a vibe, but it's okay. It happens. We don't know each other that well—"

"No, wait. I'm sorry. You..." *You weren't wrong.*

Tracy looked from the way back to Grace.

Grace breathed in. She couldn't tell Tracy the truth. That she hadn't dated since her sister disappeared sixteen years ago. Too many treat her differently after learning that. "This mob thing has me really stressed. And I'm tired." Grace hoped she kept the pleading from her eyes as she inwardly begged Tracy to say something.

The woman considered her. She had a soft beauty underneath those bangs, a quiet assurance to the way she carried herself. "Mexican okay?"

Grace perked up. "Uh, yeah."

They walked in-step to the garage. "I do have an idea for the interviews," Tracy said. "A personal contact."

"Oh?"

"Yeah, I, uh, used to date a serviceman."

"Yeah?"

Tracy smiled. She must be aware the effect that was having. "Are you always this tired? How many hours do you work?"

Crap. Grace hadn't expected this. What was a normal amount? "Uh, fifty or so," she lied.

"Perry told me it was closer to eighty."

Stupid Perry. "Somewhere in between, then."

"Sounds like we need a place with coffee."

"I hate coffee," Grace spat, more vicious than she meant. "It just tastes like liquid shoe."

Tracy looked back toward the elevator.

Say something, Grace thought. *Something nice. You're losing her.* "Tea is good, though. I'll email you?"

Tracy took forever in replying. "Sure."

Shiiiit.

Tracy left without a word once they reached Grace's car. Grace needed to say something, to stop this impossible beauty from walking away.

Speak, dammit!

But before she could, Tracy called out, "Omg, I got a date with Grace Lorraine Clemons!"

Then she slipped inside, leaving Grace and her dropped jaw. *What a freaking goof.* A goof who knew her name, her whole name. Most of her colleagues didn't know that. Grace twirled her car keys on the end of her finger and floated on air into her car.

3

GRACE HAD A DATE. She almost floored the gas pedal out of the lot. Who cared if her A/C was broken and the temp had already reached eighty? She had a date!

The conversation with Tracy played in her mind on repeat. The curve of the woman's smile as she laughed, the way she lingered in the office doorway, how her voice squeaked at the end of screaming "Grace Lorraine Clemons!"

Gods, it was nice to have something more interesting to focus on during her commute than forgotten details to add to her articles or what type of frosting to put on her comfort food before bed.

The Quarter's hideous murals shone in their blaring reflective paint. They started to harsh her mood. Each one displayed a hideous, gaudy tale of divine guardians rescuing the downtrodden. The rust from the barbed wire above had bled down and ruined the top of each image.

No, no more negativity. Today she had a date.

Grace went to shove her sunglasses on but couldn't find them. So the last mural hit hard: a benevolent soldier that looked like a white Jesus handing a cowering vampire an IV bag of blood. The words underneath read, "...give unto the least of these..."

I knew I'd have to be objective, but this is inhuman.

Tracy's words together with the mural cut through her, stirring a memory. Grace tried to ignore it, to drive on, away from the past now seeping out of the wound Tracy had opened, but a line of cars brought the world to halt. The tiny breeze blowing through her window ceased. And against her will, Grace was pulled back to another day nearly decades earlier when summer had overstayed its welcome well into October, like the sun had reached down and held the winter ransom.

***

The rotating fan in Grace's room whirred its unsteady rhythm, punctuated by the occasional *shing* of blades grinding against the wire net casing. All summer, Grace and Joy had lain prostrate before its massive frame, dragging it from room to room. But as the heat lingered, it stayed in their bedroom, as did they.

Sweat was everywhere. Grace's clothes. Her sheets. Her crack. That last place, especially. She was pretty sure hell was sweat trickling down your ass and being unable to wipe it away for all eternity.

Joy stood at her meager waist-high dresser, a determined look on her face that showed she was oblivious to her pit stains. Grace envied her sister when she got like this, unmoored and sailing beyond the tar pits of reality. But when Joy's eyebrows furrowed, Grace knew the voyage in her sister's head had ended on rocky shores.

Joy pointed at the poster over her dresser, the one of the Quarter Dad had bought two years ago for the low, low price of half his pay check. "Laura has a better one. Her cousin had a layover in Cleveland and he bought it from a dealer. It has a real vampire in it!"

Grace rolled her eyes. A rumor had been going around that someone had figured out how to photograph vampires. It would be a few years before the news caught wind of this and debunked it. But back then, posters of the Quarter were all the rage, every girl—well, almost every—obsessed with the mysterious residents.

What fueled the demand was the decision to depict the ultimate fantasy: misunderstood yet sensitive bad boys with six packs who just needed to be tamed by the right girl. Grace understood the appeal; she had been around the boys at school, with their odors and humor, not to mention their own market of disturbing scantily clad vampire posters. She couldn't blame the girls for wanting something more.

But that didn't mean she wanted to hear about it. All. The. Time. "Can we talk about something else?"

"Laura won't even let me see it," Joy went on. "Not even for a second. When I bring it up, she just stares at me. It's like she's trying to tick me off!"

"Maybe she's worried about it being damaged?"

"God, Grace! It's like you don't even care that Laura hates me!"

"Joy..." Grace propped herself up on an elbow, careful to stay in the air flow. "What is the big deal?"

"We made a promise to always show each other our crushes."

"Gods. Boys again? You didn't hear me talk nonstop about hot guys when I got boobs."

Joy's nostrils flared. "Oh, sorry! I didn't realize I was supposed to be a weird sexless loser like you!"

Grace saw red. Without another word, she snatched up the fan and walked out.

"Hey!"

The cord caught and wrenched the fan out of her hands. It fell with a loud bang and sputtered, then died. Grace looked at Joy following in her wake. "Now look what you did!"

Joy swallowed. "Me?!"

"Just help me fix it."

For a moment, Grace thought Joy would do no such thing. She continued to stand there, but finally huffed and went to the closet where her dad kept the tools. Grace unplugged the fan.

Joy handed her the screwdriver. Grace went to work unscrewing the front casing.

"...is it busted?" Joy asked. This was probably the closest Joy got to saying "I'm sorry."

Grace considered a retort but decided against it. It wouldn't fix what happened. Plus, her sister hadn't said anything worse than what she'd heard while encased in a bathroom stall at school.

It wasn't that Grace didn't talk about boys. But their loud belchy ways never really did anything for her. She was still lightyears behind her classmates at discovering her sexuality. Honestly, she still hoped to peg it down.

"It's okay," Grace finally said.

Joy let a long breath behind her.

Grace peeled the casing off. "Mom and dad don't like you talking about those vampires so much."

"What do they care? Dad bought me this poster."

"After you bugged him for over a year. He's never even come in to see it."

"Yes, he has."

"When?"

Joy said nothing, only handed over another tool.

"Why are you so obsessed, anyway?" Grace asked.

Joy twirled, her top billowing like a sail that received a sudden and needed gust of wind. "Because they're so mysterious and dark and edgy and... Laura said there's one, Rafael, who uses his small savings to paint all the beautiful women he's met throughout the centuries. Ah—" Joy placed her hand over her heart "—can you imagine?"

Grace focused on forcing her head up and down instead of on the prickling sensation at the base of her spine. "Vampires aren't what you think," she whispered.

But Joy went on, as if Grace hadn't spoken. "Laura and I have come up with a hotness scale based on hair, abs, butt, smile, and..." she wiggled her eyebrows, "...*smolder.*"

Grace checked the wires and found a couple that had come loose. "There's a video at school."

"Okay...?"

Grace reached for the cheap smartphone her parents got from a donation bin. "The first video of a vampire."

"No way."

"Way. I caught one of the basketball players showing it to his girlfriend before school. Here."

Joy took the phone with both hands. Grace went back to the fan and finished reconnecting the wires. She listened as the video—a hoax—played.

In it, a pale bald vampire with a beer gut cornered a woman in a dark alley. The woman screamed as it shredded her top and clamped its powerful jaws into her shoulder. She battered the creature, smacking its head and neck and eyes. Useless. Her body shriveled from the massive blood loss, her attempts to resist growing sluggish, then ceasing altogether. Finally, the beast wrenched her violently back and forth until a chunk of her shoulder tore off in its mouth. Blood splattered the camera lens and covered what happened next. But the audio continued.

At the sound of the blood spatter, Joy whimpered and lowered the phone. Grace counted to five, then looked at her sister. Her eyes glistened with tears.

"This isn't real," Joy said, her voice weak.

"It is," Grace assured her. "And that's not even the Quarter. That vampire got out. They hunt like that, you know, cornering people, letting them tire themselves out. That's when they have their fun." Grace looked into the whites of her sister's eyes. "But sometimes, they sneak into people's homes. And if the person they want to eat makes even a peep, they kill their entire family."

Joyce ran. "Mom!"

Grace had maybe a minute before her mom stormed over and grounded her. She turned on the fan and sat, luxuriating in the cooling gust. The video had done its job. Joy would think twice about bringing up vampires around her again.

She closed her eyes. Everything always worked out.

As if on cue, the fan coughed and died.

Grace went to bed early that night, no supper except the bitterness in the back of her throat. No one understood her. They could all rot. Her sister, her parents. Everyone was out for her, 'cause she didn't fit their normal.

Sleep eluded her for hours as the torrid thoughts mixed with the broiling heat. Joy slept, grinning, the fan circulating her half of the room into bliss. Grace would get her back in the morning.

But the sun, when it rose, brought a different unexpected scream.

Grace rocketed up and scanned her room for its source. Was she dreaming? Joy's bed lay empty, the window screen next to it slashed. A lump of green lay curled up on the floor nearby.

Grace didn't move, uncertainty gripping her. Who had screamed?

The lump unfurled to reveal her mother. "What did you do?!"

"M-me?" Grace stammered.

Her mother's face twisted and she began to crawl toward her. Grace shrank back, holding the blanket as a shield, but her mother grabbed her and jostled her. "Where's your sister? Where?!"

When Grace didn't respond, her mother shook her harder. "WHERE?!"

Her mother's glare bore into her, rage and hatred stripping her down, tearing into her flesh until she was bare. *Why didn't you wake up? Why didn't you protect your sister?*

"Let her go," her dad said, rushing into the room, dropping the phone. "Hope, please!"

"She knows! She knows who took my baby..."

"She was asleep."

Her dad pried her mom off. With each finger, her mother's scream grew, her mouth widening until it could swallow the sun. Grace thought she'd be consumed. Finally, her father succeeded, and her mother fell to the floor, sobbing, a pale withered thing.

Her father watched, regaining his breath, wary of another attack. A voice came over the phone, tinny and distant. He spared Grace a final glance, then picked it up. "Yes, I'd like to report a missing child..."

Her mother clung to her robe with white bloodless hands. "You were her keeper. You were supposed to protect her." Setting her back to Grace, she whispered the last words she would speak to her daughter until she ran away at seventeen: "Now you're just my mistake."

***

Grace entered her apartment and sank to her knees. She took a few unsteady breaths. Her apartment was probably crawling with invaders and murderers. Let them come.

Mr. Pawcy rubbed against her. *I love you,* he was saying. *Most ardently.* She forced her hand to rise and pet him in return. She was his protector. His keeper. It was up to her to keep him safe.

One more deep breath, then she went through her routine. First was the shoe box. She slid it away from the wall with her foot, making the trip wire tied between it and the side table slack. Next came the failsafes. Mr. Pawcy followed her as she checked the barred windows and locks, the hairs still set in all the frames. Only then, when she knew the apartment was secure, did she allow herself to settle into her favorite chair before her lone piece of wall art.

A few moments here, buffeted by Mr. Pawcy's purring furry mass and her sky-blue walls soothed her knots away. Finally, she looked at it, the poster of the Quarter from her sister's bedroom, framed and standing in place of a TV. The bottom right corner was starting to yellow from age.

She'd have to reseal it again. But for now, she studied it, petting Mr. Pawcy into a stupor. Every line and angle a visual promise to her sister. To be memorized and absorbed each day.

Five more victims, Joy, she projected to the picture. *Five. But hopefully, with this article, the last five. No more lost, sister. No more failed keepers. No more...you.*

She performed a quick prayer to both Gods—a lasting holdover from her father but also the only religion that made sense, the God of the Fortunate and the God of the Lost, feuding equal powers, with humans caught in the middle, collateral. Then her nightly routine was complete.

Centered, she walked over to her Arizona wall calendar in the kitchen and penned in the next couple days. Hopefully, this week wouldn't alter her sleep schedule too much. She had grown accustomed to the night shift years ago, and it was getting harder to adjust. Aging sucked.

Her eyes kept moving past Wednesday's interview to Thursday. To Tracy. The excitement earlier had coursed through her and finally settled into her stomach, where she could digest it.

Relationships were not on her radar. Attraction, sure. Who wouldn't be turned on now and again? But that was more of an errand to take care of with the same vigor as grocery shopping. More enjoyable, certainly, but anything beyond it? Not possible. Not with her schedule, her mission.

This Thursday meetup must be business, she told herself. Not a date. She'd have to get Tracy on the same page. There was no room for anything more.

But when she tried to picture telling Tracy...

This was absurd. She shouldn't be more afraid to eat out with a coworker than verbally tango with an armed mafia boss. Right?

Maybe she could reschedule. Really, the whole thing could be an email, right? Of course, it could. She was the reporter, the boss. If she wanted to cancel a time-consuming meeting, why shouldn't she?

She lifted her phone to email Tracy when a call came through. Grace went rigid, mouth agape. Maybe her exhaustion was causing her to hallucinate? She rubbed her palms in her eyes, but the screen still showed three impossible letters: M-O-M.

It was a pocket dial. It had to be. There was no other explanation that the woman who'd ignored her for years would suddenly want to talk.

Mr. Pawcy made an all too familiar hacking sound, startling her from the call. Grace set the phone down as if it were radioactive. She waited, staring, expecting the ping of a notification that her mother had left a voicemail. But time passed, and nothing.

Grace sighed. After all these years, her mother still had this effect. Like the cat throw up at Grace's feet, she spoiled everything and left her stink long after she was gone.

Crisis averted, Grace went to grab the paper towels. She may as well change the litter, too. That also meant sweeping, washing hands, and finally — joy of joys — hush puppy heaven.

Soon, the routine of chores and comfort food took over, and the need to cancel was soon buried and forgotten.

4

VLADIK KOMAROV WAS THE Russian equivalent of the Hindenburg disaster in shape and destruction. Law enforcement connected him to no fewer than thirty-six murders and countless more disappearances within the last three years alone. The ways he mutilated his victims would make the vilest serial killers wince.

This was the man Grace had to interview in Room 106 of the Economy Inn across from the dialysis center. The higher ups at her paper must have a sense of irony.

She knocked, then waited. Trying to still her tapping foot, she glanced over at the parking lot and willed a third car to join the gangster's and her own.

A disheveled rail of a man opened the door a crack. A waft of citrus undercut with black pepper emanated out, reminiscent of the rancid deodorant teenage boys like to spray. When the man spoke, his accent was light, almost American. "Yeah?"

"Room service," Grace replied, reciting the passphrase. "You requested the cardamom brandy?"

He gestured her inside with a sweep of his arm.

She rushed in. You don't keep a man who was alleged to have beaten a pro UFC fighter to death with his bare hands waiting.

A sharp click behind her, like a gun having its safety turned off. She spun, keys at the ready. But it was only the door shutting. Of course.

A quick pat down—professional in every way—and the man beckoned her on with a finger. "This way."

She did her best to hide the tremor in her knees as she followed the guard past what could generously be called the bathroom into the room. A second guard, a scar bisecting his face, leaned against the wall, peeking at the world outside from behind the cheap pastel curtains. His hands were too large for his frame. The perfect size to engulf her neck.

Grace swallowed and turned. On the lone king-sized bed, propped up against floral pillows, shoes off, was the man himself. The embroidered sign over his head read, "Kind people are my kind of people."

The rumors of his obesity were way off. His whole torso was conditioned muscle, a flood of flesh that threatened to burst through his shirt at the slightest flex.

Grace's blood rushed in her ears and she had to force herself to breathe. This was only one man. She'd done interviews before with corrupt politicians and CEOs, tyrannical leaders and arrogant tech innovators. Granted, none carried the air of authority Komarov did.

He made no move to begin. After what Grace decided was long enough to appear humbled, she gave an awkward curtsy and said, "Pakh-sir." She froze. *Oh no.* She had almost called Komarov "pakhan" – the Russian word for mob boss.

His eyes went cold.

Crap. She was going to bed in a body bag tonight, wasn't she?

"Igor," Vladik said in a gruff, ursine voice.

"Yes, boss?" the man from the window replied. He was beside her, standing inches away without having made a sound. Grace clutched her purse. The brick inside might give her a head start. Might.

"Where is your head? Give the reporter a chair."

The man pushed a chair out from a side table without a glance and sat back down. The chair slid halfway to her and pitched over.

"Igor," Komarov sighed. "Please."

"I'm keeping you safe—"

"An army won't march on this place in two seconds. Please, show our guest some courtesy."

"It's okay." Grace picked up the chair and sat down. She thanked Igor with as much confidence as she could muster. *They bicker like my cousins,* she thought. And just like that, it was another day at the office.

"I like to start my interviews," Grace explained, ignoring the dark brown stain by her left foot, "by asking for any anecdotes or funny stories you think capture who you are."

"Capture who I am?"

"Yes. Nothing life changing. Just anything you're proud of, or that you tell your drinking buddies."

"I am five years sober."

"...it's just an example."

He set his massive hand on his chin. "I think not. My stories are not for faint hearts."

"Okety dokety." *Okety dokety?* Grace reached inside her purse to cover her heating cheeks.

The door guard was behind her in an instant and bumped her elbow with his knee, sending her hand deeper into her purse than she intended. She fought the urge to cover her nose against his BO.

"Only my pad," she explained. "For notes."

He squinted, searching her purse, then nodded and stepped back.

She tried to continue as if nothing had happened. "Mr. Komarov, why did you want to meet with me today?"

"For interview."

"Of course, but why specifically?"

Silence.

"Usually my subjects have clear goals they want me to tackle." Or they were so ecstatic to be in the paper, they didn't care what she asked. But that didn't apply here. "I've been told to focus on Pride Month. Is that all right?"

"That is fine."

"Great." She took a moment to recall the questions she had prepared. "When did you first realize you were gay?"

"At fourteen."

"And your age now?"

"...I'm in my fifties."

"Who was your first crush?"

"No comment."

"Longest relationship?"

"No comment."

"Is there anything you've contributed to the gay community at large?"

"No comment."

"Mr. Komarov," she said, squeezing the pen in her fist, "why did you contact the paper for this interview?"

Komarov's eyes settled on the space above her. "I didn't."

The guard at her back coughed.

Well, this was new. She resisted turning to address the guard. What the hell had he been thinking, contacting the paper without his boss's consent?

"Does anyone want ice?" the offending guard asked. Without waiting for an answer, he left.

Komarov glared after him until the door clanged shut.

Grace took a breath, capped her pen, and set it down hard enough for the mob boss to hear. "I want to assure you, Mr. Komarov, everything I write will be sent to you for approval before it gets within a mile of publication. You have nothing to fear."

"Fear? What do you know about fear?"

Grace resisted rolling her eyes. The question was such a clichè. Still it drummed up images before she could stop them. Her sister's ruffled sheets. The nights spent sleeping in closets, or the shed, or wherever an intruder would be least likely to look for her. Begging her mother to let her in in the morning.

"More than you know," Grace replied.

"Is that so?" he asked, finally deigning to meet her eyes. "Let me tell you a story since you are so keen. Not for record. When I was eight, my father and his friends brought home two strangers. The men were drug dealers, new to the area and looking for a buyer. My father was charged with finding their supplier. I went to sleep after the dealers fell unconscious from the beatings.

"When I woke, the floor was centimeters thick with their blood. My mother had to sidestep around the pile of severed limbs in the kitchen to make my toast."

Bile tore up Grace's throat.

"I can still hear her sloshing over to me. Yet the fate those men suffered would be nothing compared to what I would face if my rivals found out a single one of my weaknesses. So, I ask you, Grace Clemons, what do you know about fear?"

Grace dug her nails into her thigh.

I knew I'd have to be objective but this is almost inhuman.

"Mr. Komarov, when I was fifteen, my younger sister disappeared from our bedroom. The window screen had been slashed. I slept less than six feet away. Some—" she held her arms out, palms open "—monster came in and decided on a coin flip to take her instead of me. After, my mother blamed me. She thought I was jealous of my sister, that I conspired to have her taken away. After, my father grew increasingly paranoid and believed whoever took her would come ba-"

"Are you saying," Komarov interrupted, "that I am a monster who takes young girls in the night?"

"What? No, I—" Had the guard by the window moved? He seemed closer now, larger. Grace realized what holding her arms out toward Komarov must have looked like, the implications that carried, and lowered them. "I meant no offense."

"But you have caused one." The behemoth on the bed held her in his gaze. This must be what those dealers felt like before Komarov's father ripped them apart.

Would the guards make Komarov toast as she lay bloody on the floor?

He broke eye contact and shrugged. "Or maybe a nervous mistake. Go ahead. Ask your questions."

Her bottom lip quivered. She bit down on it and dove in.

***

The interview lasted another thirty-five minutes. Komarov provided more 'no comments' than answers but as soon as Grace had enough, she ended it. The door guard never returned.

She held her composure until she was outside in the bright, open parking lot. No cars had joined her own. She arranged her keys between her knuckles, Wolverine-style, and readied her purse brick. Sprinting would have looked bad, but a jog was probably okay. She pretended to get an alert on her phone, then took off toward her car. Her clacking heels echoed off the walls and stone pillars wide enough to hide assailants.

As soon as she got inside her car with the doors locked, all this would be behind her. She couldn't believe she told Komarov about Joy. The mobster had an uncanny way of prying out information. Gods, she was such an idiot, taking this interview.

Why hadn't she parked closer? There her car sat, all smug and blue in the last spot, right next to the safe street. The motel cut off not far from the spot. Anyone could be hiding behind those dilapidated corners, ready to strike.

She tapped the unlock button on her key several times. The car chirped back, merry and beckoning.

A ball of desperation formed in her stomach, a craving for the familiar. Maybe the Tavern on Biddolph? Perfect little corner table there to type up the interview before nightfall.

A crunch of pavement at her back sent her spinning.

A fleshy dash slipped behind a pillar not twenty feet away.

The bodyguard! He must have followed her, laid in wait, letting her get most of the way to her car before he rushed forward like an Olympic runner at the speed of-of–

No, that was insane. If she disappeared here, now, it would be too easy to trace the mobsters to the incident.

Although...Komarov had gotten away with more. A lot more.

The car locked and she jumped. No, that was okay. It did that after ten seconds. She let out a sigh that morphed into a nervous laugh.

Lord, she needed a drink. Despite what she told Tracy, yesterday was the first time she partook in ten years. Lone woman at a bar? Too dangerous. But today called for something to steady her—

A jab of pain exploded between her toes.

She recoiled, backpedaling and stumbling until she came down hard on her butt. Sticking out of the soft skin of her shoe was a clear syringe, plunger depressed. A gloved hand disappeared underneath the car. She spun, crawling, the world blurring. But as she opened her lips to cry out, the dark of the lot rose up and claimed her.

5

Grace's body locked her inside.

*****

Something bumped against her. It was him, her kidnapper. This was his thigh. Tapping against her as he carried her along. The solid, alien warmth of these facts weighed against her and settled her back to reality like a heavy blanket during a storm.

He wasn't all powerful. She could figure her way out of this. If she struck at the right moment.

A light. He hadn't zipped the bag closed all the way. The yellow light rose, then faded, but was soon followed by another. A streetlight. They were in a city.

Wherever he was taking her, he wanted her immobile but not numb, not unconscious. He wanted her to feel what was coming.

He wanted her to hurt.

A smooth metal structure loomed into her slitted view. A speckle of white light illuminated swirls of wire along the top. The mural of white Jesus looked even paler at night, his eyes hollow.

No, she thought. *Not here.*

A clang was followed by a series of clicks. She rose into the air, the barbed wire nearing. He was taking her up a ladder.

Not this. Anything but this. Please...

He grunted and repositioned her into a bear hug. She caught a glimpse of a black shirt and ski mask. His head cocked to one side, revealing his collarbone. White skin poked out, his neck exposed. And there, running parallel along his jaw, was the slightest hint of a scar. So faint, she probably wouldn't have noticed if she wasn't so close.

This was good. She had an identifying mark. Now all she needed to do was escape.

"...help...m..."

She was confused about who had spoken until she realized the word had come from her own lips. A finger twitched along her lower spine. Finally! The drugs were wearing off. She was moving. Not enough for an attack yet, but a finger or a bite in the right place...

Heck, if she could scream loud enough, she could alert the Green Beret. Whoever this was, he was a fool for not using a tunnel.

A thick, slow sigh from her kidnapper wafted across her face. Her eyes moistened at the stinging, yet subtle, stench. An image came to her: a small, wiry man opening a motel door and ushering her inside.

Her arm twitched. The mob guard. He'd been waiting for her. But not where she suspected.

What if he paid off the Beret? Was that possible?

She'd have to get away herself. The next time he adjusted her, she'd strike. But the feel of him disappeared.

Where had he gone? She waited, readying to snap out in an instant. But then an two immense pressures spiked between her shoulders and in her lower back. He must be holding her aloft, his arms under her like columns.

"Hel...Help! I—"

Then, with a grunt, the pressure disappeared and she careened into an ocean of floodlights.

6

A DAY LATER, DETECTIVE Eugene Yukawa stared straight ahead into the Hellmouth's check-in area because if he didn't, he'd smack the top of the sausage-headed guard patting him down. What was this, the third time this guard had explored his right leg?

Eugene closed his eyes and took a deep breath. This kind of harassment was typical for Cleveland PD, especially him. If it weren't civilians and suspects barking at him over every tiny thing, then it was his colleagues complaining that he didn't live up to the model minority they envisioned. This meathead was no exception and, most importantly, not worth it.

This Green Beret was probably just reveling in a little power trip. Couldn't blame him. No civilian outside these walls would believe that under the mountain of concrete and floodlights were a mere fifty soldiers pent up in six gray rooms and a hallway. Most stood in said hallway now, watching him without watching. All good. Let the little white power cosplayers have their petty distractions. Besides, Eugene was already late for this interrogation and shouldn't be here as it was.

The guard finished patting him down. But instead of waving Eugene on toward the interrogation rooms, the guard produced a clipboard from somewhere and started scribbling.

That's it, Eugene thought. He leaned forward, making a show of reading the guard's dog tags. Private Beluga, like the whale. Must be joke tags. The guard might have been a hundred fifty pounds soaking wet.

Beluga laughed, loud and boisterous in a way that made Eugene flinch. "All right. This way, detective."

Eugene didn't need to be led to the room, but followed the guard anyway. No need for any further delays.

"I have to wonder," Beluga said as they went, his pace slowing. The detective matched, even though he wanted to go around. "How many times have you spoken to this vampire now? Six?"

"Um." Eugene had always been terrible with numbers, even counting. "Five?"

"Ha, you lost count?"

Red edged into Eugene's vision.

"Geez, and you still haven't solved that case from...when was it again?"

"...August," Eugene guessed.

"Hm. And it's what, almost June? Do you get a punch card for each unsolved month? A free phone book to use in your next interrogation?"

Eugene tightened his hand into a fist. "Is there a problem, private?"

"Sergeant First Class. And problem? No," Beluga said, looking as innocent as possible. "It's just—the boys and I have a bet."

Here it goes. "Oh?"

Beluga came to a stop and blocked the corridor. "See, I think this is a sport for you. Like watching the game on Sundays. This vampire is your equivalent to rooting for the Browns. And torturing her for info is butting your head against a lineman. One day you'll break through to the QB."

Eugene grinded his teeth.

"Course, the boys have worse i—"

"I've never tortured a suspect. Not once."

"Not with our tools, no."

"Then what are you on about?"

Beluga stuck his tongue in his cheek. "Here's my offer: You let something slip, something that will lead a few interested parties to the perp, I'll split the pot with you."

Eugene ground his teeth again. No one had access to his recordings. They were sealed behind three different confidentiality laws. So this was a massive breach. But best not to upset the few with the real power here.

He glanced over Beluga's shoulder to the interview room ahead, the heavy bank vault door wide open. "Well," Eugene stepped in close until he smelled Beluga's peppery aftershave, "between you and me, Zola is more than just a witness in a homicide case." Eugene leaned to the right.

Come on, follow me.

Like a buffering image, Beluga eventually swiveled opposite Eugene, copying his movements seconds late. Eugene grinned. "She's..."

Beluga leaned in.

Eugene held back the clincher until he had switched places with the sergeant. "...protected by the law. And deserving of our respect."

The guard's expression soured. Eugene hurried and sauntered to the vault door. *Let that be a lesson to you,* Eugene wanted to project. *Don't mess with the CPD.*

But once Eugene was out of sight in the interrogation room, he collapsed against the wall and panted as if he reached the end of an intense workout.

After a few mechanical clicks, the vault door shut him inside. *Out of the frying pan.* He took a moment to compose himself, then turned.

The room was twice as long as it was wide, drab gray like the rest of the base but with one large exception: dried blood spattered the walls on the second half. More crusted a centralized drain in a large pool at the foot of a heavy anchor at the far end. A vampire was there, chained neck-to-ankle in stainless steel, the links secured to the anchor, which in turn was bolted to the floor. Holy sigils of all faiths were carved into each link and cuff.

Vampires were in constant pain every second the chain made contact with skin: a compelling reason to confess fast and often. But nothing was foolproof. For instance, what if said vampire was a self-proclaimed masochist with a pain fetish?

"Afternoon, Zola."

"Eugene."

A demon with the appearance of a seventeen-year-old Black girl smiled as straight as she could, her lips crooked from years of torture by Eugene's more cruel and unusual predecessors. Her mop of disheveled hair parted to reveal a crown of crucifixes that had been scorched into her forehead.

He twitched at the sight of her brow, like he did every time. "Have anything new for me?" It was a dumb question. She had called him here, after all.

With a hiss, the door sealed behind him. It had been over a minute since it closed. Beluga dicking around, probably. Idiot. If Zola broke out, she wouldn't have killed just Eugene but several others before being taken down.

"Eugene, by Jove," she said, busy bobbing up and down, chains rattling along her warped back and legs. "How's the missus?"

He resisted pinching the bridge of his nose. Telling her about his home life had been a mistake. "Zola, if you don't have anything..."

"Saw a shooting star last night," she said.

Here we go, he thought. *Into the cryptic nonsense.*

"Big sucker. Made an impact in the East. Lit the sky up with a cool khaki."

"Sounds great." He pulled out his pad and wrote down everything she said. Over the last several months, he had warmed a little to her way of speaking, even catching a clue or two. Nothing super helpful, yet. "Any of the guards see this?"

"Oh, the guards didn't care about no shooting star. But the devil did. And he snatched it right up. Carried it off to safety, to care for it, nurture it. It'll grow big and strong. Shake the foundations of this place."

"Good for him." He finished his jotting. "Anything else?"

"Maybe for a Toblerone."

He sighed. Her obsession with the nougat bars was strange; everything but blood tasted like ash to vampires. Not to mention the Hellmouth was very particular about contraband. He told her so.

"Man..." She stewed for a moment, like this was news to her.

He flipped through her folder again. Numbers and dates leapt out then soared past. Data like that was his Achilles heel, even his own phone number. "What about the Martinez case, Zola? Can you tell me more about that?"

Zola shifted enough to shake her chains. "I told you about that."

"It's not why you called me?"

"You heard me about the star. Go find it."

"You want me," he checked his notes, "to find the devil, then force him to give up his shooting star?"

"No! I want you to help him raise the shooting star."

Eugene pursed his lip. This was a bust. However, he didn't want to face the asshole guard again. So he said, "I'll do that, Zola, if you go over the Martinez case one more time. Start with what you smelled."

He had asked her about smell once before. Courts only took sight and sound as evidence. Smell could only provide leads, which was a shame. Two decades after being sired, vampires' olfactory senses heightened to that of dogs. And Zola had been a vampire much longer than that.

"Man wants to know what Zola smelled again." Almost to accentuate her point, she sucked a torrent of air through both nostrils. "Brownie was—"

"Immigrant."

"Right, imminent. She was tearing off, all ziggies, you know, after all those zaggies? She was a beeline, a crooked shot of honey toward a dispatch of chuckers. Not sure why. News ain't the truth. Safety less so. But Mister Marker don't care. He barreled his stank mobile right—"

Eugene shot up. "Mister what?"

"Uh. I am a lady."

"No. The mister. He had a marker?"

"No. You asked about the smelly. He reeked of the foul."

Eugene made a note and underlined it. "Okay. What then?"

"Then her pretty blood went all silver shimmer in the moonbeams and...Zola was lost."

Eugene knew the rest. The Quarter boasted few riots except in the case of human blood spilled anywhere within a hundred feet of the fence. Whenever a guard nicked themselves shaving, they were sent to the boggy, insect-ridden Fort Polk in Louisiana for a month as punishment.

"Thank you, Zola."

"Can you get me some new paint for my house? Cubicle beige hurts my energy."

Wow. He almost applauded her. That was pretty coherent. "I'll see what I can do." The cop answer for no.

Her eyes glazed over. "Man says he'll see. Man sees nothing."

Eugene knocked on the interview room door. Marker wasn't much of a lead, but it was better than nothing. Maybe he'd take a new look at the teachers at the high school one more time, and maybe the middle school too.

If the door ever opened, that was. Eugene motioned at the camera. "Open up, Beluga. This isn't funny."

The lens zoomed in on him, but nothing happened.

Eugene sighed. His phone rang. Ice gripped his heart at the two words on the screen: Sergeant Cole.

"Shit." He huddled in the corner. "Yes, sergeant?"

"Detective Yukawa, please explain something to me." Cole's raspy voice dripped with extra respect. Eugene shuddered. "Why are you at the Hell-mouth?"

He didn't even ask how she knew; she always did. "I had a tip, ma'am."

"Would this tip be related to the new case I handed you not an hour and a half ago?"

He swallowed and eyed Zola who watched, enraptured. "Noitwould-not."

Cole's tone took on the air of a disappointed nun. "Say that again so all may hear, Detective."

"...it would not."

"I see." She sighed, her disappointment making his hackles rise. "Detective, do you ever wonder why your caseload only grows while my other officers' shrinks?"

"I—"

"Because detective, you follow wild goose chases. I thought a promotion would help to focus you but I was wrong. Have I displaced my faith? Is this position too much for you?"

Sweat broke out on his upper lip. "No, Sergeant—"

"Then perhaps you're testing my patience. How else am I to take your course of action? I hand you a brand-new missing person's case, the type of case where the first forty-eight hours are the most vital, and I find you have not only ignored my orders, but have not even stopped at the victim's apartment to go over baseline evidence with CSI."

"Well, um..."

"Stop blathering. Is there any information I'm missing, *detective?*" The way Sergeant Cole said "detective" sounded like it was a mistake soon to be rectified.

He gripped the phone so hard the casing popped. "No, maam."

"...I see."

The door finally hissed open but Eugene had trouble getting his legs to move. And it had nothing to do with the lack of guards in the hall outside.

"After you relieve CSI, report to my office. Eugene."

"Yes, m—"

There was a harsh clack like a ruler slapping against a desk. The sergeant had hung up on him.

A blob of molten lead filled his gut. He hadn't felt something like this in years, not since Catholic school. Cole always dealt with him fairly, and he thought she understood him, why he worked the way he did. But that was before. This promotion was already costing him.

Eugene glimpsed at Zola. Her wicked grin told him everything. He should leave, tail firmly tucked between his legs, sprint to the crime scene, and meet his boss before she reached Super Pissed mode. No need for any further conflict.

But the hallway outside remained empty. He was stuck here until a guard showed up to cover his six.

Zola broke into hysterical laughter. Heat flushed down his face and seared across his chest. Since he'd stepped in here, he'd been felt up, intimidated, bullied, lied to, belittled, and toyed with. Something had to give.

"Tell me about the Green Berets," he said.

Zola, who had started dancing a small jig to make her chains rattle, skin smoking in a dozen little places, went still. "What?"

"You heard me. How do they really keep you all contained?"

For the first time in the past ten months, Zola shut her mouth.

"Time to go." Beluga finally arrived at the door, two others in tow.

"I'm not done with my interview."

"Yes," another guard said, all three reaching for their nightsticks. "You are."

Eugene held Zola's gaze a moment longer before surrendering and following the guards out.

***

Back in his car, Eugene laid his head on the steering wheel and blared his meditation audiobook over the car's speakers.

Stupid. What did he expect would happen? Letting that rage out, turning his brain off. It was exactly what his girlfriend hated about him. Ex-girlfriend, he reminded himself.

The sausage-headed guard leered at him from the Hellmouth's entrance. He let the guard's steely gaze wash over him until he was covered in a layer of self-hatred.

Finally, he started the car—after sweet talking the old bird for ten minutes. If he hurried, he could buy the guards an apology six pack after stopping at Grace Loraine Clemons's apartment.

7

GRACE WOKE TO MUSTY dark. Something sharp poked her shoulder and the left side of her body throbbed.

She nearly wept with relief—she was alive. And, thank Gods, the drug had worn off. Out of habit, she reached for her phone and was rewarded with a spike of pain down her arm that left her gasping.

Down, down it took her. She fought to stay awake, but each blink shifted the warm yellow light closer to dull white. Sunlight rose through the window.

A strip of wallpaper curled down towards her and almost touched her nose. Had it been there the whole time? She glanced in the direction of the light source.

She was in a dilapidated living room/kitchen hybrid. A gray couch cushioned her, damp from sweat. Beneath this lay what must have been a blue rug but was now gray from years of sun and foot traffic. The kitchen beyond contained white countertops plopped onto jagged wood, edges now weathered and frayed. Wires poked out where appliances should stand. No windows, unless that bright rectangle next to the cupboards was a window. If so, it was the dirtiest she'd ever seen.

Straining, she caught sight of a mint green sink in the corner behind her, straight out of the 1950s.

She licked a slimy tongue across dry lips. *Take it slow.* If she blacked out again, she might not get another opportunity. She lifted herself up on her left arm, then her right, which cried out. Her sleeve rolled back to reveal a long strip of red fabric, ragged but clean, tied around a wooden stick that ran from elbow to wrist.

It was rudimentary, to say the least. Whoever wrapped this must have limited supplies but a wealth of experience. However, she couldn't remember what the purpose of it could be. Had she fallen? Experimentally, she bent her hand at the wrist.

She cursed, her temples throbbing at the sound. Something thudded above. A heavy something. A dozen scenarios flashed through her mind, none good. She was vulnerable, exposed. Unarmed. But if she had any hope of defending herself, she needed water.

Footsteps above. No more stalling, she had to move. Leaning on her good arm, she staggered to the sink using the wall for support.

The cold water valve turned easily enough, but nothing came out. She twisted it until it came off in her hand. The hot water was the same. Maybe the well needed a minute? But whoever was above could be here any—

"Clerical error."

Grace spun. A figure darkened a doorway she hadn't noticed until now. Her arm fell, striking the sink, but the pain was secondary to her terror.

"The sink. It was a clerical error." The low timbre of his voice cracked every other word like a guitar string snapping midnote, trying to tune. "Government bought and installed those before deciding vampires do not require sinks."

He stepped forward into the dim glow. He was pale despite the low light, far paler than she expected one of his kind to be. Red-pocked skin surrounded yellow eyes that protruded from sunken cheeks, distorting his features into those of a sickly praying mantis. The hems of his sleeves and pant legs were shredded and shriveling. Speckled scars dotted his wrists and ankles.

"Luckily, the mistake was rectified before purchasing appliances." He came forward. She edged along the counter, mirroring him step for step to keep the kitchen island between them. "After all, we don't need to keep a bottle of milk or to cook ourselves a four-course meal."

Some drawers were slightly open, others were pulled all the way out. She explored them with her fingers as quietly and sneakily as she could as she focused on those intense eyes of his.

"They made sure to turn off the plumbing as well. No one thought we would wish to do laundry or wash ourselves."

The more he spoke, the more alive he seemed to become. His voice evening out, growing confident. He motioned at the empty room, his arm cutting the air like a sword. "We have nothing at all. No TV. No sports or gatherings. Little to occupy our time."

Last drawer. She plunged her hand inside.

"Besides satisfying the insatiable need to feed."

Her fingers brushed metal. She stifled a triumphant cry.

A rod of iron settled into her grip. She broke eye contact for the briefest moment, a blink, no more. Then the air thickened with the scent of death.

"And not always succeeding."

A vice clamped down on her fingers. In that tenth of a second, the vampire had moved, crossed over a dozen paces in the time it took for an eyelid to flutter.

He twisted her wrist, the force great enough to shatter it into several pieces. But she held on, straining to point the rod toward him. His fangs popped out, top and bottom all at once, a gullet of twisted knives. She recoiled but his grip now held her in place, anchoring her to the drawer. He leaned in toward her neck.

Tracy flashed before her eyes, followed by Mr. Pawcy. That was it. Her life gone in a flash. Another blink and all that would remain to mark her life on Earth was an empty apartment and a cluttered office.

The vampire's breath turned to lava against her skin. No one besides an acquaintance and her boss would mourn her: not her colleagues, not her family.

She released the iron rod and went limp. *Do it.*

The vampire held her a moment longer, his fangs poking her skin, then dropped her. She sank to her knees, nausea cloying at her stomach, her insides begging to climb out of the submissive lump she'd become. This monster must be equally disgusted with her.

"I have an offer for you," he said.

"What?" Had she been killed? Or maybe her mind snapped in the seconds before the vampire drained her of the last few drops of her pitiful life.

The vampire watched her from his original position across the kitchen, moving in a blink once again. His expression was calm though appraising, teeth back to normal but with a slight edge to them. "I can get you out of here."

She said nothing, the words making little sense.

"Didn't you wonder why I patched you up?"

Because hope tastes better, she wanted to say. Instead, she remained silent. The vampire continued to stare at her like she was an exotic animal that had wandered into his kitchen. "To save me for later."

His brow furrowed. "Later?"

"Keep me in your attic. Feast on me slowly."

"Ah." The vampire chuckled. "I believe that's what befell Xavier in season fifteen of Bly Hollow. Personally, I thought the show went downhill after the first showrunner left."

"You..." She rubbed her neck, trying to reason her way through the whiplash this conversation gave her. "You watch Bly Hollow?"

"Novelizations. The only literature the guards let us ingest features people killing vampires. It's so...uninspiring." His eyebrows knitted together. "Despite all that, I find the themes quite philosophical. Plus, I like when the Butcher gets thrown into a wall."

After a full minute of her staring, he added, "What's up your gullet? Is it so hard to believe someone can like a show where he can see people like himself succeed for a change?"

She looked the six-foot-tall, white male vampire up and down. A laugh escaped before she could choke it back.

But the vampire didn't look offended, only taken aback.

"It's nothing," she said. "Just...adjusting."

He nodded and looked down at her bandaged arm. "Your left side is bruised quite badly. From what I can tell, you may have a nasty fracture in your forearm. And a concussion, of course." His green eyes met hers. "My offer expires soon."

"Offer?"

"I lead you out of here, you do something for me in return."

Grace didn't like the sound of that.

"Or I could partake of you instead. Daylight always makes one so weak." He hunched as if readying to pounce.

She slid away and knocked into the counter at her back. "What do I have to do?"

"One body. A month."

"You're not serious."

"As serious as the adrenaline pumping through your veins."

She swallowed and covered her neck. "Why me?"

"Because you're here."

"No, I mean... If you could leave, why not go?"

"Who says I can leave? I said I can get you out."

She eyed him then looked at the doorway beyond. "Maybe I'll wait. Maybe the Green Berets are on their way here right now and you want a promise from me before they arrive."

"Oh, like they picked you up on a sensor or a camera?" The vampire motioned around. "You've been here almost a day. Do you hear the cavalry breaking down my door?"

She had no response to that. The cameras should have picked her up the moment she dropped in here. In fact, the fence should have been humming with electricity last night, every inch watched. Yet here she was, like so many other victims she had covered over her career. Something was off.

A shudder coursed up her spine. Whatever was happening, this vampire lay at the center of it.

"You know the way out of here." She said this as a statement of fact.

"I do. Living forever gives you endless trial and error."

She leaned back against the counter. Could she trust him? He seemed normal enough. Of course, he might have locked his crazy in some back room. Something about this whole set up seemed off.

However, did she really have a choice? Or was that as much of an illusion as his personality?

"Who are you?" she asked.

"You may call me Diavolo."

He had to be kidding. "The devil?"

He blinked a few times. She caught him off guard. That was good.

"You speak Italian?"

"I'm a reporter in Cleveland."

He lifted his chin and chuckled. A gleam that might have been respect danced in his eyes. "What is your answer?"

"Again, why me? Of all the victims in here."

"Why not?" He leaned forward. "Come now. Ask the question you really want."

She opened her mouth to deny him, to say she wasn't even beginning to contemplate this, but stopped. Perhaps it was the concussion or the adrenaline still coursing through her. Whatever the reason, she voiced the question the logical part of her brain begged her to, the part separate from all those pesky emotions.

"Can the body be dead?"

The vampire smiled like he had won something. "No, Grace Clemons. It cannot."

What little hope she had died. "How do you know my name?"

Diavolo's tongue ran along his serrated teeth. "Let's just say we were destined to meet. Now—" he raised his hands like a carnival barker "—one live body every month for the foreseeable future. That's *your* future, not mine. Don't want you worrying about passing this debt on. Your next body will be due at 11:59 pm on the 15th of next month."

She cocked her head. "Next body?"

His smile curled until his eyes gleamed. "Any other questions?"

"What will you do with them?"

"Any *other* questions?"

Millions, she wanted to say. How did she get here? Who kidnapped her? How was he keeping the Green Beret away? Did he work with the Russian mafia? Was Komarov involved?

But none of those changed the present, changed the fact that she was stuck in here with only one means of escape. She peered at him, trying to think of a question he wouldn't dodge. Maybe if she made it personal. "Why did you rescue me?"

"I told you–"

"Don't give me that. There are hundreds dropped in here every year; most of them could supply you with bodies. Now: Why me?"

Again, he blinked at her. "Do you remember," he said after a moment's contemplation, "the article you wrote about Christie Mancini?"

"That...was years ago." The story was one of her first — a girl abducted by her stepfather and dropped inside the Quarter. Grace had interviewed almost a hundred people before writing the article.

"Yes," Diavolo said. "Let us say, I felt you were owed the same dignity for once."

It was a plausible reason—even explained how he knew her name. But had Diavolo known Christie Mancini? Or had he quoted an old article of hers to confuse her?

No way to suss out the truth. There were too many unknowns. She needed time and space to think. But she wouldn't get either here.

"Question time is over," he said. "Your answer?"

One body. One month.

Each one, someone's Joy.

The very idea made her want to shove her neck into Diavolo's mouth and tell him to bite down. But there was a story here, her existence in this house proved it.

And, more to the point, what could an imprisoned vampire do to her outside these walls?

"I accept," she said.

8

DIAVOLO, SATISFIED, LEFT GRACE to her own devices but warned: "Traipsing around outside like a prized turkey will...well, you get the gist." Then he locked himself in a room upstairs.

Fine, she thought. There had to be any number of insights she could gain from exploring how Diavolo lived.

The rest of the first floor matched the kitchen: empty, sad, aged. The only other place to sit was a ripped-up lounge chair in the parlor, green from the mold growing out of the cuts in the mangled cushions.

Upstairs held less, somehow. In a back closet, she found a massive amount of plants. Not marijuana, to her disappointment. Just regular plants you could find anywhere. Their pots were made out of discarded bottles and Styrofoam coffee cups. But the plants were well maintained. One had a delicate orange flower blooming at the top.

Wow. The first peek into a vampire's home life in recorded history and the only discernible feature was some dying plants. Her Aunt Ruth might be impressed, but no one else. Whatever Diavolo had in his room, she doubted it would make up for the massive letdown the rest of his place turned out to be. He was practically a squatter.

A presence was at her back. It had been there some time. She turned. "I was just...um..."

"Dusk has fallen." Diavolo gestured for her to back away, then closed the closet. "This way."

Diavolo led her out the back door into the night. Here, under a sliver of moon, he seemed to grow into himself with each step: his gait lengthened from a limp to a saunter, his head high, his eyes sharp.

"I thought the exit was this—"

"Shush!" He cut her off with the slice of his hand.

On they went, deep into the Quarter, through backyards, narrow alleys between houses, and pockmarked streets. The last of these was the worst. The potholes gouged the uneven asphalt, like this was less a street and more a smattering of discarded boulders tossed aside by giants. Each hole was wider than she was tall, and too deep to see the bottom in the faint light from the distant fence. Winding their way around took time. The hairs on her neck prickled, nagging her every second she remained exposed. Diavolo strolled along as if he were a tour guide paid by the minute.

Despite the danger, a small part of her delighted. She could count on one finger the number of outsiders given this kind of access. The houses sagged and bulged in spots corrupted with rot, but each one was unique. A corner had crumpled away here, a wall there. Some mixed the moss and lichen into art.

These signs of life were the best. Garbage arranged as decorative lawn statues, mud paintings splayed across entire structures, streams dug into lawns that cascaded into intricate patterns. The most curious sights were the religious symbols carved into the walls and slashed through, then over-grown with ivy and vines. Diavolo didn't respond to her question about them, only mumbled, "Failed revolution."

Interesting. One such house had tags in a language she was unfamiliar with – Urdu maybe? She was so enthralled that she almost ran into Diavolo. He hunched down at the end of an alley and motioned her to do the same.

"We have a few moments," he explained, "before the others are out. Most prefer to wait until full night. You need to leave before then."

She nodded.

"Your task is on the far side of this next line of houses. Keep up with me. I can mask our scents, but after so many decades together, we can identify each other by sight from a hundred yards out. So step lively, and walk where I walk."

Easier said. Unlike the previous streets, this one was coated in broken furniture, trash, and clothing. However, since they were two streets away from the wall, she could make out a few more details than before.

The trash consisted of discarded nursery junk: baby toys fuzzy with mold, onesies in tatters, clouded pacifiers, shattered cribs. Grace stopped. Had the guards done this? Strewn this stuff all over the street? Why? She glanced at Diavolo's retreating back. The fear of being left behind wrenched her from her thoughts. She'd have to ask later on.

Diavolo approached the best kept house on the street. It had a manicured lawn and a garden. A rarity. Some of the trash had been washed and repurposed. Flamingo birds made of broken glass and plastic lined the tree lawn. Old wood hammered into a makeshift fence. Nice. The wreath of baby doll heads hanging on the front door was a bit much but understandable.

They tiptoed around the side. Before reaching the backyard, Diavolo held up a hand to stop her, then poked his head around the corner. She glanced back at the street. Nothing moved among the trash.

Gods, it was all such a waste. And for what? To humiliate these creatures who had nothing? Children could have used all this. So many out there begged for scraps, while there were none here who could—

None here. That was it. There was not a single child in the Quarter. Vampires couldn't have them. So the guards in their cruelty had gifted everyone a reminder of what they couldn't possess. And the vampires had thrown it all here, on this street.

What kind of vampires would be okay living next to these constant symbols of loss?

Grace turned back, curious, peeking over Diavolo's shoulder. A young vampire with the body of a fifteen-year-old dug a ditch in the center of his backyard. Of course. He'd been turned too young to worry about children. Too young to be affected by the guards' tactics.

The back porch of the house was missing. Instead, bricks stood stacked in a uniform pile beside the trench. He was...renovating?

Diavolo motioned to her and they retreated out of earshot toward the front of the house.

He pulled a stake out from behind him. "Time to shine."

What? He couldn't be serious. "That's a vampire. The opposite of alive."

"I make the rules, and therefore, the exceptions. And I say, you kill the vampire."

"I...have no idea how to do that."

"Learn."

She opened her mouth to argue further, to tell him he was insane—honestly, he was no better than Perry, bullying her into an interview she didn't want. And one thing was certain: She was tired of being pushed into men's agendas.

However, right at that moment a window creaked open across the street. A face emerged from the darkness within, hair long, fangs already descended. A band of crucifixes scarred her forehead. But her eyes were closed. What was she doing? A sudden jerk of her head provided an answer: sniffing. Trying to get a scent.

Grace crouched down until grass prickled her neck.

"Time is running out," Diavolo whispered in her ear.

"Please...why can't you kill him?"

The pointed end of the stake poked her shoulder. As if to say, "Death first, questions later."

A stiffness spread through her jaw. How in the hell was she supposed to do this? To kill someone— anyone—let alone a brutal, supernatural creature with tremendous strength and speed.

Diavolo's glare shifted from needles to daggers. He must be mistaking her hesitance for obstinance. "If you refuse," he whispered, his tone somehow dripping with venom despite its low volume, "I'll remove the protection my pheromones are providing."

Her heart raced at his words. Death surrounded her. There was no way out.

No. Over the last day she'd been threatened by Komrov, kidnapped by a man with a scar, and manipulated by this fool who fancied himself her savior. No more. She dug her nails into the ground and shook her head.

Diavolo remained where he was but he seemed to darken. What little light there was dimmed. Grace found herself transfixed and unable to look away from this black hole in the shape of a person.

"Grace Loraine Clemons." His hand went to the back of his neck, winding up for some devastating blow. "If you are so adamant to refute my offer, then I will give you the proper incentive, but at a cost. For each body you bring me, I will answer one question. Anything you desire. However, your quota has now increased: one body per week."

No, he couldn't do that. Couldn't change the deal.

"You have five seconds to decide."

Despite the darkness, she heard a front door open, a vampire wandering out into the street. She may be the only one blinded by this power of Diavolo's, leaving her exposed. A rabbit in a snare.

"Please..." she begged.

"Two..."

"I need more t—"

"One."

"Yes! Yes, I'll do it."

The world flickered back on. She shivered, the cold dew of the grass soaking through to her skin. Whatever Diavolo did had blocked out the sensation.

"Kill...or be killed." Diavolo took great heaving breaths as he spoke, like he'd run a marathon. So that trick had taken from him too.

He offered her the stake. She watched her fingers close around it.

"One question, one body," he said.

"...one question, one body."

He lifted her like a discarded doll and set her on her feet. With a pat on the arm, she was off. She rounded the house, her feet carrying her past the point of no return. Ahead, the immortal teenager continued to dig.

A dozen paces away, her faculties returned in a rush. She halted. What was she doing? This being had powers beyond her understanding and all she had was the equivalent of a pointy stick.

"Now, where did you come from?" The teen who was not a teen looked at her, intrigued.

She hid the stake behind her back. Crap. Had he seen it?

He hopped out of the hole and seemed to glide towards her. His eyes were moons, feral and bright, nothing like Diavolo's. "Another discarded human, eh? How many of you are even left?"

Any second, he'd unhinge his jaw and take a bite. She needed to stop him, to throw him off. She stammered out the first thing that popped into her mind. "Diavolo."

That stopped him. "Uh...okay?"

No recognition. Gods, of course, Diavolo had given her a fake name. Well, at least she bought herself some time. It was only seconds but it was something. "Il Diavolo. Mio Dio."

"Is that so?" He stepped forward, wary.

She crouched, brought her hands together like a prayer, the stake between them. "Mi Dio! Dov'é il bagno?"

"Bagno?" His brows knitted together. "Is that like Spanish? Did you just ask something about 'the bathroom?'"

Shit.

She lunged, aiming for his stomach, but he wasn't there. Turning in mid air, she tried to find him and redirect her attack. But her foot came down and rolled, roaring with pain. She crumpled to the ground.

"You've heard one too many stories." His breath was hot against her neck, hotter thanDiavolo's. "Enough fun. Let's find you a—"

She jabbed the stake up under her armpit in the direction of his voice and was rewarded with a soft *thunk*.

"W—" His speech distorted with a burble.

She crawled out of his reach before turning to survey what she'd done. The stake protruded from the vampire's chest. It had sunk in several inches. His eyes were saucers, face as pale as a ghost. He was bent over, his hand outstretched, like he wanted to help her up.

Gods, had she misunderstood? He'd said something, hadn't he? Before she stabbed him. Let's find you a—what? A guard? A bathroom? Was he going to take her to the gate?

No. It was probably a trick. A ploy to lure her into the dark of his home.

His face distorted in such pain. Had she missed? Hitting his heart, on the first try, at that angle? Practically impossible.

A word escaped his lips: "Please." Blood dribbled down his chin.

"I'm sorry. I thought..." She swallowed down the lump building in her throat. "I had no choice."

He tried to speak again but instead coughed up more blood. She limped over and reached toward the stake. How did she stop this? The boy—and he was a boy, she saw that now—hadn't done anything. Not really. How? How did she end this?!

"What do I do?" She searched his eyes. Gods, they were terrible. "Tell me what to do."

"Patience." Diavolo was there, lifting the boy until he stood upright. Diavolo would make it right. Oh, next to him, the boy looked so small, so weak.

"You..." the boy said.

"Me." Diavolo set one hand on the shaft of the stake. *Not that,* she thought. *Ripping that out would make the wound worse.* But then, he did something curious—he started to motion with his free hand. Sign language of some kind, though it didn't match any signs Grace knew. The fingers bent at odd angles, with a nimbleness only the most dexterous could pull off.

The boy had suffered enough, she wanted to say. Mercy. But was too afraid to interrupt this exchange, to soil whatever blessing Diavolo was bestowing.

When Diavolo put his hand down, the boy's eyes widened, tears threatening to spill from the corners. "I. Take it back. Please, Fr—"

In one swift motion, Diavolo wrenched the stake out.

In the space of a breath, the boy dissolved into a mass of ash, hair, and bone. All that was left to mark his life on this planet fell onto her face, her hands, her clothing. Motes mixed with her sweat and became apart of her.

And in his absence stood Diavolo, stake in hand, the point coated in blackened blood. "Well, now," said Diavolo in his usual convivial tone. "Such excitement! I dare say, once this is discovered, the micro chips your military planted in my kind will lock us all down. So let us adjourn and get you to that gate."

She lifted her hand and stared at the gray flakes of the boy she had killed.

"Grace?"

When she didn't move, he spun her round and marched her away, steering her from behind. Her eyes never left her hand, thoughts consumed with ways to chop it off.

9

NOT HALF AN HOUR later, Grace walked up to the Hellmouth, completely unharmed, and asked in a polite tone if they would be so kind as to open the gate. One guard stared, bug eyed—though that might just be how he looked—while another tried to communicate the situation on her radio.

That was it. No secret passage or code word, the Green Beret didn't hold her at gunpoint and demand to know who she was. She just strolled up, hands held high while they administered a quick test from a distance. Nothing to it.

Diavolo had played her.

Shame boiled in her gut as an ambulance drove her to the nearest hospital. There, after hours of being prodded by EMTs and nursing staff, an Indian doctor with a sagging gut told her what she suspected: Her arm was broken in three places and required a cast, the left side of her body was badly bruised including much of her face and upper torso, but she was intact. Her concussion needed monitoring, but the aches would fade in about a week.

Patrolmen came and took her statement. She told them a version of the truth—complete amnesia. They were skeptical but left around three in the morning. She spent the remaining hours before dawn alone, curled up in her hospital bed, unable to bring herself to check out or turn on the TV.

The hospital released her shortly after sunrise. Her clothes lay on the bed, folded in a pile. They looked different somehow, wrong. Like they belonged to someone else. She needed safety, security. Hush puppies. Driving home, she stayed five under the speed limit, trying to memorize every car that didn't pass her. There were none.

Pulling into her apartment's parking lot, an attendant in a booth blocked her way in. Neither the booth nor the man had been there before. What was going on? The long faced man with silver hair and olive complexion smiled and asked for her pass.

Unsure, she flashed her apartment key and told him the floor she lived on.

"Uh, not...that. I meant your press pass."

What? She looked beyond him at the apartment building beyond. But it wasn't there, the Plain Dealer was. She sat back. This must be a joke. A steady pounding settled into her temples. She'd driven to work. She wanted to be safe and came here without a second thought.

"Is it not your day today?" the attendant asked.

"Um...what?"

"It's okay." He set his hand on the hood of her car. Hers. "Lots of people show up on their days off. Happens more than you think."

"I..." She stared at his arm. Bile rose in the back of her throat and she forced it down. A little stayed, souring her tongue with its sudden acidity. "Here's my pass."

He leaned back, his shadow pulling away from her. She was so grateful that it took her a moment to realize she'd decided to stay rather than leave.

He studied her pass—was that a cocked eyebrow? Like he was surprised. Did he wonder why she was here? Here, and not the Quarter where he'd thrown her?

She peered at him. He seemed the right height for the man who grabbed her. Strong, too. Odd for an attendant. He must have another job, one that required dead lifting a great deal.

She leaned forward and sniffed.

"You...okay, ma'am?"

The attendant gave her a puzzled look. Then without warning, his hand shot out. She screamed and curled into a ball. The attendant window blessedly fell away but the car rolled forward toward the closed gate. The angle proved difficult. The car went askew but she refused to correct it. However, she did risk one leg to hit the brake. Fortunately, the car halted a foot short of the gate post.

"Woah, there!" the attendant said after coming around. "Didn't mean to spook you. I just had a devil of a time recognizing you with all the bruises. You sure you should be coming to work?"

Grace swallowed. "A devil?"

"...uh, okay. Take it easy." He handed her back her pass, slowly this time, and she snatched it up.

Finally, the gate inched up. But the attendant called out once more, "You take care of yourse—"

Grace raced her car forward as soon as the gap was wide enough, the roar of her engine drowning the man out.

***

Detective Yukawa was five cases in and three cups of coffee down when he turned his attention back to the Clemons case. There was something about jumping from one crime to the next that kept the mind fresh, poised. To anyone else, all these folders on his desk would label him a slob. But to him, their precise positioning resonated perfect harmony.

He opened the Clemons folder. Everyone at the department knew Grace. Her articles, while well informed, often placed a great deal of pressure on the higher ups and detectives to solve cases. Opinions around here ranged from respectful to apathetic to downright loathing.

Personally, Eugene liked her. She was one of the reasons he buried himself in cold cases so often. Of course, her many public criticisms of the department meant that her disappearance was his case and his alone. Now the brass could say they made every effort without much manpower wasted. And if she didn't turn up? Yet another leech removed from the commissioner's backside.

Even his sergeant, who hated to play politics, wouldn't give him any more help than the kick in the pants she had already dished out. That was her management style: jumper cables. If a subordinate needed more than a quick spark to get on track, she didn't want them. Transfers were difficult to file and carry out, but Cole hardly cared, hating coddling more. If Eugene failed this investigation, his probationary period as lead detective was still in effect.

So, he sipped his lukewarm two creams and no sugar, flipped to the place in her file where he left off, and hunkered down once more.

The apartment was a dead end. Forensics weren't in yet but the baseline revealed no signs of a struggle, lock intact, and possessions untouched. No chance she was abducted from home. Interviews with her colleagues had yielded bupkus. Few had even spoken to her due to her odd hours, and no one but her boss had contact with her outside of work.

The last person to see her alive, an intern, spoke of various bars Grace frequented but mentioned zero specifics. Fantastic. Grace lived in a veritable nest of bars and distilleries. That, plus the Green Beret being their usual prick selves about security footage, meant creating a timeline of Grace's disappearance was like finding a needle in a city of needle factories.

If it weren't for her daily texts at midnight to her boss saying she was all right — a practice possibly related to prior trauma or, more likely, from being a woman in America — no one would have known she was missing at all.

Thankfully, her boss had sent her schedule right away. It left an eight-hour window after her interview with Komarov–speaking of which, what a fun call. Before talking with the pakhan, Eugene hadn't been aware someone could drive the deaf mad with silence. But reviewing the security tapes at the motel cleared Komarov and his men.

Eugene closed the folder and rubbed his temples. Back to square one.

Truth was he needed more manpower. If the last lead detective managed this, there'd be uniformed officers canvassing bar to bar while a partner talked theories and checked forensics. Instead, Grace had a trainee and an amber alert.

A group of officers in the bullpen broke out in laughter. One bumped his chair. No apology. Course not. How had Faison earned these frat bros respect? The old fogey's idea of a good time was an evening sherry with a jigsaw puzzle.

Eugene set Grace's file down next to the immigrant case. Oh, that one. He was close, a day or two at most. Of course, he could get lucky with Clemons and find the right bar immediately.

He needed to make a choice.

"Eugene."

That voice.

He stood. "Sofia."

Hands stiff at her sides, his ex looked out of place in a brightly floral midi dress. However, her pained expression matched the station's aesthetic pretty well..

"You're here," Eugene blurted. The cops at his back snickered. It may have been an obvious remark for a detective, but the idea of her still hadn't cemented in his mind. "Where's...?"

"With my mother."

She glanced at the cops, then shuffled in close to him. Precisely what she didn't want to do, based on her raised shoulders and thin lips.

"That's why I came," Sofia said. "She's been asking for you. When you'll come see her."

"You could have called."

"We both know how that would have gone."

Eugene nodded. "...I can do next weekend. Work is—"

Her face fell.

No, really, he meant it this time. Why wouldn't he want to see his own daughter? But the unmistakable clunk of a coffee cup on his desk cut off any chance of further explanation.

"Here you go, detective." The young trainee Eugene had sent away for coffee an hour ago grinned with visible gaps in his teeth.

In a dismissive tone, Eugene said, "Thank you, officer..." Shoot, he should really write down names. He was useless without his notes.

"Gemmel, sir."

"Right. Gemmel, can you give us a minute?"

"Sure, sir, but the sergeant wants to see you."

"Okay. One minute."

"But–"

"One. Minute."

The young officer finally slunk away.

"Sorry," Eugene said, trying to push as much sentiment into his voice as possible. "The caseload this week has been...taxing."

"I understand. But it's not me you have to explain this to. She asked for you, Gene. Do you know how many teenage girls actually want to talk to their fathers?"

"I know. And I'll be there. A movie maybe? She still like those cute pony movies?"

"She's fourteen."

"Wait, really? No, her birthday was...was..."

"Detective Yukawa!"

Eugene snapped up. Sergeant Cole was in her doorway, doing the one thing he'd never seen her do: smile.

"Congratulations!" This rang out with an air of potential sarcasm.

"How's that, ma'am?"

"Grace reported to work today. None the worse for wear."

He doubled over in relief. People clapped around him. Good news was rare here. Even those who had no clue about his case joined in.

Sofia set a hand on his shoulder. Even after all this time, she was still beautiful. He should go to lunch with her, talk about Maria, about them. Connect, for once.

But also...

He was so close on the Martinez case.

"Get me her current location."

Gemmel saluted and left. A quick shuffle through the stack of folders on his desk and Eugene had a pile of four he could work on during downtime. No hunger pangs, so no need for a break. Or was he forgetting something?

"Oh, Sofia, I—"

But she wasn't there. Across the bullpen, a wisp of a decadent rose fluttered through the station's double doors and out into the bright sunlight.

Bile hit the back of his throat, the acid taste all too familiar. He'd lost. Again.

No. He'd call. He wouldn't forget this time; he'd make a note. But when Gemmel returned with an address, Eugene still hadn't found a pen.

***

Grace entered the Plain Dealer's expansive marbled lobby. Heads turned on craned necks like vultures smelling blood. A heavy silence fell, an intake of breath, then with a dash, they were on her.

"Here we go," Grace muttered under her breath as her coworkers closed in. They swarmed and surrounded her, all speaking at once. Despite the mob, everyone kept a foot or two of distance, which she appreciated, many acting like she was made of fractured glass. They weren't far off.

The questions were the kind she expected. How do you feel? What did the doctors say? Are you sure you should be working? Did they catch the bastard?

She handled as many questions as she could with a plastered-on Barbie-doll smile. Finally, when they seemed more sympathetic than curious, Grace sidled toward the elevator. As understanding dawned in the more socially conscious, the crowd started to dwindle. Grace waved to the last stragglers as she slipped inside.

She collapsed against the back wall. Maybe she should hit the emergency stop and rest. Another crush of coworkers and she might pass out. Sympathy proved more stifling than the kidnapping.

But the doors opened on her floor to reveal a lone Perry and his jovial jowls shaking in welcome. She stepped into a half-sincere hug: full sincerity on his part, none on hers. The events of the last day still wrapped her in an invisible shell.

Rather than ask how she was, Perry explained who had covered her stories and any other business he thought necessary. Not once did he ask why she was here and not at home. Gods, she could have hugged him for real.

They reached her office and went separate ways with a "ee you later." Inside, a press report waited on her desk with hand-written notes in the margins. A human interest story. Like any other day. She swallowed the lump in her throat.

Sliding the report aside, she got down to business. A moment of awkward finagling got her laptop open. As it booted up, she let her thoughts drift back to the conversation with Diavolo in the Quarter.

***

The Hellmouth lay ahead, another block or two. Her hands still shook from the kill, the ash in her mouth caught in her throat.

"Your turn," Diavolo said.

She bit her tongue, his words startling her. Her turn? She held up her hand. Of course, he was going to kill her. The deed was done.

But he only watched her, expectant.

"My turn?" she asked.

"For a question. A deal's a deal."

She almost laughed in his face. He couldn't be serious. What possible question could she ask that was worth the gray flecked flesh on her hands?

But he stared at her, fingers fidgeting, like he was an eager school boy waiting to impress his teacher.

He wanted a question? Fine. Why hadn't Diavolo killed the vampire himself?

She opened her mouth to ask, then hesitated. Some part of her, some piece deep down, that still called itself a reporter, held her back.

How about: Who was the young vampire? No, she couldn't bear to find that out. Humanizing him would only make her feel worse. She needed to think bigger.

Why was she here? Too vague.

Who was Diavolo? Again, vague. Too easy to dodge.

How did he know Christie Mancini? That had potential but too much risk. Besides, she could research it herself.

What did she *need* to know? The question that had been bugging her since she woke up in this godforsaken place. "What's the Quarter's connection with the Russian mafia?"

A fine question, but as she thought of it now, from the comfort of her tiny office, her insides twisted. This was the moment she had started compartmentalizing the murder.

"Do you ever wonder," he'd said in a gruff tone that echoed off the houses surrounding them, "how much they spend on electricity in here?"

"What does that have to do—"

"I'm getting there. Work with me for a moment."

She sighed and tried to recall her proposal. "The city uses almost seventeen percent of taxes on the Quarter's electrical grid."

He chuckled. "That they do."

"Then what are you saying?"

"You were near the fence last night," he said. "Was it on?"

A cold jolt traveled up her spine. "You can't be suggesting...the Green Beret helped kidnap me?"

Diavolo shrugged. "These are the people who got assigned to watch over sickly undead freaks. Turning off the fence, selling little blackouts to the highest bidders. It breaks up the monotony. Plus it keeps the city clean of all those pesky dead bodies the cops would have to spend too many resources on during these recessive times."

"We're not in a recession."

"We're *always* in a recession."

Grace shook her head. "This makes no sense. They'd be caught for sure. Besides, why would the Green Beret need to do that with the tunnel network?"

"Tunnels?" Diavolo's brow furrowed. It was the first time he looked genuinely confused.

"How the victims get in. Fanatics dig tunnels under the fence."

Diavolo *tsked*. "Amazing. So that's what a well informed populace believes. I had thought, with the newspaper so close... Ah, I guess, I shouldn't be surprised."

"No tunnels? At all?" Gods, the implications. "So you're saying the mafia buys time slots to dump bodies, funneling money to the Green Berets?" She shook her head. "This reeks like a conspiracy theory." She said this not because she didn't believe him, but because she found people responded with the truth more if they had to prove their honesty.

But he simply shrugged once more, shirking her bait. "Research it yourself then."

***

So here she was, typing at a snail's pace. Her hands ached like ants nibbled at her joints and forced her to stop. It had only been an hour since she started, but already her muscles were stiff. Gods, her body must have taken more of a beating than she thought. She took a break to stretch.

Her hands had bent into hooks. Sort of like the sign language Diavolo used. He'd told her there were no gatherings, but that didn't mean they couldn't communicate.

Infinite trial and error. The vampires had their own language. Perhaps one not even the guards knew about. If she wrote down what she remembered and consulted a language expert—

A knock accompanied by an all-too-cheery, "You're back!" interrupted her thoughts. Tracy darkened her doorway with a massive bouquet.

Grace rubbed the back of her neck. "I'm here, yes."

Tracy placed the flowers on two near-level piles. "They tell me flowers are best for the sick and injured. In Alaska, I'd just pick you out like a super nice icicle."

The joke made Grace grin. Dang it.

"You sure you should be working?"

"I need to, so I am."

"...okay."

Grace finally looked at her. Dark circles lined Tracy's eyes. She regretted her bitchy tone. "I'm sorry. Come in."

Tracy glanced over her shoulder before shutting the door. "Don't worry about our date. You should take some time. For yourself. You look...haggard."

If one more person tells me to go home, Grace thought. "I'm fine." She tried not to sigh. Tracy was...well, Grace didn't know, but a friend at least, or something close to it. "Really. I need to focus on something, otherwise...I appreciate your sympathy."

She turned back to her laptop. Sympathy. Perhaps there was someone sympathetic in the city or the utility company that might give her access to records because of her—

A squeak. Tracy was leaning against her office door, face suddenly ashen.

"Are you okay?" Grace asked. "Is it your mom?"

"It's nothing. Or—"

"Hey, Grace!" Perry shouted with an accompanying knock.

Tracy jumped a little. There was more she wanted to say, Grace could tell. But instead, Tracy opened the door.

Perry strolled in. "Got a moment? Oh, Tracy! I've been looking for you. Can you wait for me out there?"

Tracy glanced at Grace, eyes wide—no, pleading.

What was that about?

Perry shut the door behind her. He waved his glasses around. "I didn't want to say anything in front of everybody, Grace..."

Grace's thoughts drifted to Tracy. The woman had been terrified. Had Perry done that? Was he threatening her?

Or was it something worse? He'd been involved in kidnapping Grace. Perry wasn't a bodybuilder but truth be told, it didn't take a strong person to lift her one hundred and sixty pounds. Perry could do it easily. In fact, almost any man in this office...

"Grace? Are you hearing me?"

She started. "What?"

"It's just, you gave me a heart attack when you didn't text." The pencil behind his ear was chewed halfway through. "A second one when you walked in here. I know you don't like people harping on you. But will you go home? Rest up? For me."

"I'm sorry." She looked away, cheeks flushing. "You're one of the few people who—I'm just a bit out of it, is all."

Grace offered him a sad smile. However, the warmth in his face was gone, replaced by a sudden harshness. Gooseflesh streaked across the back of her neck. She had known Perry for years, since she'd moved here. He didn't look worried for her. Was this an act? Stopping by her office, checking on her. Playing the good guy.

Or trying to get her alone.

Well, two could play at this game. "You're right, Perry."

"I am?"

"Yes. I'm heading home," she lied. She gathered her things, stuffing whatever fit into her laptop bag. "Forward me any info you want me to take a look at."

"I'll do that." Perry gave a toothy, wolfish grin. "Don't do what I wouldn't." He winked and left, closing the door behind him.

Grace waited until she heard muffled voices on the other side, then crept over. She inched the door open a crack.

Perry whisper-screamed at Tracy, his face twisted with rage. Tracy shrunk under the thundering Perry. He jabbed a finger into her shoulder like an assassin with a dagger. Grace rubbed the same spot on her own shoulder.

She couldn't hear exactly what he said. Whatever it was, Tracy started to tremble. Grace should stop this. Perry couldn't bully his subordinate in broad daylight.

But then Tracy might take that as a sign of affection. And Grace couldn't have that. Not right now. Not with Diavolo hanging over everything.

While she drifted on the edge of decision, a sharply dressed East Asian man stepped in front of her door and blocked her view.

"Miss Clemons?"

Oh, for fuck's sake. "Yes?" she asked.

"Hi." He waved. Actually waved. "Detective Eugene Yukawa with Cleveland PD."

"I remember. You worked a couple cases last year I reported on."

"Uh, right. Do you have a moment?"

"I already told the other cops everything. I'm not in the mood to repeat myself a seventh time."

Eugene nodded and stepped inside, ignoring her. Without watching where he was going, he tripped over two piles of folders stacked along the wall.

"Won't you come in," she mumbled.

While picking up, he motioned to one of the awards hanging on her office wall. "That an Ohio AP award here?"

She drummed her fingers on her desk. Gods, to be a man and always expect to get your way. "I keep forgetting to box those." She went back to gathering her stuff.

"And the George Polk award? Impressive. How many awards do you have?"

"I'm not sure," she replied in a flat tone.

"Humble. Now, can you recall—"

"412."

"—what?"

"Awards. 412."

"That many? There can't be more than half a dozen here."

"I know the number."

He *humphed*. "Nominations then? Still pretty impressive consi—"

"People, detective. 412 people." She set her bag down with a soft thud. "That's how many I've pressured the police to keep investigating. 412 families who no longer have to wonder 'Where?' or 'Why?' 412 given justice. 412 who weren't forgotten. I know the number, detective. I count it every day."

Detective Yukawa blinked, his stance quavering.

She held him under her gaze and waited for him to shrivel. When he didn't, she picked her bag up again. "I'm leaving, taking a few days at home. So if there isn't anything else..."

"Miss Clemons." The detective cleared his throat. "I handle all things vampire related at the department as well as missing persons."

"Odd," she said, lifting a stack of folders. "Have the police always put those two together?"

He continued as if she hadn't spoken. "I'm only here to ask if there's anything else that stuck out to you? Your account is very...sparse."

The pile wobbled between her hand and her brace. A folder slipped off the top and *thunked* onto the desk. "Can we please do this later?"

"Of course." He frowned, his mouth settling into worn grooves. "Oh, and here." He set an evidence bag on the desk. A beat up leather purse was inside. "Forensics just cleared this half an hour ago. Should probably change the phone's PIN from your birthday."

She bit back a retort and set everything down. The phone tumbled out into her hands. A cold tingling trickled into her fingers, the plastic case alien to her own flesh.

"You missed a few calls. Your mom, I think."

She crammed the phone back into the bottom of her purse. "I'll walk you out."

Once the detective stepped outside, she glanced at the plaques along the wall and made a mental note to pick up garbage bags later in the week.

10

GRACE SPENT THE REST of the day at various bars, losing any tail she might have. Not that she ever spotted one. Finally, after a few days of entering her apartment via the fire escape, she admitted she might be a bit paranoid.

Still, Grace spent Friday and Saturday diving into research at different local libraries. Sore, she tried her best to relax: a mountain of ice packs, Jane Austen adaptations, hot baths, and a plethora of comfort food.

Diavolo had given Grace two leads: the electric company and Christie Mancini. The electric company would take the most time, so she started there. After she reached out to potential whistleblowers, chased down blueprints of the power grid, verified Diavolo's claims, and almost became a certified electrician, she came to a well thought out and unavoidable conclusion: She'd still have to do that thing for Diavolo by Wednesday.

No one talked. Not at the electric company, not in the retirement community, not in city hall. Even the city archives no longer took her calls. The city archives! They were practically begging people to break the monotony.

By Sunday, she was ready to bang her head against the bars on her windows. If that was how they were going to be, fine. She slapped her laptop shut and headed out. She made it as far as her front door.

Outside, the dim light of the hallway stretched on and on until it ended in a pool of darkness. An old tingle crept up the base of her spine, one she hadn't felt since the day she decided to crawl inside a closet for the first time.

Grace slammed the door shut and locked it. Her hand shook on the knob. *There's no one out there,* she told herself. She'd looked into her neighbors the week she'd moved in. Cat ladies, poor college women, an elderly man with advanced ALS. No one could hurt her.

Perry wasn't waiting for her. He was cold, an unemotional dinosaur. With a penchant for micromanagement. Not a stalker.

Not a stalker.

But her hand continued to tremble. She took a deep breath, then went to her nightstand. She loaded five of the seven pepper sprays inside into various pockets, and two of the four knives into her sock and purse. The shaking stopped. Assured, she left down the fire escape.

***

On a good day, the Tavern was rife with dozens of horny men, and about half as many women willing to get drunk enough to sleep with them. Grace cared little for that. She was a connoisseur of the oldest sport in the world: the bar debate. When the mood was right, two morons would start shouting at each other about something they knew almost nothing about for hours on hilarious hours. If anything could get her out of her head, it was that personal little slice of heaven.

However, today was Sunday. A half-dozen bloodshot eyes settled on her when she entered. Sighing she wound her way through empty tables and stiff bodies that lumbered about like planks despite the near empty beers in their mitts.

She took a seat at the bar with enough space to work and ordered some food, her voice carrying too much in the jilted silence. A dry socket opened in her throat.

Settling in took an eternity. She only pulled out a laptop and notebook but every bump sounded like the demolition crew. Finally, the patrons turned back to each other.

"All I'm saying is," a man in a plaid trucker hat huffed out between swigs, "we should move on China after wrapping up North Korea. It's right there! We got all the manpower right at the border."

"And all *I'm* saying is, that's suicide." The woman in a Little League team jersey motioned for another Guinness. "They have us beat in population like five to one."

The man nodded. "Okay, sure, but are they mobilized? Do they have the strength of eighty-six other countries behind them?"

"Those countries won't support a war with China."

"They will if we divide it up with them. Sit down with a pen and paper for a few months–"

"You sound like a racist six-year-old."

"Fine, Janine, what do you think we should do then?"

"Only one thing to do: Iran."

Grace groaned. She knew this argument well enough to mouth along with the woman: Take out Iran for making nuclear weapons, then Syria, then back on to Russia to stick it to them for trying to stand up to us in the first place.

Where were the great debates? Like which Disney princess would win a wrestling royal rumble or how churches should offer sin incentives for showing up (AKA sin-centives)? Not this regurgitated poli-slop.

Freaking twenty-four-hour news.

Tuning the conversation out — at least until it got interesting — Grace got to work. She pulled up her old article on Christie Mancini using the public library's newspaper database.

Forgotten details clicked into place as she went. Christie Mancini was thirteen years old when her stepfather had laced her iced tea with a low dose of a sedative called GHB. After a few minutes, she was suggestible enough that he simply asked her to walk into the Quarter.

At the time, the fence was basic chain link, not electrified sheet metal. Simple bolt cutters got them inside. After Grace's article, the government invested in improved security measures.

Christie had little to no family outside her stepfather and mother. Her real father died of a heart attack when she was two after his fifth double shift as a transit driver. Besides her mother, an overnight nurse, Christie only had a distant great uncle in Sicily but he had never traveled to the United States, as far as Grace could tell.

For Diavolo to be related to her, Grace would have to dig into records from before his imprisonment in the Quarter. That was at most sixty-five years ago, before the Cold War ended in '72. A lot of records from that time were still sealed but genealogy websites usually kept a good number of the declassified ones. Christie's family was no exception.

Near the bottom of the results, Grace reached Reconstruction Era descendants. Surprisingly, a decent number of pictures were included. One of the black-and-white photos showed a dirt field filled with sharecroppers, a couple overseers, and a businessman standing in a circle holding shovels.

Grace zoomed in on their faces, the businessman in particular. He held a plow in one hand, jacket off, suit and tie drenched as if he'd weathered a storm. A carpet of beard shrouded most of his face underneath the rim of a gray fedora, but his black eyes caught her attention. They bore into her out of the grainy dark. The light of the bar dimmed around her. It was him.

The caption underneath stated his name as simply 'Prince.' She scoffed, shaking her body loose from the hypnotic glare. No way that was a real name outside of Minnesota. A quick search told her it meant 'the first to take.'

One question, one body.

"Order up!"

Grace almost fell off of her stool. She caught herself on the bar.

"Woah! Sorry, darling," the waitress said.

"No worries." Grace pulled herself up. The bar went quiet again. All the women seemed to have left during her research. The men glanced at her, then away, puffing up their chests. Time to leave.

Grace closed her laptop and waved the waitress down. "Sorry. Can you wrap this up to go?"

***

Monday came and went.

Tuesday night, Grace ran shaking fingers through greasy hair. One by one, all of her contacts she'd reached out to to investigate in her stead came up empty. The last left a curt and professional equivalent of a middle finger in her inbox. What's more, the Christie Mancini connection amounted to nothing. No information about the man called Prince could be found anywhere outside that photo.

This was it. Every avenue of investigation had been shut down.

She swore in circles until finally admitting the unthinkable: She was out of options. All except one. The one she'd been avoiding thinking about.

It took her another hour for her to accept what she had to do. Another to act. She hopped in the car, trying to jolt her mind to find another solution.

Rage flowed through her, violent and warm. She hit the steering wheel. Once, twice. On the third time, her cast cracked. She let out a yelp and pulled over.

The arm didn't feel broken, though she could only guess. That would be her luck. She nursed her arm and glimpsed outside. Uniform suburban homes surrounded her with closed curtains and empty porches. Not the best place to lose her shit.

How was she supposed to kidnap someone? She could barely drive. They'd take one look at her yellow bruises and broken arm, then push her right over.

Unless she went after someone smaller than her. Someone far younger...

No, that was out of the question. She may as well throw herself over the Quarter's fence right now.

Two houses away, a man excited from a veritable mansion that shone like a crown jewel. No weeds, pristine blue shutters, a tire swing. A picture from a magazine.

He sat on the porch, the blood red of the front door a perfect match to his outfit, the same clothes he wore the day of her interview with Komarov.

Paralysis took hold. She was in the bag again. Her limbs unwilling and unable to do as she commanded.

One body, one week.

A monster for a monster.

No, she couldn't do that. Not for ten thousand stories. She'd find some other way; this was just a rut. Driving here was a coincidence, a subconscious leak from her research on Komarov's organization from before the interview.

The man, Richard—she knew all their names—lit a cigarette at the end of his long fingers. Just a blue-collar guy who made his neighbor's annual salary in less than a month.

His sister and her five kids lived with him, their well-beings tied to a mobster and the atrocities he committed. But they were innocent, or at least the kids were. The youngest was a girl of seven. If Grace took Richard, she'd send that little girl skittering to the closet, like the monster who took Grace's own sister.

Joy's face appeared before her, still stuck at the age she'd been taken. Even back then, the divot in her jaw let everyone know she had a bite to her. Joy would be twenty-nine today.

Her sister frowned at her. No more Joys, Grace had sworn. But how many had Richard taken from their families? How many screens slashed in the dark of night? Empty sheets left still charged with a loved one's scent?

She remembered the squeak of his boots behind her, how he shifted under his boss's glare. His knee knocking into her elbow.

Her kidnapper's thigh against her side...

He ambled down the rest of the steps and out of his yard. The scent of black pepper permeated the car as he neared. The same as that night. As that bag.

She shifted lower in her seat as he passed, her whole body trembling in hot rage. Her eyes glued to the rearview mirror as Richard retreated down the block.

This was dumb. She should leave. Brainstorm alternatives. She hadn't tried Tracy yet; maybe she could find a breakthrough. Of course, that meant talking about their missed date, and that would involve explaining why Grace had missed it, and that meant telling Tracy about the Quarter, and what went on in there, and there was absolutely no way Grace would do that.

But wasn't an awkward conversation better than Diavolo's insane deal? She was clearly frazzled, not thinking straight. Sure, the vampire's deadline loomed, but what did she care? He couldn't leave the Quarter. All his talk of answers was probably bluster anyway.

She glanced at Richard one last time before reaching for the key in the ignition. Her hand touched the car door handle instead.

11

BLOOD RUSHED IN GRACE'S ears until she could hear nothing else. Was she really doing this? Following someone?

Yes, yes she was. But not to kidnap. Only to watch, to observe. She needed a break. People took breaks, didn't they?

Six weeks ago, she had interviewed a big game hunter, more interested in her chest than making the paper. As a way to impress her, he gave her a case of tranquilizer darts. She took it from her trunk and hurried to catch up. *Only for self-defense,* she assured herself.

Richard kept the steady pace, his stride a constant flow navigating around anyone and anything with ease. Even when an oblivious contractor picked up a stack of two by fours from an idling pickup and swung them toward Richard's head, the bodyguard dodged with a few quick steps. The wood missed by inches. But Richard didn't scold the man, just went on his way. He even started whistling.

When he entered a convenience store, she hung back. The front wall of the store facing the street was glass, cement bricks on all other sides. A joke passed between him and the cashier as the latter went to grab a pack of cigarettes.

He *would* be a smoker.

"Miss Clemons?"

She gasped, pulling the tranquilizers close to her chest, and turned to a sight that chilled her veins. "Mr. Komarov...?"

"I got the feeling you were unwell," Komarov said in a concerned tone. He wore a wool suit but the humidity didn't appear to affect him. Perhaps it was too afraid. "It is wonderful to see you out and about."

"How kind of you."

"And why are you out and about in this..." his eyes passed from her to the convenient store and back, "...location?"

"I—" She grew dizzy. "Th-the article. I was hoping your guy could approve it."

Komarov held her in a patient, heavy glare.

She cleared her throat. "I know I could have emailed it but I was cooped up and knew...er—suspected if I came over, he'd approve it faster, you know, me tapping my foot all naggy like."

He drummed his fingers on his forearm. "...all naggy like."

Grace nodded for a long time.

After what felt like forever, Komarov exhaled, breath stampeding out of his nostrils. "Do you know why he is named Richard? A good Russian like him?"

She shook her head.

"He picked it on his eighteenth birthday. Richard Pryor was his favorite comedian. He watched everything of the man's. Like the star, he once grew overeager and set himself on fire with his own crack pipe."

Grace's eyebrows rose involuntarily. "I never would have thought—"

"That was before I knew him. Thankfully, he is now clean. He wears long sleeves to spare others any unpleasantness. He is like that. Never showing his scars. But you," Komarov dropped his chin into his chest, scorn radiating out in waves under his steel brow, "your scars are visible to everyone."

Her chest tightened and she had to remind herself to breathe. She tried to match his intensity with her own, a battle of wills. Her jaw twitched. She bit down and tasted blood.

Komarov held out a hand and sighed, his rigid posture relaxing. "Give me the interview and go. I'll make sure Richard has my corrections back to you by morning."

She gave a grateful smile, one she didn't have to pretend, and reached toward her back pocket. "Silly me. I must have forgotten it."

"Then what is that?" He aimed a cocked finger at the white tranquilizer case clutched to her chest.

Shit. "It's...uh..."

This was going south. Could she use one of these on him before he killed her? The smooth surface was firm, unbreakable, electric. Her arm almost shook from the thrill of it. But no. Not here, in daylight. With a sigh, she shoved the case in her back pocket.

"Nothing." Her voice came out in a whisper. "Wrong fi—"

Her phone rang. Komarov's extended hand curled into a fist. She checked the screen. Her mother. *Thank Gods.* "I...I have to take this. An emergency. At work."

He glowered at her, eyes piercing through her lie. He knew something was wrong. He wouldn't let her leave.

But all he said was, "That is...unfortunate."

"I'll be back." She hit hang up but went to place the phone over her ear anyway. "Another time."

He said nothing as she walked back to her car, but the weight of his glare stayed on her long after she drove off into the horizon.

***

A full half hour passed before she took a full breath. Komarov's shadow lurked in her rearview mirror the whole way home, his weighted glare brimming with curiosity and controlled fury. A man like him could afford to bludgeon first, ask questions never.

A fumble in her purse rewarded her with a crumpled cigarette and a cheap neon lighter. The smoke coursed through her, a tepid heat massaging her nerves. For the first time since grabbing the pepper spray, her shaking fingers steadied.

A giggle bubbled up. Then another. One conversation had her this spooked and she expected to capture a mobster tonight? That one push up she did three months ago would sure have come in handy, huh? She roared so loud, a cramp ballooned in her gut. But still she laughed, the guffaws breaking into uncontrollable titters of madness.

Gods, how long had it been since she'd slept in her bed instead of the closet? Tuesday? That couldn't be right. Seven days? Then again, when was the last time she had a good night's sleep, period? In the hospital, sure, but after that? A string of bars, errands, and research filled her mind, buffeting her along like a raft over rapids.

A metallic clang made her start. Outside, the parking garage was full and still, everyone now home at the end of the day. Every spot taken. Thank Gods she had her own spot. Now all she had to do was pass the thousand hiding spots the other cars provided between here and the elevators.

Maybe if she went down a level...? No, she was smack dab in the middle of the spots, equal distance of terror in either direction.

All right. A hundred steps. Then a quick ride up and six doors down to the blissful *thunk* of engaged deadbolts. She could do this. Of course, her car at the motel was a lot closer than this...

Komarov glared at her in the mirror again. Now wearing white gloves.

No, she was imagining him. Still, she locked the car door. Plan B. Waiting. Someone would come outside to get something eventually. Then she'd hop out and accompany them back in. It wouldn't be long.

***

Morning light cracked through her windshield. She faced it with blinking disbelief. But the empty parking garage confirmed it. The night was a restless one but somehow she'd fallen asleep in her car. Her back ached in appreciation. She stretched, wondering if she should put on a pot of coffee or if it was too early to go to a shop for a sugary frothy milkshake thing that ended in –cino.

She yawned and glanced about for the phone she'd taken out her pocket to get comfy. The breath died in her throat.

A note was stuck under her front wiper. Words slashed in haphazard handwriting glistened in dull red: SEE YOU SOON

In the corner, like a signature, was a hand drawn devil face, complete with horns and a goatee. She got out, forcing her fingers to remove the clear hallucination. The note was warm in the cold concrete air of the garage. The red ink, or what she hoped was ink, smudged her skin with its freshness.

She glanced around once more, expecting to see Diavolo standing a few feet away, smiling his all-knowing grin.

This was it. Proof, the vampire could escape his prison. She had no choice now.

Diavolo must be fed.

12

GRACE BURNED THE NOTE on her stove and dropped the ashes into the sink. Blackened water spiraled down the drain under a relentless stream.

The vampire could reach her here, could reach her anywhere. Pluck her out of her apartment no matter how deep in the closet she dug.

Her phone buzzed. She ignored it, instead, shutting off the tap and setting her forehead on the counter. The cool fake marble soothed her as if she was hot with fever.

She should have known Diavolo could escape. He'd basically told her that he could skirt the Quarter's monitoring system. No gatherings, he said. Yet he walked right up and ripped the stake from that other vampire's chest.

Gods, if she failed to meet his deadline in fourteen hours...

Her phone pinged again. Groaning, Grace snatched it up without looking and dragged it over. A bright text from Perry burned her eyes. Oh, joy. Her replacement tonight had food poisoning. In his passive aggressive way, Perry explained the brass didn't like all the absences. She needed to work if she wanted her article published.

She almost texted back, "What article?" before catching herself. The article. The one she staked her career on. The one to change her world, er, the world. How could she have forgotten?

This blasted, bitch of a week. All right. For one moment—one—she would consider Diavolo's offer seriously. She couldn't take an innocent life, even a stranger's. That would be like picking up the cat at her feet and drowning it in the toilet.

That left only one kind of person. The kind that would satisfy both Diavolo's blood lust and absolve her of any guilt. But unlike yesterday with Richard, she couldn't do this half-heartedly. No, she'd have to go all in, heart and soul.

And she had the perfect person. And a little more than half a day to pull it off. Sorry, Perry. No way to kidnap the bodyguard of the most dangerous man in the city, clean up any evidence, feed him to a vampire, and work her usual eight-hour horror show.

Mr. Pawcy rubbed against her legs. She knelt down and patted his soft fur.

"If only my life could be as simple as yours," she said to him. "What would you do in my shoes?"

The cat nudged his food bowl, then stared at her, tail flicking in annoyance. She grinned at him, imagining Diavolo doing the same thing if she didn't show tonight. The grin died on her lips. But Diavolo wouldn't do that, would he? No, he'd nab the next dropped victim after sneaking out and slitting her throat.

By doing nothing, all she'd guarantee was someone else would suffer in her place.

She scratched Mr. Pawcy behind the ears. "All right, then. We'll try it his way." A quick text let Perry know she was on for tonight; after all, she'd need an alibi. Then she went to put on the first of several pots of coffee.

"First, I'll need a dolly…"

***

One hundred percent humidity lulled Cleveland into a stupor. Grace drove straight through its steel heart into Richard's neighborhood. She arrived twenty minutes before six, then circled the block twice, alert for any sign of Komarov. Coast clear, she parked on a side street two blocks from the convenience store. As soon as the car's engine sputtered off, the shaking in her fingers returned. She breathed in deep and forced herself to relax. There was absolutely no way anyone would suspect what she was about to do.

Maybe she should have chosen a different outfit: jeans with holes at the knees, sunglasses, a baseball cap pulled low to cover her bruises and an over-sized long-sleeved T that concealed an obvious bulging cast? Oh yeah, nothing to see here, people. Just your friendly neighborhood Unabomber.

Too late now. With the tranquilizers in her front pocket, she made her way to the convenience store. A storm teased on the edge of the horizon, distant enough to be a mirage.

Families lazed about. Front yards teemed with half-dressed kids and half-caring parents all high on summer. The wavy tentacles of humidity pulled on them all but Grace marched right through, not slowed in the slightest. Unlike them, she had a purpose.

And yet, the store's A/C felt refreshing. When she entered, the clerk yelled at a group of teenagers, demanding they buy something or leave. They ignored him, milling about under a vent. She slipped past to the back of the store and hid behind an end cap.

Half an hour passed with no sign of Richard. Antsy, Grace thought through her plan. The store's alleyway was narrow and butted up against the house next door. Based on the yard, the owner wasn't the leave-your-house type. She'd wait inside the store for Richard to arrive, then leave and hide in the alley. When he walked by, she'd ask him for help, then prick him.

The clerk finally noticed her. He stared at her from behind the counter, drumming his fingers. She waved, grabbed some jerky, and purchased it. After some deliberation, she bought a few energy bars.

"You've got to be kidding me," he said as she handed the bars to the teens. "Y'all are out of here the second you finish those."

In response, the teens took slow, disgustingly wide bites. She grinned. You could always count on teens to be assholes.

One hour later, Richard still hadn't shown. The clerk had been back three times to ask if she needed any assistance, hissing at her through gritted teeth. She said no, she's still browsing.

"We close at ten," he said.

"Good to know," she responded with a tiny bit of bitch thrown in.

He rolled his eyes and headed back to the counter.

Where the heck was Richard? When she drove off yesterday, he'd exited the store with a pack of cigarettes. If he was an avid smoker, he should be here.

Maybe Komarov called him in? Or the cigarettes were for someone else? Or maybe he did smoke, but not that much.

Dammit, she could camp here until Diavolo's deadline passed and never run into him.

If only she had another plan.

At quarter to ten, she set some fashion magazine down on the counter, mumbling a curse. Work had already started and she needed to change. The A/C rattled through the empty store, the clerk having forced out the teens a few moments before when they broke a jar of relish. She didn't want to, but she might need to knock on Richard's door. Too many variables there, including running into Richard's sister or one of her kids.

Grace's insides twisted at the idea. But what other option did she have? She was about to add two bags of comforting pork rinds when the bell over the door rang.

"Evening, Neil."

"Richard! My man."

Grace froze, her eyes plastered on the slushie machine. She studied the polar bear in its red and blue sweater as if it could save her. Why hadn't she worn a hood?

The ding of the cash register snapped her back to attention. "That'll be twelve twenty-two."

She paid, snatched up her magazine and zipped toward the restroom at the back of the store. She fumbled with the dart and the magazine as she went, her unsteady hands screwing up her retreat.

Misstepping, she stubbed her toe and swore, an end cap sending her careening off balance. Teetering, first overcorrecting one direction, then another, she finally regained composure as her hands clapped together, forearms banging into a shelf of brake fluid. She pulled her hands apart instantly, a small flash of pain registering a second later. Something small fell and bounced off her foot. Whatever it was disappeared beneath the shelving.

"Usual tonight?" the clerk asked.

"No, sir. Tonight, I swear off the cancer sticks."

Richard hadn't noticed. That was good. Time to leave. She went to wrap the tranquilizer in the magazine.

It wasn't there.

She paged through the magazine to be sure and came up empty, the shelf too. She went to check her pockets when she noticed a small bead of blood budding at the crux between her index and thumb. A dullness spread across her palm.

Shit.

The clerk smirked. "Good on you, man. What brought this on?"

"Hunter is taking after me too much. Thinks he's the man of the house when I'm not around, but he just ends up pissing Deb off."

The tranquilizer must have been what slid under the shelf. How much had entered her system? It was so fast, certainly only a little bit? How fast were they? If she bent down to grab the dart and check, Richard would know something was up. The numbing sensation had already traveled down her wrist and into her forearm. How long did she have? It was only a tiny prick, less than a second. Minutes, maybe? Enough to get out of here.

But when she took a step, her legs jellied. She reached for a shelf for support and knocked off a couple bags of pretzels.

"That's—careful!"

Her vision swam.

"You all right, ma'am?" Richard approached.

She nodded. But doing that made the room bounce. Her stomach burbled. "I'm... move!"

She shouldered past him. The contact made her knees buckle. She barely caught herself before banging into the door and spilling out into the street. Deep breaths didn't work, the humidity having churned the air to soup.

The store's bell rang. "I can walk you home. Women should not be out alone at night. Even here." A hand touched her shoulder, white and gloved.

"Don't touch me!" She shirked him off and scrambled away. At the mouth of the alley, she faced him. "You're a monster. You...murderer."

He wore no gloves. Had she imagined them?

"...Miss Clemons?"

She fumbled, stepping further back into the alley, hands digging through her pockets.

He stepped toward her. "What are you doing here?" His tone plummeted to the basest levels. Each word pounded together like an avalanche of stone.

This is what he's like before he kills, she thought.

"Vladik told me..." He stepped back.

Grace's breath turned to a wheeze as she tried not to panic. "I...please." Her tongue grew fat in her mouth. "I need help."

That got her a head cock. No way. That worked? No, he still looked tense, a taut rubber band ready to snap and fly off into the night. "I could call an ambulance but they're expensive. Is that okay?"

"No need. Just...help me to my car?"

He hesitated. Then, cautious, he leaned down. The scared deer look in his eye told her to wait for a better opportunity, but the numbing sensation spreading through her lower extremities begged to differ. As he helped her up, she jabbed him in the side with both of her remaining tranquilizers.

Best to be sure. Richard jerked back, tipping her off balance. Her chest hit the pavement and she bounced. She felt nothing.

"What did you—? Tranquilizer darts?"

She craned up to see him. He'd removed the darts and held them close, studying them. Not even wobbling. "If you got the dosage wrong, you'll kill me. Who put you up to this?"

His hand disappeared inside his swirling foamy body and came back out, gripping a piece of the darkness in the shape of a gun.

He was going to kill her. Why did she think he would be vulnerable here? This was his domain, his kingdom.

"Eh, I suppose it doesn't matter."

As the black hole of the barrel trained on her, she fumbled in her pocket. This was her last chance, not only to stop Richard but to get answers. Her fingers had gone numb, any feeling lost. She forced her hand closed over something solid.

Night descended in its totality. The lights from inside the store blinked out.

Ten o'clock.

Grace rolled, not willing to let the dark consume her. The gun's muzzle flashed at where she'd been. In the confusion, she thought it was a starting pistol.

She sprang at where she guessed Richard to be, all the strength in her legs evaporating as she poured everything into this last lunge. Her head cracked against something hard. From his grunt, she determined it to be his hip. The momentum kept her arm swinging up, right into him, too numb to tell where. Plastic thudded and released a hiss. A hiss? That wasn't right.

He roared in pain and smacked whatever it was out of her deadened grip. A cannister fell at her feet. Pepper spray. She'd grabbed pepper spray. The impact caused her finger to depress the plunger, shooting his upper torso.

Richard fumbled toward the street, wiping at his eyes. Grace pulled at him, desperate to keep him out of sight, but he shrugged her off.

No, he couldn't escape. Not now. Sprinting, she ran up behind and tripped him. Down he went, skidding on the pavement.

Yes! Grace lifted a foot to hold him down, but her leg weighed a great deal all of a sudden. Before she could think the word *tranquilizer,* the sedative in her system took hold and she collapsed.

13

Sensation returned to Grace in painful bits and excruciating pieces.

A walloping gust pummeled her. Its rough tendrils raked across her face, snaked down her nostrils, and pried open her eyelids. The storm had arrived.

Light blinded in a sharp spike, piercing her skull with a migraine sharpness. But the headache did not prevent her from spotting one key detail: She was alone.

She closed her eyes, waiting for them to adjust and held back a sob. The left side of her body ached like she had just been dropped over the Quarter's wall again, but that didn't compare to the ache in her chest. She'd have to leave. Get what stuff she could before the cops came. In a minute, she'd run to her car and peel out of here. In a minute.

The harsh brightness above dulled to a yellow streetlight. The moon was high and bright. From what she could tell, no one was on the street.

Her pockets were empty except for her car keys. The jerky and what little pocket money she had was gone.

Someone had walked by, saw her lying in the street and decided to take what they could rather than help. Richard's influence, she was sure.

A wonderful goodbye from the worst place ever. Sighing, Grace dusted herself off and peeked out of the alley. No cop cars yet; she'd have a few minutes, probably. Of course, her ability to judge how long before things happened is what got her into this mess. She tossed the tranquilizer dart case to the curb. It landed a few feet from a limp body on the sidewalk.

Richard. He was leaning against the front door of the convenience store. Place was shut tight. He must have tried to get help there instead of home. This was too lucky. The darts had worked. She chuckled in disbelief.

A quick check told her the time was 11:27 PM. Perry was going to kill her. But she could still make Diavolo's deadline, and that was the real concern. Something told her he'd leave more than a threatening note.

Grace dashed to her car in panic. She'd have to hurry. She drove over to the alley, popped the trunk, and retrieved the dolly inside. Once this was over, she'd have to clean this thing off before getting it back to her super. Gods, what a strange thought to have right now.

She propped Richard up, shifting his arms and head over the dolly's center bar. A long moan escaped his lips. His eyes fluttered open and pinned her in place. Grace started, scrambling. She picked up a fist-sized rock off the ground and lifted it over her head.

Richard's irises shook. Fear if she ever saw it. Then the lids closed.

After a few seconds, his breathing deepened and his head slumped. Grace dropped the rock as if it burned. Gods, what had she almost done? Her first reaction was to lash out, to kill. Hatred settled in her gut, sour and cloying: She was no better than the man who had killed her sister.

Her resolve broke, sending her to her knees. It no longer mattered what Richard had done or what Diavolo would do; she couldn't kidnap anyone, even this monster who'd wronged her. She would dump Richard somewhere remote. Or possibly leave him here. It wasn't cold tonight. He would be fine until morning. By then, she'd be long gone.

One arm came off the dolly, then the other. It was a cliché to say he looked peaceful in his sleep but he did, angelic almost. Grace ached to sleep like this just once. As she repositioned his legs, shimmying his hips off the dolly's base, she touched something hard. The gun.

She didn't want to touch it, but leaving a weapon in his pocket where thieves could steal it was dangerous. After pocketing the gun, she dug around for anything else. No phone, luckily. Instead, he carried an envelope and a wallet. Basically, he still had everything on him while she had nothing. The mugger only went for her. Even unconscious, he was feared.

The envelope's contents slid out into her hand. A lump rose in Grace's throat. She stared at the bundle of cash and the school picture of a pigtailed girl in what might be the fourth grade. This wasn't one of Richard's nieces. Grace knew them all.

This was a hit. Someone Richard was going to kill or traffic, like he had with Grace.

Grace closed her hand into a fist, crumpling the photo. Purpose flooded her with renewed strength.

She should have known better. Never doubt a monster.

Within three minutes, she had him in her trunk and was stomping the gas pedal to the floor, on her way to the Quarter.

***

Diavolo's instructions were meticulous. Disturbingly so. The drop site lay on the western edge of the Quarter, ninety degrees from the Hellmouth gate, centered between the largest gap between Green Beret stations and tucked out of sight of the Plain Dealer's office windows. How many others had gotten caught before her, fallen into snares for him to perfect this exact trade off? And had it been perfected? Or was she another guinea pig?

Grace shivered as she parked in the blind spot of the Beret's cameras. *Thank Gods there's no extraction right now,* she thought. Hopefully there hadn't been one. Then she hadn't screwed up her shift too.

When she opened her door, the wind almost ripped the handle from her grip. Dust and dirt soared into her hair, her eyes, her mouth. Shielding herself with an arm, she rushed to the back door of her car and cowered behind it. Bending down to keep herself protected from the maelstrom, she checked the ladder she'd stored here that afternoon. The ropes and pulleys she'd added hadn't gotten dislodged or twisted. That was good. However, the ladder had weighed a great deal in sunny weather, carrying it in this windstorm...

No help for it. She stretched and got started. The whole setup took several minutes and her back ached long before the end. Luckily, the wind's howl covered up sounds of clanging and, well, dragging metal, even from her close perspective.

One minute to go. That sent a tiny trill through her chest. Maybe she could do this. As she went to retrieve Richard, she kept a constant vigil on the guard stations. Nothing stirred. In fact, she hadn't seen anyone since she passed out. Had she died outside the convenience store and entered some sort of endless ghost world?

Gods, late night horror marathons were not good for her psyche. But as she tied a rope across Richard's chest, a more unsettling thought wormed its way in: Diavolo got the Berets to look the other way. A prisoner with control over his captors.

Anyone, human or vampire, who had that kind of power was enough to make her want to drive away fast. For the first time, she wished Richard had killed her outright rather than subject her to this.

She climbed to the top of the ladder and peeked over the wall. Diavolo paraded out from the line of houses, coming straight toward her. He stopped at the edge of the floodlights and bellowed over the roaring gusts: "My apprentice! You have returned."

"Quiet!" She scanned every shadow and guard tower his voice might have carried to. But the task soon proved impossible – there were too many places for someone to hide.

Was he really this confident in his control? She responded as quietly as possible, "Let's get this over with."

"Why so hasty? New rookie to train?"

Her heart hammered against her chest. "What?!"

"You're late, Grace Clemons, but I'll forgive you this once. We must celebrate! One moment."

"No—" Grace called out but it was no use. Diavolo raced out of sight.

He knew about Tracy. No, it was okay. He didn't know about their date. Unless...

Grace groaned. Unless he heard Tracy scream it from the parking garage a few hundred feet away. Everything Diavolo said was a threat. So now if Grace screwed up, there was a second life on the line.

A loud crash made her jump. Three houses down from her position, a screen door clattered against a wall. The windows, dark. Nothing stirred.

So many homes. Were other vampires watching? Or did they have their own victims to play with?

"Here it is." Diavolo was at the fence. She hadn't seen him approach. He stood in the floodlights, his skin unmarred from the artificial sunlight.

Diavolo was right. The lights were turned off at certain times.

He waved a long metal tool with dull hooks on one end, then raised it to the top of the fence, shimmied a bit, and peeled the barbed wire away. Soon a three-foot-wide hole materialized. Diavolo's hands filled the gap. "Give him here, my lady."

Grace nodded and climbed back down. A quick double check told her the rope was tied around Richard's chest. That secure, she tied the opposite end of the rope around her waist. As she stepped back — exerting more effort than lifting the bag of sand she practiced this on— Richard rose to the top of the fence. Inches before Richard snagged against the pulley, the vampire leapt and snatched him up. Grace cut the rope in fear of being pulled in too.

One monster down.

"Ah! Perfetto! Un lavoro ben fatto." Job well done.

Grace climbed to the top of the ladder. "The electric company lead was garbage," she shouted over the wind, "and I think you knew that. If you could–"

"My dear reporter. Always on task, aren't you?" Diavolo set Richard down, grabbing the man's chin and angling his head toward her. "Look at your captor, my friend. She's the last good you'll ever see."

"Do you have to do that?" Grace kept her eyes fixed on Diavolo, but she could feel Richard peering at her from half-lidded eyes.

"Take pride in your work, Grace Clemons! This man is a testament to what you can do if you try. If you continue to seek the truth as hard as you have. So look, and revel in your triumph."

"I don't–"

"Look!"

She flinched, eyes falling away from Diavolo and onto Richard. Already, he was a tiny, shriveled thing. A scarecrow wrapped and dressed to haunt the wide-open plains of her mind.

A must. For his sister and her children's sake, she'd burn every inch of him into her memory. His shrunken eyes burrowing into his ashen face. His chin red from streams of drool. His receding line of auburn hair. His stiff jaw line with the – wait. No, that wasn't right.

"Where's the scar?" she asked.

"Scar?" Diavolo restrung the barbed wire. "I don't understand. Is that your question for me?"

Question? How could she ask a question when everything was so wrong? Richard had no scar. He wasn't the one who abducted her. Her monster was still out there.

"This is not the man I thought. I-I take it back. Give him to me."

"Sorry," Diavolo lifted Richard over his shoulder. "No refunds."

"But—"

Fangs shot out. "You try my patience. Ask!"

Grace swallowed. She looked at Richard as she voiced not the question she had rehearsed, but the one that assuaged her guilt. "Who kidnapped me?"

"He didn't know?" Diavolo gestured toward Richard.

Grace opened her mouth, her jaw trembling.

Diavolo set his hands behind his head and stretched. "No, I suppose not, what with him unconscious and all. But this time, I will not beat around the bush. The answer is simple: I don't know."

"But-but you have to know. The deal—"

"Our deal is for me to answer your questions, which I have. If you don't find my answers satisfactory, that is on you for wasting your efforts. Now, I must digress..."

His mouth sprouted more crooked, shark-like teeth. Rows upon rows, more than she'd seen before, as if he'd been holding back. He tore into Richard's shoulder in a spray of red mist. Richard woke and screamed, a death rattle that shook Grace's soul. Every possible emotion crossed his face. She couldn't watch anymore yet she was transfixed, unable to tear her eyes away. It went on and on. The surprise in his eyes grew to agony, then anguish, and finally, after a far longer time than Grace could stand, to quiet, accepted misery.

Diavolo pulled away from the slumped form. "Ah. Never thought I'd taste a goodfella. I applaud you, Grace Clemons, and admit I underestimated you. Farewell."

He turned and dragged Richard behind him by the shirt collar. Grace watched the two until they disappeared behind the row of houses, swallowed whole by the shadows beyond. Despite what her mind told her should be, no trail of blood followed in their wake.

14

GRACE STARED AT HER bedroom wall until the sun rose. Red streaks stretched in bloody rivulets, then morphed into burnt orange veins that crept ray by ray into deathly pale-yellow seams.

No memory of driving home. No memory of the rest of her shift. Only the void and the blood that should saturate it.

Something landed on the bed, at her back. Warm and firm, yet soft. A shadow. Her lungs hitched, breath coming in short gasps. She could see it in her mind, leaning toward her neck and opening its razor wire mouth to whisper its threat: *"Meow."*

She blinked, then rolled over. Mr. Pawcy licked her nose.

One week. The countdown had reset. Seven days tick tick ticking down, each second booming in relentless rhythm: *Who. Next? WHO. NEXT?*

Unable to take it anymore, she tossed off the sheets. Mr. Pawcy skittered to the floor. The previous day's clothes were still on, stained from sweat and grime, but she didn't mind. They felt right.

She meandered to the kitchen. Mr. Pawcy twirled around her legs in apology. She petted him mechanically. A set of muddy footprints led across the kitchen and down the hall to her bedroom. Guess she left a trail.

Unlike Richard.

Her hand clutched around Mr. Pawcy's scruff and the cat hissed. She forced herself to let go. He sprinted behind the couch and hid.

Richard was guilty, she told her twisting gut. Even if he hadn't kidnapped her specifically. She'd heard the monster in his voice, found his next target, almost fell victim to his gun.

So why wasn't she leaping for joy?

She opened the freezer. Nothing inside jumped out at her. So instead, she started chopping some peppers and onions.

The way she felt had nothing to do with last night. Nothing. This was exhaustion from days of work without rest. Richard deserved his fate.

But someone else deserved it too. Yes, that must be it. She'd bagged a monster but missed her own. So her psyche punished her with insomnia.

All right. Richard's jaw lacked a scar. So if he hadn't kidnapped her, who did?

As her omelet sizzled, she played through scenarios. Assuming Komarov ordered the hit, maybe Richard had acted as a courier to someone outside the motel she hadn't known was there. It made sense: hide some extra muscle nearby in case a rival learned about the interview.

But how could she verify any of that? She couldn't exactly walk up to Komarov and ask.

The spatula screeched against the pan. Komarov. He had seen her two nights ago. Had marched right up to her and asked the time of day. How soon before he figured out she was connected to Richard's disappearance? Were men on their way now?

Something clicked in the outside hall. She paused, listening. The rational part of her knew it was the A/C turning back on through the old vents. However, that part was not in charge.

The part in charge knew a man like Komarov wouldn't have to connect her to the disappearance. Men like him rarely needed evidence. That click sounded an awful lot like the safety on a gun being turned off.

She tiptoed to the front door. Gods, the bolts were undone! How long were they like this? She quickly relocked them and peered out, ears perked for the slightest creak.

The hallway through the peephole seemed to stretch on forever. Empty. She smelled a faint burning. But no smoke appeared in the hallway. Maybe it was downstairs. Komarov's men must have set a fire to smoke her out; she'd run out of here and BAM!—lights out.

Her smoke alarm blared. "Shit!" She rushed back to the kitchen to find the eggs black and smoking. Quickly, she dumped the whole mess into the sink and ran water over it. The black tarry remains of her breakfast hissed under the sink's spray.

She sighed. The wrong thinking had put her here. Bad thoughts crowding out her training, her expertise. Going slow, she prepared a bagel. The slow spread of the cream cheese under the knife calmed the excitement. That done, she could replay her options in her mind without fuss.

Hiding was out. She had no one she wanted to risk. Killing another guard might work, but then they'd be on to her. And none of her former subjects were quite as terrible as Richard's ilk.

Frustrated, she said aloud, "Well, I guess I could...kill Komarov."

She chuckled. Kill Komarov, sure. Find one of his dozen safehouses, get past an army equipped with more weapons than both Gods, and take down the man with a giant pectoral for a torso. Komarov's neck alone could probably lift her entire body. Could Diavolo's teeth even break through something like that?

She laughed, cream cheese dribbling down her chin as she pictured the image. Like a dog trying to chew through an insulated pipe. Ha! YouTube would flip.

Tears ran down her face, she laughed so hard. Man, she was tired.

But as she bit into her crunchy bagel, she had to admit, Komarov's death would sure make things easier. With him and that other guard of his gone, no one could connect her to Richard. She would save hundreds. The police might be suspicious, but more likely they'd conclude everyone connected to her interview was being targeted. She might even earn some protective custody.

Her phone rested next to her plate. She half expected an ironically timed call from her mother, but the screen remained dark. She opened it, stared for a moment, then scrolled through her contacts.

For research purposes, she told herself, as she dialed the first one. *Simply research.*

***

One hour-long shower, an attempted cat nap, and two whipped cream smothered waffles later, Grace nestled into a booth at JP McGee's, tucked away in a corner on the side of the entrance. JP McGee's was upscale enough that people actually came to eat the food and listen to the live music, which wasn't just the closest white man with an acoustic guitar.

Grace nursed a locally brewed ale and tried to look bored. The ale was a habit. When she came to this town over a decade ago, she had to wear the bartenders down. A customer working instead of hooking up lowered morale and drained tips. So Grace stuck to the corners, ordered something expensive, then tipped heavy. Soon enough, she became part of the scenery.

She took a small break from a crossword to rate the beer on her phone. She hesitated, her finger shaking before hitting submit. A small ding notified her she'd earned her tenth drink medal; she'd only registered one before her abduction. The post went public to anyone using the app nearby.

"Grace?"

Looking up from her screen, Grace met an impossibility: "Tracy."

Her colleague held a glass between both hands, like she was afraid the beer would jerk out of her grasp. "How have you been?"

"Uh, fine." Grace looked around. A few at the bar glanced in her direction. None lingered for more than a few seconds.

Tracy gestured at the booth opposite Grace. "May I?"

"Um." A man at the bar glanced back her way. She needed to hurry.

"Please."

Desperation leaked into her tone and caused Grace to falter, causing her head to fall in a nod.

"Thanks," Tracy said, sliding into the booth. Her voice dropped as she said, "I'm not equipped for this, Grace."

"For what?"

"I've...filling in for you."

"Oh."

"It's...hard. I tried being objective, tried focusing on the good I was doing, on the families. But it's too much. And I know you said writing is amazing, but honestly, it freaking sucks."

Grace held back a chuckle. Tracy looked so beaten down, Grace wanted to reach out a hand to grasp hers. "Did you tell all this to Perry?"

Tracy groaned. "He's useless. 'Short staffed,' and 'You got no seniority.' It's bull. I think he's just mad you wrote my name in that byline."

The byline. Grace blushed. That's why Perry had yelled at Tracy.

"But I thought," Tracy said, "you hold some sway. That's why I texted so much. I'm sorry about that. By the way."

Grace crossed her arms. Of course that was why Tracy texted. "Perry rarely listens to me." The man at the bar walked out the back way, toward the bathrooms. And the far exit. "Anyway, I can't do this right now."

"Oh, God, I just walked right over here, didn't I?" Tracy glanced around. "I didn't even ask how you are or what you've been up to."

"Oh, nothing. It's just I have a, um..." What could Grace say? "A date."

Tracy reeled as if slapped. "Oh. Let me...know how it goes." She slinked out the front door, half empty pint glass clutched to her chest.

Shit. What was she thinking? Should Grace follow? She turned back toward the bar. The man hadn't returned. She punched her thigh, cursing at herself in English, French, and Spanish. This mistake was worse than any one language could contain.

She cycled through what few swears she remembered from that spring she dated a Russian varsity player when a firm thud made her look up. A different man than the one at the bar had set his glass down on her table. She hadn't noticed him before. Somewhat attractive, in a wrinkled kind of way. The graying hair at the temples helped.

"Buy you another round?" he asked.

"No, thanks." She turned her phone so he could see the screen and her username, distracting him while she straightened up. "It's only two out of five shot glasses for me."

"I would have expected more. A cultured one like you."

"Culture is all about perspective." She slid her laptop over an inch, letting the corner of the envelope that was underneath poke out.

The man's stance shifted and she felt a paper bag against her shin. "And I thought it was all theater and tights."

"That's toxic masculinity for you." She angled her laptop away from the man, leaving the envelope bare.

"Ah. Another empowered liberal broad."

The man turned to leave, the exchange complete. She resisted doing a little dance, instead vying for a victory sip. That was surprisingly easy. Almost a good thing that Tracy didn't—

"Oh my gosh. I'm so sorry."

She started. Tracy and the man had bumped into each other. Spoiled beer soaked the man's shirt front, rage clear on his face. The scene froze before Grace, a snapshot of where everything went south. She felt weak.

The man looked at Tracy, then at her. The payment envelope was aloft in his hand, gripped in a squeezed fist. "No problem, ma'am. Happens to the best."

Tracy grinned and nodded a few too many times. The man grinned through gritted teeth and made his way toward the bar.

"Where do you get off?" Tracy leaned over the table and stuck a finger in Grace's face.

The paper bag at her feet burned a hole in her pant leg. "W-what?"

Tracy slammed down an empty glass. "Sorry, I don't hold my liquor well. But no, I'm mad. I know you were hurt, and I gave you space after...what happened, and you date someone else? What, did I come on too strong? Not strong enough? What?"

"I..."

The bar went silent. Only a couple turned her way, but she knew every patron here was listening.

Fire stoked inside her, a heat that she wanted to let roar. But her contact remained, just out of sight in the dark of the back exit. Waiting. If she played this wrong, this situation may get her and Tracy killed.

"I'm sorry!" She hadn't meant to shout. More swiveled her way but she didn't shrink back. A few embers from the smoldering rage pushed her on. "I'm not good at relationship...stuff. My usual go to when something bad happens is to hide away. I'm sorry I lied. I...wanted to be alone."

This was so close to the truth, Grace's cheeks burned from the embarrassment. Tracy stood there, glaring, probably thinking the worst. This must be what ants feel like under a magnifying glass as the sun beam closes in.

Grace closed her laptop. "I should go—"

"You are skittish." Tracy giggled. "Sorry, standing here like a deer in headlights. I was trying to wrap my head around how humiliating this is. Didn't think I could feel embarrassed when drunk." She rubbed her eyes with the palms. She slunk into the booth. "Let me try this again. I'm sorry. I hope you're better soon. Shoot me a text when you're up for it. Doesn't have to be a date. We could chat about smart people topics."

Grace grinned. Gods, was she falling for this? "...smart people topics?"

Tracy peeked out from behind her open hands. "Yeah, like red wines and fancy cheese. You know, Kobe cheese. Or the opposite: live text garbage television. Whatever you want."

"This is what dating people do?"

"Only the good ones."

Tickled pink, Grace agreed to contact her soon.

"After while, crocodile."

Grace grinned. *What a nerd.* "See you later, alligator."

Tracy departed, Grace following a few moments later, once she could hold the paper bag without wanting to leap into the air.

***

Inside her locked car, she tore into the paper bag. The sleek, black surface of the tranquilizer gun absorbed the dulled light of the cloudy day. The barrel and trigger were wide, the grip a hollow shell. Not much weight to it, honestly.

All in all, it was pretty...disappointing. The whole gun had a plastic feel to it. She expected more Colt .45, less Red Rider BB Gun.

She tossed the expensive toy onto the passenger seat, too flustered to even put it back in its bag, and drove home. She had another contact. Maybe she could get a second opinion after she stashed this–wonderful, more time down the drain. If the gun wasn't such a necessity—she could not risk unconsciousness again—she would forget the whole thing.

Too bad other knock out drugs had one key downside: range. With her targets' hand-to-hand experience and strength, the risk of close contact was too great.

On the elevator ride up to her apartment, her stomach rumbled as she stuffed the gun back into its bag. A sudden craving for greasy breakfast foods high in fat and deliciousness struck. Fluffy pecan waffles drenched in maple syrup with a side of crispy bacon. But sadly, reality never lived up to her dreams.

The elevator lurched to a halt and she wiped drool from her bottom lip. Maybe a quick meal and a cat nap was in order before she called the next dealer.

When the doors slid open, she froze. A grim faced but well-manicured man waited at the door to her apartment. He pulled back his suit coat to reveal the badge at his waist.

"Miss Clemons," Detective Eugene Yukawa said, "do you have a moment?"

15

SHE DUG HER FINGERS into the tranquilizer bag, knuckles turning white as Yukawa followed her movements.

Say something, Grace thought. *Your mouth has been hanging open for like ten minutes. Say something!*

She forced a smile. "Detective," was all she managed.

His eyebrow rose.

Too big a smile, you look like the Joker. Dial it down.

"Call me Eugene," he said. "Sorry about the delay in following up. New cases take precedence. Especially since your case has been downgraded from missing persons. Are you all right?"

Lie. "Just fine. Except I have cramps and...the shits."

Wow.

Eugene looked at his shoes. "Uh, sorry to hear that..."

"Y-yeah." She looked at her hands. "My case is now a kidnapping, right? I assume you called the FBI?" *Stupid.* Why did she ask that? Now he'd bring more investigators in, if he hadn't already. She focused on digging her keys out before she said anything worse.

When he didn't respond, she glanced over. Eugene mirrored her, fumbling through his suit jacket until he pulled out a notepad and pen. "O-of course. This was more of a...social visit. Uh, extending any local services you might feel warranted. And a few questions to close out my report."

"Oh." He hadn't called anyone. This was good. Time to up the charm. "Would you like some tea?"

"That would be great." He sighed and smiled, a pleasant, Hollywood type knockout of a smile. If she was into that.

She led him inside to the kitchen. Mr. Pawcy was nowhere to be seen, probably hiding under her bed, terrified of the new person. Lucky jerk.

"Caffeine or herbal?" She set the bag containing the gun on the counter like it was nothing. Some peaches she'd picked up. Now if she could grab the tea cupboard door without her fingers spasming.

He leaned against the counter, hip inches from the gun.

"Never mind," she said loudly. "You're probably still up from the vamp beat. Gosh, detective, I wish I had your big, strong energy." Oh Gods. What the crap was that? Her experience of straight people flirting came from Hallmark movies and bad sitcoms.

"Uh...huh," he said and glanced away, swallowing.

Wait. Had that worked? Damn, straight women had it easy.

"Can you start with any details of your assailant?"

Her lip trembled. "I already told those other c–"

"This will be the last time. I promise." His eyes were steady, sure.

She turned toward the cupboard and its relaxing blend of scents. A deep breath, two. He probably thought she was gathering her strength to relive that night. The truth wasn't too far from that.

"He was a tall man," she explained. "Strong, too. He only dragged me on the street once while carrying me. Of course, I'm not exactly huge but I'm not nothing either. But I didn't hear him grunt or strain at all."

"How did he knock you unconscious?"

"Some sort of needle?" The memory of the white glove disappearing beneath the car surfaced and she shoved it away. "A pinch in my foot. That's all I felt."

"You didn't see him?"

"No, he hid under my car. Attacked me after—" she swallowed, realizing she'd almost implicated Komarov in her disappearance "—after I finished at the bar. I don't even remember what bar it was. Some nearby hole."

Eugene frowned. He didn't like her answer. What exactly about it, she wasn't sure.

As he scribbled in his pad, she forced the conversation away from the topic. "The duffel bag itself may have been black or dark blue but at night, it was impossible to tell. He drugged me with a paralytic so I couldn't move. My mouth was buried in the duffel's fabric. I could only breathe through one nostril."

She sniffed, then turned to wipe at her eyes. It surprised her, despite giving these rote details, how much the terror of that night still bled through.

"Have you ever been afraid?" she asked. "Like, 'I'm going to die,' levels of afraid? Where every cell in your body screams in panic, and you try to force calm? Ignoring those instincts you've trusted your whole life that tell you to run and never stop? All so you can take in every detail you can. Because you know if you live, there's a chance he can be caught. The slimmest chance. And that's all you have. So you cling to it. And never let go."

Grace realized she was trembling. She let go of the cupboard door. The muscles along her arm were sore.

Eugene stepped next to her. For a moment, she thought he'd put an arm around her. One human offering solace to another. But instead, he said, "Do you need any help?"

Grace shook her head. They broke apart. The detective made a few notes while she waited for the hitching sobs to fade.

"What happened after you woke up?" he asked, like nothing had happened.

"No idea," she said while filling the kettle.

The scratch of his pen stopped. "No idea?"

"That's what I said." She chose her least favorite tea among the many on her shelf — a homemade dandelion from last spring. "I woke up at the Hellmouth and a day had passed."

"Ms. Clemons, there were cameras."

The hair on the back of her neck rose. To cover, she flicked the gas stove top on and waited for the spark.

Rumors abounded that the military had cracked the vampire on camera mystery but no one had any proof. Grace wasn't sure if the detective was admitting to such a feat, but that wasn't the issue: Cameras would capture her no matter what.

The stove top burst with sudden heat.

Diavolo had tricked her. If the police had footage, than the Green Beret weren't under his thumb, like Diavolo led her to believe. But why the deception? With her on camera, the Green Beret had her dead to rights. What purpose did that serve Diavolo if she was captured now? Was the detective here to arrest her?

Someone was lying here. She just needed to find out who.

"Cameras?" she asked. "Good. Maybe you could tell me what happened?"

Silence. "Do you remember the gate?"

A deflection? So either he didn't know and was trying to get her to confess something, or the Berets had confessed ignorance. Or something else entirely. Her head was starting to hurt.

"The gate..." She stared at the wall behind him, trying to give the impression she was looking at something beyond. "Yes, vaguely. It was like I had been walking for some time and just became aware of myself. Does that make sense?"

He nodded, pencil flying for a few seconds. Then he shuddered and pointed at a cabinet. "Sugar in here?"

She nodded and shrugged. He took that as the go ahead to rifle through it. At least he asked this time.

"Thanks." He rifled through her cupboard. "Do you spend many nights at bars?"

She ground her teeth. "Are you insinuating something, detective?"

The metal in the kettle tinged as the water expanded.

"...not at all, Ms. Clemons." He filled his mug with copious amounts of sugar and honey. "I had a hell of a time establishing a timeline for you. Besides a general text to your boss that you're okay each night at midnight, no one knows where you are."

"I work the Quarter, detective. As you know, it's not glamorous or sociable."

"I understand. But the dangers–"

"I have mace on my key ring and a blade strapped to my ankle. I know perfectly well the odds a woman has of not making it home each night. As much as your lot yells at us about safety, I don't see you going after the men who commit these crimes with half as much gusto."

"...that's not what I meant."

"It never is."

Yukawa ripped open a black tea bag with too much force, sending it falling to the counter. "I admit the police in this city don't handle cases like yours...well. But I'm trying. I only want to understand how an injured woman can be dropped inside a nest of ravenous vampires and come out a day and a half later without a scratch."

"That still sounds like an accusation." The kettle whistled. Grace glared. "Ask the question you've been burning to, detective."

His face took on a sorrowful, almost pleading, look. "You really don't remember anything?"

"I've been a reporter for ten years. I've interviewed a lot of people who blacked out their assaults. No one believed them. Except me."

"Are you saying you were assaulted?"

Grace almost lifted her broken arm and yelled about his detective skills but didn't. Instead, she turned off the kettle and said, "You're the one with the cameras, detective. Not me."

His hand paused as he reached for his mug. Only for a second but noticeable.

"I understand your frustration," Yukawa said, dipping his tea bag in and out. "My predecessor could make a stick confess to tripping a pedestrian. I'm not him. My skills lie in understanding. For instance, I can see how someone who has been attacked may feel the need for protection."

He shifted toward the paper bag. "I'm not one to judge. The way we act is based on our past so much, it's amazing we can even walk around."

Grace bit her lip. Odd place to pause. He must be waiting her out, that thing old detectives on TV did when they wanted a confession. Well, time to see what he thought of what she really had to say.

"Congratulations on the promotion, by the way." She raised her mug in a toast-like gesture. "I really do appreciate someone on the force looking into cold cases."

"Is that so?"

"Oh, yeah. It brings me a lot of hope that you continue to do that even with me sidelined."

He offered a not unpleasant smile.

"But." She raised a finger. "You're in a position to do so much more. There's no excuse for the rate at which these cases are solved and the minimum staff they're given."

He pulled the mug from his lips as if its contents had turned bitter.

"I'm sorry but it's true. Siblings...loved ones need answers." She cleared her throat and hoped he hadn't noticed her error. "They can't just be left in the dark for years. It's inhumane. When people see cops nowadays, they see either brutes, neglectful guardians, or keepers of the status quo. And no matter how many words I write or how many people protest, it only gets worse. Do you not see the path you could make toward healing and reconciliation?"

The detective held the mug aloft, as if debating whether to take a sip or not, then set it down. When he spoke, it was quiet but clear. "I'm not the detective who worked your sister's case, Grace."

The mug in her hands almost slipped from her grasp. "What did you just say?"

Yukawa held up his hands in surrender. "I'm sorry, that came out–"

"Get out."

He opened his mouth, then seemed to decide against whatever he was about to say. He nodded and retreated, her front door clicking softly shut in his wake.

She held herself upright. Steam curled up out of the detective's mug in a thin wisp. She hurled it across the room where it smashed into Joy's poster and erupted into porcelain shards.

Grace let out a howl somewhere between a sob and a shriek. Leaping over the couch, she patted at it, hoping to undo the damage. The picture inside was soaked through, splinters impaling its center. A shard of glass sliced her finger. She sucked on the cut, barely aware of it.

Bleary eyed, she sank to her knees and cradled the tattered wreckage to her chest.

16

After Detective Yukawa left, Grace plodded down the street to the nearest bar. Drink after drink, she felt her inhibition drift away, her body becoming less hers. But it wasn't enough. Her thoughts continued, relentless. So she visited another tavern. Then three more. Eventually, the staff refused her on sight. Morose, she crawled home and curled up in the closet, everything still in its place from last time.

Hours or days later, her back groaned, its stiffness so demanding that it woke her from a black, dreamless sleep. Grace unfurled from a tiny fetal ball. Bright sunlight broiled her eyes from the crack in the closet door. She rubbed her temples, trying to pacify the skyscraper-sized hangover the morning—evening?—sun provoked.

Her gut gurgled. She cradled it. The sour churning garbage inside clawed its way up her throat. A hand over her mouth held back what it could. But that was a freeze frame solution. If she moved, she'd vomit. If she didn't, same result.

She thought soothing thoughts. A breeze, cool porcelain against her forehead, a white mug resting warm against her palm. A lemony mint aroma suffusing throughout the apartment.

I'm not the detective that worked your sister's case, Grace.

Those ten little words curled up into fists and socked her in the gut. She burst from the closet and half ran, half crawled to the bathroom, arriving a second too late.

After an hour inside and a sad attempt at cleanup, she shuffled back to the closet.

The door was closed. Had she done that? She went to open it when the mattress inside squeaked.

Her mouth went dry. Someone was here. They'd broken through. And found her heart.

There was no running. Not now.

She pushed open the door. Joy sat on the mattress, but not as a child. No, it was as she'd be now. Hair long, face still containing a small flare of the attitude of youth. Then the skin grayed and eyes went milky white. Richard was next to her, his shoulder torn open to reveal bone. Their hands clasped together in her lap.

Grace spun, covering her face. They weren't real. Hallucinations. *No one's here. I'm alone. Alone. All alone.*

Slowly, at the only speed her spine allowed her to turn, she looked back. The two were gone. All that remained was the poster from Joy's room, still in its shattered frame.

She kicked the closet door closed.

Work. She needed work. To busy with some meaningless task. An encyclopedia's worth of Komarov's financial records sat on her desk – numbers that ran circles around the best investigative accountants in the country. But she had something they didn't: a C+ in high school algebra.

Another gurgle doubled her over. Gods, even jokes hurt.

Her phone blared. She groaned. Probably Perry again. She dug and dug and dug through her purse. How could something so loud be so hard to find? Her arm disappeared past the elbow before her fingers grazed plastic. She dragged the offending brick out and smacked it until the ringing stopped.

"Grace?" a tinny voice asked.

Grace groaned. She thought she'd hit End Call.

"Hello?" The word snaked through the cratered minefield of Grace's throat. She wrenched herself up in search of water. The dick of a sun was finally down.

"Grace, honey."

"Mom?" This was worse than the ghosts in the closet.

"I've been trying to reach you."

All Grace had to do was tap End Call. But her mother's voice froze her stiff.

"I'm sorry if you're busy." Her mother paused. This Grace knew. The silence from her mother. The unrelenting quiet of apathy. "Look, there have been some podcasters asking about your sister and—"

"No."

"Well, that's what—"

"I'm not talking to anyone for you." The script Grace prepared over and over again in case this happened started spewing out: "Or making you the hero who never gave up. I'm done. You had your chance with me. You don't get another. Have a nice life."

She tapped the screen so hard, it hurt. But the pain felt right, justified.

Podcasters. Trauma tourists. She'd seen enough of them over the years. And if her mom was calling about them, there was no doubt she'd want to be cast in a positive light. Maybe her mother would appreciate a picture of the bars on her remaining daughter's windows to see how great she was.

The fucking nerve.

Grace texted Tracy, *I'm not going to make it in today. Got one of those on again, off again bugs. Cover for me?*

Tracy replied with a thumbs up.

All right. No more pity. It was time to hunt some monsters. Her mom should be thankful she was in another state.

***

Several days later, Detective Eugene Yukawa banged his knee into his boss's desk a third time, rocking the sergeant's computer monitor. Cole, phone still pressed firmly to her ear, glanced at him the same way someone would notice a fly. Eugene offered an apologetic smile. She turned back to her call.

He wrapped his spindly legs around his chair legs to prevent another bruise inducing thump only to lose his balance, unwind, and whack harder than before.

Cole glared, exasperation clear.

Eugene cleared his throat. "Sergeant, if I could ask what this is in reference to..."

She silenced him with a swivel of her chair.

Eugene acquiesced. Why hadn't he applied for Organized Crime? The mobster Obolensky went missing recently, so they were celebrating with cake. Sergeant Cole celebrated with a job well done and a firm handshake. Not that he was going to get that here.

No, it was pretty easy to tell what this was about. He had screwed up Grace's interrogation—er, victim interview. Geez, he hoped he didn't slip up like that when Cole got off her call.

I'm not the detective that worked your sister's case, Grace. Why had he said that? Grace had pushed his buttons, sure, but wouldn't he have done the same thing? He'd ignored her for almost a week to get a collar on a year-old case. A little thrill rushed through his veins at the thought of that solve but a flood of guilt snuffed it out cold.

No, he deserved to be punished. Grace probably – rightfully – filed a complaint. Honestly, he wasn't sure why she'd waited this long, but that was up to her. He would accept whatever punishment Cole dished out.

He bounced his knee, rattling the desk and accidentally tilting the computer monitor his way. Politeness took hold and he averted his gaze, but not before catching the headline splashed across the screen.

A mob boss interview for Pride Month. Grace's article. The idiots actually published it. The Plain Dealer was probably getting eviscerated online over this. Maybe that's what they wanted.

Cole continued to ignore him. Bored, he speed-read a few lines. What was the harm?

The interviewee, anonymous of course, had a familiar cadence to their speech patterns. They avoided all personal issues, protecting themselves with every answer they gave, or lack thereof. No surprise, but there, at the bottom of the screen, Eugene felt a connection spark. Two lines of an anecdote were cut off by the monitor. He swore he knew that story.

His first few years on the beat, before meeting his ex, he studied mob case files over microwaved dinners. Something more interesting – and yes, more fun – than watching one of six different procedurals on basic cable. He analyzed the worst of the worst's social interactions, traffic stops, childhoods, articles of clothing, groceries. It humanized them. It provided hope. These weren't monsters or demons from myths. Just regular people who took regular bathroom breaks.

That was how he got to know Vladik 'The Hermit' Komarov. That legwork had given him an advantage when he spoke with the Hermit about Grace's disappearance, which was why he was still alive. Same stonewalling here. And if he could identify it, then–

"Sorry about that." Cole hung up the phone. "Commissioner chews my ear off every now and then about some budget line or other. All I can do is listen and nod. Anyway, I suspect you know why I called you in here, detective."

Eugene tried not to blanch. "No, ma'am."

"Really? That's surprising." Cole shuffled through a few folders and brought out a familiar one. "But I guess you're a better person than I am."

"Ma'am?"

"It's actually refreshing. Giving me the benefit of the doubt after I chewed you out about this the other day? I would not be so magnanimous."

He had to think before he realized that Cole was referring to the interview with Zola. "Ma'am, I–"

She raised a hand to silence him. "I don't dole out enough compliments to let my detectives undo them by talking. Now, I need you to walk me through the Martinez case real slow so I can walk through it again for the toddlers." Cole's nickname for the press.

Not believing his luck, Eugene relayed the latest interview with Zola as succinctly as he could, particularly the mention of a new clue: the scent of markers on the perpetrator.

"But you have more than that, right?" Cole made a play toward opening the file. "Seeing as vampire scents aren't admissible."

"Correct," he admitted. "But with that new lead, I did some digging. Alessandra's school switched to smart boards two months before her kidnapping. The science teacher was one of three holdouts who still used a whiteboard on principle. But he was the only one the victim had classes with. We found a stash of burner phones behind the insulation in his attic. He was careful. He only texted students at other schools. But he made a mistake with Martinez." Eugene leaned forward. "It still throws me. The guy's record was spotless; he wasn't even a person of interest."

Cole nodded. "Stranger danger murders are the worst."

"Yeah," he said, voice subdued. "Anyway, the lab found a match to a single cell found on the scene. His DNA was also connected to two unsolved rapes."

"Excellent!" Cole pounded the desk in contradiction to her voice. "So excellent, in fact, I believe this calls for a commendation."

He balked. "Ma'am?"

"Don't get overexcited. I can only recommend you for one. Or—were you expecting something else?"

"I just—I mean, I've never..."

"I am capable of showing my officers praise, Detective Yukawa. So long as it's earned." The sergeant fixed him with a piercing glare. Eugene tried to maintain eye contact. "You have some slack in your leash, detective. Try not to strangle yourself."

Eugene swallowed and nodded. He may already have.

"Dismissed."

The clacking of Cole's computer keys reached him before he stepped into the bullpen.

He had almost forgotten. "If I may, ma'am—" he turned back "—that article you have opened. Can you send it to me?"

"Hm? Oh. Sure thing."

A quick scroll through at his desk told him the rest of the story. But that wasn't what leaped out. Komarov wasn't alone in the hotel room. No, two bodyguards were there too. One at the window, the other who wore long sleeves despite the A/C not working.

Long sleeves. The trademark of Richard Obolensky.

Eugene was out the door faster than a greyhound out of a kennel.

17

FINALLY, A CONTACT REACHED out. Grace muttered a silent thanks as she drove. Digging into Komarov's finances proved a horrible decision that practically cleaved her brain right down the center. And it wasn't one, but two days before a body was due. Things were looking up.

According to her contact, a recent crackdown on illegal drugs by Ohio's tough-on-crime governor was pushing the Russian mob to "diversify their portfolios." Not so unusual really. This kind of crackdown happened all over the world, Grace found. The Mexican cartel had expanded to avocados, the Milwaukee mob gobbled up fish, and the pakhan before Komarov had weaseled into the steel union. But Komarov, he aimed big.

His target? Coffee.

Six independent coffee shop owners were "invited" to a secure location for a deal: twenty percent off the top and the corporate coffee chains in C-town disappeared forever.

Extra security detail was brought in on the day of the meet. But after? The coffee shop owners slunk back to their homes under surveillance to protect them from any "self-aggression." Satisfied, the pakhan returned to his men, a job well done. That's where Grace came in.

Komarov's current home was a four-story apartment complex shaped like a grave, an onyx behemoth at the dead end of a short street. One of his shell companies purchased the property a decade ago and conducted heavy remodeling inside.

Try as she might, she found little information outside of rental records, many likely fake. Zero blueprints.

Well, if she couldn't scope out the architecture, then she'd focus on what she could: guard schedules and security routes. That meant getting eyes on the place. Google Maps helped in part. A boarded-up sheet metal factory sat on the corner at the entrance to the street. Social media posts around that location showed a heavy metal door in the back, partially hidden from nosy neighbors by a tall fence. With that knowledge in hand, all that was left were a few instructional videos, a call to an old friend, and a stop at the hardware store.

Time for an undetectable B&E.

She parked a block away. Despite what meteorologists predicted, the night promised rain. She examined her outfit in the side mirror. The sunglasses looked dumb under the rising moon. What was she, on a mission from God? She took them off, revealing the sickly yellow bruising across the left half of her face. Ugly, but it matched the hue of the streetlights.

Enough stalling. It was midnight on a weeknight for Gods' sakes. The only ones up were the arthritic old and the beyond drunk. Still, after exiting the car, she kept her focus straight ahead. Any suspicious behavior on her part and the Victorian-style homes teeming with Komarov loyalists would sound the alarm.

She didn't loosen up until the abandoned factory stood between her and the street. Now for the fun part. She took out her two pokey sticky thingies—technical terms—and set to picking the lock.

After a few seconds, it was abundantly clear the how-to videos were a load of the utmost crap. The urge to chuck the stick thingies as hard as she could mounted. Course if that happened, she'd wake up a neighbor, which was bad, but silver lining: she could stab their mafia-loving butt.

"Mind if I take over?"

Grace spun around. The yard was empty. No detective in sight. It was all in her head. Gods, she was losing it. The God of the Lost must be—

No, she wouldn't think about Him. Not for a second.

Finally, the back door opened into what must have been the staff break room based on the tacky carpet and stripped kitchenette. Here she waited for her goosebumps to settle, her ears perked for the wail of a siren.

When none came, she continued on. The place was stripped of machinery. Obscured windows on all sides splashed moonlight on rust-colored puddles across a concrete floor. Rotting ceiling tiles hung from rafters thirty feet high. No sign anyone except rodents had been inside for years.

On the second floor, a hallway extended between two offices. It had a narrow window opening that looked out on the street and Komarov's apartment complex. She set her perch up here.

If her intel was right, Komarov would arrive home four hours before her deadline. It was one a.m. now. The meeting started at two this afternoon. If she gave him a little time to settle in, and subtracted half an hour for travel time to the Quarter, her margin for error neared zero. Add to that, Komarov was a hermit encased in a tank. No matter how much studying or recon she did, hiccups were inevitable.

But what other options did she have? So for the next several hours, she watched. The guard patrols outside the apartment complex were like clockwork: seamless with lots of moving parts she didn't understand. Who knew the mob would be so good at complicated security techniques? Despite this, she found minuscule gaps where she might wriggle in.

Grace leaned back and stretched as the sun crested the horizon. It was too soon for her muscles to be so stiff. She thought the soreness was over, her last serious ache days ago.

Maybe it was this place. She hadn't noticed before, but the air carried the faint whiff of tangy ass. She could even smell it through her shirt.

She pulled out her thermos and took a swig—then spit the contents onto the floor. It tasted disgusting, worse than disgusting. Like the place had somehow seeped through her metal lined thermos.

This seemed like an omen. But which God sent it?

Rather than dwell, she swapped the drink out for one of three door-knobs from her bag and busied herself picking its lock. She timed herself, then spent the rest of the early morning trying to beat that time. Soon, she called it quits and tried to sleep on the carpet in the better smelling office.

In twelve hours, Komarov would return and she'd be free of this hell hole.

***

Eugene stretched. The vinyl of his car's back seat had melded into his back an hour ago. Besides that and an urge to pee, he was exhilarated.

Grace leaned forward in her surveillance nest, binoculars aimed at the apartment building down the street. Eugene snapped a few shots with his telephoto lens.

He'd been following her for almost a day at this point, though he hadn't meant to. Tended to happen when a person hangs outside another's apartment building, trying to get the courage to walk up, and she just happens to come out. She carried a massive plastic shopping bag. Sure, it could have been for a story, but Eugene made out a couple doorknobs through the semi-opaque plastic.

So Richard Obolensky went missing a few days after an exclusive interview, the same event Grace is abducted from. Maybe a rival witnessed the exchange, wanted information from the players involved. No matter the motive, Grace needed placed under protected custody.

However—and this was a big-bag-of-doorknobs-sized however—there was another way of looking at it: Richard went missing less than a week after Grace returned. Her selective amnesia cover story was garbage. None of her coworkers knew anything about her except that she knew how to get to the bottom of things.

So which was it? Victim or perpetrator? Well, here she was, staking out one of Komarov's known residences from an abandoned warehouse. Guess he'd take door number two.

The urge from Yukawa's bladder grew too large to ignore. But stepping out or turning his car on would alert Grace. So, he rummaged around for an empty bottle. As he went, he played with the idea of arresting her now and ending this charade. He could pull Cole in on the interrogation. She loved those.

But he shook his head. Grace was up to something. Last night, she had headed into the woods behind Komarov's building. He tried following, but the place was littered with sticks that would give him away. Before he found a silent way through, she was coming back out, hands caked with dirt.

Zipping his fly, he sipped at the last of his lunch from yesterday, a cup of cold roasted garlic potato soup. He took tiny sips, a poor attempt to trick his brain into thinking it was more.

Another knot formed in his back. He prayed Grace would get on with it soon.

***

Night shuffled its way in, draping the street in darker and darker blankets of umber. Komarov returned hours ago. A quick meeting. Guess coffee makers didn't have spines when their families were concerned. Hard to risk death over pastries.

Grace picked up the thermos, sipped, and set it down. Still tasted terrible, but she was getting used to it. After a moment, she took another sip. Full dark was coming soon. Komarov snuggled up in his castle, safe in his stronghold. For now.

Bottle empty, she shook herself and focused on the tranquilizer gun. Yep, the safety was set—no more accidental self-doses. Unfortunately, she needed her good hand for the lock picking, which left the gun to her bad arm.

She tested the weapon. It was a nice fit, lightweight. The muzzle ended just shy of the end of her sling. Moment of truth. She squeezed the handle and gasped as shooting pain crackled up her forearm. Useless. The sling would have to do most of the holding. She could at least appear threatening without wincing.

Cautious, she tested the trigger with a slight pinch. No pain. Silver lining.

Grace tucked her ski mask in a back pocket, then smoothed out her all-black outfit. When the moon slipped behind a cloud, she set out.

A strange woman strutting with the wrath of hell at her heels would set off every alarm Komarov had. So instead of heading north toward the apartments, Grace exited the factory and headed west.

The trek took nineteen minutes, through backyards and overgrown trails. She had walked this path before, but tonight felt different. Like the universe was on to her. Every cricket chirp made her heart lurch. But nothing stopped her. Not yet, at least.

Soon, the safe covering of the overgrown forest behind Komarov's estate engulfed her. The fifty-foot-tall dirt ridge stood right where she left it, handholds chiseled into its face. She climbed up with relative ease. However, at the top, the coverage from the trees was sparse. From below, the forest always looked a lot thicker.

It couldn't be helped. She crouched and hurried forward. If her timing was correct, the first patrol should pass by in three...two...

A pair of guards strolled out from around the corner to the right. Wait, why were there two of them? Grace knelt. That wasn't right. There had only been one last night.

The guard on the left shivered. The night carried a chill that brushed Grace's cheeks. Her cheeks? Crap! She clutched at her back pocket, ski mask still tucked inside.

Too late to put it on now. The guards now faced her direction. Even as far back as she was, any movement would alert them to her presence. But they might spot her regardless if she remained exposed. The choice pumped ice into her veins, freezing her in place. Their gazes pierced the darkness, pierced her. One reached toward his belt...

And scratched his hip. Then they turned as one, their path running parallel with the apartment wall until they turned the corner and disappeared from sight.

The thunder in her chest steadied to a thrum. A quick tap started the forty-five-second countdown on her smartwatch. She dug out her mask and charged forward. Two guards were more than she planned, but she could handle them. They weren't all that different from one, really. She repeated that thought until she believed it.

The service entrance lay directly ahead, a big concrete slab of a door. This entry was her best bet to get inside undetected–hidden enough by the corner of the building to block her from the street, yet open enough to hear any guards' approach.

The lock looked like the smattering of knobs she had practiced on from the hardware store. That was good. Ninety-nine percent of locks were identical. So said the internet, anyway.

Grace readied her comb pick. Its long metal handle and five short teeth shone copper in the yellow light. Thirty seconds until next patrol, seven to make it back to the safety of the forest. Time enough for a quick test. As she worked, she tried to keep her thoughts from what awaited her on the other side. One task at a time.

Almost immediately, the doorknob made a clicking noise. Her comb pick popped out. Tightness clutched her chest. Ninety-nine percent of all locks were identical; the other one percent were rare, expensive, and only available by special order...and also, on this door.

She wrung the tiny comb pick handle in frustration. Of all the times to have one and a half hands. She took a deep breath. Patience. She hadn't had a clue how to write an article when she started at the paper–

Voices. She checked her watch. That couldn't be; they were almost fifteen seconds early. Either the guards were sprinting around the front or...

She dashed toward the woods. A fallen log a few feet in might be enough cover. She dove headfirst, arms splayed. The ground rose up faster than expected and she landed with a thud. Her whole body seemed to vibrate from the impact. She wheezed for air as quietly as she could while listening for the clomp of soft earth under heavy boots.

The guards were early. Why? All the time she had observed them, they kept to a rigid pace. Why change now? Maybe Komarov brought in new guys from out of town? Trainees walking too fast without realizing. Still, it could be fortunate. This might mean a larger gap between them and the next patrol.

Like before, the guards' footsteps continued past then faded. But rather than risk another attempt, she stayed where she was, catching her breath. She kept her eye on the time, testing her theory.

Sure enough, the next patrol arrived early too. Instead of forty-five seconds, she was down to thirty-three. There were only supposed to be three guards out, but instead, there were eight, working in pairs. Who brought in more guards after a meeting with middle-aged baristas?

Coast clear and stopwatch adjusted, she jogged back to the strange lock to examine it. Seemed ordinary. She sunk the comb pick in and tried again, more cautious. The allotted time passed before she could do much of anything.

Spinning to hide once more, a hitching yank pulled her back. The comb pick stuck. She grabbed it with both hands and wrenched. It didn't budge. If she left it here, the guards might spot it. However if she stayed, the guards would definitely see her. Cursing under her breath, she abandoned the tool and sprinted for cover in the nearby brush.

As she rolled, her mask rose up. She struck something soft and pillowy. Bitter air and tiny particles flooded her mouth and nostrils. The urge to cough was immediate and dire. She clamped her mouth shut.

She glanced back. The two guards seemed to loll, their steps slowing. Her pin comb nearly glowed under the lone wall light.

moveassholesmoveassholesMOVE

Unfazed by her telepathic urging, the guards stopped. One bent down to tie his shoe as the other lazily glanced about.

A gremlin was clawing its way up her throat. After all this running, she could barely keep it contained.

Maybe if she let out a small cough? Just a tiny one? She lowered herself to the ground, buried her face in the mask an inch from the dirt and opened her mouth a crack.

Something primal tore loose inside her. Coughs barreled out, great hacking ones that commandeered her whole body, contorting it, folding it in on itself. She wrestled to regain her composure but failed. Whatever dust or spore she struck, it now had control.

Eventually, the hacking relented. She rolled over, spent. No possible way the guards hadn't heard that. She turned to check if they approached and barked. It came out on its own, reverberating through the silent woods.

But the men were gone.

More would come. She traveled as deep into the woods as she could and coughed freely into her mask. Once she was sure everything was out of her system, she returned.

Rather than return to the lock, she timed the patrols from the shadows. If any so much as turned in the comb pick's direction, she was ready to haul ass.

But when it became clear the guards would do no such thing, she gave in. She wasn't getting inside, not tonight. Of that she was sure. But if they found her comb pick, Komarov would change location and she'd lose any shot of catching him in the future. If Diavolo let her live. She'd have to retreat and figure out some other victim. She had a few hours. Although the thought was enough to cause her to hyperventilate through her raw throat.

No dignity left now. She walked up and smacked the stupid pick, soothed it, stroked it, everything short of worshipping the damn thing and bowing prone before it. But still, it wouldn't come out.

Voices murmured from around the corner. She'd lost track of the time. The next patrol was seconds away. She set her hand on the comb pick one last time.

Please.

If the monster at the top of this limestone tower lived, he'd abduct more like her: whistle blowers, survivors, those trying to change this world. Those just trying make it through to another day. He needed to die.

But not her. She meant nothing in this. Let her own life pass if it meant his ended.

Grace took a deep breath and gave the slightest push. The comb pick sunk a half inch into the lock. A soft click. A small flicker of hope rose in her chest. She turned the knob. The door opened.

Amazed, she floated inside as if in a dream. The comb pick slipped right out into her palm.

Darkness descended as the metal door shut without a sound. *Okay,* she thought, then swallowed. *Easy part done.*

18

Knee deep in mud, Eugene dropped the dirt clods in his hands after sliding down the ridge face yet again. He spit out the clumpy, earthy sludge he'd tasted too much of over the last fifteen minutes. How the hell had Grace climbed this in the dark? She'd marched up to this monstrosity and zipped over it on the first try. This was Eugene's tenth. There must be some secret.

He shivered and shucked off his mud-smeared jacket, then reached for his flashlight. He stopped himself. It wasn't worth the risk of being seen. Not yet. He wiped his hands on his dirty khakis and tried again.

This time, he took a few steps to the left and started up. His fingers sunk into a tiny cleft in the face. A handhold! He felt around and discovered another. This must be what Grace had made the night before. Clever. He probably should have figured that out. Detective, indeed.

Halfway through his most successful attempt yet, someone started coughing at the top. He shrank against the ridge, hoping it was enough to block him from sight. No cry of alarm rang out. When the coughing ended, he continued on.

By the time he reached the top—sweaty, ragged, and more than a little pissed – he saw no one. Despite the sparse woods, there was enough foliage and fauna along the ground to completely mask anything below the knee. It wasn't until a guard patrol passed along the apartment building ahead that he spotted Grace, or who he presumed to be Grace, dressed all in black, sprinting for a maintenance door. She stooped down, her hands busy with the knob.

Guards wielding flashlights approached from the right side of the building. What was she thinking? He almost called out but held back. Getting her killed helped no one.

Right as the guards rounded the corner, Grace managed to get inside, closing the door behind her. The guards continued on, none the wiser.

Eugene waited, thighs and forearms burning, staring at the grand arc of a building for some sign of her. After a few minutes, he decided it was time for his least favorite part of the job—decision time.

Unfortunately, this was less a shoot-first-ask-questions-later kind of situation, and more an ask-loudly-first-or-get-shot plea. Every cop's dread. The mere thought of these circumstances caused him to stare at his bedroom ceiling into the wee hours at least once a week.

Did he call for backup and wait? Or rush in, gun drawn? Regulations stated the former, but every cop with a medal pinned to their chest had picked the latter.

The seconds ticked on and Grace Clemons kept doing God knew what in there. Eugene tiptoed to the edge of the forest.

He waited for a patrol to go by. While the next pair were still a good deal away, he stepped out. He tapped his phone's flashlight and tilted it toward his badge held out in the other hand.

As the guards' flashlights rounded the corner, Eugene sucked in through his teeth. God, he hoped this worked.

"Police." He spoke soft but forceful. A whisper not meant to startle, but with the power of command behind it.

A flashlight shot up to his face. He made no sudden moves. Not even a wince.

Despite the blinding light, he could make out the silhouette of one of the guards. The man's hand inched toward a holster.

***

Grace flipped a switch inside the mobster's fortress. Fluorescent lights flickered to life, revealing a concrete room. Tools hung on the wall to the right above a wooden work bench, while an adjacent electric grid of meters and switches stretched across the wall opposite Grace.

A maintenance closet. Fantastic.

An open doorway to the left led to a gray hallway beyond, where the rest of the complex waited. Curious, she crept out to see what she was up against.

Komarov had done his due diligence on this place. Besides the missing blueprints, the architect had died in a mysterious accident, the construction company had gone out of business, and everyone on the crew had moved out of the country within six months. All of Grace's intelligence gathering concluded only two things with a low degree of certainty: Komarov was here and most likely on the top floor.

Now all she had to do was wander through long hallways past endless wooden doors that ticked up into the hundreds to find the elevator. She only hoped there wasn't the faint smell of spoiled Indian food from everywhere and nowhere all at once, like her apartment building.

She stopped shy of the end of the hall and gazed on. No slew of narrow hallways. This place stretched wide open, up and up from the ground floor to the ceiling. Every apartment on gaudy display.

The gray slab roof held a skylight at its heart, stenciled angels framing a black sky. Four floors of residences lined three of the walls, each "hallway" connecting them in a continuous, open balcony guarded with ornate railings. A waterfall mosaic of colored tiles covered the final wall, bookended by two marble columns. No elevators. Instead, three staircases cut through the center of each wing.

Along the marble floor, wide paths directed residents between rows and rows of beautiful plants with a check-in desk at the center. Grace saw nothing but thorns.

Every apartment looked out on the ground floor, each one equipped with wide windows and thin curtains. While plentiful, none of the plants on this floor were tall enough to conceal her. Out there, she'd be exposed. Like a nerve.

It wasn't hard to guess that many of Komarov's men lived here. Most likely, rent free. The pakhan not only trusted the neighbors' watchful eyes outside, he made them a certainty inside as well.

Sneaking back to the maintenance room, she removed the ski mask, then the black sweater and pants, until the electrician uniform was visible and unfettered. The Mr. Ohm Electric logo and name tag were a little wrinkled. She smoothed them out as best she could.

She had triple checked this was the mob's contractor, though that seemed moot now. The slogan for the company, "We put the OHMMM in your life," curved around a picture of an overweight man meditating in jogging pants. It reeked of bad Russian humor.

She'd used a disguise like this once before for an exposé and it had worked amazingly well. Of course, that was a beauty shop committing food stamp fraud. But the same principle applied: A contractor was one person that could slip in anywhere without notice and stay however long she liked. Besides, even if someone did watch the lobby, no one did so constantly. Why would they? This was a castle. If they spotted her, they'd reason that they missed her entering through the main doors and shrug it off.

Hopefully.

Feigning confidence—er, no. Not confidence. Faint boredom. This was another day of wires and switches and stuff. She shuffled out into the complex and made a beeline for the central stairs. The clack of her shoes echoed off the apartments and bounced back, impossibly loud. Her breath quickened with every step. She forced herself to maintain a slow, but deliberate pace.

As she entered under the shadow of the landing above, her shoulders relaxed. On any other day, she'd scoff at stairs, but now she was all smiles.

The first two flights went fine. She started to feel the burn at the top of the third, when an apartment opened. A white man with a serious unibrow and wearing dungarees stepped out holding a clipboard. His gaze fell over her.

"And who might you be?" he asked in a syrupy drawl.

Her practiced answer leapt from her mouth: "Contractor. Faulty electric on three." Shit, she meant to say four.

"Ah." He looked her up and down, admiring the little flesh she showed. He hadn't heard a word. "Name?"

"Sorry?"

"Gotta check in. Did they not tell you?"

A twinge of panic made Grace's heart leap. "Right. That. Uh, Tracy." *Sorry, Tracy.*

"I like that name," he said, jotting it down. "Height and weight?"

Grace cocked her head. She rose on her tiptoes and glimpsed at the paper in the clipboard. Large red letters at the top of the form proclaimed PETITION FOR ISSUE SIX in all caps. He tipped the clipboard back and away from her.

Her mouth set into a thin line. "Height: six foot five. Weight: two hundred and eighty pounds."

The unibrow furrowed.

"Oh, wait. That's my boyfriend's measurements. Silly me. Here." She volunteered a phone number. "That's West Park Station in Lorain. He's working right now, but he'll be happy to answer your questions. Ask for Chuck. The bouncer."

"The...the bouncer?"

"You know what?" She reached into her pocket. "Let me text him. Tell him you're calling."

"No," he said, hiding the clipboard behind his back. "No, I think that'll be all. Have a good day."

"If you're sure. Bye!" Grace marched past him, while the man's caterpillar lips undulated.

Crossing the third floor wasn't part of her plan, but it couldn't be helped. The stupid unibrow man made her misspeak. Hopefully, he'd believe her and scurry back to his hole. She tried to melt into her uniform. This was just another day in the exciting world of patching shit up. *Ohm Life, bitches.*

She reached the next set of stairs going up. If Unibrow saw her, this mission was done. She glimpsed over her shoulder. He was below, staring at his phone as he walked to the front desk.

Fast little weasel. If she failed and Komarov tossed her off the balcony, she knew where to aim.

Komarov's floor was empty. She expected no guards, but no cameras? Not even Komarov was that bold. Unsettled, Grace tried to keep a grasp on her fleeting calm and counted the doors. The third from her position was the target. Furniture storage. The curtains were pulled back in that room, giving her a clear line of sight from the factory window. No one had entered there in the last day.

The lock only took her a few moments this time.

Dim moonlight greeted her, lighting a path through sheet covered furniture. She crossed the darkened room, then felt along the wall for a handle into the rest of the penthouse. The metal bumped her ring finger. She opened the door the barest crack.

The grand hall held furnishings made of the richest mahogany she'd ever seen, and the artwork she was sure cost more than this building. A grand ballroom-level staircase glided down the center to the floor beneath.

Earlier, she worried she'd have to search for some time before finding Komarov. But there he sat across from her, on a leather bench at the top of the stairs, next to a familiar guard. The same guard from the interview, but instead of watching the outside, he held his boss's gaze with a blank expression. Dark shadows creased Komarov's face. His limbs sagged under some unseen weight.

Then the boss of the Russian mob, orchestrator of the All Saints' Day Massacre, the one whom she had sneaked in here to kidnap, said two words that stole the warmth from her blood:

"Grace Clemons."

***

"Hold, Viktor."

Eugene recognized the speaker as the man lowered his flashlight, distinct scars streamed along both cheeks that made it look like he cried molten lead. He had spoken to Eugene at the precinct about a missing persons case a few years back. His name might have been Roman.

Possibly Roman held up a hand to stay his comrade, but Viktor was having none of it. Eugene held his shield up as if it could actually stop bullets.

"We have seen no missing persons," Possibly Roman said in restrained politeness, "or vampires, detective."

"What a strange choice of words." Eugene almost asked how Possibly Roman could know he hadn't seen either but decided against it. Nitpicking in this situation was a bad idea. Eugene was already in trouble based on the twitching in the other guard's trigger finger. Best not to push.

Eugene spoke with all the authority he could muster: "I have a witness that claims you've been infiltrated."

"Mistaken, your witness is."

A deflection. Eugene tried a new tact. "What would your boss say? Hm? You not helping the police?"

This had no perceived effect. Another patrol passed, eyeing the exchange. Eugene had to wrap this up. He held his shield out a moment longer, then lowered it. "Fifty bucks."

"A hundred," Possibly Roman countered.

"Deal."

***

"Grace Clemons."

Grace tightened her grip on the tranquilizer gun in her bad hand. The act made her wince but she didn't loosen her hold.

"It was Richard's idea. Talking to her." Komarov let out a heavy gust of air from deep within. Grace did the same. "Maybe that's what killed him. He was always doing that. Thinking outside the box, cracking jokes. Adding spice to this dull life."

"I don't think he's dead, boss," replied the bodyguard. "You can't know something like that."

"I appreciate the optimism—" Komarov tightened his robe "—but I can. I offered him a job in city demolition. His own company. He would answer to no man. Always, that was his dream. He had no reason to run. That is how I know he is dead. If you and the boys don't find him, the police soon will. Or worse," his voice cracked slightly as he said, "the Quarter."

The guard reached out a hand toward Komarov's shoulder, then seemed to decide against it. "Let me get you something to drink, boss. Take your mind off things. We'll toast to Richie, swap stories. The whole shebang."

Komarov gave a slight nod and with it regained all his steel and temperament, sloughing off any vulnerability with the same amount of energy it took to remove a jacket. The guard exited down the grand staircase, his face hopeful. But his eyes spun in the tiniest roll.

Alone with her quarry, Grace watched Komarov proceed to stare at the floor. Her chance had arrived. No guards, no killers. Just the two of them. Like he'd been dropped into her hands.

A pain laced up Grace's jaw and made her temples throb. She forced her bite to loosen.

Why was she hesitating? With Richard, she had had no problem. Granted, he'd placed her in a difficult position. Literally.

Somehow she'd assumed this would get easier. Richard had a family, those he loved. But Komarov. He was one man, alone on a bench in his own empty home. The men he paid barely tolerated him.

Why couldn't she push aside this door and end him? She knew his crimes, the horrible atrocities he unleashed on her city. She could only guess at Richard's.

Maybe that was it. Richard suffered for perceived wrongs. Whereas Komarov's offenses were legends. His agony should be a hundredfold. Not some quick shot in the dark.

And here she was, with a means to administer it.

Let's start with my abduction, she thought, stepping out into the light, *and work backward.*

***

The man with the long brow leaned over the concierge desk. "Yeah, no. It was this contractor. Tight piece of...ah..." He cleared his throat as Eugene bored holes in him. "Anyway, she said she had work on three and then marched right past me. We didn't speak. At all. Wouldn't want to mess with her if I were you. She's got a bouncer for a boyfriend."

"You didn't speak," Eugene said, scratching an itch, "but you know she has a boyfriend?"

"Uh..."

Eugene thanked the man and turned back to the guards. Roman—definitely Roman—leaned against the lobby desk while the other guard remained at strict attention, a rottweiler awaiting commands.

"Any contractors ordered?" Eugene asked.

"Anyone can order one," said Roman. "This is not prison."

His partner repeated, "Not prison."

"Right," Eugene said. "What's on the third floor?"

"Apartments, detective."

Eugene turned at the words. Another man came down the main stairs, this one dressed in a blue striped polo and khakis. Cheap clothes, but if you were going to beat someone to death, you don't want blood on your finest. This must be Komarov's newly appointed second, Alexei Sokolov. Alexei drilled Eugene with a glare that said he was ten seconds away from being strangled. One of the guards must have radioed on the way in.

"All sorts live here," Alexei continued. "Teachers, bankers, accountants. Same as anywhere. If you'll excuse me for a moment." He mumbled something to the guards in Russian.

"The cop thinks someone broke in," Roman explained in English before switching languages.

Eugene picked up a few swear words and a couple yesses, but that was all he knew. He addressed the unibrow man. "Can you describe this contractor for me?"

"About this tall," the man said and held a hand up to his nose. "Brown eyes, dark hair. That boyfriend of hers is a piece of work."

"Uh huh." *Geez, this guy.* Eugene couldn't wait to be done with this. Sheer habit made him ask the next question. "And why do you say that?"

"I could see these bruises all over one of her hands and half her neck. All yellow like they—hey!"

Eugene ran for the stairs, not glancing back to see if the guards followed.

19

GRACE SHUFFLED FORWARD, CROSSING the hallway with the smallest of steps, getting close enough that her impaired aim would no longer be a factor. This was it. Komarov remained impassive. He was completely caught off guard. Free for the taking.

And yet...

She couldn't pull the trigger. Not until he knew who was about to cause his suffering.

"Bet you didn't expect to see me again."

"Hm?" Komarov shook and looked about. Finally, he settled on her. "Miss Clemons? How did you," —his gaze fell on the gun— "get in."

"This is for kidnapping me." She squeezed the trigger. The gun gave a soft click but didn't fire. The safety. She left the safety on!

"You're here." Komarov rose. "I did not kidnap you."

"Your man screwed up." She fumbled with the gun. No time for this. He was close, too close. Where was the safety on this fucking thing?

"My man?" He consumed the space between them, sucked away her air, leaving her breathless. "Do you mean Richard?"

"S-stay back."

"My Richard was taken down by some yellow journalist? One who threatens me with a gun? Me!?"

"He deserved it! For kidnapping me!" Her voice cracked.

His face was a hammer at the end of a sledge. "You're still alive. He did not kidnap you."

"That's bull—"

He fell on her. She tried leaping out of the way but it was too late. The gun went off in her hand as it was knocked away. She cried out, her broken arm throbbing from the blow. Hands snapped tight around her throat. She clawed at him, nails raking his face, but he was made of stone, his skin a mask that hid the gargoyle beneath. Her feet kicked as she left the ground.

He squeezed. The pressure built until she opened her mouth to scream. Nothing came out. Any second, her neck would snap. And worse, she wanted it, craved for this to end.

Darkness swam, closing in until there was only the warmth of his hands and the boring hatred of his eyes. She detached from her body, floating above, watching her tiny body spasm, growing stiller and stiller.

I tried Joy, she sent into the ether. *I really did.*

Then the pressure lessened. Not disappeared but lessened. Enough for her to take in the barest teaspoon of air. Her toes touched down. The burning weight of him fell away. She crashed down, crumpling to the floor. Oxygen burned down her damaged throat, the sweetest pain she'd ever felt.

Vision returned all at once. She lay face to face with Komarov. His fingers fumbled towards her. She rolled away. But he didn't follow. His limbs flopped around, useless. Something feathery stuck out of his shin. A dart. The gun. When it went off, she must have hit him.

"What is this?" he asked.

"Curare," Grace croaked. "Mixture. A paralytic. What your man. Gave me." She massaged her throat, finding the gun and holstering it. "Your adrenaline. Made it. Act fast."

Komarov licked his lips. "I can still talk."

"Not. Long."

"My man will be back soon."

She picked up the gun and reloaded it. Komarov's face darkened. He understood: His man was coming too.

He chuckled. "Then you have it all figured out."

"Talk."

"Oh? And if I do? You *let me live?*" This last part was said in a mocking tone.

"Then I. Tranq you. Before. Your lungs give out."

Komarov closed his eyes. A sort of peace overtook his features, as if he'd been waiting to hear those words for some time. "You have no idea what you've walked into. Richard did not kidnap you."

"Bull."

"Check my tapes. There," he said when she pointed to the right room.

She opened the door slowly, cautious for traps and, finding none, went in. Flipping on the light revealed a massive bedroom with a large flat screen and open cabinet with shelves of DVDs inside.

Grace scanned the shelves: Basswood Inc., NIKE Managers, XXXperiment, Oxygen Workout, 20/20, DOWNS. Some kind of code, and a bad one at that. The case marked 20/20, the old news show, was clearly her.

But she hesitated. The code was too simple, too obvious. Komarov would know that. Maybe her DVD was the one next to this one? Or beneath it? Or four down.

Or maybe Komarov did nothing of the sort because he never expected someone to break in here. After all, investigators would only need to pop a DVD in to figure out its contents. It was crazy to even have this treasure trove of evidence right out in the open. Komarov must have a lot of the law in his pocket.

She picked up the case titled 20/20. Maybe this was her interview, maybe not. No time to check. Better to take the lot. She put the DVD and all the surrounding ones into a duffel she found in the closet. The irony wasn't lost on her: Her life had been upended by a duffel bag, now one held her salvation.

She cinched the bag tight around her and went back to Komarov. He lay unusually still. The only sign of life was a twisted snarl that made his eyes gleam with rage.

"R-Richard didn't suffer." Were those her words? They must be. A kindness. Yes, that was it. Because she was better than him. "It was quick. No pain."

A creak of a floorboard broke her train of thought. The bodyguard! Where was her gun? She scanned the area around Komarov before remembering she had holstered it under her uniform.

She crouched behind a pillar. The guard may have brought backup. She'd need to take them by surprise. On three, she popped out and brought the muzzle to bear on the stunned face of Detective Eugene Yukawa.

***

Eugene and Grace spoke at the same time:

"What the hell are you doing?"

"You work for *him?*"

Too much to unpack here. Eugene caught his breath, thinking fast. The mobsters would storm in here any second. They almost overtook him on the stairs before his second wind kicked in. No time to get Grace out. No time to hide her. No time to check on Komarov.

Only one option.

Eugene muttered a silent prayer and positioned himself in front of the stairway. "Find cover."

But Grace didn't move. "What are you–"

All three guards burst through the fourth-floor door. Crap. They were supposed to come from the bottom of the stairs. Now, the guards had a clear line of sight on Grace and, worse, on their possibly dead boss.

Eugene leaped into motion, "Wait. Wait!"

But the guards aimed their sidearms regardless. Grace ducked behind the unconscious Komarov.

Eugene raised his hands as he stepped in between the guards and their target. "Stop?" His voice rose in pitch, turning his command into a plea. *Nice work,* he thought. Maybe he should add a please at the end. That should stop the violent hit men from unloading on him.

But his luck held. Everyone froze.

Roman spoke first. "Move, police man."

"We can work this out," Eugene said.

"She is next to our dead boss and you want to talk?" Roman asked.

"He's not dead," Eugene hoped. To Grace, he muttered, "Tell them he's not dead."

Silence.

Say it, he wanted to scream. Komarov's breathing body was the only thing between the two of them and a wall of bullets.

Grace mumbled.

"Louder."

"He's alive. Sedated."

The guards' shoulders relaxed but their guns remained trained.

"See?" Eugene studied each guard in turn. "Nothing's been done that can't be undone. All that's happened so far is a misunderstanding. I can arrest her–"

"I'd like to see you try," she interrupted.

"I can arrest her," Eugene repeated. "You file charges. Trespassing, assault, whatever you want. She'll be put away." He looked into Alexei's close-set, hazel eyes. "Work this out legally. There's no need for bloodshed."

The guards turned toward Alexei. He flexed his jaw. "Impersonation?"

"Of course," Eugene agreed.

"Hell no," replied Grace.

"Attempted murder?"

"This is a tranquilizer gun, dumbass!"

Eugene held his hands up higher. When both sides quieted again, he said, "We can discuss it all down at the station."

"Whose side are you on?" she spat.

He ignored her. "Do we have a deal?"

"Hm." Alexei bit his lower lip. He looked as if he was trying to pick out a flavor of ice cream rather than decide if a person should live or die. "Deal."

"No, we fucking don't."

"Grace." Eugene took a few steps toward her and reached for his handcuffs. "Make this easy."

"This–this can't be for nothing!" She gestured at Komarov. "Do you know who this is? Do you think any other cop would negotiate to save this piece of shit's life? You won't last a week."

She was right, Eugene knew. This was the right thing to do but no one would commend him for it. Recent arrest or not, he would be removed in record time once this came to light. And not in a fancy new desk job kind of way.

But sometimes that was what justice was: fair to no one.

He took a step toward Grace. "We're almost out of this, Clemons."

Her eyes threatened war. "We could be." Her finger twitched toward her gun's trigger. She stared at Eugene's holster, then at the mobsters.

Eugene gave his head the slightest shake. What did she think? That he would suddenly turn on three professionals because she asked? She clearly wasn't well. This was his fault. From the moment she smacked the Quarter's asphalt, she was his responsibility. He should have called a therapist for her the day she left that hospital.

But there was plenty of time for guilt trips later.

A phone went off behind him and he jumped.

Alexei sighed and answered. "Yes?" His eyes went wide. "Yes, of course, sir."

Sir?

"But we can avoid...I see, but Komarov has exceeded..."

Exceeded? Why was Alexei talking like Komarov was his employee instead of his boss?

"I understand."

Eugene didn't like the look on Alexei's face when the man hung up.

"What is it?" Roman asked.

Alexei leaned over and whispered.

"Eugene," Grace whispered. Eugene turned to her. "I'm here for a story. A story I won't live to tell without your help."

"What kind of story?" he whispered back.

She looked past him toward the other side of the room. "Conspiracy."

The detective turned back to the mob men. The shift in their stances was subtle but noticeable. Whoever had been on the other end of that call had shaken them.

"We still have a deal?" Eugene asked.

"Change of plans."

Three guns swiveled in his direction. Eugene's jaw locked up. Another, more dignified officer might make a joke here, but jokes were the furthest thing from his mind. Instead, some inane memory rooted its way into his thoughts. Something so dumb, he had to voice it aloud.

"I just remembered." He pointed at Roman. "You owe me a hundred bucks."

The guard glanced at his comrades, cheeks reddening. "I don't–"

In that split second gap of uncertainty, Eugene drew his gun and fired.

Muzzles flashed, the reports deafening in the enclosed space. A singe of heat cut across Eugene's shoulder. Another along his hip. He lost all sight of Grace as he dove, hand cramping as he fired shot after shot. He never ceased, even as his arm went numb from the constant recoil.

A click. He was empty. He rolled, trying to reload as he went. But the new clip slipped from his grasp, his palm slick with sweat. When he came to a stop, he raised his arms to shield himself from the swarm of bullets coming his way.

Silence reigned. Finally, slowly, he risked a glance. Three bodies lay sprawled, bullet holes and darts littering their torsos, and the walls and floor beyond. A dull click. He followed the sound to find Grace squeezing the trigger again and again, her gun clicking empty. If it wasn't, he was sure she would have shot him too.

"Clemons..." He knew he spoke but he couldn't hear himself over the ringing in his ears. He cleared his throat and spoke louder. "Clemons, it's done! It's okay!"

Okay was pretty far from what it was, but he needed to silence her gun's cry for more ammo, more death. He made his way over and knelt beside her, his hand lowering her gun. "Grace."

The clicking stopped. Her shoulders remained tense, as taut as a tightrope over an abyss. He pulled her back. Tears threatened at the corners of her eyes. She was mumbling something. He leaned in.

"No no no..."

Her dark eyes stared down at less of a body and more of a bloody mass. Holes the size of fists punched through Komarov's center, the exact area Grace cowered behind. It was a miracle she'd survived unscathed.

She gasped and dropped to the floor. Eugene checked over her, afraid she had been hit after all. But then she wailed a long, "Noooo..." and frantically applied pressure to Komarov's wounds.

Dumbfounded, he looked on. Hadn't she wanted the mob boss dead? Why else would she break in here? Something was going on. If only he had the time to figure out what.

"Grace, we need to leave."

She continued, sticking her hand inside his chest.

"Grace! Other people will have heard the shooting. They could have guns. We need to go."

"No. This can't be for nothing."

Whatever that meant would have to wait. He bent down and grabbed her shoulders.

"There's nothing you can do. He's gone. They all are."

"All? But I need a second one."

Eugene ignored this; she was clearly in shock. "The building will be alert now. We need another way out."

"All gone. But they weren't punished enough."

Eugene shook his head. Of all the times for a psychotic break. He went to check the halls outside. No one yet but there were too many places to hide.

"But my story," Grace said. "It needs this."

Maybe if they explored these other rooms? There had to be some weaponry around here somewhere. Maybe on the bodies?

He swallowed. That was wrong, but wrong was better than dead. He gathered up their guns and rooted through their pockets. Five guns total, most near empty, and two backup clips. But that wasn't the most interesting find. "Alexei? Holy... This guy's alive."

Eugene heard the unmistakable sound of a gun being reloaded. He spun, hands too full of his finds to draw his effectively. It didn't matter. Grace already had him dead to rights. "What are you doing, Grace?"

"I told you. I have a story." She pointed her gun at his chest. "And I need a body."

"Tranqs aren't instant. I'll shoot you before I pass out."

"I lied. This isn't a tranq." She smirked. "I trust my chances."

No way he could pull on her before she fired. He needed a new tactic.

"What are you gonna do?" He removed his hand from his sidearm. "Hold me hostage against the mob? They'll kill us both without flinching."

She scoffed.

"You're not well, Grace. I can help you."

"Help? You saw what happened. Someone just ordered the mob to kill their own boss in a ten second phone call. What hope do I have with the police?"

A queasiness bubbled up in his gut. The phone call had disturbed him too but he locked it away to pick apart later, like so much of this night.

"Then work *with* me, Grace," he countered. "You infiltrated a Russian mob fortress. You have a better handle on this situation than anyone. With my resources, we could take down whoever's behind this."

The gun in her hand wavered.

"I will be there every step of the way," he went on. "You know how much I focus on a case. You will be my obsession. I guarantee it."

"Detective..." She backed away, toward the stairs.

"Okay, it sounds weird when I put it like that. But I'm one hundred per–"

"Run."

He faltered. "What?"

"Run!"

He turned. The guard he didn't know, the rottweiler no longer lay in a pool of his own blood but was up in a seated position. Eugene yelped and fired. The bullet tore through the man's tie and into his chest. But other than a dabble of blood, it appeared to have no effect.

"That...hurt." Fangs jutted out of the man's gums. The newly formed hole stitched closed.

Eugene stared. What had Grace said before? Conspiracy. That was one word for it. Insanity was another.

A shuffle of footsteps brought Eugene out of his stupor. Grace disappeared through a side door. With a curse, Eugene leaped over the banister into the grand staircase and fled, the vampire close behind.

20

GRACE BURST OUT ONTO the fourth-floor landing. She cursed, nearly tripping over her own feet. But she reached the stairs without pursuit. As she hit the next floor, a crash made her jerk up.

A figure in a dark brown duster tore off away from her and toward the central staircase. It was Detective Yukawa. He ran hunched over, hands patting his pockets. What was he doing? Looking for his car keys?

An explosion of splintering wood rent the door he'd come from off its hinges. A roaring blur rushed, not for him, but her.

She fled, tearing down the steps, feet blurring with speed. A shadow blocked the landing. Grace tried to stop, almost smacking the clipboard from their grip.

"I called that bar and there's no boun—hey!"

She shot past Unibrow. No time, only speed, only the rush of wind, the burning in her lungs, the growing ache in her thighs.

"I don't like being lied to!" Unibrow called after her. "I'm a decent guy! Give me a ch-"

His words cut off in a gurgle, punctuated by a clatter of plastic.

On ground level, Grace bolted for the light of the lobby, but a shadow dropped into her path from above. She ducked. Claws passed so close, Grace felt the gust of their wake rile her hair. She'd be dead if she was a tenth of a second slower.

She pushed on through the plants. The front desk lay ahead, the path splitting in three directions. She went right, pretending to head toward the back room where she'd entered originally. A snarl shot at her from behind. She ducked and turned so fast, her toes cried in protest. The vampire careened past her and into the garden beyond. It landed in a bush with tall, skinny pink flowers. The vampire howled when it struck. Whatever the plant was, it tore through skin. Grace wasted no time, sprinting toward the front door.

Cramps bloomed in her sides. But she was almost there. The metal handle cool to her touch.

Then a blistering yank sent her flying back. "No...!"

Her vision filled with teeth. So many teeth. Claws shredded her uniform at the shoulder in a heartbeat, the vampire's breath hot against her now exposed flesh as it closed in.

She resisted, but it was like trying to hold back the tide.

This was it. Dead without anyone around who cared. Like so many victims from her articles. No life flashed before her this time. Funny, that, like she'd already gotten it out of the way.

Glass shattered and the vampire vanished in a cloud of steam and fury. In the mist, Eugene appeared, pulling her along by the elbow. She let him lead her outside.

"How...?"

"Holy water," Eugene replied. "Every Quarter cop carries a couple of vials for emergencies."

The guards outside were gone.

"They-they..." she stuttered as she grabbed Eugene's waist.

"Yeah."

"They added more at night."

Eugene said nothing for a moment. "...they sure did."

She tried to explain but was silenced by a shiver. All of the guards were gone now. Driven away by a phone call.

Soon they passed the abandoned factory Grace had shored up inside of and made a beeline for a dark red sedan, police radio on the dash. Eugene set her against the rear passenger side door and patted his pockets once more.

Grace hugged herself. "I'm sorry."

"Tell me at the station." His tone was flint, hard and sharp.

She supposed she deserved that. For what happened. For what might.

In a moment, he pulled out his keys and opened the passenger door. "For what it's worth, I'm sorry too. It's never easy when a gun's in your face. But we're almost out of this."

"I'm not sorry about that." She stood upright. "I'm sorry about this."

His brow knitted together. Then the dart hit him in the chest. Eugene teetered. She braced her body against his to prevent a fall.

"A sedative," she explained as she lowered him into the car seat meant for her. "Should kick in any second now."

His hands fumbled toward his holster. She offered him a sad smile. "Looking for this?" Then pulled his gun out from behind her waist.

His mouth turned into an O.

"Again, sorry." She took the keys from him. "But it's like I said; I need answers. And this story I'm working on will solve everything." The door shut with a *thunk* of finality.

As she got into his car's driver seat, she wanted to explain how much good this would do. Sure, Eugene was sympathetic, but terrible at his job.

Someone better would come along, someone more effective. This way, his life would have meaning, and lead to better justice down the line. A win-win for everyone. She opened her mouth to say all this, but a sour taste in the back of her throat made her hold back.

She checked the time instead. Damn. If she sped, she could reach the Quarter with three minutes to spare. After that, she'd figured out some way to dispose of Eugene's car. Probably.

As she turned the ignition, a roar erupted from the front gate of Komarov's apartment complex. Covered in blood and froth, the vampire guard rocketed toward her at inhuman speed.

The engine failed to turn. She pushed the accelerator to the floor, trying the key again. The vampire neared. Five houses away, then three. He sprinted on all fours, speeding on like a jungle cat.

"Work!" Grace screamed, turning the key again. The vampire howled, the whites of its eyes visible in the night. Blessedly, the car's engine started and finally drowned the fucker out. Cranking the steering wheel hard, Grace peeled out. Gravity pinned her against the door as the world spun. The reek of burning rubber scorched her nostrils.

Something slammed into the car, stopping it in its tracks and shattering the back window. Eugene slumped forward and banged into the dashboard, blood gushing from his nose.

Grace mashed the gas pedal to the floor but the car stayed put. She turned, trying to see what was going on. She froze. The vampire's chin rested on the trunk. The street behind him was gone, replaced with a dark sky. He must have the car by the bumper, lifting it into the air.

His head rocked one way, then the other. What was he doing? Before Grace could piece it together, Eugene fell onto her with the weight of a dead man, pinning her. That was until the car started to shake. A slight rocking at first until it grew into a quaking tremor. She lost all ability to discern which way was up or down, tossed about like a flake in a snow globe.

Something heavy struck her across the face. Stars ignited in her vision. Static roared, then faded. The detective's radio. She grabbed on to a door handle only for it to slip from her grasp almost instantly, the violent frenzy overwhelming her waning strength.

Then, without warning, everything stilled. Grace found herself on the floor in the front seat, the detective's foot in her face. She pushed it away, nausea forcing bile up her throat. Lucky Yukawa had been passed out during all that. Though it might be her dizziness but his other leg looked bent at an odd angle. Nausea threatened however, and Grace had to close her eyes to make the bile ebb.

The sound of straining metal sundered the narrow space. She tried, but couldn't determine the source. Was the vampire trying to crush them?

With one last grating screech, it stopped. Nothing seemed different. No, not true. Her door stood open. Had she forgotten to close it?

No, not open. Gone.

The vampire's thousand jagged teeth filled the gap. A clawed hand clamped down on her ankle. She screamed as it wrenched her out. The sidewalk flew past beneath her. Grass rose up. She ducked her head, on instinct. Her shoulders struck first, the impact filling her lungs with foam.

A hand seized her by the hair and slammed her into the hard earth. The vampire pulled her up and screeched in her face.

"P-please–"

It brought her down again and again. Her strength left her. She was a rag doll in its arms. Blackness threatened to descend in totality with each blow.

She had been so close. A body in the car. Diavolo waiting. Her answer over the horizon.

"Little bitch," the vampire said in a garbled Russian accent.

I'm sorry, Joy. A shaft of lightning split her skull as her nose broke. *I failed.*

The vampire hoisted her up, bending her until her back strained and she cried out. A bleary fist seared towards her.

The hollow pits of its eyes swelled, swallowing her. This was her end. She'd expected it ever since she had been dropped over the fence. But it didn't need to take so long.

A roar from far away. Strange. She always thought death would be silent. But maybe what little life a person had left raged in their final moments. Gods' last failsafe to mark a person's passing, that noted they were here and cried out in justice. It helped, if she was honest. But why did it sound so...mechanical?

A silver beam lit up the night. The vampire gave a bark of surprise. One second, it's fist was about to cave her cheekbone in, the next, she was tumbling to the ground, alone.

She lay, the sky spread above, light blaring away its starry essence. A familiar, impossible face broke it down the middle.

"Diavolo?" Grace asked. "How—"

He was upside down to her, yet unmistakably chipper under his dark disheveled hair. "Ah, ah, Miss Clemons. You haven't yet paid for your question, even a partial one. Now," he glanced about, "where is that detective? Ah!"

He disappeared, only to return with an unconscious Detective Yukawa over his shoulder, the man's leg dangling and bent at an odd angle. "Bit of a smell to him. Do you...oh, yes. Of course." He fished in Grace's pocket for the inhibitor to the paralytic, then continued on. She lifted herself up. The detective's car lay mangled, its front end wrapped around a tree trunk, wheels still spinning. Pieces of bumper and engine littered the surrounding lawn. The arm of the Russian vampire poked out from underneath the wreckage.

"Here you are, detective." Diavolo set the detective down in the driver's seat. He tossed aside a large rock and the rev of the engine suddenly cut out. But when he approached the front of the car and the mangled hand, Grace turned away. She didn't need to witness another vampire's death.

The wail of police sirens swelled as Diavolo strutted back to Grace. "They'll be here soon. Three minutes by my estimates." He leaned forward, his smile bright despite the violence on his hands. "Now, where's my body?"

Eugene started snoring right then, the light growl audible over the approaching sirens. She watched as his head rose and fell with steady breath. Diavolo shifted and blocked her sight. "Body, Miss Clemons."

Grace continued to study Eugene. The vampire wanted a body. She'd give him one.

Her finger pointed up. "Fourth floor. Penthouse."

"Excellent!" Diavolo clapped. "And I must say, you really know how to show fear. Someone like me could smell it miles away."

She blinked, not sure how or even if to respond to that.

"Evening," he said. He tipped an imaginary hat and walked off.

He couldn't leave, not like this. The police would lock her away. She sucked in all the air her damaged lungs could manage and shouted the only thing that mattered:

"Question!"

But his footfalls continued to recede. The police sirens intensified to an incessant pitch. Grace tried to sit up but failed. Her insides felt like they could explode.

A sob escaped. She had been prepared for death. But this—guilt, capture, imprisonment—was so much worse. Having to live with her failure every day.

"Ask."

She looked up. She hadn't heard Diavolo return.

The word was a command, the tight line of his mouth telling her he wouldn't accept any nonsense. That this needed to end quickly.

But she couldn't think of a thing to say.

"Ask," he repeated, more forcefully.

Question after question poured into her mind: the surveillance tape, the man under her car, Diavolo's escape, the mysterious voice on the mobster's phone. But she held her tongue. Because she was staring at Diavolo, at his bottom lip and the budding fang biting into it, the tiny bead of blood swelling at the tip. In that drop, she saw all the blood she had spilled tonight and all the potential blood she would give this man.

And she held her tongue.

"I see." Diavolo swallowed, his jaw quivering a little. "As I do not yet have a body, your question is moot."

"If that's true," she said, measuring every word before she spoke, "then leave."

In the distance, pinpricks of blue and red police lights twinkled into view. Neighbors trickled out of their homes.

He cursed. "Fine."

In a flash, she was lifted, her face buried in his chest, the stench of dirt and sweat immense. When he set her down seconds later, she found she was on the rooftop of the apartment building.

"Stay here." He lifted a window in the skylight and jumped in.

"No, wait You can't leave–"

The dark that had been beckoning for far too long finally took hold.

21

GRACE WOKE, EXPECTING TO find herself in the same spot on the roof of Komarov's apartment building, awaiting Diavolo as he retrieved Alexei's body. Instead, she was inside a hospital room, an unblinking golden retriever inches from her nose.

She held still. Based on the warm drool under her cheek, she'd been here some time. This must be Diavolo's sick idea of a joke. Or perhaps something far more sinister. One doesn't fall asleep on the top of a mob safe house without consequences.

The dog continued to stare. Retrievers were supposed to be friendly, but there were always exceptions.

"Nice, doggie," she said, raising her hand one slow inch at a time. "No need to—"

In a blink, the dog snapped forward and stuck its great big red tongue in her open mouth.

"Blech!" She pushed the golden retriever away and wiped her lips on her sleeve. Guess that answered that question. The dog bowed its front, tail wagging. What did it want? Didn't matter, because it barked. In this small of a room, the sound made her ears ring.

"Oh, piss off."

It barked again.

"Okay!" She set a hand on its head and it shut up.

Where was she? Someone had changed her into scrubs. She didn't *feel* violated, but it was hard to tell. A vampire had slammed her head into the ground a half dozen times, she was lucky to still breathe without assistance.

The place stank of antiseptic and piss, which almost caused her stomach to flip. The posters on the wall showcased people with their pets under massive block letters that asked if they've been spayed or neutered. Based on the people's expressions, she couldn't tell who the question was directed at.

A TV sat in the corner with a DVD player underneath it. Maybe she could find a news station, check the date. The dog leaped up, setting its paws with their raking claws on her legs.

She shoved it back down. "Go. Away."

The retriever, finally realizing she wasn't going to play, left through a doggy door Grace had failed to notice until then. The instant the dog's tail slipped from view, the door opened. A tall, older man with a russet brown complexion, thinning hair, and bifocals came in holding a small duffel bag. His lab coat hung over loose khakis and a plaid shirt. He looked uncomfortable, his clothes wearing him instead of the other way around.

"Miss Blockwell."

"Clemons."

He didn't apologize, only nodded. "Our mutual employer has asked me to keep an eye on you. Bring you up to health and speed. Are you recovered?"

"...I'm awake."

He nodded again as if that was enough. "Well, your boss, Mr. Peer—"

"Who?"

"Peer, miss." When she still showed no recognition, he rolled his eyes. "First name Van."

"Van P—Oh. Clever."

"He told me to give you the works. Here's your duffel."

She took the offered bag and unzipped it. Inside was a small roll of cash and a cheap flip phone with a charger.

"Please make only necessary calls," the vet explained. "It should last the day. Longer if you are more selective. Now, I see no reason to destroy the pants you wore. They're washed and in the dryer now. The shirt, however, was a lost cause. I—question?"

She lowered her raised hand. "Why are you doing this? Besides him, I mean. Why do I need a burner phone or cash? What's going on?"

The vet sighed. He must not have expected her questions. He brought out his phone, swiped a few times, then turned it to face her.

The headline splashed across the top read 'Journalist Wanted for Attempted Murder.' She quickly scanned the article. Most of the details were correct, which meant one thing:

"Eugene."

"I'm—I don't know who that is. Komarov had a vast camera network throughout his complex. Cameras smaller than a grain of rice. Captured everything."

That was why she hadn't seen any security cameras.

The vet continued. "You are now public enemy number one. State troopers have been called in, Amber alerts sent out, roadblocks scattered about every few blocks. The net has been cast, Miss Clemons. I'm here to see you aren't snagged."

Everything sounded so foreign, like he was talking about someone else instead of her. How could she cause so many ripples? Enough that strangers would study the intimate details of what made her tick. Or worse, not strangers, but those she knew. The bar regulars would squawk their lungs out about the strange woman who sat in the corner and typed until last call. The patrolmen who offered a shoulder or an ear after particularly brutal murders would rifle through her bedroom, her closet, her under-wear drawer.

She knew she should be horrified, feel some semblance of disgust or betrayal, but all that reached her through the din was a sense of fi-nality. She was done. No more story, no more stake in Diavolo's crazy schemes—though last night made it clear he still had something to gain.

But she could leave. Get out of this job, this city, this life.

An involuntary sigh escaped her as all the tension in her dissipated at the thought. She'd been burying herself for so long, holding on because of her promise to a sister so long dead, Grace barely remembered what she looked like. And now, with her reputation destroyed, her shred of power stripped away, she could let go.

"What can I do?" she voiced aloud.

The vet answered, "Step one: get dressed." He pulled clothes out of a drawer and set them on the counter. "I'll be back with lunch in fifteen minutes." He made to leave, opening the door an inch, then stopped. "A little at a time. Just focus on the next little at a time."

He offered a sympathetic smile that she resented every inch of. When he left, she went to the sink. A yellow note with a familiar curved handwriting was left on the clothes pile: TWO PER WEEK. She crumpled it up. The sink water soothed like fresh aloe. She must have been crying because the skin around her eyes was puffy and sensitive.

Refreshed, she checked the duffel bag. It was the same one she'd nabbed from Komarov's apartment. She dug through it. Maybe it still contained...yes! The DVD case marked 20/20 lay hidden under the clothes inside, shiny as the day she nabbed it.

But her enthusiasm soon soured. What did she do now? Watching it would mean nothing. It's not like the contents would give her any clue how to escape the authorities, and she couldn't publish her findings. Plus, most of the people on this were dead.

Or were they? Grace set the DVD in the player. Komarov had been so adamant Richard was innocent of her kidnapping. More than likely the claim was a stalling tactic he'd used to get close to her. But what if Komarov was right?

She had a few minutes before the vet returned. Enough to put this to bed once and for all.

The motel came on screen. Four camera angles broke the screen up in equal parts: one inside Komarov's room, another in the hallway outside, a third in the parking lot, and the last in the motel check-in office with a window looking out on the vending machines and a tiny slice of the parking lot.

He'd stolen the motel's security footage and spliced in his own.

She fast forwarded to the interview, to the moment Komarov sent Richard from the room, then hit play. Richard made his rushed exit, then entered the lobby. He asked the employee at the desk something; the woman disappeared into the back, and came back out with an ice bucket.

Richard promptly filled it outside next to the vending machines, then dumped it over his head.

Grace bit her lip. The interview went on, unabated. Richard continued to stand there, bucket beside him on the ground. He stayed like that for half an hour, filling the bucket twice more, soaking himself, then staying put. No checking his phone or speaking with anyone else.

Eventually–*finally*–he turned and darted behind a column, only his foot still in the shot. What set him off? Komarov? No, he was on the bed still, talking to his guard. In the shot of the parking lot, she neared her car. So that scrape of shoe she'd heard had been Richard, hiding from her.

The abduction took place. She ignored it, staying focused on Richard. The man didn't move. He remained hidden while she was kidnapped in broad daylight.

Any guilt over Richard vanished. He deserved to have his blood sucked out.

She hit rewind. This time she would keep an eye on Komarov. So what if Richard hadn't taken her? Komarov had more than one man working under him.

Except Grace had accidentally hit fast forward. In a rushed frenzy of movement, Richard returned to the motel room, the guard watching the window hurried out, and Komarov and Richard made passionate love on the stained mattress.

Grace cleared her throat. Thank Gods the TV was on mute. She re-wound the footage. So that was how an underling talked a mob boss into a news interview. This explains why Komarov was so broken up over Richard's disappearance. Why Komarov would stop by Richard's home the day she tailed him. The pakhan must have known Richard was gone long before the police. Maybe even called them himself.

If Komarov weren't dead, she'd have let the chill in her spine take hold. Instead, she started to dress.

When she looked at the screen again, the tape had gone back to the beginning. She hit fast forward, paying more attention this time. All three mobsters arrived, acquired the room key, did a quick canvas of the area, and then waited for her.

Once she pulled in, Grace stayed focused on her car.

Not long, maybe a minute after she headed toward the room, a man stepped into view dressed in a hoodie and jeans, face masked, gloves on. Not an inch of skin exposed. The angle of the cameras didn't get the street, so she hadn't caught him walking up. She checked the other camera feed. There she was, knocking on the motel room door, while this stranger crawled under her car. If she'd turned her head, she would have seen him.

This had to be Komarov. The timing was too precise. That's why Richard sat back; he was in on it.

Whoever kidnapped her, this masked man, was still out there. Getting away with his crime. A monster still needing to be reaped.

No. Grace was done. Someone else would catch him. Komarov's organization was in shambles, the police sifting through the pieces.

She finished dressing. A bulge in her pants pocket poked her hip. She reached in and pulled out her old phone, the screen now sporting a dozen fresh cracks. It was off. She pushed the power button. The low charge icon flashed. Still had some juice.

Any number of people in her contacts had enough resources to get her out of the city. But the blackmail notes were in her office. It wasn't like she could stroll over and pick them up. The whole newspaper building would be compromised. That's *if* the police hadn't ransacked her desk yet.

She would need a courier, a go-between. Someone who wouldn't betray her. A friend.

Or someone who was a little more than that.

Nausea burbled up her throat and burned. After the night Grace had, no one deserved even a small slice of this hell. Especially Tracy. She was a good person. While Grace had betrayed a detective.

Her old phone buzzed and lit up. She must have been holding the power button without realizing. The battery blinked empty in the corner. Before she could tap her contacts, two texts popped up. The first, more recent one, was from Tracy.

Call me as soon as you get this mom. We have to talk

Stay safe xox

What in the God of the Lost's world had she done to deserve this woman? Too bad Tracy fell for one as broken as Grace. If Grace could repeat all this, she'd get on that elevator with Tracy and never get back off.

The second text she tapped without thinking. It was from Perry:

Congrats! The powers that be granted your article! Can't wait to read it.

She stared. This text had been sent yesterday evening after she left the factory, right after she silenced her phone. She laughed. To think, if she had gotten this before breaking into the penthouse—

Wait. The article. It was still alive. All it needed was a new byline. She found the number she needed and let the phone die.

On her burner, she dialed and set her thumb on the call button.

The article had the power to change everything. Even if she wouldn't be the one to write it. It could still do the most good. Make all of this worth it. Make everything up to Tracy and Joy in one fell swoop.

And all she had to do was avoid blowing up one more person's life.

How difficult could that be?

***

The first day after Komarov's death, Eugene woke in a hospital bed to a mountain of get-well cards, edible arrangements, and an assortment of mini pastries. He asked the nurse if they had put him in the wrong room. She chuckled and patted him on the shoulder. Throughout the day, coworkers stopped by to sing his praises and drop off more little gifts.

The second day, the hospital became a ghost town.

That was when he knew: Word had gotten out. The security tapes of him negotiating to save Komarov's life had leaked. He performed by-the-book and tried to mete out justice for the courts to decide. But every cop knew that the courts never dolled out anything of the sort. In this situation, you threw the book out and turned a blind eye.

However, a couple of officers did visit. They made small talk with plastered on smiles, their jaws hard. The flint in their eyes asked, "How could you?"

By nightfall, Eugene wanted to crawl up the walls. He begged Sergeant Cole to bring him some work. Anything, so long as it kept him occupied.

A diligent worker bee herself, and with enough power to not care about any of the frat boy politics, she came through.

The case involved a dead vampire in the Quarter. The victim was a Caucasian male, teen in appearance, with brown hair. After a quick head count, the Berets determined the victim to be Conroy O'Brien.

Eugene couldn't recall any other case like it. Vampires were chipped with what was essentially GPS shock collars. They could do little more than think about hurting another vampire before they were overwhelmed with ungodly amounts of pain. That must have been why the Quarter had dished it out to local police: They were stumped.

To begin with, pinpointing the time of death was nearly impossible. Vampires were partially dead and in a passive state of rot, growing catatonic after a thousand years or so.

But this case had another fun factor thrown in. When a vampire caught the sun, they were vaporized from the UV radiation, no remains to find, even when dead. Most of the teen had vaporized away. However, ash remained. The Green Berets managed to collect a few flakes from a shaded spot. This vamp had died by removal of the head or a wooden stake to the heart.

The shade offered another clue. Judging by the position of the sun, the time of death was in the last two weeks. Possibly a day or two earlier based on heavy cloud coverage.

Eugene jumped to Grace as a suspect right away. Probably a side effect of his tired, addled brain.

The squeak of his nurse's old tennis shoes roused him from his thoughts.

"You have more visitors," she said, bored.

"Tell them to wait. Need to pee."

He positioned the crutch under his right arm, opposite his damaged leg, like the medical staff advised. Despite the leg with its torn ACL and the many broken bones he didn't remember the name of, he was lucky: surviving a car wreck, no catheter required. Sure his nose was broken, as well as two ribs, and a concussion sent him running to empty his guts every few hours. But the most painful injury wasn't any of those. No, that was covered by the tiny bandage on his chest: the hole from Grace's dart. Even now, the cold dead in her eyes when she shot him sent a chill down his spine. How had he been so wrong about her?

When he came back from the restroom, Sergeant Cole was there with an older woman Eugene recognized from press conferences: the police commissioner. He hoped his hospital gown was tied in the back.

The commissioner's eyes, already large, swelled with excitement upon seeing him. He felt exposed under her measured look, like she could see inside him to what made him tick.

"Ma'am," he squeaked.

"I can't tell you how fine a job you performed, detective." The commissioner beamed. Her teeth hurt to look at. Had she grown a few extra somehow?

"Thank you, ma'am."

"Have a seat."

Aware of a sudden breeze on his backside, Eugene shuffled crab-like until he reached the bed.

The commissioner's tone never changed. "I can't tell you how much I wish I was behind the wheel of your vehicle, detective, smashing into one of them piss suckers. Plow through 'em all, I say."

"...yes, ma'am."

"God, the thrill you must have felt."

"Uh, yes, ma'am."

"Mhm. Which is why I'm excited to share that you've been moved off active duty."

Sergeant Cole, who had remained silent throughout this exchange, looked down at the floor.

"Ma'am?" Eugene asked.

"That didn't sound right, did it?" The commissioner leaned forward, hands clasped together in her lap. "We're moving you up. Desk duty. With a sizable raise."

"Ma'am, I'm more than capable."

"Hell yes, you are. Hence the promotion. The desk stuff is more PR than anything. Shows I keep the health of my officers in mind."

"The health of your officers, ma'am?" Cole still refused to meet his eye. "Or me?"

A crack in the veneer. "Can't tell you how little I appreciate your tone."

Cole exhaled sharply. A soft rebuke. This was not the time to fight.

"Sorry, ma'am," Eugene said, hating every word. "Still not quite right. The accident and all."

The beam returned, brighter somehow. "No need, detective. That's why this desk job will do you good. You need to recover, mentally and physically. A commendation plus some time off your feet will do you wonders."

When neither he nor Cole showed any reaction, the commissioner scoffed. "Celebrate, you two! This city just lost a major criminal. You act as if someone important died."

Cole finally spoke. "I'm sure Detective Yukawa is ecstatic and will be fully able to express his enthusiasm at the commendation ceremony, ma'am."

"Excellent," the commissioner said without waiting for a response from Eugene. "And with that, I'm due for a press briefing. I can't tell you how much I enjoyed your company."

When she was gone, Eugene turned to Cole. "I think she accidentally set her track on repeat."

She cocked an eyebrow.

"The whole 'I can't tell you' thing," Eugene explained. "Has she always been like that?"

"A lot of politics," Cole said, "is about letting people think you're giving them your whole attention when really you can't do a damn thing. While the rest—" her eyes scanned the halls outside, a shadow falling across her face "—is damage control."

Eugene took a moment to swallow that. He thought the most his fellow officers would do was give him the silent treatment, maybe stiff him at social outings. What Cole said hinted at something worse. That an armed officer didn't have to fear an unarmed public, but the armed people beside him.

Cole opened her mouth to expound further when a knock rapped on the door.

A uniformed officer entered without waiting for permission. "Ma'am, we've received a tip. It's her."

"Thank you, Officer Jenkins. Please, wait for me outside."

After the officer left, the sergeant kept her back to Eugene. A heaviness settled in his gut as all expectations of receiving a straight answer evaporated the longer Cole refused to face him.

Then she called out: "Officer!"

Jenkins returned.

"Find me a wheelchair."

Eugene smiled and stood. Maybe Cole would play straight with him after all.

22

THE PHONE RANG SEVERAL times. Grace cupped her hand over the earpiece, afraid the tinny sound would echo out into the hallway and bring the vet back.

The person answered.

"Tracy?" Grace asked.

"Hello? Who is this?"

"Sorry this wasn't exactly what you pictured when you said, 'Let's get drinks.'"

A pause. "Mom? Shouldn't you be on vacation?" Tracy's voice dropped to a whisper. "Like in a foreign country?"

"Probably." Grace let a beat pass before saying. "I need help."

"I don't know if anyone *can* help you." A swish fell across the speaker. A deep voice rumbled in the background, too faint to discern. After a beat, Tracy said, "What is it?"

"Who's with you?"

"No one."

"Tracy..."

"Clearly I don't mean as much to you if you kept whatever all this is from me. Trust is a bridge, and you smashed it right down the middle. You need to start building from your side."

Did Tracy talk like this to everybody? Like they were in a decade-long relationship? Gods, Grace didn't know this woman at all. "I know. I have no right, but you're the only one I can ask."

"Then ask."

Grace laid out exactly what she needed and how to go about getting it to her. That done, the other line remained silent. She imagined cops bent over laptops, wires connected to Tracy's phone, tracing the call. Grace held the phone so close, it hurt, trying to pick up some hint as to whether Tracy was betraying her.

Finally, Tracy said, "After while, crocodile," and hung up.

Grace swallowed. "Hope to see you later, alligator."

The vet returned soon after, dog in tow, carrying a ham sandwich and chips on a plastic tray. A small vase of water contained a lily in the center. She had to resist a laugh—was he worried about a Yelp review?

Still, Grace gobbled up the food, unaware of how ravenous she was. After, an exhaustion deeper than anything she had felt before took over. Her eyes drooped.

"Well, my dear," the vet said.

Dear? She stopped sucking the last bit of mustard off her thumb. He might be older, but he wasn't *that* old.

"I would have given you more time to rest but it appears the game is up. The police know you're here."

"What?" She stood, sluggish, then settled into a defensive stance, hands in karate chopping position.

He laughed. "Down, Grasshopper. We have a few minutes. I caught the call on the police scanner relaying this location. Are you finished?" He gestured toward the plate.

His calm demeanor caught her off guard. She replied that she was.

"Good. This way. Stay, boy."

They left the dog and entered a labyrinth of white hallways. Grace did her best to keep up. The old man was more spry than she'd guessed. Eventually they reached a staircase leading into a dark underground room filled with cleaning supplies. "The sewer entrance is at the back behind the shelves with the toilet paper. It will take you wherever you need to go. I suggest taking the fourth right and then two lefts to put you out in Parma. Careful of any sudden floods."

She exhaled a shaky breath and proceeded down.

"Oh, and Miss Clemons?"

It was a mistake to turn back, but she did. He blocked the doorway, an outline darkened by the overhead lights from behind. Like Death finally came to escort her on.

"No matter where you go, no matter how far, your debt will always be owed." Then he was gone, and Grace was left to scrounge in the dark.

***

Sergeant Cole gunned the accelerator of her tiny green Neon out of the hospital garage and onto the pockmarked asphalt of Memphis Avenue, cutting off a green SUV in the process. The angry honk barely cracked her stoic facade.

Without looking away from the road, Cole said, "Time to tell me why you have a death wish, Detective Yukawa."

Eugene opened his mouth to speak but the sergeant cut him off.

"And if you say ma'am one more time, your face will meet my wedding ring." The half inch thick band of metal wrapped around the sergeant's middle finger like a coiled snake about to snap.

He cleared his throat. "W-what makes you think I have a death wish, ma—sergeant?"

"You think I don't know what my boys are saying? Normally, they pick on your absent-mindedness or your service record. Occasionally, a few throw in a splash of racism but I trust you to report that if it gets too out of hand."

Eugene nodded. She had told him as much when he signed on. It had made him feel respected at the time; most CO's either infantilized him or ignored his complaints entirely.

"But this is different," she went on. "The whole precinct has a hate on for you. The commissioner likes you now, but don't expect it to last past a couple press conferences."

The matter-of-fact way Cole explained his situation unnerved him. "Should I run?"

"What you need are allies. Tell me, detective, your first three years—" the sergeant held up three fingers for emphasis as she gunned through a slow yellow "—your arrest record was higher than anyone's in the department by a mile. The fourth year, a few months before I came on, it tanked."

The unasked question of "What happened?" hung in the air. Eugene inhaled. "Do we really have to talk about that?"

"If you want my help..."

The light ahead changed to red. Rather than run the siren, Cole brought the car to a halt.

Eugene braced himself against the dash, then held on. "Do personnel files mention relationships?"

"Only marriage."

"Guess that's a relief." He lowered his hands slowly. "Sofia and I met right after high school. Church speed dating event. We had two children: Maria and Fonda. The younger got leukemia." His heart already ached saying those few words. He curled his hands into fists. "At first, treatment made her better but that turned quick. It tore us up, the constant...reality of it. I tried to fix everything, bolster everyone's spirits. Searched for every treatment option I could find. But soon I realized what my wife had months ago: There are no miracles. All you can do is wait. Witness. Try to endure."

He sniffed and tasted tears. "Have you ever seen a seven-year-old shrivel up before your eyes?"

The car drove on, slower than before.

"After..." He took a deep breath. "After, I was lucky to string two sentences together. I went dark, started reading about other people's success at chemo. Punishing myself, I guess. Sofia moved in with her parents, neither of us able to lift a finger to save what we had between us. It was the same with Maria, in a way...

"I was ready to quit the force if I could have pulled myself out of the pit I was in." His fists loosened. "Instead, I picked up cases no one cared about. Impossible murders no one expected any results from. My record went in the toilet, my career halted but I didn't care. Solved a few of them and people got off my back. Then they assigned me to vamp detail. All I had to worry about there was one naggy reporter. Then the worst happened."

"...Faison retired."

Eugene wiped his nose on his sleeve. "Now I see all of it for what it was: attempts to fix the impossible. Trying to save my kid one obscure cold case at a time."

Sergeant Cole patted his arm, a tissue between her fingertips. He took it. She appeared to have tears forming but by the time Eugene composed himself, the small chink in her armor was gone.

Cole asked, "You ever turn to the bottle?"

"Sofia drank enough for the both of us."

A veterinarian's office came into view ahead. Yellow caution tape blocked off the entrance. Two uniformed officers corralled a horde of reporters inside a taped off area near the sidewalk. The group rounded on Cole's car as it pulled into the lot.

The swarm overtook them before Cole set the parking brake. Eugene sank into his seat. "What...?"

"I need you on this, Eugene." Cole made eye contact with him for the first time since they left the hospital. "This is your case, regardless of what the commish says or your physical injuries. We are gonna see this to the end. Now, follow my lead. I promise I won't feed you to the wolves." She smiled. "Shall we?"

Eugene swallowed. "Lead the way."

23

GRACE SLEPT IN THE sewers that night. After the noise of the last few weeks, the quiet down here settled over her like a weighted blanket. On a high up, semi-dry spot amid the dark and the stink, she curled up using the duffel as a makeshift pillow–zipper side down, of course.

She'd find a way out at first light, head inside some thrift store, and purchase a new wardrobe. Oh, wait, she'd have to shower first. A rec center was the obvious choice. Or she could skip it, let the mothball aroma of the thrift shop overwhelm her BO.

None of that truly mattered but it was better than thinking about Tracy. Who was she speaking with? Could Grace really trust her? Was this a trap?

She shoved the troubling thoughts aside. They weren't worth mulling over until she laid eyes on the place. But no matter how much she tried, the questions gnawed at her like ticks, making her roll over and over.

***

The next morning, cops swarmed outside the Plain Dealer in the same way that bees swarmed a hive: en masse with tiny moving parts.

Officers wore plain clothes and grazed about, but Grace saw through their act. She had been on enough ride-alongs and listened at the edges of enough cop circles to know what undercover looked like.

Even if she hadn't, these fools weren't exactly subtle. A couple stopped to stare into each other's eyes every ten feet, but never smiled. Two chess players sat on a picnic blanket, one didn't even know how to play. The worst was a jogger who stretched for twenty minutes straight.

Grace squinted through binoculars from a quarter mile away, separated by an intersection under a highway overpass. A skinny maple tree rested against her back on a strip of landscaping outside a Buffalo Wild Wings. She bounced on her toes. No one could spot her, but these last three weeks had taught her how fast events could go south. So, yes, the cars provided excellent cover but there was no way she wouldn't be ready to duck inside the bustling restaurant at the merest hint of foul play.

Her fingers played at a loose thread on the hem of her Cuyahoga Community College sweater. Everything was fine. If anyone asked, she was Ann Stevens: amateur bird watcher, empty nester, pun lover, and bored housewife ready to get back into the workforce. She was fanny packed and raring to go. Just don't say anything about her bad dye job.

Another ten minutes passed with zero change. Grace pulled out a new burner phone from her shoulder bag. The phone the vet provided, the one which probably tipped the cops off to her, was now surfing a wave of shit down to the lake.

Tracy answered on the fifth ring. "Where?"

"Outside," Grace responded.

"Jesus..."

"When?"

"Any minute. Watch the entrance."

Easy to do. Grace set herself up for a clear view of the entrance, right in line with the drop off spot: a public bench on her corner of the intersection.

She shot off one last text to Tracy, focusing on the individual letters rather than the message, because she'd never type it otherwise: *Now run from me*

Immediately, the phone blared with text after text. Grace snapped it in half and ripped out the battery. A driver climbed into a pickup parked in a nearby spot, staring at his phone, oblivious. She sneaked over and slipped the broken burner into the truck's bed. He never turned. She returned to her post, never chancing a glance behind her.

Then the front of the building stirred.

"Son of a bitch."

A security guard exited and charged across the street. Right towards her.

She was going to kill Tracy. Saying goodbye was not the worst thing; in fact, it was inevitable. Did Tracy not get that? There was no way the cops weren't paying attention to this.

Yes, the undercover agents stopped in their mechanical routines, avoiding the guard without avoiding him. When he passed, they glanced at each other, unsure what to do. The guard ran full tilt across the intersection, immune to their confusion and somehow unhindered by traffic, and barreled onto her block.

Wonderful. She would have to wait forever after he dropped her flash drive on the corner bench. It would be watched like crazy. She'd have to find her own way out of the city.

But the guard zipped right past the drop site. And straight toward her.

Bark scraped Grace's back. Tracy had betrayed her. She risked a glance toward the restaurant. Could she slip in? Maybe pretend she saw someone?

No, that wouldn't work. He'd seen her, she was sure of it. The cops would notice him change direction.

She swung around the tree, grasping the trunk for support. He was incoming, a well-dressed bomb about to blow away her cover. Was this all she could do? Hide behind a tree like a child caught during a game of hide-and-seek?

Her knees gave out. The police would hightail it over and find the subject of their manhunt, taken down by an idiot in a blazer sent on the word of an intern.

A quick shuffle, the booming footfalls landing close enough for her to feel the vibrations through the ground. She braced for a hand on her shoulder, a cry of discovery. But neither came. She looked up. The guard has rushed by, his retreating back slipping inside the darkness of a coffee shop.

Grace bent over, an uneasy chuckle escaping her lips. A coffee run. He'd been sent on a coffee run. She'd forgotten. It was a tradition of the older guards to haze a younger one by making him get all their coffee orders in under three minutes or lose OT for the next month.

She shook, her body went slack, releasing the tension in an uneasy laugh. Toxic masculinity for the scare. After a count of twenty, she resumed her observation.

The cops had gone back to their normal routines. But something else had changed outside the Plain Dealer: Perry was halfway across the intersection. Because of the guard, she had missed him. His face was twisted in a snarl. The center of Grace's chest contorted in a similar manner.

The weeks since she'd last seen him had not been kind. His skin was blotchy, the bags under his eyes puffy and flecked with purple, like he had been in several fights. The buttons on his shirt were mismatched. Small, gray discolorations spattered his cheeks, jaw, neck, and hands. She couldn't recall hearing of any medical condition but that didn't mean anything.

He ambled across the street this way and that, like he had lost all sense of direction.

There was no way this could be because of her, could it? Perry always seemed so indifferent to the reporters under him. But maybe Grace hadn't given him the benefit of the doubt. After all, he had called the police the night she went missing, had responded to every midnight wellbeing text she'd sent over the years. It was strange, watching him near her block, to finally realize someone cared about her. That her absence brought out the ugly in him.

He ducked down next to the corner bench and tied his shoe. *Oh, Tracy,* Grace thought. *Picking him was almost cruel.*

Perry looked up without warning, his gaze traveling up, then down the street. When his eyes swiveled in her general direction, she shrank back, hoping the shade of the tree and disguise obscured her enough. Letting Perry see her might do him some good, lift him out of whatever despair he'd sunk into. But she couldn't risk it. It took everything in her to walk toward the restaurant patio.

She took a seat at a table with a view that blocked Perry and the police. Next to her, a table of teens shouted at each other over a basket of fries, the racket muffling. If Perry had spotted her and alerted the police, they might be crossing the street now. She'd have no way of knowing.

Why had Tracy sent him? Did Perry know what was happening? She might have to leave the flash drive at the bench for a few days, though the idea didn't sit well with her.

"Excuse me."

Grace glanced up to find a waitress towering over her, a group of sharply dressed men in tow. "Yes?"

"You need to see the hostess before being seated."

Apologizing, Grace got up from the now claimed table and headed inside in the direction of the hostess. At the front, she enjoyed an unobscured view of the bench and the Plain Dealer. She cursed under her breath. She should have spied from in here.

Perry was nowhere to be seen. The police had trickled to another side of the newspaper building. All of them settled in and began their routines again.

She counted in her head. When she reached two hundred, she made her way out to the bench. She remained alert for any sort of trap, the hair on the back of her neck on end. A manila envelope a little larger than an index card rested behind the back leg. She bent down next to the bench and went through her backpack, removing a water bottle. When she stood, she pocketed the package.

She'd done it.

Now to escape. *One foot in front of the other*, Grace thought. *Slow, steady, like your heart isn't trying to escape through your chest.*

When she thought she was far enough away, she pulled the envelope out and opened it. Two flash drives rattled about inside with a small note: *I'm sorry*

***

"I can't tell you how angry I am." The captain's impish frame swelled and filled her office, dwarfing the bunker of a desk and gorilla-sized chair. "Just what in the hell were you two thinking?" Her fist slammed down and Eugene swore the massive portrait behind her wobbled.

Like Cole, he remained silent.

"I give a press conference," the captain roared, "praising how much of a hero our man here is, how much headway we've made into this investigation, how you're in recovery. And then you two come storming in and shit in my pie."

"Ma'am," Cole replied in a subdued tone, "Detective Yukawa was confused. The crowd of journalists...it can be very disorienting."

"I can't fucking tell you how little I care." Pulsing with each word, the vein in the captain's neck purpled. "Yukawa, you are on leave, effective immediately. Sergeant, the same, except yours is without pay. Dismissed!"

Cole scampered to the door. Eugene knew he should follow, but something hitched his steps: "Ma'am, I don't mean any disrespect. I just need to know: Did the vet confess anything?"

The captain, who had buried her head in a file cabinet drawer, stiffened.

"Eugene..." Cole put a hand on his shoulder.

Eugene shrugged her off. "Please, ma'am."

The captain spoke to the wall. "Our officers had the vet on the ropes. A cell phone belonging to Grace Clemons pinged inside one of his offices. He started pouring his guts out, but before he said anything incriminating, you burst in." She turned, her face dark at the edges. "He has since clammed up and asked for his lawyer. Suffice it to say, this is no longer your case. Major crimes will take over."

He gasped, her final words like a fist to the gut. "Captain, major crimes only arrests low level pushers. Half of them are owned by the mob–"

"Careful what accusations you level at your fellow officers, Yukawa."

Cole was pulling Eugene out of the room by his shirt collar. He shouted, "You can't let them have this case! Everything will get swept away in a week!"

But Cole dragged him into the hallway, the captain's office door shutting with a sharp click.

24

GRACE SPENT THE EVENING on the stoop of a sandwich shop. Hard to believe a little over three weeks ago, she'd been a respected reporter, shortlisted for major awards and shoving the marginalized in the faces of people who'd rather forget. Now the only respect she received was from true crime fans as her fugitive status climbed the Most Wanted list, all while she could barely shove down a four-day-old "Mystery Meat Club w/ Special Sauce" from some rundown deli's garbage bin.

The flash drives were tucked safely away, one inside her fanny pack, the other inside her shoe. A tiny voice inside told her to run, hop inside some internet cafes, and find the closest person to smuggle her away. Anything but face what she had planned.

But she needed to stick this out. Not because of altruism, or obligation to the victims, or pride. But self-preservation. In a forest of wolves, best not to wake the pack at your back, not until you're out of their cave.

Once full night arrived, she trekked over to the Quarter. Her hands and feet shook despite the humidity. The ladder was in the trunk of her car locked away in some evidence lot. It was just as well. With her anxiety, heights would probably make her dizzy.

Time to confront the asshole who did this to her. She reread the note she had scrawled on scrap paper:

I'm a hooked fish. All you gave me is worthless. I'm done.

She had more to say but didn't want to give away too much in case a Beret found it. Better to be vague, yet confrontational. She fastened the note to a rock with a rubber band, then chucked it over the Quarter wall. Without watching where it went, she ducked, squeezing in close to the curb that ran along the Plain Dealer's driveway.

A distant clatter of rock on asphalt. She counted to twenty, waiting for an alarm to ring. Nothing.

She settled in. Cold started to seep into her limbs. Maybe he hadn't seen it? The Quarter was a pretty big place. She should have made a second note.

Something struck the curb near her right ear and came to a dead stop. She glanced over. The smooth white surface of the note glistened within reach of her hiding spot.

She picked it up and undid the rubber band with shaky fingers. Two small pebbles slipped out. She managed to catch them before they fell. In the dim glow from the border lights, she could make out their shape: two sharp teeth. She gasped and dropped them.

The words *Do you like them?* blared up from the note in a sprawling script. She peered in close to read more.

Alexei screamed a little when I pulled them out but I told him they'll grow back. He continues to whimper, regardless.

Alexei was still alive? Diavolo had told her he wanted live bodies but she'd assumed it was some kind of kink. But this... If he imprisoned them inside, what was his endgame? She turned back to his note, desperate for more.

Unfortunate news for you, Grace Clemons. I am no fan of the law, myself. However, I am confused. Was our deal meant to rocket your career to new heights? To win you a Pulitzer?

He was trying to goad her. Unsettle her. Well, screw that.

She scrawled: *It was implied,* repackaged everything and chucked it back. She brushed the teeth away and hunkered down. Let him chew on that for a while.

A familiar *thunk* hit the same spot as before less than a minute later. The words were darker, like he'd pressed the pen to the paper with every ounce of strength.

I IMPLY NOTHING.

Your conscience inferred a way to keep itself unburdened by guilt. That is your doing, not mine.

It must be frustrating to live on the dredges of society. Allow me to play the smallest of violins.

I imagine this was all worth your while before, the quid pro quo, but now you are forced to ask yourself: how many lives are worth your own?

When you can answer that – and I admit, I'm curious – then, and only then, will our deal end.

She read his words twice. The last question pierced her heart like a spike. Finally, she replied: *If I go, I'm taking you with me.*

His answer was several minutes in coming.

Is that so?

I believe you are under some false pretenses. Allow me to be your illuminator.

First, there is the matter of my note on your vehicle, the only evidence against me, though it's circumstantial at best. I hope you destroyed it, but if not, no matter.

Second, vampires are chipped. We cannot hurt one another. Didn't you ever wonder how the government was able to bring bags of blood in here safely for so many years? We are monitored, controlled, leashed. Yet somehow, one of us was incised. And in a camera-free zone, no less. The authorities are running themselves in circles trying to deduce that.

Goosebumps prickled across Grace's skin at the next words:

I think your idiot detective might be interested in my side of events. Or should I say, these two lovely gentlemen's sides?

I'm afraid I own you, Grace Clemons. For a very long time to come.

His writing sprawled along the margins of the page, encircling their correspondence. She rotated the page, breath growing rapid as she read on.

Oh, and if you think you can start delivering hobos or strangers or some other riff raff, don't. I have acquired quite a taste for wise guys.

How had she been such an idiot? Trying to beat Diavolo at his own game. She curled into a ball, wishing to sink into the earth beneath her. All her chances at survival were gone, stolen away with the pierce of a stake.

Maybe she should crawl over to the Green Beret outpost and turn herself in. Cut off any hold he had.

She almost didn't perceive the dull thud that followed. It was faint, like a cracking stick in the dark of the woods. She checked around to make sure she hadn't imagined it. But there, about ten feet away, the was another rock, wrapped inside a strip of fabric. She had no desire to unfurl it but knew she had no choice.

It contained only two words: *I'm waiting.*

Waiting? For what? She scanned the murals, hoping for a clue.

A sharp pain rose in her right knee. She lifted it to see one of Alexei's teeth with the fang end jabbing into her. She knocked the tooth out and rubbed at the spot.

The reality of Alexei's situation sunk in. She swallowed down bile. Torture. Gods, she would never get used to this. Despite knowing Alexei deserved this, he had made his own bed. She knew, in her bones, that if it came down to it, she'd exchange him again.

An exchange. That was it. She had provided a body; Diavolo was waiting for a question.

She had no idea what to ask. Unlike before, she hadn't prepared for this. Besides, what was the point?

Her eyes traveled to the dark building where she used to work. Over three weeks shut outside it's doors, since she'd been a reporter. Her calling. Promise to Joy or no, she knew now, journalism was her life.

So who cared if she didn't have the job or not? She was still a reporter. She just needed to remember her training. What would the Grace from before all this ask?

She wrote: *Alexei took a call before he tried to kill me. Who from?*

The next reply took the longest time yet. All this because of a promise to her sister. The promise came years after her disappearance too. It was more of a means to justify running away than redirecting the anger and blame. Grace used to wrap the promise around her like armor, reciting the Quarter's victims like a prayer every night before she went to sleep. Now she conked right out. Or at least she used to. Now she shot detectives.

When had she changed? The instant the dart hit Eugene's chest? Maybe. Or was it earlier, when she'd decided to kidnap Richard? Or when she'd taken the stake from Diavolo? Maybe all of them, maybe none.

Perhaps there was no initial moment, no jumping off point. Each choice was instead a step down a gradual slope she didn't realize she was on until she neared the bottom. Until she was stuck in a place where only the ends mattered, screw the means.

A rock plopped down, rousing her from her thoughts. The note tied to it was scribbled in a writing Grace had trouble discerning. She almost thought it was written by someone else but the loops on the y's were identical to before.

He doesn't know the specific person. The caller gave a code word used by an authority among the traffickers.

This code is used only by those in the Hellmouth.

By the Green Berets.

Adrenaline surged through her veins, screaming for her to run, to get away as fast and as far as possible. To hide in the deepest corners she could reach and never come out.

This went past anything she could deal with alone. A person could be exposed, dealt with. But an organization of special forces? A disciplined powerhouse who could make a vampire tremble in his boots? Who could force the mob to turn on their boss with one phone call?

She was nothing against that. A speck of sand trampled underfoot. She'd be lucky to survive the week.

Diavolo's note flew through her fingers. The scrap of fabric tumbled end over end, up to the top of the wall, where it snagged in the barbed wire. There it thrashed. No matter which direction it tried to escape, it only wound its way in deeper, the barbs tearing it to shreds.

Part Two

25

TODAY WAS THE DAY. The day Eugene and Cole returned. The day he would start making it up to her. She'd ignored his texts and voicemails, but couldn't ignore a face-to-face apology. He'd arrived extra early, just in case. No way she escaped him.

And then she entered the room. Posture rigid, pace brisk, she brushed right past Eugene without a word. He slumped in his chair. No one else noticed anything wrong as Cole passed desk after desk, but he did. That second of hesitance before she opened her office door? She may as well put her fist through its window.

Three weeks had passed since the two of them were disciplined. And Cole still took it this hard? Guess he couldn't blame her. Komarov's organization had been broken up and sold for parts. So many mobsters went missing, no one could tell which Grace had a part in. This was Eugene's fault. If he'd kept himself in check, none of this would have happened.

But Cole wouldn't accept his apology, he was certain of it, not now or in the future. Between that and with Grace out of his hands due to her crimes, he figured it best to concentrate on what he could do.

Eugene forced himself to focus on his workstation. The mess on his desk was organized by a method only he understood. The intermixed case files jolted together possible connections he couldn't otherwise make. But now, so long removed, he saw it the way others must: a hoarder's overflow bin.

He dug in and sorted what he could. Best to return everything to its subsequent place in the evidence locker.

One pile rested atop a box full of Quarter interviews. The file in front boasted an all-capital ZOLA written across it in bold letters.

He sighed. Her interview should have been filed in the high school teacher case as evidence a month ago.

He opened it, double checking he'd crossed every i and dotted every t.

A loose sheet slipped out, a page from the last interview. He skimmed one of the lines. His stomach roiled.

***

Grace rolled one of the flash drives back and forth in her palm. Three weeks she'd been on the run. Three weeks and still alive. But what else could she hope for? Sure, these little plastic containers held so many options, but all except one was a lie.

First, they were a life raft, a plane ticket, an unmarked car—anything she desired. All she needed to do was choose and off she'd go, a life on the run. A life with numbered days.

But the flash drives were also intel, leverage, a crowbar to pry her into the lives of the warm bodies Diavolo desired. But this held risks: capture, torture, death. A last resort to get whatever answers she could before going down in a hail of bullets.

Two choices that weren't really choices at all.

However, the vet's existence provided a third option, one that made her toss and turn the most. If Diavolo had roped in a morally bankrupt veterinarian, then he had others under his sway. Some possibly on this little device. But finding them might prove too difficult without more resources. They didn't exactly advertise.

Still, it helped to believe she wasn't alone. That others might know of the situation in the Quarter. Others who might not be content with their lot. Would they speak out? She certainly would, but she was always the exception.

That left option four: all of the above.

Find someone Diavolo wanted, who had answers they might be willing to share, and a means to keep her from being discovered.

However—and this was the kicker—she'd already taken the fourth option five times already. Six times, if you counted the person who's home she was breaking into right now. Still, here she was, with no escape.

But option four was getting easier.

A former foot soldier of Komarov's, this guy—no names anymore, not ever—was a low-level enforcer who started three months ago, no incidents or illegal activity. So new police and rivals weren't aware of him. Perfect for her. The only downside was his occupation: He defected to private security after the pakhan fell.

Well, Mr. Security had a back door that opened in ten seconds flat, no blaring alarm or attacking dog. Maybe this wouldn't be such a problem.

Everything inside his home suggested the remnants of a family leaving in a typical weekday hurry: half eaten breakfast left out, toddler toys spilled across the living room floor, shoes carpeting the front entrance way. The place was lived in and still thrumming with a residual static aura that hung in the air. Like any of the home's occupants might come down the stairs at any moment.

Grace had grown accustomed to this feeling over the last few weeks, fed on it. Zipping through the mess, leaving all undisturbed, she navigated easily through the first floor. Mr. Security's office segmented off the laundry room.

God—not Gods, for she was far, far too deep into the territory of the Lost to pretend any longer—this guy was bad at his job. Blueprints to a half dozen businesses were left on his desk. His trash held all his last pay stubs, unshredded. What was next, the large drawer down there had a false bottom? A reach inside gave her an affirmative.

She rolled her eyes. If the suburbs gave people this naive a view of their safety, she hoped to never move out here.

The hidden folder contained the locations to four safe houses the mob used. A quick snap with a disposable digital camera got all the details she needed. Finished, she replaced everything, then wove back through the house toward the kitchen. A quick slip of roofie in their fridge's liquids to wrap it all up. Then she'd be back tonight for retrieval.

Excellent. They were an iced tea family. Different juice boxes meant the kids likely didn't drink from these pitchers. She hadn't witnessed them doing it either over the last few days.

A creak of bed springs on the floor above made her freeze.

"Samantha?" The voice was old, elderly, possibly senile. "Did Oliver forget his lunch again?"

Grace glanced at the kitchen knives. Too messy. Better to retreat. But she still hadn't spiked the drinks. She was risking too much already.

"Anyone? Jeff forgot my medication. Lord knows, he would. Being up all night with my old bones. It's on the kitchen sink. I have to go to the bathroom."

Steps traversed the room above and ended in a door slamming shut. Grace still held the fridge open. On the freezer, pictures of the mark's–Jeff's–family adorned all available space. Taken on an old Polaroid but somehow dated last year stuck out: an old woman behind a birthday cake adorned with dozens of candles. A bald man with sleeve tattoos, Jeff, hung his arm around her shoulder, face aglow, staring into her eyes with pride.

Underneath, in shaky pen scratches, was "My Perfect Son."

Grace looked from the photo to the iced teas, the roofies ready to slip through her fingers. All she had to do was choose.

***

Eugene read the line again:

Saw a shooting star last night. Big sucker. Made an impact in the East. Lit the sky up with a cool khaki.

He scoured the file, hoping his instinct was wrong. But a quick check confirmed his fears: This interview took place hours after Grace had been abducted. He read on.

...the guards didn't care about no shooting star. But the devil did. And he snatched it right up.

Carried it off to safety, to care for it, nurture it. It'll grow big and strong. Shake the foundations of this place.

A sliver of night clawed out of the depths of his memory. A harsh whisper that cut through the effects of the tranquilizer: "Diavolo." A quick search on his phone confirmed his worst fear.

He dashed towards the exit, his workstation forgotten. Grace had sworn she had no memory of what happened in the Quarter. But she lied. The aching hole in his chest proved it. And now, he knew her endgame.

26

A CRICK BLOSSOMED IN Grace's neck. Sleep had proved elusive last night. Park benches were simultaneously comfortable and not. She couldn't find any newspapers to huddle under. If she were in a better mood, that might be ironic.

Clouds stampeded overhead. Looked like a big storm.

Might be nice.

Around her, a few oblivious couples continued to laugh on blankets, all keeping their gazes deliberately away from her. She considered getting a drink from the water fountain, but that meant passing the refurbished jungle gym made from a mammoth skeleton and a dozen playing kids. Their parents might not be so blind to her then.

Thirty feet away, a man wearing a thousand-dollar T-shirt relaxed on a checkered blanket with his wife, the two casually watching their son swing on the monkey bars. Compared to the Polaroid, Jeff looked much better in person.

What happened next depended on the choice she made. And there was only one she wanted to take.

She took out her phone. The number practically typed itself despite the fact she hadn't entered it in over a decade.

It rang twice. "Clemons residence."

The voice was the same, though had gained a rasp, the throat weakened from age and countless nights wailing into a pillow.

Grace cleared her throat. "Hi, Mom."

The pause lasted so long, she worried her mother had hung up. Grace wiped a clammy hand on her pants. Was her manhunt national news? She listened for any sign the police monitored this call.

But then her mom said, "Grace?"

"Is this a bad time?"

"No! No. It's-it's a great time. I–um... Your father's out picking up groceries. He won't be back for another hour."

They were still together. That was good. "He's...well?"

"His gout acts up every now and then. Usually before something bad happens on the news. He says with that and his arthritis predicting storms, the Gods are trying to tell him too much at once. He tries to weasel out of chores by saying he can't hear me over all the divine chatter."

Grace smiled but her head drooped. Her dad was almost sixty by now. "How's the house?"

"Fine, fine. I'm trying black-eyed Susans this year."

"Those were always Joy's favorite."

Both fell silent. Grace's palm itched. "Do you remember that camping trip? When I was ten or eleven? We had to borrow Grandpa's tent and it smelled like marijuana and farts."

Her mother laughed. "You made a s'more out of a donut."

"Joy wanted to go so bad but I just tried to get out of it. I read a book most of the time, probably only said two words the whole week."

"I shouted at everyone," her mother said in a gleeful tone, "and your dad never shut up. He always does that, never lets a silence stretch. I wanted to smack him."

"Right." The light tone, the playful words. Grace hadn't heard her mom speak like this in so long. "But Joy kept her spirits up the whole time. Came up with games to play, kept wanting to go on hikes. Always doing the most good, no matter what. The way I never did."

"Oh, honey. That's not true." Her mother sounded sincere. She had always been a good liar.

Grace eyed the mob man and his family. "I have this choice to make. One that will affect a lot of people. And no matter what I decide, it'll end up hurting someone."

The line went quiet. Grace pulled the phone away, but her mom hadn't hung up — she had just paused to think. Impossible. Her mother was probably preparing a geyser of hate to spew into the receiver and berate Grace into a stupor like the final time they spoke.

"Then choose whatever does the least harm," her mother said. "Sorry, did that sound too forceful? I've been doing couples therapy with your dad. The doctor is an idiot, but it helps."

Therapy? The weak woman's crutch?

"When...whatever this is, is over," her mom went on, "will you come home? Er. That is, if-if you want to."

Thank God the bench was under Grace because every taut muscle in her let go at once. "I will...Mom."

"I love you, Gracie. And I'm sorry. More than you'll ever know."

"I love you, Mom. Give dad my best." Grace swallowed. "And Mom? Me too."

She hung up and stared at the screen, the ghost of her mom still lingering in its glow. The buoyancy inside her almost lifted her into the air. Empowered, she felt she could walk back to Arizona.

She kissed the burner phone's screen before tenderly placing it in the trash.

The least harm to all involved. That she could do. But she would have to break a promise.

The sky opened up as she strode out of the park. The mob man and his family sprinted for cover beneath the skeleton of the ancient beast, crying out about a ruined day, none of them knowing how close they had come to something far worse.

***

Eugene barged into the Quarter's interview room to find Zola already chained, a crooked smile playing across her lips.

"Well, well," she said. "The famous trapeze artist returns. Still with his blindfold on! Now that is dedication. Ladies and gentlemen, boys and girls–"

He cut her off. "Who was the woman you saw?"

"Uh," she said, taken aback. "Specificity breeds...something. Probably answers?" She added under her breath, "Or Toblerones."

Eugene caught his breath. He had stopped by Grace's apartment before this, expecting to find a clue, but the instant he opened the door to the darkened living room, he knew. She was gone. His drive around the Quarter yielded similar results, though that was more desperation. She could be floating down the Ohio River in a barrel for all he knew. So, he came here. Time was slipping through his fingers.

"The shooting star," he said. "The khaki one. You saw it crash just inside the fence and the devil carried it away. Who was the star? What did she do while she was here? Who rescued her?"

"Woah, too much too soon, fella. You can't just hop on the champion bull. Gotta woo me first."

He tapped his foot. "What do you want?"

Zola licked her fangs. "Extra blood."

"Done."

"And new clothes."

"You got it."

"And a new car! Come on down! You're the next contestant—"

He smacked her. Once, twice, three times. The smile cracked then faded. None of it hurt her, not physically. Human strength compared to a vampire's constitution was like a fly smacking a window. But she had to know how upset he was.

He wrenched her up by the cusp of her shirt collar. She rose an inch before the chains went taut. Her eyes went hazy, vacant, like she disappeared into herself. Slowly, as his breathing calmed back to a regular rhythm, she returned.

"Breath mint, Eugene."

His jaw trembled. Her shirt was in disarray, revealing pockmarks poking out in criss-crossing patterns.

"Tell me where she is." He leaned in close. "Or I'll request a kit."

Immediately her temperament changed.

The spacious leather kits contained everything needed to maim, but not kill, a vampire. Each device designed to inflict maximum damage to drive the tortured insane. He could see the gears churning, the memories of all the different instruments she'd experienced over the years.

Eugene had long suspected Zola's pain fetish was just talk. But he never had a reason to test it. Until now. A sick wave of disgust washed over him as her pupils shrank to watery dots.

"Y-you'd never..."

"I haven't before, no." He put as much salt into his words as he could muster. "But desperate times."

"All right. All right!" she relented. "It's no fun when you get all serious."

Eugene pulled a chair out from the corner, unplugged the camera, and took a seat across from Zola. "Talk."

***

Grace slipped the remainder of her cash into Richard's sister's mailbox. No way of knowing if Richard had left money to her or the kids in his will – if he had a will – but Grace didn't care. Granted, it wouldn't cover her sins or make restitution. But she couldn't think of anyone else to give it to.

She borrowed a new ladder from one of the neighbors. It was wonky and cheap but would do the job. The rain finally came to a stop after an hour of deluge, leaving the streets wet, empty. Calm. She stayed hidden until she could be sure there was no chance of accidental discovery. She didn't want anyone trying to stop what was about to happen.

Once in position, she set up and climbed atop the metal contraption. She hoped she might have a moment of peace at the top, but when her head cleared the fence, there he was. She sighed. It was better this way, she told herself. Less time for second thoughts.

Diavolo's clothes were damp, dark hair clinging to his face. He must have been out in the storm. But when he spoke, his voice gave away nothing. "Grace Clemons. To what do I owe the pleasure?"

She stared up into the light-smothered night. "You know, after my sister was abducted, my father escaped into books. Any and all kinds to bury his head in and not come out. The one that had the most impact was this little novel by Stephen King. It was about this nine-year-old who got lost in the woods. But her radio broadcasted baseball games to her every night. They kept her going. She loved the pitcher, this Christian guy who thanked Jesus at the end of every game, win or lose. But in those woods, there was no pitcher, no Jesus. But there was a capital G, God. A wasp-faced monstrosity. The God of the Lost."

"...and you feel I am this God?"

"You?" She shook her head as she turned her gaze back to earth. "No. But my father worshiped Them both. Would kneel down next to me in my closet and whisper Their truths. I pitied him. But soon I understood. He was right. The God of the Lost does exist. I used to think both Gods controlled my life, taking turns with a castaway toy. But no. I've only belonged to One. And I have been in His Domain for far too long."

Diavolo blinked. "And how does this relate to our rendezvous?"

"It means I have an answer for you."

"I see. And the question being?"

"You asked how many more lives were worth my own." Her hand shook as she spoke. But it wasn't from fear, only the lingering chill.

"Ah. And you're, uh, sure," Diavolo said, his voice unusually high, "you have the answer?"

"I am."

"Then I do not accept, Grace Clemons. Turn back."

In response, she pulled out wire cutters from her pack.

"Grace–"

"I've made my choice." She severed the first wire. "This ends tonight."

27

EUGENE SWORE AS HE left the Hellmouth. Grace might have delivered another victim to Diavolo while he was getting the story straight. He berated himself for taking so much time with Zola, but he had to be sure, especially with her nonsensical ramblings. Parts of her story provided much needed context, but exactly how guilty Grace was would have to be sorted out later, by a jury of her peers.

No use taking the patrol vehicle he'd been lent. She'd flee from sight long before he could catch up to her. That left going on foot. His crutch slipped off a curb and clacked the asphalt lot. Wonderful.

At night, under the shaky beam of his flashlight, The Plain Dealer and Beret outposts stood as still as photographs. No one looked out, no one questioned him. Where was everyone? A cold sweat broke out on the nape of his neck.

He hobbled on. His left leg spasmed when he put weight on it. He refused to slow. If he did, he'd be done and he couldn't stop now. Somewhere along this fence, Grace was going to commit another terrible crime, if she hadn't already. She was too smart for the Berets. Too connected. It was up to him.

His flashlight pierced the dark around the next bend. The fence ran another thousand feet before cutting to the right. He huffed along, each breath agony. A second pain hitched in his left side and he clutched his chest.

Why Grace? All that talk she had filled him with. Her noble infiltration of Komarov's. Meting out justice, rooting out corruption. She was nothing more than a cheap vigilante, playing with fire in an oil drum. She probably killed Richard Obolensky, too.

Silver glinted in the distance. He increased his pace, pain temporarily forgotten. Metal lines began to take the shape of a capital A: a ladder. Straddling atop, hands obscured by the fence's barbed wiring, was his suspect.

"Grace!" Eugene sped up, a cramp roared in his stomach like a fist trying to burst through. He slowed, still dozens of yards away. "Grace, freeze!"

She turned.

He picked up speed, his lungs burning, hating him. No kidnapped victim in sight. Was he too late?

Her features went slack as she recognized him, settling into an expression he couldn't quite read. Pity mixed with sadness. Or was it some kind of resigned joy? She gave a sheepish wave.

No. She couldn't–

"Grace!"

In one swift motion, she grabbed the top of the fence and leaped over.

28

DIAVOLO'S ARMS WERE SURPRISINGLY soft. That was Grace's first thought. Her first thought in hell.

Diavolo had hesitated when she dove, the pavement growing in her vision until it almost consumed her. But before she struck, he appeared.

His hands searched her, an impossible feat as he kept her suspended in the air, four feet above the ground. Yet there was not a single second she didn't feel wholly supported.

His breath stank of decay as he hissed, "Where is it?"

"What?"

"The stake."

She understood. To him, the only way she could give herself up, to not exchange another in her place, was if she tried to kill him. The story of his life spread wide before her. Not the details, but the motives. Why he did all this. How alone he must be, hardening himself against pain and betrayal. No family, no companions. No one to speak to except abusive wardens, helpless prisoners, desperate murderers, and those he threatened into deals.

"I don't have any weapons," she said.

He caught her eye as he finished searching. "That makes you a fool, twice over."

"Halt!"

The detective waved a flashlight at her from atop the ladder.

But Diavolo carried her away toward the line of housing. He gave a slight nod to a dark yet familiar shape. Alexei?

The former bodyguard set a fist over his heart, then dashed off. What the hell was going on?

"Stop in the name of the law–" A series of hacking coughs cut Eugene off.

Diavolo turned. "The law is what put me here, detective."

A roar erupted from somewhere nearby, accompanied by a shattering of glass and cracking of wood. Grace looked in the direction of the sound but determined no source.

"And unjust laws deserve to be broken."

The world blurred as Diavolo raced off. Grace gasped and didn't hear the sound escape her own lips. All she could do was cling to Diavolo as the violent chilling wind tore into her and pray for it to stop.

***

The vampire faded into the night with the perp. For a moment, Eugene considered pursuit, but who was he kidding? There was a battalion of Green Berets a quarter mile away who weren't about to fall over. Let them handle this.

If they'd help him.

Uh uh, none of that paranoid stuff. This was the exhaustion talking.

Still. Why had the Berets abandoned their posts?

This investigation was two steps forward, one leap back. He sank to the ground, feet half-stepping, half-slipping down each rung of the ladder. He just needed a minute to figure this out, to catch his breath. Then things might make sense.

One minute.

***

The world returned to Grace in the center of a raging sea of rioting vampires. Acrid fumes thickened the air into boggy soup. She covered her nose but it was no use, the mass of bodies was too compact.

This was insane. She'd waited all her life to see a vampire, and now here stood dozens. Vampires danced on rooftops, broke second-floor windows, and tore off shutters. Every time glass shattered or siding cracked, thunderous applause broke out from those on the street below.

It was violent, it was loud. And to the untrained eye, it would appear genuine. But Grace had covered enough protests to see an invisible hand directing it all. How the crowd swayed in unison, the heads all turning in the same directions right before something happened. This was staged.

Everyone wore the same metal plate on the back of their neck. Some kind of uniform or symbol she couldn't ascertain a meaning to. All of them were identical except the lack of one on the back of–

"Alexei." Diavolo's lilting voice rose over the din. The former bodyguard materialized out of the crowd and stepped in close to Diavolo. The two spoke in a hushed tone.

"A-aren't you going to bite me?" Grace asked. "And since when are you friends?"

They ignored her.

A hard thump in the small of her back sent her sprawling. "Hey!"

A vampire spun on her, snarling. She shrank back. He wore no shirt. His face and neck were covered in horrific, mangled scars of various shapes and sizes, like the ones on Diavolo.

His eyes focused on her and his face softened. "Sorry. Reflex," he muttered before being absorbed into the crowd.

As she stared at the space he'd vacated, she noticed everyone bore similar scars to his, peeking out from rips and holes in their dilapidated clothing, cleaving their faces into horrid masks. Each mark was too long and too deep to be self-inflicted. Or at least, most of them.

She thought only Diavolo bore such wounds, remnants from his upbringing. But this...

The scope of it silenced her.

"What the hell did you think you were doing, Grace?"

Diavolo finally faced her. No Clemons. No fancy grammar. His voice had changed too. All manner of his character shed like a second skin.

"I don't–"

"Didn't you understand a thing I told you?" His eyes were wide, alert. On edge. "Didn't you investigate?"

Her brow knitted. "Of course I did, but I don't see–"

"Of fucking course, you don't." He sighed. "I suppose I played too good a villain."

Played a villain? What did he mean?

"It doesn't matter. If this plan is going to work, we have to go."

She opened her mouth to object but before she could, he picked her up once more in his steel grip and darted off. She waited for the world to return as her mind raced with questions.

***

Eugene was going to puke. One more step and every organ would spew out of his body like a broken fire hydrant. And he was only halfway.

He stumbled forward, reaching out to the wall for support. He stopped just shy. A thrum hummed through the air. Frying himself alive would certainly solve things. Sizzle his flesh into a gaseous ball of putrid meat and puss–

His dinner came up in a burning gush. Once, twice. After the shame and heat melted away from his face, he felt better. He wiped his mouth on the back of his sleeve and straightened his tie.

Careful not to repeat the event, he plodded along until he reached the Hellmouth's lobby. The metal detector shrieked. The guard from earlier who'd let him in had gone. Now, the sausage-headed asshole from a few weeks prior – what was his name? – sat behind the Plexiglass at the check in station, waving Eugene away. "Interview hours are over."

Eugene licked his lips and replied in between gasps: "I have pertinent information. Time sensitive."

"Oh, 'time sensitive,'" the guard mocked. "ID in the slot and wait for your pat down." The guard went back to his crossword puzzle.

"I need immediate—"

"ID and wait for your pat down!"

Eugene bit back his next reply and slid his card into the slot. The guard moved at a speed a sloth would call lethargic. Eugene paced. How long had passed? A few minutes, ten at most? He resisted looking at his watch. The barest glance might send him hurtling at this asshole, despite his exhaustion.

Instead, he snuck a glance out the facility door's window slit into the compound hallway beyond. Two lines of Berets stood at attention, dressed in full tactical gear.

"Step back," said the sausage head.

"You guys are fast." Eugene inched closer to the window. "The whole thing only just happened. I'm impressed."

He faced the guard and was met with a bewildered expression. The man had no idea what he was talking about. So what was this? Well, maybe orders hadn't reached the front desk? He was only the door guard, after all. Chain of command was need-to-know.

"I know it's against procedure," Eugene said, crossing his arms around his jittering frame, "and I don't want to step on anyone's toes, but can I join you guys?" He coughed and it felt like a tiny piece of him died. "Like in the situation room. This case has been...a load and a half. I'd like to see it through."

The guard gave him a once over and shook his head. "No can do, det—"

A phone rang behind the Plexiglass, cutting him off.

"Wait here."

Eugene waited until the guard was absorbed in the phone call before collapsing against the door. His forehead rested against the cool glass. Through it, soldiers were decked out with the usual crosses, faux-sunlight flash-bangs, and crossbows. But a few had strapped on shotguns. How did those work against vampires? Guess he had a lot to learn.

"I think we could find a place for you."

Eugene started. He hadn't noticed the guard slip out from his booth. Unsettling as the man stood inches from Eugene. Had he passed out?

The guard sneered. "If you can manage."

"I'm more than capable." Were his knees literally knocking together? "Lead the way."

After a quick scan of a keycard, the door gave a sharp click and they were inside. The commanding officer between the two lines of soldiers cut off mid-sentence and angled Eugene's way, dark faceplate hiding his expression. Eugene shuffled behind the closest guard in line until he was concealed from the CO's sight. Still, the officer did not continue.

A side door opened, a guard cutting the tension with a jangle of metal. She carried dozens of handcuffs, their metal shimmering in the fluorescent light, religious symbols filed into each one. A second soldier followed the first carrying a similar amount but with one exception. Two handcuffs lay over his shoulder, separate from the rest. Eugene couldn't make out any symbols on these. In fact, as far as he could tell, nothing separated them from the pair tucked into his belt right now.

Maybe it was the paranoia, or the residual adrenaline from the rush over here, but a connection sparked.

Useless shotguns. Two sets of handcuffs. Two unauthorized humans:

Grace.

And him.

"You know," Eugene said, turning back toward the door guard. "I should radio this in."

"My CO is already handling it."

Like hell. "I have a few other cases to check up on. Lab results coming in. You know how it is."

The guard continued to stare. The exit lay at his back. He had positioned himself to block the door, the space on either side of him narrow and tight.

"I'm just gonna..." Eugene sucked in his gut and stood on tiptoe. The guard refused to budge. In fact, he didn't even turn his head as Eugene stepped around.

"This is getting to be a habit," Eugene said as he made it through to the other side.

He took one step before a loud whistle from behind made him pause. A bird? In here?

Next he knew, he was on his knees. The top of his head felt warm. His fingers brushed his scalp and came away red.

A shadow covered him. He looked up to see the guard, his baton raised, the tip the same impossible red.

"You should have waited for your pat down."

The baton rose and whistled back down, splitting the air.

29

DIAVOLO CAME TO A stop in a cloud of dust and stale light. He set Grace down on a gray lot surrounded on all sides by houses. No Plain Dealer or Hellmouth in sight, which meant she was tucked into the far southeast corner. Years covering the Quarter and she had never noticed this empty spot. It felt strange, like finding her name misspelled on her mail slot after a decade.

Wooden crates tagged with government logos lay stacked in neat rows around her. Blood ration boxes. A stocky figure bent over a tiny computer monitor from the 90's, their hands flying over a keyboard. A twisty mustache poked out on either side of a round head.

"Are we all set, George?" Diavolo asked.

George shook their mustache in the affirmative. "Cameras are mine, playing on loops."

Cameras?

"How long will they hold?"

"No idea," George said. "Unless you can show me how competent their tech guys are, then I'm basically racing a go-kart against an invisible Ferrari. I can tell you when they hack me but that's about it. But they should be confused temporarily."

Diavolo groaned.

George's voice took on an annoyed tone with a slight accent budding through. Hindi, maybe? "Hey, this ain't the movies. There's no countdown or dumb CGI graphic I can show you. We have now, and 'now' is beyond temporary."

"I don't know what half of that means," Diavolo said. "How long do we have on response time?"

"Based on what the others told me, thirteen minutes. More or less."

"Ah, and escape route–"

"All right!" Grace had been patient, but she was beyond done. "Can someone please tell me what the hell is going on?"

Both vampires looked at each other, some unspoken agreement passing between them. Then Diavolo turned to her as George stacked some crates.

"We have thirteen minutes. What do you want to know?"

Grace folded her arms. "I don't need to give you a body first?"

"No, that plan's done. You obliterated it the second you jumped the fence. Now, ask."

She stared him down.

"Ask."

"Fine. Why aren't I dead?"

Diavolo fixed her with a look that simultaneously made her want to crawl away and slap him repeatedly.

"To tell our story," he said. His words came out fast, blurring into near gibberish if she didn't pay absolute attention. "You're a reporter. Why do you think I made a deal to answer your questions?"

"Are you serious?" She matched his speed. "I forced you into that."

He laughed. "If that's what you want to tell yourself." When Grace's expression remained unchanged, he said, "Come on. We needed to move before a patrol found us and you weren't exactly complying. You're the first reporter I've nabbed since I rescued the tech wizard over there—" he pointed at George '—I couldn't let you slip away."

"You didn't play villain with him too?" she asked, pointing at George.

"No, *they* recognized the truth much faster than you."

Grace pursed her lips.

"Granted—" Diavolo raised a finger "—they had the advantage of being stuck in here and witnessing firsthand how we're treated. After that, they began hacking into the cameras for us. Though it did take some time." His face took on a knowing grin. He looked younger, fuller. "George's first trick was looping a few seconds during a rainstorm over a holiday weekend. They had a pretty good handle on it by the time you arrived.

"Still, we needed to be cautious. No way of knowing if the guards discovered the tampering. Might catch a snippet here or ghost audio there. So I had to act the villain no matter what."

So it was George playing the cameras on loop that prevented the Berets from retrieving her, not neglect on special forces part. Clever. Well, one mystery solved. "So this is all an elaborate escape attempt."

Diavolo shrugged. "More or less."

"And if you succeed? I don't think the public would be too keen on a bunch of ravenous blood drinkers roving the country."

"We stayed hidden for millennia before all this. But I understand the concern. Most of us took a pledge to only drink animal blood. The government stipend is half pig anyway. We survive on it just fine. The one vampire who refused has been...dealt with."

Her hands shook. The boy she killed. His pleading eyes as the stake plugged into his chest. "You made me kill someone...because he disagreed with you?"

"It's not that simple."

"Oh, it never is!"

"You don't understand. Luke was a stubborn thrill seeker from the Pioneer days. He followed whims. Raced buffalo, blazed trails across unexplored territory. He survived more cycles of crushing poverty and soul-sucking wealth than any of us. But he never heeded advice or listened to a single bit of counsel. Once he set his mind to something, there was nothing...nothing anyone could do."

When Diavolo finished, he stooped over, his breath haggard, hugging himself. Like that story had taken everything he had.

Whatever his and the boy's relationship had been–and it was far more than friends–Grace couldn't bring herself to care. She peered down at Diavolo. Even here, at his most vulnerable, dishing out all the answers she could ever want, she hated him. This rake of a man who had forced her to do such terrible things. A glimpse into his past changed nothing. He'd destroyed the life she'd carefully built up with one wave of his hand, all for his own self-righteous ends. There was no forgiving that.

"Did you..." Did he pay to have her kidnapped? She couldn't bring herself to say it. The answer might break her. He'd probably lie anyway. Just like what he said now were lies. Another way to manipulate her.

"Why didn't you run?"

He cocked an eyebrow at her. "What do you mean?"

"When you planted that note on my car. You were free, so why not leave? One vampire is easier to hide than eighty."

"Ah," Diavolo said. "Let me be frank: I didn't plant that note."

Her cheeks burned. "What? But...the handwriting..."

"Oh, I wrote it. But the actual planting was done by an obsessed vampire fan. You think you're the first to throw a rock in here and hope it gets answered?"

"But you got out and saved me at Komarov's."

"Ah. That. George needed a trial run to see if they effectively hacked the GPS chips in our necks. I was almost caught, though for different reasons. As for the timing, evolutionary quirk. I could smell you from here once I had your scent. Sensed your terror. And I know, you're going to ask why I didn't flee then. But the goal isn't for me to escape alone–it's all or none. We've been stuck in here so long, our suffering has made us one. Without the others, I'm nothing."

Rousing speech. She's sure he practiced several times in front of a broken mirror. "That's it?"

"What else is there?"

"I find it hard to believe you'd save my life for practice. You could have gone anywhere. Rescuing me is the harder option."

"It was the *only* option."

She scoffed.

His eyes met hers. "Your reporting is at the center of all this. Exposing the Green Berets would create enough chaos to let us slip away. Maybe even provide a legal way back into society. Heavily monitored of course, but better than this. Nothing pulls the heartstrings like a good story. And you tell the best around."

Grace frowned. Flattery aside, all his boasting came off as naive. Any bad press her story caused would be white noise the instant the vamps in here bolted. But she played along. Best not to upset the seasoned killer. "I'm wanted now. All the information you gave me is useless."

"I assume you have others who could publish your work? Ones you trust?"

She opened her mouth and closed it. Sure, while Perry wouldn't risk his neck, Tracy might. But without Grace, without sources, the military could claim fake news and discredit everything. If only after twelve years, Grace had other, more respected colleagues she could ask for help on this besides a single intern.

"There's no one," Grace replied.

"But–"

"Sorry. Turns out you picked the most introverted and traumatized reporter and tormented her into a paranoid shadow of herself. Congratulations."

"I..." For the first time, Diavolo looked at a loss for words. "...for what it's worth, I'm sorry."

"Shove it." She would have preferred the horrible villain to this apologetic ideologue. "This plan seems slapdash, at best."

"Only because you rushed it."

She flipped him off, tired of all this blame.

"I meant—" he held his hands up in a placating gesture "—we were going to wait until the night before your article was published. Then, after we escaped, your words would give the public doubts about our recapture. An investigation would give us a head start."

What a naïve load. Grace couldn't stand here anymore and listen to this. She needed to walk. But as she was stuck in the middle of a vampire prison camp, she resorted to pacing instead.

Centered, she focused, put herself in Diavolo's shoes the same way she had all those missing people. These events could make sense from a certain sort of view. Most of these vampires had last seen the outside world in the mass protests of the sixties, when people marched in the streets in solidarity. Problem was public outcry nowadays resulted in a hashtag or a halfhearted boycott, then life went on as usual. No change.

The vampires in the square with their scars and ragged clothes were the most bodies in the street this issue might get.

"You're a fool," Grace said.

He sighed. "Perhaps. But your fate is tied to mine now."

"Great. More blame."

"I'm not blaming you." He snarled the words out with enough force to take Grace aback. "This was my doing. I needed numbers to strengthen our cause. Able bodies. George is good, but they're only one person. I needed vampires, undetectable by any camera. The perfect stealth agents. And those I sire have a compulsion to obey. At least, for a few weeks after transformation."

"But you couldn't know who I'd abduct. You were potentially condemning innocent–"

"Does it look like I've slept much to you?" His darkened, wizened frame seemed to bow from its own weight. "These last few weeks have been torture. Even with the mafia men you provided."

Grace almost asked if he had to transform Richard right in front of her but decided against it. "I've seen Alexei. Where's Richard? And the others I've given you?"

"The others are keeping watch. Richard..." Diavolo looked down and mumbled something.

"What?"

"...deceased."

She bent over as if struck in the gut. "What?"

"Not everyone survives transformation."

"You..." Her lip quivered and she bit it. "I asked you for him back."

"I know."

"He had a sister and five kids, you piece of shit!" She marched up to Diavolo, raised her hand to strike, thought better of it, and balled it into a fist instead. "I took him away from them. Do you know what that's like? What that will do to that family? Those kids will turn in on themselves, ignore each other until they've become strangers under the same roof. They'll seek comfort wherever they can. Build up walls so thick, they're numb to everyone and everything." Her voice cracked. She bent down, unable to take his pitying eyes, and their condescending sympathy. "Until those kids are no longer themselves. No longer hurting. Or able to be hurt."

She was on the ground, knees hugged to her chest.

Diavolo crouched down next to her. For a moment, she thought he might place an arm around her, which she was ready to shove right off. Then he said, "Three thousand, seven hundred and eighty-six."

She wiped her nose on her sleeve. "What?"

"That's how many I've transformed. Most with families. I keep track because they're all that matters. Them and my people. They are the reason we're staging this revolt."

"Why not just tell me all this? Why turn me toward the tunnels and the electrical grid?"

He offered a sad smile as he glanced toward George. Ghost snippets. The Berets might catch wind of Diavolo's plan. And that would be the end.

"It was still risky. What you told me."

"Yes, well, I needed to tell you something or you'd never return. And George needed time. Blocking the high-tech signal to our control chips with scrap metals was the easy part. Getting enough in here to block everyone at once? That took some ingenuity."

"All for this."

"All to tell the military," Diavolo explained, "they can no longer use my kind as super soldiers."

"What?"

"Haven't you ever wondered why there's a camp full of vampires in the middle of a major city?"

Grace bit her lip.

"The government *wants* people to drop their undesirables inside," Diavolo went on. "Society trims some fat and the United States builds an empire on the back of the greatest killers evolution has ever produced. Spirited away inside blood ration boxes none would give a second glance. The Quarter you see is only the tip of an iceberg. Experiments are done on my people. Beneath our feet, a quarter mile of facilities houses unspeakable atrocities." Diavolo shook his head. "It wasn't the public who started calling this the Quarter."

A few more pieces of the puzzle clicked into place. But one still bothered her: the vampire at Komarov's apartment, the phone call. Why move against him now? What had changed? She voiced this thought aloud.

"When you asked me about that call—" Diavolo's jaw trembled "—I almost confessed everything right there. I thought the Berets were on to us. But nothing happened. It must have been something else, something Komarov did. Something the Berets didn't want out."

Grace thought. Her interview had come out that day, but that could have been a coincidence. Komarov didn't even mention the military. A warmth itched up the base of her skull and with it came a memory, half formed. Then it was gone.

"It was a good thing Detective Yukawa was there," Diavolo said.

Grace tried not to laugh. "What?"

"Most cops are controlled. Others are so inept, they can't do any harm. They're usually assigned to missing persons or vampire crime. You're lucky there's an actual decent detective on the force."

The corner of her mouth twisted. Eugene? "Yeah, he's a hero." She watched George work for a moment, the Quarter beyond conveying a false sense of serenity. "I was out here every night for ten years. Couldn't you have sounded the alarm before it got to this?"

He smirked. "Because people are so inclined to believe vampires?"

He had her there. "Okay, then why not give up? Passive resistance? Hunger strikes?"

"You think we haven't tried that?!" His fangs shot out without warning. The teeth sliced into each other, a gnarling mess.

The outrage more than the fangs made Grace back away, hands up. God, she'd grown so used to those teeth already. But something was off about his fangs: a tiny gap in the bottom set, where a tooth should be.

After a moment, his face softened. "Sorry. That was...unbecoming." The fangs retracted. He sat back down and motioned for her to do the same. "Please."

She refused. No telling what might set him off again.

"Guess I asked for that." He cleared his throat and tried to look relaxed. "We...have tried everything. More than once, but still, we try again. In many ways, we are slaves. Cogs meant to churn victims into vampires for their war machine. The chips on our spinal cords can fry our neurons up to the point of death. Or the guards torture us in one of their cells. Every time we enter those tiny rooms, they take a small piece of us. A tooth, a nail, a toe. Leaving us a little less than whole each time."

The deep scars on everyone's bodies. She looked down at Diavolo's hands. The marks were as numerous as splinters in a tree.

"They reward us for recruiting by letting us live pain free for a week."

Anger radiated off him in waves. His eyes were distant, looking back at decades of abuse and pain.

"That tooth you gave me," Grace said. "It was yours, not Alexei's."

Diavolo spoke so softly, she barely heard him. "Yes."

"Why?"

"The pain I dish out every day, it's all...not white noise, but more of a dull gray. But when I chose to save someone from harm, then a dash of color, a speck, fluttered in. Like a cherry blossom from a distant land. Does that make sense?"

She nodded. Throughout her teens, the world emitted a similar hue. As if she had wandered inside her sister's poster, awash in monochrome. Then Grace made the promise.The surge of purpose that flooded her at that moment was greater than any high she'd had before or since, including her acceptance to the *Plain Dealer*. However, she would find, no victim she memorialized ever truly delivered such raw passion again. Sure, there were wisps, here and there. Fleeting glimpses of her sister in the work she carried out. Enough to keep her going. Scattered pieces of Joy stretched across humanity for her to dig down and excavate like fossils.

Diavolo crossed his arms, hiding the knot of scars on each.

Maybe she hadn't dug deep enough.

"So how can I help?" she asked.

"You don't."

She pulled back from him. "I thought you had a plan."

"Yes. *Had.*"

"The detective saw me-"

"SWAT is only allowed in when called by the Hellmouth. And that's only when a body is found who fails to undergo the change. That's about one in nine."

"One in...nine?" That couldn't be true. "The number of people I've written about... You have to be wrong."

"I wish."

Her whole life had been about not leaving anyone uncared for. Giving the voiceless a voice. And she only helped one in nine?

Her rage returned twofold. She wanted to scream. To put her fist through every crate she could find until her hand was nothing but a bloody stump.

"Then everything was meaningless! Shooting Yukawa. Abducting those people. Leaving their families to...to..." She swallowed. "And now I'm stuck here because some dumbass is trying to break out of prison with a deck of playing cards."

Diavolo watched her, nodding along to every word, which only pissed her off more. "Don't give me that. *Do* something."

He shrugged. "Endless trial and error, Grace Clemons. Is this escape perfect? No. But we've been imprisoned for decades before you were even born. If this doesn't work, we'll–"

"Don't give me those bull platitudes. This is my life!"

Electricity crackled through her veins, an energy she hoped to amass into a bolt that scorched him right between the eyes.

"I'm sorry," he said. "You're r—"

"It's time." George waved from the periphery.

Diavolo sighed. "I was afraid of that. We need to get started. Please, this way." He stood and walked away down the center pathway of boxes, letting the conversation end on his terms.

The urge to scratch his face off rose.

"What I said before? I was lying somewhat. I can't get you out of here. But I can give you a chance to help yourself." He lifted a sewer grate, revealing a dark pit. A slight odor of sewage filled the air. "You hide in here. Once the soldiers pass, run like hell to the gate. The place should be empty. You can escape out the front door, with no one the wiser. The odds aren't exactly in your favor, but at least this way, you *have* odds."

The anger in her boiled down to a simmer. "I have more questions."

"I'm sure. But that's all the time we got. You'll have to piece the rest together on your own. And hopefully, your article will do what I planned and not be a memorial."

She took a step forward and stopped. "Wait."

"We don't have t—"

"What's your name?"

His eyes narrowed, then relaxed, turning pleasant and kind. It looked much better on him than the villain persona. "Francesco. Parisi."

"Francesco. I'll finish the article and get it into the right hands." She pointed at the surrounding houses of the Quarter. "For them. Not for you."

"Wouldn't ask for anything less."

She nodded at him, then at George. "Nice meeting you."

George gave a half wave. "A pleasure."

Grace hopped down inside. The pit was shallow, only waist deep. She squatted. From what she could tell, it was little more than a ditch where water exited into a narrow pipe on one end. The space had been cleaned out except for small tufts of dirt and a patch of grass growing in a crack. A bit of cloth lay folded up as a makeshift pillow near the pipe.

Grace shrugged. It was only temporary. She made herself as comfortable as possible.

The grate clanged down and boxes shifted around, covering her up. A final crate went on top. She tested the weight and found it manageable to lift, not easy but manageable. She'd have to put her back into it.

Two knocks from above. "Farewell, Miss Clemons."

Bye, asshole, Grace thought, listening to his footsteps fade. *And thank you.*

30

EUGENE'S CHEEK ITCHED: GREAT, he was still alive. He tried to scratch it and his wrist flared with hot needles that spread up his arm to the shoulder. Huh, alive and bound then.

Those last few moments before he blacked out danced across his vision. He cringed. At least his memory was intact. And cringing meant his nerves weren't firing all wrong. Small victories. Now to assess the damage.

He peeked out one slitted eye. Harsh white light barricaded every detail around him. Steadily, it peeled away: first his arms, pinned and chained to a steel block beneath him. His feet likewise. A drip of drying blood stained around his collar but that was the extent of it.

He knew this place. The concrete walls that engulfed him on all sides. The blood that pooled at his feet, hardened and black from the past victims of this place. The crisscrossing splatter patterns that decorated every inch beyond, including the open steel bank vault door. All marred crimson except for the two figures that darkened the recess to the hallway.

The sausage headed guard sneered. What was his name again? Beluga! Like the whale.

Or the vodka. The *Russian* vodka.

Shit.

The other figure looked strange outside her chains, the crown of scarred crucifixes less pronounced under her frazzled hair. "It's a shame," Zola said.

"Yes," replied Beluga. "Such a decorated detective. To fall in the line of duty in the Quarter. He'll be given full honors, I imagine." Beluga *tsked*. "I'll leave you to your interrogation. Oh—" he motioned to someone in the hallway and a medical bag with a skull and crossbones on the side was wheeled over on a silver tray "—the full kit you requested."

"Zo...a..." Eugene's tongue was thick and stubborn, smearing his words to gibberish.

Beluga took the offered tray. Leaning to the left as far as the chains allowed, Eugene managed a slight glimpse of those outside. A soldier trained an automatic rifle on him. It was unlikely she was alone.

Zola put on latex gloves from the tray and took the bulging leather bag with a thank you kindly.

Then they were alone.

"Zo, le me out—"

A fist soared at him faster than a starter pistol and knocked his head back into the metal bar behind him. White noise roared in his ears and he struggled to right himself.

"That was for the most recent crimes against my person."

"Z...Zo..."

She silenced him with a finger. With her foot, she wheeled over the small table with the bag on top. With a flair, she unlatched it, her hand disappearing inside. A smile crept up her face the longer she rooted around, then snapped full. He gulped, her eyes massive. She inched her hand out, slowly revealing an impossibly long metal stake.

Setting the stake on the tray, she buried her hand once more. Again and again, she fished around inside, bringing up more and more instruments from a nightmare. The stake was soon joined by syringes filled with mysterious fluids, brass knuckles etched with various religious symbols, holy water laced with acid, and on and on and on.

Eugene had seen these implements only once: orientation at the Cleveland Police Department. They sickened him then, thinking about what people would do when a government declared a group not worthy of humanity.

When the tray filled, Zola began laying the items along the wall. Eugene expected to grow bored after a time but the opposite occurred–the terror mounted. Zola's swelling glee didn't help.

With her first task complete, Zola sauntered in front of him, prancing with a crooked smile. In one hand, she held a meat cleaver serrated with tiny sharpened crosses. The other held a very large, very long pink rubber dildo, the word COEXIST written out multiple times in different religious symbols. If his heart wasn't about to escape out his throat, Eugene might have thrown up.

"Show time."

***

Grace did not wait in her pit long.

A great burst of light announced the Berets arrival followed by a chorus of screams. Even in her shelter, it was bright enough to rob her of what little night vision she'd gained. Probably a solar flare, something the local news covered last year that replicated sunlight. Not painful enough to kill a vampire, but powerful enough to shred the first few layers of skin, incapacitating even the strongest. Sure, vampires healed rapidly, but based on the cacophony of wailing, not fast enough.

Maybe they needed a moment to rally, gather their wits, form ranks. Grace would never know as gunfire split the night. She clutched the grate in surprise. It sounded so close. The Berets weren't taking any chances here. Cries of mercy were met with the emptying of clips. This rebellion might be over before it began.

She needed to get out of here, to do something. What kind of person would stay back while prisoners were slaughtered? But instinct told her to stay, to hide. To listen to Francesco.

Snarls rose from somewhere to Grace's right and heavy footfalls filled the night around her. More gunshots. A loud thud came from a box above.

It couldn't be time yet. Or had Diavolo decided to use her as a hostage instead?

Crates started to shift. Impossible, they couldn't have found her this fast. She raised a hand up to the grate, willing whoever it was to leave.

They only grew closer. The box above her was knocked aside and a man collapsed on the grate. She didn't recognize him, but he was definitely a vampire based on the shabby jacket and torn scarf.

"All clear in the third quadrant," said a baritone voice from above. "Bravo company, move out. Alpha company, gather bodies for interrogation and reeducation."

A cold drop plopped on her cheek. Rain? She wiped the moisture away. Too dark to see, her fingers smeared the warm liquid around. Another drop fell. From the vampire, she was certain. She hoped it wasn't blood. Holy water, perhaps?

The vampire was pulled away in a rush, revealing a full moon lighting up her now exposed spot. A shadow rose and eclipsed it: a soldier. Staring straight at her. Grace bit down so hard, her jaw popped. She froze, wishing the sides of the pit would close in and bury her.

He bent over. To do what, Grace didn't know, but she could think of a few cruel and unusual reasons. But the soldier's hands fell to the vampire's body, patting up near the shoulders and neck. A quick jerk and metal tinged on asphalt. The neck protector.

Grace held her breath as the soldier continued to search, moving down to the vampire's feet, away from her. He remained quiet. Had he not seen her? No, she was certain he had. So why...?

She debated calling out. But if Francesco was right, she would be exposing herself to a worse monster. The cruel methods the guards used to tamp down this riot bestowed little confidence. But would they actually kill her? Or was this another part of Francesco's game? Who was he really? Villain, or revolutionary?

God, she hated not knowing who to trust.

A flare burned the night away. Grace sucked in sharply from the suddenness of it.

"Well, hello, reporter lady."

While she'd stared at the one guard, three others had sneaked up to the grate on the opposite side. The Berets ripped open the grate and yanked her out of the crawlspace, dragging her up by the shirt collar. She snarled. That was all she could do; they were too well trained and subdued her in a blink.

One guard knelt down. "Allow me to introduce myself." He dipped his head. "My name is Leonid Beluga. Yes, like the drink. And this..."

Two guards brought over a limp, bloody body between them. She started.

"Oh, you've already met Francesco, I see. Say hello again."

Francesco was out cold. The putrid smell of garlic radiated off of him in waves. Beluga clapped a hand over Grace's scalp and wrenched her up. She cried out. But the pain didn't stop until she was at Francesco's feet.

"Say it!"

"H-hello," she said.

"Good." Beluga leaned in until she felt his hot breath on her face, then shouted: "Do it!"

She cowered, her ears ringing. When she looked back up, the metal shield from the back of Francesco's neck was on the ground. A second guard stomped down until the disk fractured.

"HQ," Beluga said. "We have a green light on inmate two six. Permission granted for surge."

A voice replied back over the radio: "Green light is go. Thirty seconds."

Leonid flashed a wolfish grin, then released her. She collapsed, palms smacking the pavement at the same instant as Francesco's face.

"Francesco?" She reached out. His breath was shallow but steady. He was alive.

The guards retreated, their steps hurried and out of sync, until she was alone with the vampire. Why hadn't they killed her?

A low hum rose. It grew in volume and pitch until it became a growl.

What had Beluga said? Something about a green light. A surge. That was right after they removed Francesco's metal card, the one that blocked his chip. A chill curled her fingers. If it could monitor a vampire, what else could it do? Back of the neck, right on the brain stem.

The Berets couldn't shoot her. Too many questions. But if a vampire were to kill her...

Grace rose on shaky legs and scurried away. Behind her, the growl inten-sified until the earth shook.

***

"Come on, detective. I expected you to play the game a little better than this."

Zola slapped him with a rubber club. Eugene's teeth knocked together and clanged through his head. An alarming amount of blood spat onto the floor. Despite that, he was thankful Zola had set the cleaver and dildo down. Perhaps she had wanted to scare him or thought them too much too soon. Still, they rested on the tray at her back, never more than an arm's length away.

"Next question," Zola said, stuffing ear plugs into her nostrils. Eugene swallowed. He could only guess why she'd want to block her sense of smell. "If Jack Sprat could eat no fat, and his wife no lean, what did their children eat?"

Eugene vaguely recalled the nursery rhyme, but couldn't remember anything about children. He swallowed. Time for another guess. "Um. Packaging?"

Zola's jaw went slack, her mouth opening in a wide O. Then she broke into raucous laughter. "That—" A fit of giggles overwhelmed her. "That's the dumbest thing I've ever heard. No, Eugene. The children ate the cat and then their parents and finally the policemen who came to investigate."

She turned and picked up a stiletto dagger. Eugene fought his bonds again but like before, only succeeded in rattling the chains.

Zola grinned and pointed the blade's tip at his chest. Step by measured step, she neared, the blade never straying. He held his breath. She was trying to break him, toy with him before the final blow. To savor it. But he could resist, stay strong. She couldn't mangle him too bad yet. Right?

But the dagger didn't stop. The tip almost pierced his flesh when Zola lifted the blade over her head and brought it down, slashing his chest. He winced, expecting pain at any moment.

None came. He glanced down to find his shirt front opened. The buttons of his shirt were sliced off. He almost shed a tear in relief. However, she circled around, starting again, blade straight for his gut. This time, as she neared, the tip pierced. He shuddered, trying not to cry out as lancing heat seared across his abdomen.

"Hold still," Zola said, slicing his right side. "Or I'll have to start my pretty picture all over."

Eugene bit his tongue as she carved. Maddened glee lit Zola's face. There was an almost carnal, sadistic pleasure to it. Just when he thought he couldn't take another cloying second, she pulled away.

"This game brings out the artist in me." She left to trade the stiletto for something worse.

The tears came as he took in her masterpiece. In the streams of red, a stick figure held a knife over a pile of limbs. A severed head at its feet stuck out a tongue, bloody X's for eyes. It wasn't hard to tell which one he was.

Fear gripped him then, the kind of way it does once or twice in a lifetime, forced him to scour the room to break free. Every weapon lay out of reach, the door bolted from without, an uncaring security camera observing everything. No one was coming. No cavalry arriving at the eleventh hour. He was a previously suspended cop who was hated by his colleagues and hadn't even bothered to file his paperwork before bolting from the job the first day back. He was stuck in here, forced to play Zola's twisted game with its ever-changing rules.

He refused to give up. If the rules always changed, then this wasn't a game. This was a puzzle. And every puzzle could be beaten, no matter how impossible. Like asking Zola what she smelled in the teacher case, he just had to find a way to cheat the system.

"Next question." Zola came into view carrying a large metal staff with a sharpened end; a glaive he thought it was called.

Before she could get another swing in, he blurted, "How long have you been here?"

She cocked her head to the side, a finger tapping the side of the glaive's edge. Then, whether because of her own rules or the months he'd spent questioning her, she answered, "Man wants to know Zola's been here fifty some years."

"Yes. He does."

Immediately, he knew he mis-stepped. A red flush rushed into her cheeks. "WRONG!"

The glaive wound back, tip almost striking the wall, then swung. It was in his calf muscle in a blink. At first, he thought it was fake. A trick. Then everything rushed in. He roared. Hot tears flowed. Blubbering spittle flew.

Every inch of composure he had fought for slipped away. Then, for a time, so did he.

Something warm patted his cheek, its surface callous and rough. He was in his childhood bedroom. His mother was finally home. She worked so many hours at the hospital, they hardly saw each other anymore. He was a good boy, never argued, always kept the bad outside on the streets. Never made it hard for her, she didn't deserve that. One day, he'd earn enough money to move her out of the projects. He'd be respectable, a cop like on that show she lov–

"Wakey wakey," said a voice like glass shards. A hard slap ripped him from his dream.

"Sorry, Eugene," Zola said. "Lost myself for a minute. Oh, quit your whining." She *tsked*. "You act like I cut off the whole thing. It'll stitch back up in no time."

Eugene muttered some response.

"Next question it is, then." The glaive clanged to the floor. She lifted her next torture device: a chain with small hooks interlaced throughout, then pointed it at his groin. "Who played Detective Frank Columbo's girlfriend in season three, episode fifteen?"

Eugene gasped in a sharp breath.

Zola brought the chain back. "No answer?"

A small sense of self preservation eked through. He forced out the only thing he could think of, anything to stave off losing more of himself: "No one."

She twisted up like a baseball pitcher about to send a heater his way. Heh heh. A baseball to take off his baseballs. Eugene chortled, a crazed, wet laugh.

She held the chain back a moment, measuring him in that cocked head-long look again. The chains rattled to the floor. The mad recognized one of their own.

"Correct," she grumbled.

"It...it is?"

"Kate Columbo. She was his wife. Half bat, half sheep though. Played by Kate Mulgrew. No girly friend." This last part was said with such despair, Eugene wasn't sure what to make of it.

She turned her back to him, then rooted around on the floor, leaning one way and then the other, trying to make a decision between an axe and the end of a fire hose.

The pain threatened to pull him under. If that happened again, he was done. One more hit, and he'd likely reach the same end. He needed to win this, now.

For that, he needed to be bold. "When they captured you, who did you leave behind?"

Zola straightened, back tensing. "Why's man want to know?"

He almost answered but hesitated, his throbbing shred of a calf enough of a reminder to keep his mouth shut.

"...Krystal," Zola replied after a minute.

"Was she your girlfriend?"

"It's my turn." She bent over and scooped up some unseen object. When she swiveled around and brought the full weight of it to bear, Eugene blanched. It was a hefty iron club that ended in a massive metal ball with long spikes hammered throughout. Zola swung the whole mess around as if it was made of Styrofoam.

"When did Zola become a vampire?"

Eugene blinked. Her voice sounded level, sane.

"You've gabbed this lobster up six times this past year." A nail almost pierced his throat. "Read my digits. When did I become a vampire?"

He cursed. Numbers. Why was it always numbers? He could do this. Every time he came in, he had memorized hers and sure, like oil, it slipped right back out when he reached his car. But he could see the file, the lines of script where the Date of Origin should be. It was a rectangular blur.

"Maybe a New Year's countdown." She took hold of his left ear and leveled the mace. "Three seconds before you get the best piercings in your life. Three."

He winced as a sharp heat impaled his ear.

"Oops." She aimed at the other side. "Two."

"Jus—ah!"

The mace spike went through. She sighed. "Cops all the same."

She stood before him, club leveled at his center. No more playing around. "One."

"October!"

A whoosh of air.

He closed his eyes. "October nineteenth!"

He was dead. The impact was so massive, it killed him instantly. His sharp breaths were the first he took in the afterlife. But when he peered out through one slitted eye, he encountered no pearly gates, but a mace hovering right above his heart.

Zola watched him, expectation curving her brow.

"Y-you were coming back from a friend's house."

The nearest spike tapped his chest, not hard but noticeable. *Go on,* it said.

"Girlfriend's house," he corrected. "Krystal. The two of you had tried LSD for the first time. She hid under the bed, claiming a tiger was about to jump out of the closet and eat you both. You said she was full of it. You'd put her in your pocket and walk outside to keep her safe. Then you left, thinking she was tucked into your bell bottoms when really, she had passed out in the tub."

He licked his lips with a dry tongue. "An unmarked van picked you up a block away. You were trying to smoke the grass on someone's front lawn. The driver most likely noticed your promise ring. It wasn't worth much, but it was enough. He stole it and the little money you had left from babysitting. Then he..." Eugene swallowed, forcing his eyes to shift from the mace to Zola. "He raped you and dumped you in the Metroparks to cover up the crime."

She continued to stare at him, her eyes pleading for more. But that was all her file contained. Anything after that, Eugene would have to guess.

"A-a vampire found you," he went on, "before you died. And turned you. A week later, an abandoned van owned by a street preacher was discovered. The seats were covered in blood. The driver was never found."

A cold case from the sixties he hadn't connected until now.

Zola didn't move, not a twitch in her expression or involuntary flex in her extremities.

The vampire who turned her probably saw the act as a mercy. They couldn't have predicted the hell Zola would experience as a result. Enough for her to call him the devil. An eternal seventeen years of life and Zola had endured three times that amount in these four walls. No wonder she was insane.

In a flash, Zola's demeanor returned to its usual jovial nature. "You don't get points for extra credit, dummy."

The mace punched a hole in the concrete wall and stayed there. A breath escaped Eugene that made his entire body shudder.

"Let's see. Let's seeeee..." Zola whistled a tune. Jimmy cracking corn and no one caring.

Eugene had secured himself one more question. But that hole in the wall meant she was done playing. The next blow meant death.

Zola lifted the rubber dildo again and swung it around and around. It knocked into a light overhead, making the fixture swing. She cackled.

The light.

An idea took shape. He could smack himself for not thinking of it earlier.

"Why don't you leave?" Eugene asked.

"Man wonders why I don't leave. Negative, officer. The vodka soldier awaits without, the gates sealed."

"Did the vodka soldier tell you about the release switch?"

Zola swooned, fangs flying out. "Tell us or man dies."

"I will. Camera first."

The little box shattered in an explosion of sparks. Eugene hadn't seen Zola move but the dildo now protruded from the camera's lens.

"Second, Zola lets me go."

A head cock.

Crap. Zola grabbed the meat cleaver instead. But he refused to cower. He'd done that too much already. All he hoped as Zola closed the distance was that his daughter attended his funeral—if there was a funeral.

A clang. The tension in his right hand slackened. Needle-like sensations prickled down his arm as blood pumped through constricted veins. The cleaver had sliced through the chains on his wrists. It was quickly followed by the other three.

Eugene sank to the floor while Zola brushed all nearby weapons out of his reach. "Release switch?"

"It's...you."

Her eyes went dead. "What."

"Listen. These rooms were designed to contain vampires, it's true. But there are certain pressure points that will give you the right leverage to open the door."

"Man fibbing?"

"Trust me. I think through a lot of worst-case scenarios as a hobby. But before I explain, you'll need to patch me up. I can't last much longer."

"Tell first."

"I..." Eugene sagged, trying to make himself look awful. It wasn't hard. "I don't have time to argue."

She growled. "Eugene talks. Zola fixes."

"All right," he compromised. He motioned toward the ceiling. "You'll need to get one of the wires from the light up there. And a metal bar. Keep those gloves on..."

31

GRACE SPRINTED THROUGH A tangled maze of vampire bodies and shell casings, the air heavy with garlic, spent gunpowder, and burnt flesh. The Beret-controlled Diavolo snarled behind her, claws scraping against asphalt as he gained and gained.

An hour ago, she'd thrown her life away, leaped into a vampire's waiting arms, but now she ran, a cramp ballooning in her gut so large, it practically doubled her over. But still she ran, her lips mouthing three words over and over in time to her heartbeat: Not. Like. This.

She zigged and zagged. Massive potholes with inch-wide paths. Twisted trails clogged by debris, garbage, and uneven pavement. Identical houses zoomed past on either side. Had she gone this way before? It didn't matter. Diavolo shrieked, his wail so near, her back trembled from the force of it and almost sent her into one of the pits. He was not troubled at all. But the end was in sight. One last hole to go.

Then the lights winked out.

Despite herself, she spun, encircled by black in every direction. Something snagged her ankle. She kicked high, trying to break its grip, twisting her hips for more leverage, but whatever had her refused to let go. Instead of a clumsy shuffle and torn hem, Grace fell far enough for her whole body to feel airborne.

Down, down she went, before slamming into a solid, coiled mass. Cold vines broke her fall and ensnared her in an instant. She tried to tear herself away but her arms were pinned. Tighter the vines wound until they fastened around her waist, her limbs, her throat. She wriggled to get free, but to her horror that only sank her in deeper. These weren't plants. She drowned in flesh. A mass grave of vampires thrown into a neglected pockmark, sliding down the gullet of the earth.

This was where the guards would find her. Suffocated amid teeth and claws.

The floodlights buzzed back on and finally she could see the leg bent around her throat. One of her feet rested against something solid. Using whatever it was for leverage, she pushed herself up while clawing at the leg. Finally, she gasped, free.

A pebble fell from the opening above. Diavolo. It must be, searching for her among the dead. She hadn't lost him. Grace clamped her eyes shut and choked back a sob.

A scrape from a pair of heavy, thick boots. A soldier? No, two pairs.

"I'm not hearing anything from dispatch," one said. "No telling why the lights are doing that."

"Probably stepped out to piss." This was the guard who spoke to her before. Beluga. "Dispatch, call in. Turn off blare on two six, over."

No response.

Beluga repeated himself to no avail. He sighed. "I'll check in. See what the issue is."

Boots retreated into the night but she couldn't tell if it was one set or two. One soldier might have stayed behind. God, why did she close her eyes? Now she had no chance of knowing. The remaining guard could be looking down at her right now. She had to remain still. Act like the undead around her.

A wrapper crinkled, followed by the faint sound of chewing. That answered that. There was one left, snacking. Taking a break from genocide with a nougat.

A click of metal. Maybe a safety being turned off? She strained her ears for any further details. The silence stretched on. Maybe he'd gone. This might be her one chance to get to the gate. She needed to take it.

Or she'd die in a blaze of holy bullets. She assumed the bodies surrounding her were dead. But if not, this was the worst place to be. Not after what Francesco had become.

Aches prickled in her back and demanded she shift. Or had something shifted below? Someone was walking.

She blinked the quickest fraction of a second. A snapshot of the world seared into her mind. The walls of a pit around her. A guard standing on the edge above, his back to her, assault rifle pointed away at the ground. His tactical gear made him appear massive.

He wouldn't leave without a very good reason. Meanwhile, Grace fought the urge to shiver as she lost feeling in her toes. All the undead were stealing her warmth. She was running out of time.

God, how had this escape plan gone to shit so fast? Clearly the soldiers were in on Francesco's plans. The one, Beluga, called her reporter lady, meaning he was aware of her and possibly the deal.

Or was he messing with her? She'd worked the Quarter beat for a decade, maybe he knew her by reputation. But that gleam in his eye when he found her didn't seem like a flash of recognition. More like the twinkle Perry got when he lorded something over her. When cruelty and fun mixed. Best to act like every one of the Berets knew about her and the deal, even the answers she'd ascertained. They'd been listening.

But did they hear Francesco when he told her how to get out? Yes. Not assuming so risked death. Which meant the front gate was out.

Of course, if this guard spotted her, then that didn't matter. She waited, counting to a hundred, then two. Finally, she blinked.

The guard swiveled a little, his side to her now. A skeleton tattoo danced along his forearm up to the elbow. Ironic as his gun did just that: made these undead skeletons around her dance.

A dark shape rose halfway out of the mass of bodies a few paces from her, equidistant between the guard and her hiding spot. A vampire must be waking.

As it stood to its full height, her breath caught. It wore soft brown rags topped with a dash of red at the neck. Francesco. He must have fallen in after her, trapped in the bodies. He faced the guard, his back to her, his intent clear. She wanted to run, leaving her enemies to destroy each other, but if she tried to flee, she'd be caught in the crossfire.

Francesco sprang toward the guard with an audible snick, a sound as familiar now as her own heartbeat: his fangs. One leap and they'd be on each other, then Grace could tear herself free and find shelter in a surrounding house. But before Francesco could scale the deep sides of the pit, the guard's gun rose.

rat a tat tat tat

The rifle split the night. A bullet whizzed past Grace's ear. She raised her arms up to shield herself and only succeeded in lifting her shoulders. Francesco collapsed back into the bodies and did not rise.

"Gotcha." Grace looked up. The guard stared straight at her, his barrel swiveling her way.

Fear, primal and uncontrollable, sizzled through her limbs. *Not like this.* Grace jerked, trying to free herself. But her legs were still pinned and buried. She lunged and smacked into the wall of the pit. Not good. She tried to trick him, dodging one way and then another, but the end of the barrel never strayed.

A cackle ruptured from the guard's lips, his shoulders shaking. "Roll over, little doggy! Fear the gun. Fear it! Ahahaha!" His taunts grew in volume and regularity until he was practically barking.

Soon, she tired, her chest hurting from her heart doing back flips. But loathing burned in her gut. She latched onto it, converted it into fuel. The gun barrel no longer scared her. She was beyond it. Every lunge pried her loose another fraction. Soon, she'd be out, then he'd learn what a dancing skeleton could really do when life itself meant nothing.

The force which she popped out of the pile surprised even her. She landed face down in a pile of armpits. The guard's laughter ceased. She was up in an instant. But the guard brought his flashlight to bear, blinding her.

He held her in the beam, catching the last glimpse of her before the bullets tore through her and left her leaking on the ground.

A single thought passed through her head. It wasn't profound, or philosophical, or meaningful. Just a bad punchline. And in a way, it felt right. It was this:

What a shit way to die.

A clack of metal. She winced. It didn't sound like the gun had fired, but what did she know? Maybe military guns had silencer modes. A hard slap struck her shoulder, the jagged pain of it prying a whimper from her. She hadn't expected a bullet to feel so much like a slow-motion fist.

"It's over."

What did "it" mean? Her life?

A hand touched her shoulder, not a bullet. The guard must have climbed down here, out of sight of those above, wanted to take his time. End her the ways he chose.

"Grace. It's over. Grace!"

Wait. That wasn't the guard's voice.

She lowered her arms to discover a weary, blood-stained Francesco. His grip on her loosened, leaving behind a phantom ache. Behind him, the guard lay dangling over the edge of the pit, his eyes staring, vacant. Every part of him still massive except the gaping hole where his throat had been. Despite that, there was minimal blood. As Francesco wiped his mouth with his sleeve, she could guess where all of it had gone.

"The soldiers will return soon." His tone worried her, like everything she had witnessed so far was nothing compared to what was coming. "You need to be in the wind before then."

"The plan's gone to crap. They know about everything."

"Not...everything. Help me."

Together, they crawled and dragged themselves out of the pit. The Quarter in all its dirt encrusted glory came back into view. Grace wanted to get down and kiss the asphalt. She'd never seen such a beautiful sight. Francesco trembled beside her, then spasmed until he collapsed onto all fours.

Grace knelt. "Is it the soldier's blood? Was he sick?"

Francesco dug around under his shirt for a moment. Then with a wrench, a metal plate clattered to the ground, four spent rounds sliding off. "Made from the crates." He motioned toward the dead guard. "His gun."

"I don't–"

"Get it."

She shook her head. Did he want her to shoot him? But she sprinted over and pilfered the sidearm. The lightweight gun fit her grip if she choked up high on the handle. After clumsily checking if it was loaded — action films were her only reference—she gave the guard a justifiable kick and he toppled into the hole.

When she returned, Francesco's breath came out haggard. "The guard didn't do this to me. Well, not just him. The few wounds I received will heal...enough. Help me up."

She draped his arm over her shoulders and hoisted him to his feet. Shoulder bones protruded like wings from his thin frame. How did he even stand, let alone kill a special forces soldier?

"Changing humans into vampires," he said as if reading her mind, "leaves us weak. Do it every other day, and you get this. Add to that, the government's tiny ration of blood...and I have just enough stamina...for a short sprint."

"You need rest. We can hide in one of these houses, get your strength back."

"They'll find us."

"Oh? With what, heat sensors?"

"Not them." His gaze dropped to the vampires below. "The cut on your cheek."

Blood. It set vampires into a frenzy. Once the effects from the Berets' weapons wore off, she'd be torn to pieces.

"Where, then?"

"This way."

He directed her through the streets and backyards. Mud squelched with every step. Gore and rain ran in steady streams along the curbs. Bodies choked the nearly impassable trails between the potholes. Grace kept her head down and tried not to think.

Easy enough since Francesco needed assistance over the slightest obstacles. On top of everything else, patrols passed by, their flashlights sweeping every dark nook. They were nearly caught several times. The journey never went fast, but it went.

After some indeterminate time, they reached a concealed alley where they crouched down between a small porch and a row of overgrown weeds that blocked the view from the street. Grace peered out to find the Hellmouth.

"Not this way," she said. "They were listening in on us. They'll be expecting me."

"I doubt they'll be too worried in a few moments." He grinned. "You think I'm the only one to sire an extra vampire or three? Still, let's be cautious. When you step out, they'll see you. No blind spots exist around the gate. You'll have to move fast."

"You mean *we'll* have to."

He stared at her blankly.

"You can't be serious." Was he insane? That was the only explanation someone wouldn't want to escape all this. "You have to come."

Francesco sighed. "The floodlights have a secondary feature: sunlight mimicry. And unlike the grenades, it's the real deal. If even one soldier is inside, they could flip the switch and I would be ash in a heartbeat."

"But the lights came back on earlier. Something is going on the soldiers don't know about." She told him the conversation she'd heard between the two soldiers.

"They could have been messing with you. Lying to catch any vampires who were faking being unconscious. But even if that weren't the case, I need to return. My people need me."

"You'll die."

"Possibly. In fact, it's inevitable."

"Then why go?"

Francesco fixed her with a bewildered expression. "Because they're my people. They're me. I'm them. After fifty some years together, we're thicker than blood. I...We...are."

She looked at him then, this man with his worn shoes and disheveled hair, his wide eyes that took in every shadow. A survivor with trauma etched across his skin. There was no reasoning with a man like this. Maybe she could give him something.

She offered him the gun.

He chuckled. "I think you'll do better with that than I will."

She lowered her hand. That was it. She was unsure what to say — goodbye sounded too ominous, and a handshake too tacky. Instead, she took in his face and the surroundings, trying to memorize everything to reference in the future.

Thin lips. Brown eyes. Dark hair. The scent of olives. A blackened house at his back. Three religious symbols painted in succession under the window, each with an X crossed through it.

The warm feeling at the base of Grace's skull from earlier returned and with it, a word: "X-X-X-periment."

"What?"

"In Komarov's place. There was a DVD— a video called X-X-X-periment." No time to explain what a DVD was.

"I tell you I'm about to die and you bring up Komarov's porn collection?"

"Yes. I mean, no. Shut up for a second." Grace massaged her forehead. "Komarov had all his videos in code. A weird, stupid code, but code. Like one was labeled DOWNS in all caps, which thinking about it probably meant UPS."

"UPS?"

"Yeah. United Parcel Service."

Diavolo set a hand on his chin. "So if he wrote X-X-X—"

"–it probably meant something else. Something obvious."

She tried to think back through everything Francesco had told her, but nothing leaped out. There was simply too much.

Francesco scratched his chest, shirt shifting to reveal a bit of waist.

Grace leaned forward. "Your scars."

"What about them?"

"You said they took a little piece of you every time they tortured you. What if...what if they experimented with your DNA? Tested it in those facilities underground. And Komarov, not willing to let anyone own him outright, stole some footage?"

"So XXXperiment is just a plain old experiment on tape?"

"Right! His code is stupid so the Hellmouth bugged the place and figured it out. Then when I stole the videos from his case–"

"—they figured a reporter just took proof of their illegal activity. Before their vampire agent could get to it."

Grace nodded. "And with Detective Yukawa there, the situation went beyond their control. Everything had to be destroyed." A chill went down Grace's spine. "And everyone."

"Where are the videos now?"

"Hidden in a sewer recess."

Francesco sat back, a slight grin on his face. It was the first time his smile didn't turn her blood cold. "Look at that. You solved a mystery I didn't even know existed."

"Now let's see if I live to tell about it."

Francesco put a hand out and she shook it. "It was a pleasure to meet you, Grace Clemons."

"I wish I could say likewise."

He gave a curt nod.

She offered a curt smile. "But at least some good might come of it."

Then with a parting word, she slipped through the weeds and headed toward the gate.

The gun grew heavier the more she held it. She grabbed the handle with both hands and squared her shoulders, the way the police held theirs. A car passing on the street outside honked and she almost shot at it.

Instead of a sprint, as Francesco suggested, she went slow. Too many news stories of falls and accidental gun discharges made her cautious. She hadn't sacrificed everything only to trip on a piece of debris and blow her brains out.

The heat from the floodlights made her sweat. The tint was more of a bitter mustard shade than pure white. On her approach, the heavy gate whirred to life with the squelch of oil and steel. Grace raised her gun.

The gate stopped, the gap only a couple feet across. A woman stepped through. Her hair was pulled back in a tight bun, black pants and suit jacket uniformly crisp over the white blouse underneath. Not a soldier. But Grace didn't dare relax.

Their eyes met across the bright, charged space. A cry of sirens rose somewhere in the city beyond, faint and distant. The woman drew her gun and aimed the barrel at Grace. The suit jacket opened to reveal a police badge clipped to her belt.

"Police! Put your hands up. Now!"

Grace almost dropped her gun, but she caught herself in time and tightened her grip.

The policewoman's finger slid toward the trigger and Grace copied. Why couldn't this stranger have come two minutes from now?

The door to the Hellmouth bounded open. A figure stepped out, directly in the middle of their dueling ground.

Was that—? No. It couldn't be. Was God playing a practical joke? Except...

What happened to him?

Eugene hobbled up using a plank of wood as a crutch. Blood matted his hair, gluing it to his face, which was covered in a mass of bruises and gashes. He panted like he had run a marathon. As if sensing what he had walked into, he turned in both directions, first towards Grace, then to the strange woman.

His shoulders tensed. "Sergeant Cole?"

32

EUGENE LOOKED FROM GRACE to Cole, then back. Then once again. Then twice more, just in case. And almost burst out laughing.

The sheer irony going on here. He had strolled from one life and death situation to another while looking for the person who was supposed to have killed him in the first place. And Grace was pointing yet another gun at him!

He snickered. It was all so funny. Or maybe funny wasn't the right word. But Grace and Cole had to see it, right?

They both gave him the most horrified expressions. So...no?

"Detective Yukawa," Cole said, immediately straight faced. Figured. Cole always did know how to leech the humor from any situation. "Your leg."

He glanced down. Oh. Right. That explained a lot. So blood loss was giving him the giggles. Or maybe it was the head injury. Or watching Zola eat that security room technician. So many choices. Each one an anchor pulling him back to the present.

Eugene cleared his throat. "Sorry. I'm j—sorry."

Cole took a deep breath. "I think it's time to go, detective. You're clearly unwell and the situation here has grown terminal. We need you out."

His head still felt light but he managed to hobble forward until he stood between the two women, letting the door swing shut behind him. Hero time. "Not without my suspect. She's been feeding men to a vampire calling himself Diavolo." A snicker escaped. Eugene tamped it down, even if that was the dumbest name ever. "We need to take her in."

"She could be infected. You know she can't leave—"

"—unless we test her first. I found the equipment inside while looking for my service weapon." Which he hadn't found, but he left that part out.

Cole shook her head. "No time. It's best to let the military handle her."

"They won't–"

A clatter of metal cut him off.

He turned to find Beluga grappling Grace from behind, holding her around the throat and twisting back the arm back that had previously held a gun.

"I've got it from here, officers." Beluga jerked Grace and she whimpered. "Thank you very much."

"See?" Cole asked. "Everything's taken care of. Now let's go before any vampires show up."

But Eugene ignored her, focusing on Grace instead. She was mouthing something he couldn't quite decipher. Beluga held her too tight, cutting off her air. But finally, a croaked whisper managed to escape: "No...others..."

Beluga shook her again.

No others? What did that mean?

Cole tapped her foot. Behind her stood a human sized gap in the front gate, a chink in the otherwise rigid armor of the Hellmouth. An absence Eugene had not created.

"Sergeant, where's backup?" he asked.

"Ten minutes out," she answered without a skipped beat.

"And your vest?"

"No time."

She had said that before, "no time." And yet she stayed put, not moving to help him despite his obvious injury. In fact, she hardly seemed agitated at all, even with Beluga's cruel handling of a murder suspect.

"Tell you what," Eugene said, "why don't I go grab some handcuffs and a muzzle, and we can take Grace to the station? A couple cruisers have vampire proofing."

"No," Beluga snapped.

"You can come with us," Eugene offered. "More than enough room."

Cole sighed and holstered her weapon. "I didn't come for a murder suspect, Detective Yukawa, I came for you."

"You mean," Eugene said, "you're politicking. Like the chief. Giving me your whole attention, when really you can't do a damn thing. But for that to work, you'd have to know you can't do anything." With the blood loss, he hadn't noticed. She didn't react to anything he said. The leg, yes, but the lack of a service weapon or handcuffs? He cocked a loaded finger at her. "You made a deal."

Someone was behind him, heavy and fast. Before Eugene could flinch, a loud bang sent him wobbling. He caught a flash of amber hurtling away to his right. His makeshift wooden crutch. Gravity asserted itself over him like he was a cartoon coyote noticing the absent ground beneath his feet. He took a step to reorient, realizing too late he did so with the wrong leg.

Eugene fell to the ground and writhed. Whatever happened next was second to the lava coursing through him.

Cole barked, "Was that necessary?"

"Be more persuasive next time," Beluga replied.

"Are you all right, Eugene?" Cole leaned over him. "I didn't want anything like this to happen."

"You..." Eugene swallowed. He wanted to curl up, to give himself over to the pain, but he had to stay conscious, had to understand. "You called the mobsters."

Cole offered him a sad smile. "When a person is in an impossible situation, they do what they must. You forced someone's hand and that person, in turn, forced mine. I thought you might hear me over the speaker; a part of me, if I'm being honest, hoped you would. But here we are."

The throbbing in his leg began to ebb. The sirens that cried out in the city died.

"I tried to help you," Cole said. "Every once in a while, I can do good. Your suspension made it easier." Her eyes pleaded with him. "Let me give you an out, detective. For your little girl."

"But Grace..."

Cole glanced in the reporter's direction. "She's burned her last bridge. Besides, you just told me she committed multiple felonies. She's as good as dead. Why risk your neck?"

Eugene hesitated. She was right. All that was left for Grace were a few months of jail and a trial. Mere formalities at this point. The Hellmouth must have loads of footage of her crimes. Was it really better to risk his life so she could die in prison rather than here?

Looking at it that way, it was hardly a decision at all.

"She comes with us," he said.

Cole straightened as if slapped.

Beluga whistled through his teeth. "Your protege's got balls, I'll give you that."

Cole shot the guard a dirty look before resettling her gaze on Eugene. "I like you, detective. Not in a mushy, romantic way, but in the way that counts. Why do you think I kept you on after so many bad annual reviews?"

Eugene breathed in deep and swallowed. "She comes with us."

The tight rigidity Cole always carried in her shoulders softened. "If that's your decision..."

She set her hands in her pockets and turned her back on him. Steps heavy, she trod out through the exit wide enough for a lone person. Once on the other side, she pulled a remote out of her pocket, pushed a button, and the gate closed.

Before the final clang, she saluted. "Farewell, detective."

***

As Sergeant Cole's car engine faded, the last flicker of possibility in Grace died. At least she wouldn't be alone. It was a selfish thought, one that should make her feel bad, but she was beyond caring. Eugene had stayed for her. Little good that did, but she wanted him to know that she appreciated it all the same.

Grace wanted to reach out, thank him, but a pat on the back might put him in the hospital. The detective looked beyond wrung out. Whatever kept him alert and defiant was waning. It was clear that woman, his sergeant, had dealt him a serious blow.

"How touching." Beluga grabbed her by the hair and dragged. No screen this time. She knew this move. "Now let's finish this, little cow bitch."

The guard cackled for well over a minute, high and squeaky yips that grated her nerves. The laugh almost covered the jangle of handcuffs.

She kicked at his leg, but that only made the guard laugh harder. Metal clapped around her wrist. She twisted, trying to break his hold, but he seemed to anticipate that and shoved her hard, his grip still firm on her scalp. A chunk of hair tore off but didn't slow her. She yelped, hurtling through the air backwards, until she hammered into the concrete wall of the fort. Her lungs filled with rocks. She collapsed onto Eugene.

The blow still reverberated through her skull when there came another click. Slowly, like her brain was rebooting, she realized Beluga had handcuffed her wrist to Eugene's.

"Tell you what," Beluga said, dangling a ring of keys between his fingers. "You treat me nice– and I mean, *real* nice–and I might just let you have these."

Bile seethed up her throat. Everything spun in a sickening dance: the ground, the blood, the detective. Her gun too far away to be of any use.

She closed her eyes. The pounding in her skull not abating, but not increasing either. If she didn't do something now, it would be too late.

Not like this.

When she looked out again, her gaze had settled on the darkness outside the floodlights. A crumple of red drifted around in the black. Francesco. He'd come back for her. The Hellmouth could fry him to a crisp in a second and he came back. For her.

He stuck a toe into the Hellmouth's white light, then back, like sticking a toe in water. A trembling overwhelmed him, his hands clenched, as he looked from Beluga to the detective and back.

The blood rage. Despite his morals, Francesco had trouble resisting.

Please.

She forced herself to stare into the smug little face above her. She was alone. Her jaw trembled. "P-please. I'll do anything."

"Oh, baby." Beluga grinned. "Hearing women say that never gets old."

Disgust steamed out of her nostrils and she glanced back toward Francesco. He crept up, still near the edge of the light. But his eyes settled.

"Do your worst," Grace said.

Beluga moaned, thinking she was talking to him. "Oh, I will."

In a single fluid motion, Beluga spun, drawing his gun and firing. Francesco took off, stumbling at first, then building speed. Beluga fired twice more; Francesco modified his course. He closed the distance, a juggernaut of claws and fangs, hurtling toward the guard's throat.

Grace let out a small whoop. They'd be saved. She could still make it out of here.

Then her cheers died in her throat. Beluga dodged, stepping out of the way so fast, Grace didn't see him move. The guard walloped Francesco across the face with the butt of his gun. What should have only redirected the vampire a few degrees sent him skidding back the way he'd come like a rock across a pond.

Grace's mouth dropped.

"Think you can take me?" Beluga laughed, his high-pitched squeaks deepening into guttural chuckles.

"Eugene," Grace said, shaking the detective. He stirred but didn't open his eyes. "Eugene, we need to go."

Francesco shook off the blow, then charged once more. Beluga grinned. The two met with a thunderclap. Impossibly, the guard held his ground against the superior strength of the vampire, their hands locked in a contest of force. Francesco's face went from shocked to strained.

"Eugene!" Grace shouted.

The detective sat up with a start.

"We gotta run." She put his arm over her shoulders. "Inside. *Now!*"

As she got her feet beneath her, another deep smack boomed across the asphalt. It sounded like a clash of two beasts in the wild. She wrenched open the door to the compound. "Hurry!"

Grace shoved the detective inside, then toppled in herself. The door swung shut as the last sliver of an image dwindled through the crack: fangs jutted from Beluga's gums. Then the door closed and locked with finality, but Grace knew it to be a lie. Nothing about this was remotely over.

33

GRACE AND EUGENE HAD entered into an armory, now emptied of its weapons. Only the hooks inside the gaping cabinets hinted at what lay absent. And oh, how many hooks there were.

She half led, half dragged Eugene out into the main concourse of the Hellmouth. The large hallway lay quiet, the air stale and stagnant, like the fort was gathering its breath. She glanced at each of the five other doors, expecting someone to jump out and demand what they were doing here.

She limped over to the entrance.

Eugene stiffened. "Locked. Electronically."

"I can smash the little window."

"It's reinforced."

They both fell silent. There had to be a fire exit of some kind. They couldn't expect to pile out into the Quarter if the entrance went up in smoke.

Grace was about to ask when a sound stifled the question in her throat: Someone was jangling a doorknob. *The* doorknob. Eugene met her eye and a wordless conversation took place. Then they were moving, Eugene pointing toward a room opposite them and Grace hoofing toward it.

"There's only one way," he whispered in her ear. "Deeper in. We found a hidden passage at the back of the security station. Over here."

Who "we" was became evident when Grace entered the security room and witnessed the little of the dead guard still left inside. Who had Eugene befriended? And were they still here? Head down, she plowed on, the answers too terrifying to know.

A set of stairs ran down some indeterminable length into the Earth. *The public was not the first to call this the Quarter.* A quarter mile of mystery. A plethora of secrets Grace had wished existed since she woke next to an empty bed and a slashed window screen.

Looking down at this impossibility, something budded in Grace's chest, something terrible, something she swore to never put her faith in again: hope.

"What are you waiting for?" Eugene asked.

Grace looked at his bloodied pantleg. "Are you sure you can do this?"

"It's not all mine," he said. "And what is, is superficial. Mostly." Eugene chuckled then, unnerving Grace to the point where she almost set him down and went on by herself. "Guess she was putting on a show."

Whatever that meant. But Grace didn't argue. Because even though he might slow her down, she didn't want to face what lay ahead alone.

She started on the stairs. Eugene continued to chuckle, clearly insane. Well, maybe they both were. Two Mad Hatters who got lost in a nightmare land and decided to try the tea.

Every door on these stairs held promise. Joy could be behind any one of them. Or a computer terminal with her information. It tore Grace's heart to pass by the first two doors, but if they didn't travel far enough, fast enough, Beluga would catch up. Every floor they passed was another the guard had to check. In that uncertainty, Grace would gain time, enough for her to find a weapon, to plan, or, in Eugene's case, to rally.

However, Eugene started to get winded by the third floor. She pressed him, practically carrying the man two more flights, then called it and ducked inside. This level spread out into a large emerald room, the central lights above flickering on as the two of them entered.

Motion activated. This was bad. If every floor did this, Beluga could follow them with ease, popping his head inside each door until he found the right one. On a more immediate note, he was a vampire. He'd never set off a sensor since his skin didn't emit the kind of light that activated this kind of tech. They'd have no way to tell if he was coming.

More lights activated as she moved, revealing hallways that diverged a dozen different ways. She was in the center of a labyrinth. No signs directing her where to go.

Eugene pointed toward a hallway, mumbling about how the air didn't smell so bad down there. He giggled so bad, she almost dropped him. The blood loss must be making him delusional. Yippee.

Grace went his proposed direction anyway. One thing she learned to never do is argue with a drunk. Or the equivalent of a drunk.

The emerald tiles stretched on and on, turn after turn. Darkness lay thick beyond the edge of the light, as if it were solid, unable to be pierced by anything except the bulbs directly above.

Eventually, there was a break in the monotony. A cage materialized, about waist high and two feet across. The bottom was lined with shavings of wood similar to the kind used for hamsters. But that is where the similarities ended. A human fingernail lay on the ground near the cage door. Blood and feces soiled the inner circle of the shavings.

She sidestepped around it, trying not to gag at the stench. The next light flickered on as Grace bumped into a glass wall. Inside lay another cage, but this was occupied. Three teenagers were crammed inside, back-to-back, skeletal arms and legs poking through the tiny holes in the bars. It was cartoonish, a warped version of reality too grisly to believe. Grace wanted to throw up and laugh at the same time. *Who would do this to corpses?* she thought.

Then one spoke.

"Ajuda."

Grace almost fell backwards, clutching onto Eugene for support. He gave under the pressure and they landed hard on the tile floor.

"Por favor, ajudem-me! Ajuda!"

She continued to stare. The only other sound her rasping breath.

"That wasn't Spanish," Eugene said, breaking the silence.

Grace wanted to smack him. That was what he noticed? But like a rock in the middle of a raging sea, she clung onto this bit of information.

"It's close, but…" Eugene said.

"It's Portuguese." Grace studied the speaker, a malnourished girl that looked to be about twelve, more ribs than torso, hair matted to her scalp. *Eighty percent of the Quarter's victims are female.*

"Do you remember," Grace asked, "about a year ago, the attempted coup in Brazil? Some rebels tried to oust the president there."

"Vaguely."

"The president asked for American aid." The girl in the cage lifted her head, sniffing. "I think that's what we're looking at."

"You're saying our government kidnapped some Brazilians and brought them here? To what, experiment on them?"

"That and more."

He scoffed in response but didn't reply.

Grace set a hand on the glass. The girl started to paw toward her, fangs meekly slithering out of her gums. The other two in the cage started to grab at the air but they seemed to copycat the first girl more than sense Grace.

Francesco had said only one in nine were retrieved from the Quarter. She assumed he meant locals, or maybe those in surrounding states. But the Quarter was international. How long had this been going on? A decade? More? Since the Quarter's inception? The amount of people and logistics involved threatened to engulf Grace. And for what? Empire? That couldn't be all. What were they doing down here that could keep so many silent for so long?

"We should get moving." Eugene stared at where they'd come.

Grace followed his gaze and cursed. The lights stayed on behind them. How long were their timers set for? Beluga could follow the trail right to them.

"Police will clear all this up," Eugene said as she hauled him to his feet. "We need to survive. He can smell us. *Everything*...can smell us."

Grace swallowed and nodded. Addressing the three in the cage, she said, "We'll be back for you."

The hallway made a sharp right and ended in darkness. She stepped forward. The lights flashed on. She growled in frustration. The original central room lit up before her. The timers had turned off the lights and she'd started them once more.

Eugene cursed quite profusely. It was almost impressive. She didn't know he had it in him.

"I have an idea."

Grace led him along the perimeter of the room. Hallway lights flickered on as she went. When half the branching hallways glowed bright, obscuring their chosen path, she went down a wide one with a blue arrow on its wall. Best place to find something to defend themselves was a place everyone went. Probably. Anything was better than the bolt cutters in her pocket.

"Damn it. Hold on." Her face hot, she set him down out of sight of the main room, then pulled out the bolt cutters she had forgotten about until now. The handcuff chain proved a little too thick. Of course it did. But she kept trying.

"Doesn't make sense," Eugene muttered again and again.

At first, she thought he meant the malnourished teens but when he didn't elaborate, she asked.

"If Beluga is a vampire, our blood should have sent him into a rage. Just that scratch on your cheek would be enough to do it. So why is he so in control when my bleeding leg is practically dangling in front of him?"

Grace shrugged. Even Francesco struggled despite his system stuffed full of bullets and garlic. "Maybe you can ask him before he eats you."

The handcuffs broke with a snap. Grace pocketed the wire cutters. They might come in handy, though if Beluga ever got close enough for her to use them, there wasn't much they could do.

The two soon arrived at a lab with a metal table at its center, a cadaver on top, cut open and bound. The walls on either side contained cages from floor to ceiling. As before, vampires of various ages and ethnicities were shut into cells only slightly larger than they were. As the light turned on, they scurried to the back of their cages and hissed.

The back wall lit up too, full of cupboards and drawers in all their white dazzling glory. The God of the Lost gifting his favorite disciple.

She set Eugene down and shuffled forward, keeping her gaze on her feet. The tile would keep her in a straight line, out of reach of any vampires. She reached the back without incident and started rifling through the cupboards.

Little to find inside: a few syringes, a fire hydrant. She set them on the counter. Anything else that could even remotely be used to fight, along with some gauze, went into a pile next to Eugene who huddled under the cadaver table. He started to wrap up his leg.

Next came the folders. The ones inside the first filing drawer were marked with dates from the late sixties. This place wasn't quite finished then. There must have been some other lab or holding cell back then, taking people and storing them to utilize in the future. She shut this drawer and went to the next.

"Grace?" Eugene asked. "What are you doing?"

Did she tell him? Probably not worth it, he'd only talk further.

"I really need you here, Grace. I'm...I'm starting to lose myself. Zola missed the main artery, but I'm slowing down. Can't keep my eyes open..."

"Finding some notes," she elaborated when it was obvious Eugene wouldn't let this go.

"On?"

"Beluga and the others. The vampires above are meant to change people over, then send them down here for experiments. The ones that failed their conversions to vampires were retrieved by CPD. The mind control chips ensure the vampires stay docile and obedient. I think, sometime in the last few decades, the Berets made a breakthrough."

She could tell Eugene was enthralled. "In what?"

"Vampires without faults. Or without negative side effects, whatever you want to call it. They can walk in sunlight, withstand garlic, maybe even survive a wooden stake to the heart. And they keep all the horrifying pointy bits, except the need to feed on blood that is."

"That sounds like…"

"A conspiracy theory?"

He shrugged.

"You told me," she said, "that the Berets didn't give you any video footage of my time in the Quarter." She opened another drawer. "Ever wonder why? I'd stand out like blood on bathroom tile. I think it was to keep from exposing their vampire guards. Because the military still hasn't figured out how to get vampires to show up on cameras."

Eugene scoffed. "No way. People must have taken pictures of the Berets at some…" The words died in his throat as the truth hit.

Press weren't allowed cameras within range. No one was. Only special night vision goggles. Darkness at all times during retrievals. All rules the Berets set and enforced under penalty of imprisonment.

While Eugene had a minor revelation, Grace continued her search. Five drawers to go. She'd gotten the hang of their filing system now, but each drawer was still a surprise. She picked a random one and pulled. The dates here started a few months before what she needed. This was it. This was it!

"You're trying to find a flaw then?" Eugene asked. "Something they're weak against, something the scientists couldn't debug."

She took a long breath before replying. "No."

"What?" Eugene almost stood bolt upright. "Then why—"

"I doubt they'd leave something like that lying around." She paused. He wasn't going to like what she said next. "I'm finding some information about my sister."

"How does that help us?"

"It doesn't."

"It—what? Then what are we doing here?"

"Spending my last moments trying to find peace. Do that however you see fit."

"Don't say that. We're gonna get out of this."

"I appreciate the optimism," Grace said, closing the drawer, "but we have nothing solid to defend ourselves. And if Beluga is as powerful as I think, he's already found us." She turned toward the hallway outside the lab. The lights had gone dark. "He just likes to play with his food."

A slow clap emanated out. "Well done, reporter lady."

Beluga stepped out from the darkness. To Eugene's credit, he didn't react beyond turning toward the guard. He'd probably be dead if he did. One of his hands remained behind him, reaching towards something tucked into the back of his waist.

Grace studied the guard. Not a mark on him. She felt a pang in her chest, worry for Francesco, but didn't let it show. This monster didn't deserve to see her vulnerable.

"Did you find what you were looking for?" Beluga asked. "Closure is important. Wouldn't want you unsatisfied when I snap your neck."

A roar made Grace flinch. A vampire reached for her from the nearest cage, fangs poking out, ensnared in the mesh. That one set off a chain reaction. Others went feral, their hands outstretched between her and Eugene.

"Blood lust," Beluga exclaimed. "Sets them right over the edge. Takes a few minutes with the drug fog." In a flash, he had Eugene in the air by the scruff of his neck.

"Leave him alone!" Grace shouted.

Beluga cocked his head at her. "Huh. All noble all of the sudden. Where was this when you shot him in the chest with a dart? Yeah, I know about that. Won fifty bucks. I got you pegged, sweetheart." Beluga held Eugene out until he was almost within reach of the vampires. The tips of an old woman's fingers graced the back of Eugene's collar.

Grace held up a hand, her ribs tight inside her chest.

"Maybe it was that betrayal upstairs." Beluga shouted to be heard. "Watching this guy's sergeant turn on him must have made you pause. Reflect that you're some self-appointed good guy for all these victims you wrote about. Gonna solve the world's problems all by your lonesome."

The bolt cutters in her pocket were useless from here. If she went for anything else, Eugene would be dead.

"Please." Grace's voice cracked.

Beluga's eyes narrowed. "Tell me where you stored the DVD or Detective Yukawa here goes through the vampire shredder."

Bull. The instant she told him the whereabouts of the video, they were dead, she knew. But what choice did she have?

She knew the option the detective staring her down would take. He already had. Picked her over himself without a shred of doubt. But that wasn't the same, was it? He only had himself to think of. She had every single person stuck in these cages to consider.

What was one life against theirs?

Everything, she fired back. The answer shocked her, its terrifying nature sent a flood of emotions through her. That couldn't be right. Then why did parts of her long dead or numbed by compromise begin to awaken? The torrent surpassed even the maelstrom of purpose of her promise to Joy.

Under this crippling deluge, there was only one answer she could give. One answer this new self could voice. "The DVD is—"

Eugene whipped a hand out from behind his back and struck Beluga. At first, it appeared he missed, passing just underneath the guard's arm. Then there came a sizzling pop and Beluga's hand fell off at the wrist. Eugen fell to the floor. Something metal and rectangular clattered under the table.

The guard stumbled backward, clutching his sizzling stump of an appendage.

Grace didn't hesitate. She flew to Eugene and hefted him up. Whatever Eugene had hit Beluga with, it was lost beneath the cages.

Beluga groaned. "How? I-I don't believe..." He convulsed as the muscles in his arm spasmed.

She yanked Eugene toward the central stairs. "What did you do?" she asked.

"Hit him with a cleaver. Serrated religious symbols for teeth." Eugene chuckled. "The person who sliced my leg off gave it to me." His laughter turned wild.

Worried, Grace leaned into the exit door and pushed. If Eugene continued to cackle, the next part of her plan was ruined. "I'll lead him up," she said, louder than she meant to.

Eugene snapped his mouth shut, his giggles humming in his mouth like bees.

She cinched his tourniquet tight.

"Lead him?" he asked when he could speak. "You...you can't be serious."

"It's the only way."

"Won't work. He'll smell me out. I'm bleeding too much."

"Not if I'm bleeding more," Grace said. His mouth dropped as she slashed across her belly with the bolt cutter.

"You're insane."

"Thanks. Now, go down–" Grace sucked in through her teeth. She must have cut deeper than she thought. "Go down one level. Hide until he goes after me. And here." She whispered the location of the duffel bag of DVDs. "Make sure the story is leaked."

"You have my word." He started down the stairs as she ascended. "And Grace? Thank you."

She nodded, then went her separate way. Despite the pain in her gut, she allowed herself a smile. *No more Joys. No matter what.*

***

She only reached the next level up before Beluga barreled out. "Where are you, you bitch?"

One more floor. She rushed up, taking the stairs two at a time. "Olly olly oxen free!"

Snarls shook the complex beneath her feet. He was coming much faster than she expected. She ducked inside her desired floor as fangs flashed on the landing below.

The door slammed shut behind her, lock engaging with a click. That would buy her a few heartbeats at most.

Stucco walls split into three directions. Grace went right. The atmosphere felt almost homey, but somehow off, like the builders learned of what a home looked like through books and academic study. Her heels clacked on ceramic, the popcorn ceiling's dome lights causing her to break out in sweat instantly.

She passed wide windows showcasing playrooms full of toys, walls bedecked with crayon-drawn artwork, and offices plastered in cartoon characters and plastic furniture.

The hallway cut left, then extended for a couple hundred feet. The whole floor must be laid out in a giant rectangle. This stretch boasted living quarters, bedrooms with few signs of occupancy. She hurried a quarter of the way, then slipped inside one at random, closing the door behind her as gently as possible.

Huddling down, she weighed her options. Joy was here. The folder with her name on it said so. Grace's earlier disappointment of discovering she had passed her sister was surpassed by the terror that she may die before reaching her.

"Hello."

Grace started. A small Hispanic girl of about seven years of age stared at her from the bed, eyes almost bug-like, her hair done up in pigtails. Somehow, Grace hadn't noticed her.

"Are you new?" the girl asked.

"Um..." Grace wasn't sure how to respond. She had very little experience with children. "Shh. There's a bad man chasing me."

"Bad man? From the...Outside?" The girl pronounced "outside" with the revulsion one might hold for a mashed cockroach in your drink. "I used to be from there. I was bad. Then Dr Schneider helped me."

"Do you know a girl? White? Brown hair? Her name is Joy."

"Are you bad? You said you're being chased." The little girl went on as if Grace hadn't said anything. "Only bad people are chased. You must be bad."

Footfalls outside. Heavy, like combat boots. Grace held her finger up. "Shh..."

"Let me out of my room."

A shadow fell under the door and stopped.

"If I catch a bad person, I'll get treats for a month. Suckers. My favorite are the red ones. They're so yummy on my tongue."

Grace wanted to slap a hand over the girl's mouth. But Beluga was right outside. Watching.

"I wonder if they'll let me have my dolly too. Oh hi, Mr. Beluga!" She waved.

Blood rushed in Grace's ears.

"Everything all right, Sally?" Beluga asked through the door.

"Oh yeah, I was talking."

"Oh?"

"There's this bad white lady. She asked about Joy."

Grace's hand tightened in a fist.

"Is that so? Did you see which way she went?"

"You didn't see her? She came from the Outside."

"No, I didn't."

"Do I get a treat?"

"I'll make sure of it. Bye now."

"Bye!"

The shadow receded. The sounds of footsteps faded down the hall and went silent. Grace sagged against the corner.

"So how do you know Joy?" Sally asked.

"I'm her sister."

Sally's eyes went so big, they practically engulfed her face. *"You're Grace?"*

The relief at hearing this girl say her name was almost too much. "I am. Does she talk about me?"

"Only *all* the time. Oh, I'm sorry. I called you bad."

"Where is she?"

"She has a session with Dr. Schneider today."

The ground fell away. If this session was anything like what Grace had witnessed on the other floor, this doctor was about to face God's wrath.

Grace swallowed, her throat dry. "Where is this session?"

34

SALLY GAVE DIRECTIONS TO Dr. Schneider's office where "sessions" were conducted. She informed Grace of service hallways that criss-crossed the floor so staff could get to patient rooms quickly in case of "extreme accidents." According to her, these corridors all led to the main hallway, which bisected the floor. One such access lay two doors down from where Grace was right now.

Grace almost commented on the young child using words like "bisected" and "access," but knew it wouldn't help. In thanks, she promised to return with a doll. Sally leaped up with such enthusiasm it made Grace's heart ache. Grace silently prayed she would make it back alive.

Gripping the bolt cutters, she checked the outside corridor for any sign of Beluga. All clear, she tiptoed over to the secret hallway. Light poured from the gaping hole, a bright white. Coupled with the equally white drywall slicing through the homey stucco design, the hallway gave the illusion of an angelic passageway sent from God Itself. All that was missing was the Gregorian chant. No doubt the workers here believed they were celestial beings doing divine work.

Halfway down, a voice called out. She flattened herself against the wall. A conversation began, too low for her to discern the individual words but not the speakers themselves. One was Beluga, the other another adult, probably Dr. Schneider. They sounded muffled, tinny. The longer they spoke, the more her curiosity drove down her panic until she couldn't help but creep closer. Finally, straining, she could just make out what they were saying.

"...have this under control," Schneider said. Her voice was older, slightly gruff.

"You just keep doing what you do, doc. The boys know how to handle a few aggro vamps."

A loud mechanical click. "I still don't see how it got this far. With all your recordings. Seemed neglectful to let them even attempt this breakout."

Recordings. They must have bugged the Quarter. So that was how they'd known about Francesco's plans. But something about that seemed wrong. Grace couldn't say what.

"That's the thing about hope, doc," Beluga said. "You have to let them try with all their might and fail spectacularly. That way you squash any future rebellions."

"If that were true," said the doctor with another click, "this wouldn't be the fourth rebellion in my tenure."

Beluga had nothing to say to that.

A door opened. "All right, dear. How are we feeling?"

"Okay, I guess." Grace almost dropped the bolt cutters. This new voice cut through the air and pinned her in place. It hurt, like finding an ancient knife still sharp enough to draw blood.

"Wonderful," Schneider said. "The X-rays should be done in a few hours but in the meantime, I'd like to play a few games. Are you up for it?"

"What kind of games?"

"First is a memory game. Take a look at this." Something beeped, then hummed. Grace chanced a glimpse. There, in an open yet standard X-ray room, complete with technician booth and metal table, sat a small girl who hadn't aged a day in years. She appeared healthy enough, no outward signs of harm, no scars. But also, no growth. She should be a woman in her twenty-fourth year by now. Not this child who appeared to have been kidnapped only yesterday.

Beluga and a woman in her late fifties stood on either side of the table, looking up at a projected image of hundreds of rectangles on a white screen. "I've made it a bit harder than last time."

"Nah, this is easy."

"Is that right?" Schneider laughed. "Show me."

Grace readied. The two were distracted; she'd never get a better chance. Once Joy reached the screen, clear of any danger, she'd attack. But then her sister started swiping.

"It's amazing, isn't it?" asked Schneider after a moment. "Not only does she remember where cards are across nearly five hundred possible locations, but she can intuit where matches might be at a near seventy-five percent success rate using a predictive algorithm she created instantaneously."

Beluga yawned. "Yeah. Real impressive."

"Do you have any idea the potential this has? Predictive police? Stopping crime before it starts. Or fighter pilots? Soldiers? We're only a few years off from creating a utopia on earth."

"Uh huh. And this will make me how good at *Service of Call?*"

Dr. Schneider rolled her eyes.

Joy finished the game, eyes growing dull when she'd eliminated all but the last quarter of the tiles. "Next."

"Why don't you recalibrate your tablet while Mr. Beluga and I finish our conversation?"

Joy jumped at the chance. When her head was bent over the flashing screen, Schneider pulled Beluga aside. They approached Grace's hiding spot. She hunkered back down the corridor.

"What do you want?" Schneider snapped.

"You need to fix my arm. This shouldn't have happened."

A pause. "The wound is cauterized. There's nothing I can do."

"But it was made by a religious blade. It shouldn't be able to do this. I'm an atheist."

"Hmm," Schneider said, voice dripping with curiosity and zero sympathy. "Fascinating."

"Will it still be fascinating when I shove this stump up your ass?"

"No need to be vulgar, sergeant."

"It's sergeant first class."

"My apologies," she said but didn't correct herself. Another pause. Grace pictured the doctor checking the wound more extensively. "Well, I'm afraid you must be mistaken. Some part of you believes in one of the Gods represented by those symbols."

"That's bull. Everyone assigned here is an atheist."

"Were you always?"

A shuffle of boots.

"I see. Well, even if you don't believe now, that doesn't negate your earlier experiences. There must be something your inner child bows to. Or perhaps, your mind makes a subconscious connection you aren't aware of. For instance, the crescent moon and star that represents Islam could be interpreted as an atom with an orbiting electron. As such, a belief in science as God is enough to cause your current disfigurement."

"That's a crock of shit," Beluga said through gritted teeth. Heavy footfalls again. He was coming toward Grace.

Grace gripped the bolt cutters with both hands. Not the best opportunity, attacking an angry Beluga. Plus, after she'd incapacitated Beluga, she would have to get to the doctor before she called for help. She should have taken the earlier chance. Grace took a deep breath and steeled herself.

"You don't want to do that."

Joy's voice made Grace start.

Dr. Schneider asked, "Do what?"

Joy hesitated before responding. "Beluga was about to hit you with his stump."

"I-I was not."

But Grace couldn't be sure Joy was talking to him, the timing too coincidental. Did her sister know she was here? Or was she intuiting Beluga's actions, like a card match on the screen?

"I want to go to my room," Joy said.

Dr. Schneider rankled at this. "We've only just begun, dear. We have three hours yet."

"I want to go now."

"See what you did?" she hissed at Beluga. To Joy, she said in a cheerful tone, "What if I had Sergeant First Class Beluga leave us? Would it be all right then? I have a few more games to play with you. And you haven't had your supplements yet. I bet you'd like a sucker."

"I want to go," Joy repeated, softer.

"This isn't like you. What's the matter, dear?"

A sharp intake of breath—a sniff—from around the corner made the hair on Grace's neck rise. *"Reporter lady."*

Grace cursed. She'd waited too long. Heart in her throat, she sprang, bolt cutters high. But Beluga wasn't there. Instead, ashen faced and glaring, was Joy. She redirected her attack, the cutters barely missing her sister's forehead.

Grace blinked, taking in this new situation. Beluga grinned so wide, his smile took over his face. He knew. He wanted this to happen.

"What is the meaning of this?" Dr. Schneider asked, her stout frame shaking her glasses down her nose.

"Just a rat, doc. We know what we do to rats, don't we, Joy?"

A snap to attention. All emotion died in her sister's face. Joy grabbed Grace's wrist, then Grace was on the ground, weaponless, and arms pinned behind her back.

"Good girl."

Joy thrummed with satisfaction. Who was this guard who made her sister a beggar for his attention? God, he was going to die for this.

The guard bent down. Hot, putrid breath spilled across her face. "You actually thought you had a chance, didn't you? Poor girl."

"Will you please take her away?" Dr. Schneider asked.

"Don't move a muscle, kid," Beluga ordered.

Joy obeyed, her tiny hands now clamps.

"Joy, please–"

"Sergeant First Cla–"

"Ignore them," Beluga said, spittle pooling across his teeth, a sucking hiss under every threat. "I listened to you, Reporter Lady. Your love of the gods. Their dual nature of morals and debauchery. It's what drew me to you. To show you what I've become." To Joy, he directed, "Stand her up."

Stepping a few feet back, Beluga unbuttoned his fatigues. "Watch as evolution swallows the divine."

Flesh burst through at his clothing's seams as he transformed. His throat and chest split down the center. Knife-like teeth flooded the cavity, shredding and consuming his T-shirt from the waist up.

Grace wanted to flee, to fumble away from what Beluga had become, but Joy held her fast. Instead, she was forced to take everything in. Not only the bulk of him but the sloshing, oozing bits in between. Puss streamed from his tear ducts, his ears, the corners of his mouth. A putrid stank overwhelmed the sterile lab fumes with a miasma of rot. Beluga's face took on a gray pale.

Evolutionary, maybe, but divine he was not.

"We are *gods,* Reporter Lady." The open maw spoke in garbled English, but she understood if she tried. It was the lowercase "g" gods he used, she could tell. Then, he hadn't truly listened before. "Gods who can do what they want, if we're willing to take the power we need. No need for a sacrificial messiah. We rule as we see fit. Your sister has already learned this."

Her sister. That was the way out of this. All she had to do was bet on Joy. On knowing her sister. "How about a wager?" she asked.

"A wager?"

"You want to prove to me that my faith is misplaced? Put it to the test."

"Or I could kill you."

"Oh, you would have done that already. You want me to suffer. Destroy my trust in the beyond first. Secure your control over my sister. What do you say?"

At the word sister, Joy flinched. But Beluga had his head cocked, distracted. "What's the bet?"

"If I get my sister," Grace paused, letting the word sink in more, "to say she'll leave with me, then you let us go. If not, I'll stay. I will do whatever you want."

The grin returned. "You'll regret promising that."

Grace ignored the creep of disgust up her spine. "What do you say?"

"Count it, doc."

Schneider, who'd been hiding behind the X-ray table, rose. "W-what?"

"You heard the Reporter Lady. We need someone to keep this fair. Be the judge. In case of a tie."

"...as to whether the girl goes with her sister? How could there be a tie?"

"*I don't know,* doc. I'm covering the options."

"Uh, then yes. I'll judge." Schneider took a seat on the table, the promise of rules and order restoring the woman's demeanor. "Begin."

Joy dropped Grace's wrists at Beluga's nod. *Okay,* Grace thought, rubbing the blood back into her limbs. *Now what?*

"Joy..." Grace faced her sister. God, she was so young. "I–"

"Over here, Reporter Lady." Beluga motioned to a spot next to him.

"What? Why?"

"We're gonna do this old school. Whoever she comes to is the winner."

Like a fucking dog, Grace almost asked. But best not to piss off the super soldier. So to her spot she clomped.

"Joy," Grace began. "Listen to me. Do you remember the poster? The fight we had about it?"

No acknowledgement. She'd need to be more specific. But what would Beluga do with this information?

"The poster of the Quarter. You were mad because Laura had a better one, one of an actual vampire. I yelled at you." Grace pinched her thigh. "I yelled at you that Dad wouldn't buy another. That he hated this one. I hurt you. I'm so sorry I did that, Joy. I'm so..."

Sobs choked out the rest of what she said. As Joy watched on with dry eyes. That memory had weighed Grace down for so long, it was difficult to think of anything else for a moment. The nights wishing she could apologize, to speak the words "I'm sorry" to Joy's face.

"I–"

"Time's up!" Beluga shouted. "Time to choose."

"That can't be it, I haven't–"

"Argue better rules next time, Reporter Lady."

Biting her cheek, Grace turned toward him, her hand reaching to the bolt cutters in her pocket. So many men telling her what to do. Perry, Diavolo, the vet, and now this sad excuse for a soldier. All of them relegating her to the background. Well, this was her story. And no one was going to shut her out of it.

"Your middle name," Grace declared, "is Louise. After our grandmother. You wanted to be a scientist when you grew up."

"Shut up." Beluga held up a finger. May as well have been a green light.

"Dad taught us how to fix things around the house. Because we shouldn't depend on anyone, even him."

Lightning quick, Beluga seized Grace's arm in a vice. "I said *shut up!*" His stump hit her cheek, sending her flying but she caught. He'd held on. Her arm almost tore free of its socket. Finally, she angled the bolt cutters up. One last distraction.

"The fan! We fixed–" The pop as her index finger broke made her wince. Beluga used that split second to slowly–impossibly–rip the cutters free of her.

Then he turned them back around. She tried to dodge but it was no use. The cutters closed around her middle finger.

Not like this! Grace clawed at his face with her free hand, fingernails digging into his eyes, but it was like trying to bend a rock in half.

"The fan."

The cutters bit into her flesh, enough to draw blood and no more. *"What?"* Beluga hissed through his teeth.

"We fixed the fan," Joy's voice was tiny, unsure.

"Yes, Joy," Grace said, equally uncertain, not wanting to break this spell. "We did."

"And you..."

"Yes."

"That video."

The tears she tried holding back finally fell. "Yes, Joy. I showed you...that video. I'm so sorry."

Joy said nothing. Beluga looked from her to Grace, eyebrows higher than they'd ever gone before. That fucking video. Why had she done that? She was a teenager and a moron, that was why. But did she have to pay for her stupidity the rest of her life?

"Grace," Joy said. "Your name is Grace."

The lightness in Grace's chest brought the tiniest giggle with it. "Yes."

And there it was: a future. A place where she and her sister could exist beyond here, live without the constant stress of everything, just be. Sisters once again; messy, but a mess of their own making. Beyond the years and the scars.

"Well, then," Beluga said, voice guttural and resonant. "What an answer."

The cutters closed on her finger and red drowned her perfect picture. Beluga shoved her by the throat against the wall and pressed. Her air cut off. But only for a moment. As soon as it started, his hold loosened. It was Joy. She bit into him, sprouting fangs shredding through the flesh of his calf. He raised a fist, hesitated, then muttered, "Joy. Execute code: Phantasma."

Joy shrank back and froze, eyes blank.

"What a waste." Beluga tsked. His rank breath made Grace's eyes water. "Where was I? Oh, right."

A second finger followed. Through the pain she managed to force out Joy's name. It was like calling a mannequin.

Beluga took hold of Grace's thumb. *No,* she wanted to scream. *No more!* He was just a little twerp with a magnifying glass. Well, she was no fucking ant. He wanted to break her? Then he better try harder.

She reached with her free hand and slathered it in the red streaming down her mangled arm. *See how you like this.* Slick with blood, she rammed her fingers into his open eyes.

Beluga howled and dropped her. Her damaged hand burned as it struck the floor, the very air like acid in her veins. But there was no time to rest, she had to press what small advantage she had. The bolt cutters had clattered to the floor in the confusion. They proved elusive, the blood making her grip as slick as oil.

Maybe this should be it. Poetic justice. The answer she'd devoted her life to ended up costing her that very thing. What else was there?

Everything.

Grace didn't want this. She wanted to live. Her life had little, practically nothing. She may have nothing to live for, but she wanted to live long enough to have something to live for. To be a person.

There was only one thing stopping her. She clutched the slippery bolt cutters.

Beluga raged, the center of chaos. Her resolve sharpened to a point. She pounced. The bolt cutters went true, straight into Beluga's left eye.

He screamed and batted her aside. She struck the wall again, the wind knocked from her lungs. Sucking in took all her strength and weakened her at the same time. But she was still conscious. His mistake.

She wrenched a syringe from her pocket, stolen from the lab below. Beluga's convulsions ebbed as his enhanced healing kicked in. If he recovered, he'd kill her. Or worse, Joy. Snap her sister's neck in front of her just because he could. Because he faced the possibility of loss.

Francesco created a villain, but Beluga embodied it. A man who would kill for pleasure, who bet on and tortured others for shits and giggles. This was the real Diavolo.

Mustering everything, Grace brought the syringe up as close to Beluga as she could.

"There's..." Grace growled, her lungs punishing for every word she choked out, for the truth—the lone God—she now accepted. "There's no running from God."

Beluga turned his head like a whip. If he'd still had his human speed, he might have avoided what came next. But with his enhanced abilities, he snapped around so fast, the syringe entered his left temple without the slightest resistance. The needle went through his punctured eye, forming a cross with the bolt cutters.

His head erupted in flame.

The sergeant first class squealed. He attempted to tear the instruments from his skull, pulling until his fingers melted. The holy fire consumed his motor controls, senses, and nerve center. Viscous fluid pored out of every orifice as his yowling morphed into mewling whimpers then finally cut off.

In no time at all, the charred stump of Beluga fell to the floor with an ashen sigh.

Dr. Schneider backed away. "What...what..." She repeated again and again. She wrapped an arm around Joy in a protective gesture but the other hand held a taser. Guess the good doctor wasn't so trusting of her patients. Joy stared on, wide eyed and oblivious.

Grace raised a hand to shoo Schneider away and fell to her knees. Breathing pained her. The smoke from the fire sapped her. Even in death, Beluga held her back, stealing her last chance—the chance she earned— to rescue her sister. But she refused to let him win. She wrenched the bolt cutters from Beluga's charred head with a squelching sound and dragged herself forward.

Dr. Schneider pulled Joy away, inching closer to a red button on the wall. "You-you don't understand. This facility has cured numerous diseases. The world is better for the work we do. If it ends, humanity goes back into the dark ages. Sickness, genetic mutations. How would you like the average life expectancy to dive into the mid-70's? It would be godless barbarism."

"Jo...Joy..." was all Grace got out between wracking coughs. She was going to lose her sister again. And this time, it really would be her fault.

Please, she prayed to whichever God would listen. *Spare her. Let me die, but spare her.*

Schneider reached the button but refused to take her gaze away from Grace. "S-stay back. I mean it." She fumbled behind her, holding onto Joy with her unarmed hand.

"Freeze!"

Schneider jerked.

"Unhand her."

Francesco?

The vampire shuffled into view, gun aimed at the doctor, the same gun Beluga had knocked out of her grip outside. Eugene gasped behind him, leaning against the wall, his own gun held at hip level.

"Cleveland PD. Drop your weapon and put your hands on your head."

Dr. Schneider grimaced, possibilities playing out across the lines of her face. Then she threw the taser to the ground and bawled. Joy took one step away from the doctor and no more, like she was stepping around trash.

"Look at that," Francesco said as he helped Grace up. "I found a use for this gun after all."

***

After securing the good doctor to her X-ray table, the four of them made their way upstairs, Joy catatonic the entire way. The smoke damage proved too extensive and Grace couldn't explain about the codeword, in fact, she could barely walk. But Eugene held onto her sister, directing Joy around with gentle pushes and pulls.

Joy had recognized her, and that was enough, had to be enough. Grace wanted to go back for Sally, but decided that was better for the police. Unlikely the girl would leave with Grace and these two strange men in tow, even for the promised doll.

Francesco filled the silence as they climbed, gums flapping with wet popping smacks. Grace would have punched him if she could have formed a fist.

Apparently, Beluga had beaten Francesco soundly then snapped his neck and left. No clear reason why; maybe the guard thought another patrol would happen by, but no such luck. Quite the opposite, in fact: His people found him. Francesco's neck was set and allowed to heal. Then he followed Grace's heightened scent down into the underground. Eugene was nearly to the top of the stairs when Francesco almost bowled him over. A quick explanation and they came running, Eugene piggy backing.

"The whole revolt worked out well," Francesco said when they reached the security room. "We figured out some time ago that the guards monitored us by sound. But we didn't communicate by sound, did we? The trick was to let them think we did, whispering to each other from window to window. The real hard part was saying one thing and signing another. Drove me nuts the first few months. But it was worth it."

He slowed to a stop as Eugene signaled for a rest. "We vamps can take a licking. So that's what we did. Let them think they'd won. Then, when all the big flashy grenades and whatnot were used up, the vamps we'd changed and concealed over the last few weeks came crawling out of the woodwork." Francesco scoffed. "The Berets thought they knew how we ticked, how to strip us of everything including our dignity, but their cruel tactics worked against them. They're too used to fighting weakened vamps. But a fully fed group of us? We'll tear them apart like tissue paper."

Francesco's words seemed to have no effect on Joy, as far as Grace could tell. Though her eyebrow twitched at the mention of the dead Berets.

"My people woke to the blood of Berets, blood lust run wild. You've never seen such a beautiful sight." He trailed off, eyes gleaming as they stared off at something in the distance. "Killing can be such an art when timed just so..."

The change in Francesco's posture unsettled Grace. Like the violence he didn't even witness, only imagined, transformed him back to a creature of substance, no longer a gaunt survivor, but a man craving his addiction. "So, the vampires..."

"Are in the wind."

Grace didn't know how to take this news. The guards were brutal, yes, deserving the harshest punishments the law could give, but letting eighty vampires go seemed absurd. Especially with how Francesco acted now. If this was their leader after a hint of death, then how would the other vampires keep themselves from feasting on humans? A pinkie promise now impossible to enforce? Some third alternative must be attainable, something Grace might have come up with if she hadn't been worked to the bone kidnapping mobsters. She stated this last sentence aloud.

"You've had years to rally the public," Francesco said, "to investigate and determine our state in this prison. My people and I lingered in here for decades. Bleeding, weeping, screeching until our lungs gave out for salvation, and no one heard. Some of our own started to believe we deserved this. But I took ahold of our fate. Myself and a few others schemed, and planned, and revolted more times than I can count. If there was some other alternative, we would have reached it." He looked at her, the far-off glint now gone, replaced with a rage that set his pupils to pinpricks. "Sometimes the only way out is blood."

Grace let out a breath she'd been holding while he spoke. The words and their truths stung. What were her last few weeks compared to all he'd been through? She really was only a distraction. "This was never my fight."

Francesco bit his lip, then shook his head. "If that disappoints you, then I'm sorry. Though I expect you'll recover."

"What about those in the underground?" Grace asked. "The experiments?"

In response, Francesco leaned down and helped Joy along.

"Francesco—"

"The humans will deal with them."

Grace's mouth went slack. "You're leaving them?"

"I must. I can free them from their physical cages, but the cages that matter, the ones that the people of this place installed in their minds over years or decades of conditioning? There, I'm powerless. Even this one—" Francesco motioned to Joy "—may seem stable to you now but wait. The scars will show."

Grace refused to accept that. Sure, looking at her sister, this unchanged relic of the past, there would no doubt be issues to work through. She had been here for all these years, longer than she'd lived out in the world of middle school and cartoons, but they were still sisters. Still blood. And that cut deep. That flash of recognition Joy had earlier, that was real. And Grace would be damned if she'd let that go.

The foursome entered the main hall of the Hellmouth and stopped short. The locked door to the lobby that had obstructed Grace and Eugene before now stood wide open.

Eugene sucked in a sharp breath. "How–"

The rest of his words were drowned out in concussive blasts of gunfire.

35

EUGENE CALLED OUT AS Grace and Joy disappeared in a cloud of red mist. The vampire followed after, brains flying out the front of his skull. Without its support, Eugene fell to the floor, swallowing the pain.

All hope of surviving this died in a blink. There lay Joy, eyes staring. Gore spattered across the front of her shirt. So much for such a small child. Grace collapsed beside her, gurgling, a gaping wound in her neck pumping blood out in a river.

His sidearm, Eugene needed his sidearm. But though he patted his waist again and again, he came up empty. A chill shot down him, ending at the leg which bled once more. He'd given the gun to Grace.

The vampire spasmed. A death throe? Impossible, but there it was, trying to get his legs under him. Then, with brain missing, basic functions compromised, what was left of the vampire crawled, claws clacking across the concrete, towards Cole. A thousand generations of evolution pushed the corpse past death.

Cole aimed at the shambling torso, then reconsidered. Instead of firing, she slammed her elbow into the wall, depressing a hidden button in the shape of a rectangle. The room brightened to harsh white.

The light tore through Francesco, boring holes through his malnour-ished frame in a blink. Snarls gave way to a single muddled scream as his body disintegrated. Before the scream could echo back, Francesco's skeleton clattered to a stop, its insides swollen with ash.

Cole lifted a boot and crunched through Francesco's skull, cracking it to miniscule bits of bone dust. Eugene blanched as she rubbed her heel into the ashes.

He crawled toward Grace. He needed that firearm. This was a fool's errand but there were no other alternatives; sometimes all survival was only an attempt at saying "no."

Two pockets. Time enough to check one. Fifty-fifty chance. Tired and unsure if he could reach the farther one, he picked the closest.

Empty.

He clambered for the next pocket anyway but the hard end of the rifle clubbed him in the cheek.

Broken, head pounding, Eugene blinked about as Cole dragged him by the foot across the room. His two charges still lay. Joy. The faux sunlight proved to have no effect—the twisted scientists here had figured out how to beat the sunlight weakness. What's more, there was no wound on her shirt; her breathing appeared regular and she was stirring. She was fine. Better than fine: unscathed. Her eyes popped open and fell on Grace. Her sister gurgled, reaching for her. Joy stared back with the same bland expression of a child watching a cartoon.

Cole propped him against the wall, then went back. What more could this woman do? Everything was already lost.

With a sigh, Cole dug out the firearm. So that was how she'd play it. A me versus them scenario, where he lay shot against the wall, dying a hero preventing vampires from escaping. He'd like to believe people would see through it, but no, the story was too irresistible, too good.

Rather than aim the pistol and cement the lie, Cole did the unexpected: she crouched down next to Joy. "It's okay." She held out a hand. "I can take you home, away from these unclean people."

Nothing. Cole waved her hand in front of Joy's face. "Ah. I see. Leaf jet on the Cuyahoga."

The girl snapped back to herself. A light turned on in a dark room.

Eugene didn't think this betrayal could hurt so soon after the last, but he was wrong, this latest piece a little twist of a knife. How total her involvement was.

Cole repeated herself. Still, Joy sat, her eyes gleaming as her sister's convulsions started to dwindle.

"I know. You're afraid," Cole went on. "But Dr. Schneider told you, didn't she? The Outside is a terrible place. Wouldn't you like to go back home? To be with Tabitha and Debra and Sally? I'll get you as many dolls as you can carry."

Joy looked at the sergeant for the first time. "I knew you'd come."

"You've suffered so much today. We'll get you back downstairs in a moment. Now, wait here. I have one more thing to deal with."

The girl nodded, then mumbled.

"What was that?"

"The...shimmer."

"Oh." Cole glanced at Grace and him. "We do have a little time. But only a little. Be quick."

Joy beamed, her smile a knife blade. He didn't like that, happiness in this girl felt amiss, sinister.

"Go on. It's okay."

Joy lunged. For a moment, he thought she would bite into her sister. Instead, the little girl fell on the puddle of blood and began lapping it up.

Cole strutted over to him until she eclipsed the girl, a third gun drawn from an ankle holster. Serial numbers scratched off, no doubt. Always two steps ahead.

"Cole...Jen, please..."

"I'm sorry, detective, but I did try to warn you. And if it helps, that little girl," she motioned toward Joy, "the research they've done with her? It will save thousands who had the same disease as your daughter."

A lie, but it didn't matter. He kept his eye on the dark barrel. A peace settled over him. He was tired of fighting, of doing the impossible. Tired of filling up every moment. Tired of trying not to think about her.

I'll see you soon, Fonda. Daddy's almost there...

The gun raised. A final flash. An end. Eugene raised his arms for an embrace.

The lights above dimmed back to normal. Cole blinked and glanced about, brow furrowed. "Who's there?"

A dark form sidled up to Cole, lithe and silent. She barely had a chance to turn before claws raked out her windpipe. Guns clattered to the floor.

"...the man is happy Zola returned."

Eugene forced himself to breathe, his heart restarting. Somehow, he was alive. He almost didn't believe this was real despite Cole's blood warming his chest. To think, Cole had almost killed Francesco, Grace, *and* him–

Grace.

"Help me," he said, trying to take Zola's hand but it was like trying to catch a fish. Instead, he pointed at Joy. "Stop her. Please."

Zola rolled her eyes and sauntered back toward the hallway.

"Zola!"

The vampire reemerged a moment later, towing a stranger dressed in a medical gown behind her. Dark hair stretched down to the stranger's waist, her fingers wizened and gray.

"Zola paid back her silver. Wash clean."

"Zola...Zola!"

But she and her companion left without a second glance. He crawled over to Grace, pain in his leg forgotten. This girl, he had to speak to this little girl whose fangs now jutted out from her gums. The one licking at her sister's blood—oh, there was so much blood. Less as Joy slurped greedily. He pushed that thought away.

"Joy."

The little girl paused in her lapping for a single beat, then continued.

"Joy, I need you to help your sister. This—" Eugene pointed "—this is your sister. Do you remember Grace?"

The girl didn't stop. And why would she? He was a no one, a failure at basic human interaction, a failure as a detective, a failure as a father. This pitiful act another in a long line of disappointments. She could smell the mediocre on him.

Grace gurgled. She was still alive! He wanted to scream, in happiness or shock, he wasn't sure. Despite that he didn't believe in a god, this seemed like a sign from above. That gurgle may as well have been Grace shouting, *"Finally do something, you worthless bastard."*

"I had a little girl your age," he began. It seemed a strange place to start but he knew it was right. This was how he'd do the impossible, by starting with the small. "Her name was Fonda. She got sick. Instead of staying by her side, I went to work. Her illness had no cure. I was powerless. Do you ever feel like that?"

Joy continued her lapping. He almost asked again when she mumbled, "A long time ago."

"So did your sister. Your sister, Grace," Eugene elaborated, pointing again. "Every day, she's looked for you since you left. She even became a reporter just to find you. Wrote about all sorts of boys and girls who disappeared so their mommies and daddies, and brothers and sisters wouldn't be sad."

In response, the little girl froze. He'd done it. No, Fonda did. Joy wiped the blood off her chin with her sleeve. The police might be suspicious but Eugene could explain that away. The events of tonight couldn't be dissected by the best minds. He could slip Joy through the gap created by that uncertainty.

Joy grinned her knife-like grin. But, he was realizing, maybe that was just how she looked. A little girl growing up in this place would undoubtedly be a bit of a monster. She needed the best care, no matter her actions.

Then Eugene's jaw dropped. Joy latched onto her sister, and began to gulp down the last drops of life.

Without thinking, he forced his hand between the two. Joy hissed. Eyes darkened, the full black of blood lust. The scientists in their infinite wisdom had removed every weakness of the vampire, except this. Eugene couldn't hope she'd overcome it like Francesco, not with her lack of experience.

"She's your sister!" he shouted.

"Liar!" She struck him. He lost his grip, the blow surprisingly strong. "My sister isn't old. Stop trying to trick me." Joy darted in, resuming her feeding, her fangs now fully extended.

He stuck his hand in her way again. He winced as her fangs sliced through, but he was prepared and held his ground. Frustrated, she struck him again, harder, leaving him dazed. She could break him.

Still he crawled back and blocked her without hesitation. This was what he was meant for. Serving others. His life for the innocent and the guilty alike.

This continued several times. Resisting her was like trying to stand in a rock slide. She broke his grip, his ribs, forearms, collar bones.

But he got back up. Each time. Never relenting.

Joy growled in frustration. "Let me have her."

"You'll have to kill me," he whispered.

She accepted his request. The snarling mass of teeth leaped onto him with crippling fury. Strength failed him. It hurt far worse than he thought. His fingers grazed something metal and sharp: the bolt cutters. These could save him. One quick jab, somewhere vital, and he could escape. Joy would survive. Probably. Maybe...

He let go of the sharp object, letting his hand fall. And touched Grace.

She lay still next to him, his hand having fallen on her shoulder. Her mouth drooped slightly open, her last words dying on her lips. A plan formed. A stupid one, based on movies and TV shows from his youth, but a plan. If it meant saving someone, he wanted to try. He picked up the bolt cutters once more and sliced Joy's palm. Joy growled and dug in her claws. He writhed. Cold flooded him, soon ending the coursing torment.

He took hold of Joy's hand with its measly cut and forced it toward Grace. The girl fought at first, but when he didn't hurt her, her arm grew slack.

He pressed the cut to Grace's lips. Her eyes remained clouded and unfocused.

Come on, he thought. *One of us has to live through this.* He tried to will the tiniest contraction in her throat. *Drink!*

The weight of the arm grew too heavy. Shaking, Eugene released it. Luckily, Joy's arm stayed where it was. After a sickening length of time, Grace's throat fluttered.

Eugene wanted to dance. She was going to live. He had saved someone after all. He closed his eyes, satisfied. Images flooded in, but not from his past life. Instead, the future stretched before him. Grace would leave here, saved by the boys in blue. After her transformation, she'd wake, escape, and release her story of the Hellmouth for all to hear. Her sister would undergo psychological counseling. The prison camp now tainted, the vampires' fate would be decided by the nation. A nation unlikely to change its decades-long stance on terrors of the night.

Unless shown proof. Proof too substantial and massive to be discounted. Eugene slipped a hand inside his coat pocket. The item in there was difficult to grasp, fingers not quite securing around it. Problem was he couldn't feel, his limbs growing numb.

A siren rose in the city. It must be close to hear it through these concrete walls. It wasn't deep or reverberating like an ambulance or fire engine. The police were near. Their first step would be coordinated containment and elimination. No exceptions. Not even for ten year old girls.

He snatched up the proof with his whole fist. Everything hinged on this. He cupped hope in his palm. Shaking now from the amount of strength he needed to keep it steady, he shoved the proof into the waistline of Grace's pants. He settled back, one job done.

Now for the second. "Joy," he addressed the small vampire. "When you're done with me, go back downstairs. To your family. And..." He choked back a sob. "And wash off my blood."

Joy gave a nod. Or maybe he imagined she did. He opened his mouth to ask when exhaustion overtook him. It would be fine. If Joy had lived here all these years, she could survive what was to come.

Eugene took a deep breath and closed his eyes.

Hello, Fonda. I missed you...

Epilogue
Three months later

TRACY SIGHED AND DUG through her purse to find her apartment key. Her eyes refused to focus, making the task difficult. Three months since Grace's death. Yet it felt like twice that, and at the same time, only yesterday. Since everyone believed that she and Grace were BFFs, Tracy was hired on to fill in Grace's old role. For a fraction of a second, her excitement trounced her grief. That fraction twisted her up like an old rag to this day. The crushing amount of hours did nothing to assuage it.

She was given every story tied to the Quarter, of which there were now hundreds. A trove of classified documents had leaked, thousand of pages, the length of several hefty novels. Enough information for a team of six working round the clock. Guess how many the understaffed paper put on it.

Today's story, the first in a wave of indictments of the four lead military perpetrators – acting independently from high command, of course – made Tracy's head hurt. She had sat through her share of civilian grand juries, but JAG preliminary hearings were something else. It didn't help that the whole thing ran twelve hours straight.

The only part she understood was the end. Each of the four guards charged had been recommended for a general court-martial, the highest court in the military. However, two of the major charges were dropped: human trafficking and consorting with the mafia. The public would not be happy about that. Or Tracy would make them not happy. She'd inherited that much from Grace, at least.

Finally, Tracy found her key, unlocked the apartment door, and went in. She hadn't been here in three days, sleeping at the office as it was closer to the trial than her East Side flat.

The scent of rotten death struck her before she could set down her purse. Had that damn Mr. Pawcy killed the goldfish? Her niece was going to kill her.

Her hand clutched her purse tight, her body identifying the odor before she did. However, she did notice the impenetrable mass of darkness that blanketed the living room despite the hallway light.

Tracy backed away. She didn't care if the smell came from the vents, she wasn't about to be another Black lady in a horror movie. She'd get her super to check the place out.

Something clamped down on her wrist and wrenched her inside. She exhaled, a sharp and brief gasp, before toppling over a soft yet solid waist-high object. The door slammed shut, the light extinguished. The relief of landing on couch cushions vanished as a cold hand clamped over her mouth.

"Shh." A lamp clicked on.

"Hey, Tracy," Grace said, taking her hand away. "Long time."

"You're dead." Tracy said the words as if she could force the issue. As if, by believing enough, Grace would fall over and rot.

Instead, the woman smiled, baring row upon row of teeth. "I was."

"Are you here to kill me?"

"Not this time." Grace eased into the recliner, a plume of dust escaping from its dilapidated cushions. She held a finger over her nose.

The gesture calmed Tracy somewhat. An ancient predator who hunted humans since prehistoric times was vulnerable to hay fever. Whatever Grace had become, she was still her, still imperfect and prone to human weaknesses. Hay fever never killed a vampire, though.

"How long did you and Beluga date?"

The question sent every hair on Tracy's neck on end. "What?"

Grace pointed to a frame on the wall. "I found that in the back of your closet."

A framed selfie of Tracy and Beluga hung there, the two of them smiling arm in arm in front of the zebra enclosure at the zoo. The photo was in the precise spot she had hung it years ago. How had Grace known?

"Um." Tracy sat up. "It lasted six months. Or so. He was an ass. I ended it. That's it."

Grace stared at her, eyes unblinking. Tracy shifted uncomfortably.

"That's all?"

"Yes."

Grace shook her head and fixed Tracy with a frown.

"I swear."

Sighing, Grace reached into her pocket. Tracy straightened, wondering what weapon Grace might pull. Instead, a cheap phone came out. She pressed a button.

"I heard her. She's going to the police commissioner."

Tracy started at the sound of her own voice. It was hoarse. She hadn't caught that at the time, how the first all-nighter on Quarter duty made her rasp. A faint hum of cars could be heard in the background. If this was what she thought, she didn't want to hear what came next. Wanted to rip the phone from Grace's hand and stomp it into oblivion.

"I'm too tired for this." Beluga yawned. *"Can't we let this go for another day?"*

"You know what happens if she writes this article. What those in charge will do to us if she uncovers anything. We'll be–"

"Fine, Jesus. What do you want me to do?"

A pause. One long enough for Tracy to think the recording had ended, that it hadn't caught her reply.

"I can tell you where she'll be."

Grace hit stop. "The Hellmouth recorded everything near its guard stations. Blackmail was a somewhat lucrative means of income for them."

"My friend's cousin was raped." The words rushed out. But no matter the speed, they hurt, like picking at a scabbed wound. "The cops were gonna let the guy off, so I took matters into my own hands. Alaska is an easy place to stash someone. Beluga tricked me into telling him. I thought he was being kind, that he loved me. Then the blackmail started. It wouldn't have worked but my mom got into a car accident, then the hospital bills and long-term care..."

Grace looked down. "So when you asked me out..."

Was it Tracy or did she see sympathy in the lines of Grace's face? "I wanted to talk to you, warn you really. All these decades. You don't think there've been other reporters who've wanted to look into the Hellmouth?"

A flash of strain. "You played me pretty well." She opened a folder resting on the side table. A picture of Tracy splashed across the page. The lists of her sins. And it was so thick. "I really believed you knew nothing about vampires."

"I thought it would be endearing..."

Grace leveled a glare. Tracy hadn't meant to defend her tactics—only to keep Grace talking, though that backfired. But then Grace shook her head, the side of her mouth cocking up in a grin. "I see. Well, sending Perry to give me the flash drives was pretty inspired. The man was an asshole, but not a criminal. Though he did throw me for a loop."

"I guess," Tracy said, fighting back tears, "I got pretty good at what the Berets made me do. I'm sorry."

"So your note said."

Tracy lifted her hands in frustration. "What would you have done? Beluga had me dead to rights. And you were so..."

"Bitchy."

"Absent. No one knew you. You were the night girl. Sure, Beluga was a dick but he wasn't a stranger."

"Oh. Great." Grace shrugged. "Glad I made it easy for you."

"It *wasn't* easy." Tracy pounded her fist into her knee. "Not after I spoke to you. You were so kind, Grace. I regretted my words. I practically begged Beluga to talk to you after that, to get you to back down. But I should have known what he'd do. After you disappeared, I had every intention of quitting. Getting my mom and running. But then..."

"I came back."

"...I figured you cut a deal."

Grace watched her, silent for several moments once again. Tracy tried not to squirm.

"Beluga pushed you to do a lot." Grace pulled out a folder. She opened it to reveal Tracy's resumé. "All those jobs you mentioned having: law offices, retail, real estate. All over Ohio. The paper was just the latest."

"Beluga, he..." No, Tracy couldn't stomach another lie. Beluga hadn't made her as good as she was. The people she betrayed, sabotaged, gaslit. She never wanted any part of it, but the demands from her mom's spinal injury, the need to keep afloat, she couldn't walk away. She'd watched her grandmother wither to a stub under Medicaid, the distant stares from medical staff as her parents begged for their attention. Tracy was determined to not let her mother go like that.

But she promised, once her mother died, she would turn herself in. Give up the whole organization. It was too bad Grace had beaten her to it.

Tracy considered telling Grace this, but doubted she'd believe her. All Tracy could manage was another wimpy, "I'm sorry."

In a blink, Grace was before her, slipping into Tracy's personal space. Somehow, Tracy had forgotten she was speaking with a vampire. "You need to learn to stop repeating yourself."

Grace lifted a hand and tenderly stroked her cheek. Fear tightened Tracy's spine into a rigid column, forcing her as still as marble.

The vampire leaned down, her lips nearing Tracy's neck. Tracy tried to rear back but Grace's hand became a brace that held her fast. She closed her eyes and waited for the sting.

"I forgive you."

Tracy leaned back as if slapped. *What?*

"You were stuck in an impossible situation. For a lot longer than I was. That changes a person. And I can't hold you to account for that."

Tracy swallowed. This was the last thing she expected to hear. She had ruined this woman's life, more so than any of the other people she'd manipulated over the years. And Grace was forgiving her?

As if sensing Tracy's conflicted response, Grace held up a DVD case. "If you want a chance at doing some good, this is it. Publish everything on this disk. I would have done it, but it needs to come from a credible news source, someplace they can't dismiss or debunk easily."

A cold lump of plastic slipped into Tracy's hand, accompanied by a pounding in her chest. This was surreal. There had to be a catch.

She looked up to find Grace at the door. "That-that's it? After...every-thing?"

"That's it."

"But you're wanted now." The words were a whisper, but they stopped Grace flat. "A vampire outside of the Quarter? They'll find you in a week. What will happen to me then?"

Grace frowned and stepped back inside. A shudder traveled up Tracy's spine as the door closed once again. She bit her tongue to keep from shaking.

Then Grace told her about the others: the escaped vampires, old contacts of Grace's, and those in law enforcement who'd be watching, protecting Tracy like her own secret service. Humans and supernatural immortals ensuring these stories saw the light of day.

Tracy slumped back, like someone had put a fist through her heart.

"See you later, alligator."

Though Tracy had no idea why Grace said that. After all, Tracy wasn't the one with teeth.

The front door opened and shut once more, descending the apartment into a new level of darkness. Tracy sat for some time, staring at the plastic case in her hand. After all the bad, a shot at redemption had fallen into her lap.

She opened her laptop, her chest light for the first time since she didn't know when, and got to work.

***

Grace reached the street and entered an idling blue Buick. It worried her, leaving the car running while she went inside, but she couldn't depend on having enough time to hot wire it again. Fortunately the street was clear.

Tracy was right—Grace *was* wanted—but she was wrong too. The major crimes division in charge of Grace's case was a little overwhelmed at the moment due to some leaked documents purging dirty cops like rodents in a storm. Plenty of room for her to slip through. However, to be safe, she'd abandon the car in an hour and find something else to get her out of the city, then another to leave the state.

In Arizona, Grace had plenty of places to hide. Her mom would help with that. Grace hadn't listed her on any government documents since she'd left. Juvenile teen rebellion for the win.

Eventually, once things settled down, Grace might return, chip away at the power structure bit by bit. Not for any promise she made but because habit was hard to break. Justice now encoded in her fibers.

Leaving Joy set a sliver of ice in Grace's heart, but Grace had no idea how to help her sister through that kind of brainwash. The next few months—years more likely—would be agony, sitting on her hands as Joy pieced herself back together. But Grace would suffer in silence. No telling her parents, not yet. Better to save them from the same misery. One Grace could more than bear.

In a few hours, she'd pull over and get in a trunk before dawn. That was if she wasn't impervious to sunlight, like her sister. For now, she turned on the radio. A hopeful, not at-all-ironic, song about a new day came on. Grace settled back, letting the uplifting melody wash over her.

She stopped at a red light. Ahead lay the on-ramp to the highway.

The song switched to a somber tune, all violins and solitary piano riffs. An ache rose in her chest, prodding her once again all these months later. It first started when she woke in the ambulance. She thought the paramedic had done something to her, hurt her in some way. But there was nothing physical. For the life of her, she couldn't figure out what it was.

Eventually, the ache lessened until it faded away altogether. But here it was again. What did it want from her? She'd forgiven Tracy. Her promises fulfilled. Her sister found. The bad guy defeated. Vampires were on their way toward autonomy for the first time in decades (although if they'd achieve full-fledged freedom, who could say?).

So why did she feel like she was still standing at the top of that ladder, ready to jump into the Quarter? Forgiving Tracy felt like a step toward the solid ground below. She couldn't see the floodlights reflected on the black-top anymore. But the gap in the barbed wire remained open, welcoming her.

What did it take to step off the ladder entirely? She didn't know. But she had time. The one thing she had in abundance. Now, all she needed was courage.

The light turned green.

She pulled onto the wide-open lanes ahead, the horizon stretching from end to end under a dark blanket of sky. But Grace knew day would come.

A new dawn was inevitable. So long as she kept moving forward through the night.

Acknowledgements

What's in a name?

The first name of the protagonist in this story, Grace, is borrowed from a prisoner I used to exchange letters with. The two bare little resemblance in terms of personality or physical appearance or anything else, really. But both are survivors of abuse. My fictional Grace dealt with trauma, neglect, victim blaming, shaming, and (to a degree) gaslighting. The real one dealt with far, far worse.

If you or a loved one are in danger, please call the National Defense Violence Hotline at (800)799-7233.

The idea for this started with a woman being dropped over a fence into a sea of monsters. I wasn't sure who the monsters were, or the woman, and my attempts at trying to tell their story were pulpy and grew pulpier. When I finally hit on the idea of one body-one week-one question, I knew I had to write it as fast as I possibly could. Joy's disappearance and Eugene Yukawa's cat-and-mouse chase with Grace evolved from the writing, seeping out of the black ink on my screen, from that place writers never fully understand but are somehow in tune with. Refining all this took time and effort. I started typing the first word of this when my daughter was born, and now she's almost 5 years old.

A book is a ship an author is chained to for weeks, months, or, in this case, years. I appreciate everyone who helped keep me from sinking, provided nourishment, and/or pointed out the several cracks in the hull.

First, to my editor, Amanda at River Run Editing. I never once regretted taking a chance on you. Your skills are unquestionable, magnificent, and had me scratching my head at how I could let so many errors through.

I'd like to thank everyone who read this book in its many drafts and half-baked ramblings. My wife, the best and harshest critic who refined the confusing nature of this book's mystery into a diamond. My critique partners Monique and Rebecca, without whom this would be 300 pages of violence and a half-baked Dexter imitation. The writing group at Lorain Public Library, your critiques of the early chapters helped me dig deep into Grace's psyche and world. And my brother, Nate, who doesn't like reading but still beta read the hell out of this.

My mother and in-laws for watching my children so I could work on this. I hope to celebrate soon.

To Lit Youngstown for giving me a community for the first time. To RW and Katja, thank you for the time each month to devote to my dream. I never would have finished this without those writing sprints and refreshing tangents.

Finally, thanks to you, dear reader. Without you, none of this would be possible. It's a cliche to say that but it's true. Stories are for you. Be careful with this one. It's someone's baby now grown up and sent out into the world.

Afterword

REVIEWS! MAILING LIST! SOCIALS!

Please leave a review anywhere you can. Authors literally live and die by them.

For news of future books, signings, appearances, and general ramblings, please sign up for my newsletter on Substack @zljohnson.

If you want to be more casual than that (or hate email), follow me on TikTok, Instagram, and Bluesky at zljohnsonwrites.

About the author

Z.L. Johnson is the writer of this book and not much else, really. That should change soon. He's held a couple dozen jobs over the years and will most likely hold more, but the most related to this particular book (in no real order) would be librarian, library assistant, intern (at a library), and librarian. He's developed a healthy love of book hoarding, horror, cocktails, and being a doormat to small children (his own).